THE DARK BACKWARD

Gregory Hall

MICHAEL JOSEPH
LONDON

MICHAEL JOSEPH LTD

Published by the Penguin Group
27 Wrights Lane, London w8 5TZ
Viking Penguin Inc., 375 Hudson Street, New York, New York 10014, USA
Penguin Books Australia Ltd, Ringwood, Victoria, Australia
Penguin Books Canada Ltd, 10 Alcorn Avenue, Toronto, Ontario, Canada M4V 3B2
Penguin Books (NZ) Ltd, 182–190 Wairau Road, Auckland 10, New Zealand

Penguin Books Ltd, Registered Offices: Harmondsworth, Middlesex, England

First published in Great Britain 1995

Typeset by Datix International Limited, Bungay, Suffolk
Printed in England by Clays Ltd, St Ives plc
Set in 11.5/14.5 pt Monophoto Bembo

A CIP catalogue record for this book is available from the British Library

ISBN 0 7181 3905 4

Epworth Mechanics' Institute Library
Tuesday 10a.m – 12 Noon
Thursday 1.30p.m – 4p.m
Friday 7.30p.m – 9.30p.m

1 · 6 · 17

vith | Please return books as soon as you have finished v
them so that others may read them

THE DARK BACKWARD

For June, Richard and Katherine

'What seest thou else
In the dark backward and abysm of time?'

– Shakespeare: *The Tempest*.

Part One

I

I might as well begin with the advertisement on the country property pages of the *Sunday Times*.

On that wet, wintry Sunday morning I was propped up in bed on a pile of pillows reading the book reviews, drinking some very special Jamaican coffee I had paid the earth for in Fortnum's and eating a butter and Oxford-marmalade-smothered croissant which Geoffrey had bought fresh from the patisserie in Hampstead High Street. He liked to get up early, even in freezing February, to find these treats and pick up the papers.

He sat on the other side of the bed, drinking strong tea, surrounded by newsprint.

'I suppose they mean Thomas,' he had said, tossing the folded paper to me across the bed.

He watched with eagerness as I searched the densely typeset column to see if I could find what had caught his eye. He liked these little games. He was ever alert for the reference or the word play which he had spotted and hoped no one else, particularly me, had. I put this trivial competitiveness down to early potty training or English public school education, if there was any difference.

'It's the wrong title, then. Giles Winterborne is in *The Wood-*

landers. But that seems even more appropriate.' I could be trivially competitive too.

'Yes, I know.' This meant he didn't. 'It's pretty good for an estate agent, anyway.'

'Do we know them?'

'I think it's that ratty office down by the side of the church-yard in Queen's Hythe. It was closed last time we were there. There was nothing in the window except an out-of-date auction poster.'

'I don't remember. They all seem the same after a while. I suppose you think we ought to look at it.'

'Right. Sounds just the ticket. Let's go today. No time like the present. Before half London gets down there.' He picked up the bedside phone and was punching out the numbers before I could reply. Geoffrey could sometimes make quick decisions, particularly when they involved deciding to do what he wanted. For once, although I felt like it, I didn't argue.

But the truth was I didn't in the least want to get out of bed and go haring off again into the depths of the country. I was getting pissed off with weekend cottage hunting.

It had been Geoffrey's idea. He had suddenly said to me about four months before, as we were dozing quietly on the sofa after a particularly good Sunday lunch, 'I think it's about time we got a place in the country.'

I was completely astonished. I didn't see any need to change the habits of my perfectly well established weekend existence to sit in some hovel in the middle of a field. I said as much to Geoffrey.

He was fairly miffed. 'I did hope you wouldn't react like that. After all, you're always saying how set in my ways you think I am. Now when I suggest we have a real project to stop us getting stale and middle-aged, you go all conventional.'

I had to laugh. 'So we're a stale old married couple already, are we? For God's sake! After only four months, not counting the prior cohabitation?'

He encircled me with a fond arm. 'Darling, of course not. Don't

4

take it the wrong way. It's only that we're awfully comfortably set up and –'

'You want to make us uncomfortable.'

He got up from the sofa and started to pace irritably in front of the fireplace. 'No, no, no. It isn't like that. I think it would be good for us. Stuck here in London, we're not in tune with nature or the seasons. The past few weeks, I've felt that more than I ever have before. It may be part of the process of ageing. I just feel the need to get out and get my hands in the soil. You know, a garden, land even.'

The idea of Geoffrey as a horny-handed son of toil had never remotely crossed my mind. I couldn't even get him to water the window boxes I balanced precariously on the window sills in the summer. But as I looked at his earnest expression, almost pleading for understanding in his little-boy way, I was touched. If that was what he wanted, then I guess I had to persuade myself to want it too.

He caught the look in my eye. 'Go on Molly, give it a whirl.'

No one but he had ever dared or wanted to call me Molly. For some reason best known to him, he was fascinated by the play on my given name Mary, and my alleged resemblance to the heroine of *Ulysses*. Sensibly, he reserved its use for special occasions.

'OK, OK. Now you can tell me two things: what are we going to use for money, and where are we going to find this passport to eternal bliss?'

I thought I had him on the first one, but he was undismayed. 'Don't worry about the money. I've got a little nest egg. Some shares and gilts and stuff my Aunt Edith left me. Before we got together,' he added hastily. 'After all, this is your place. We agreed to keep things as they were before. So if I buy the cottage, that will even things up.'

I had never heard of Aunt Edith or her nest egg. It was nice for him he had that kind of dough, even if he hadn't seen fit to tell me about it until now. 'Fine, so you have hidden resources. What about the place?'

'Well, I had in mind something genuinely rural. Unspoilt. Real. Norfolk.'

I burst out laughing, nearly spilling the rest of the wine in my glass. 'Norfolk! Isn't that very, er, flat?' I strangled the vowel in this latter word into what I imagined was the right Noël Coward -style British accent.

Geoffrey waved a deprecating hand. 'No. It's the Fenland that's flat. I certainly wouldn't want to live there. Very boring. No, Norfolk's got gentle hills and the most marvellous coast. Miles and miles of white sand beaches, completely empty apart from the seabirds.'

'You sound as if you know it well.' I was surprised to find a possessive note in Geoffrey's voice I had hardly detected before. He was usually so laid back about everything. I was a bit jealous suddenly of my exclusion from so much of his previous life, particularly a special part. I was surprised. It was something which had never troubled me before. He turned to look out of the window down on the sidewalk plane trees.

'Only as a child. We went for holidays. Cromer. Hunstanton. The Broads. I haven't been back.'

There was a note of emphasis in the way he said this that I didn't think anything of at the time, but which I remembered later. Then he turned back to me, his face alight with his most appealingly boyish beam. 'We'll go back together. You'll love it. You'll see. We'll find somewhere really special.'

And because I was in love with him, I agreed.

Well we did go there. And we didn't. Find anywhere special, that is. Up to that Sunday we had made numerous weekend trips, all to no avail.

Geoffrey, however, was not in the least downhearted. He waded through newspaper ads and sheaves of real estate particulars. He became adept at translating their pretensions into the harsh reality we invariably found when we got there. He drew up lists and timetables for visits with an enthusiastic concentration quite foreign to the reluctance he usually displayed when asked to do anything that approached domestic organization.

That Sunday morning, we were on the motorway an hour after

seeing the ad. Slumped in the hard front seat of Geoffrey's slightly dated but jealously preserved BMW, I felt like a tender plant rudely ejected from its comfortable hothouse and kept alive only by warm annoyance. I didn't speak, in the hope that this would convey something of my mood. Fat chance. He was oblivious. Anyway, he didn't like to talk much when he drove. Perhaps it was just as well as even without this distraction he ignored speed limits and regarded red lights as advisory. Instead he played music on the stereo very loud and hummed along with it. Fortunately he was hardly ever moved to do full conducting. That day it was Beethoven's Seventh.

I watched the countryside unwind past the window like a strip of grey-green wallpaper. There was something desperately depressing about this part of the journey and the string of towns we passed through. Even the names struck a chill into the heart: Hatfield, Stevenage, Harpenden, Hitchin, all redolent of rabbit-hutch houses, plastics factories and video-hire shops. It was times like these when I missed the sheer cheerful outrageous immensity of America, the not always so beautiful. Out of London, England looked only small-scale and low-rent. Even the tackiness was half-hearted.

I wondered for the zillionth time what I was doing here. Why wasn't I lying on a beach in the Bahamas drinking daiquiris? OK, my mother had been English, but that hadn't made me want to leave New York to work in London. I had had to be bribed and bullied into taking a job with an English publisher. But in the three years I had been here, I guess I had gotten resigned to England and English ways. Which was just as well because, to cap it all, I had gone and married a man who couldn't be more English if he tried. Why had I done that?

One reason was very simple. Geoffrey, although not exactly handsome, was a very attractive man. And a not inconsiderable part of that attraction had been that he was attracted by me. As every unattached woman of a certain age in London knows, men, non-cretinous, non-gay men without a bagful of other hangups or a chorus line of current and ex-relationships with or without children dogging their heels are as rare as virgins in Soho. And for one of these elusive specimens to be interested in a not especially good looking, not especially slim ex-New Yorker thirty-eight next birthday is an event on the Halley's comet scale of frequency. I was flattered by his attention, and I succumbed to his charm.

God knew why he was interested in me as more than a reasonably pleasant interlude. I wasn't dumb; I had read more than *Cosmopolitan*; I could cook and enjoy eating what I had cooked; when offered a drink, I didn't say 'Just a very small sherry for me'; I liked making love; I had a good job which I did well. But all those and more could be ticked off by a whole raft of man-hungry women in the circles in which Geoffrey and I moved. Perhaps, I thought then, the difference was that I wasn't actually looking for anyone or trying to be attractive myself when I quite literally bumped into him in the lobby of the McAllister's building.

It was an odd place to begin a relationship. It had all the romantic charm of an aircraft hangar. The architect had been plainly hung up on Meccano or something similar in his formative years. The lobby or, as we were supposed to call it, the atrium, was a ten-second sketch version of the dome of St Paul's done in white steel girders and plexiglass panels. Like objects being observed under a bell jar, we scurried about, frying in summer and frozen in the winter, as the management were too mean to do anything about the lousy air conditioning that Meccano man had pencilled in on the back of the same envelope. Sharing our torment was a forest of tropical palms which every week shed more fronds and turned browner under the griddle of the dome as the automatic watering system regularly broke down and no human agency admitted any responsibility for doing the job by hand.

Even so the actual scene of our encounter could have come straight out of some sloppy forties movie. In the Judy Garland role, I was coming out of the glass-sided lift that slid down one of the white steel pillars like a soap bubble. Geoffrey, a slightly portly Cary Grant, was headed into the same lift. As usual, I was late for my lunch appointment. I also had a hefty typescript in a cardboard pocket file under my left arm, my attaché case insecurely grasped in my left hand, while with my left forearm I was cradling an open Filofax, anxiously flicking over the diary pages with my right hand to find out where the hell my secretary had decreed I should lunch with Thomas Sanderson, the doyen of London literary agents and dickhead extraordinaire.

The result was that I was, as the lawyers say, failing to keep a proper look out and consequently collided heavily with the solid form of Geoffrey Reynolds. I am no lightweight myself and we both went sprawling. The cardboard file burst open and pages of typescript fluttered around, blown aloft by the fans of the air conditioning which as luck would have it was working overtime that day, despite the early spring chill outside.

Geoffrey was first on his feet, and the perfect gentleman. 'I say, I'm most awfully sorry. That was very clumsy of me.'

He held out his hand and pulled me to my feet, then busied himself with collecting the scattered pages.

I desperately straightened my skirt, searching for and finding the inevitable ladder in my tights, and tried vainly to reconfine the mass of black hair that had escaped from my comb. Bending down, I joined him in scrabbling about on the fake marble floor.

'Hey, you don't have to do that. It was my fault.'

'Oh, knock for knock, I think. That seems to be the lot.' He handed me his jumbled pile of paper. I stuffed it clumsily back into the file with the rest. I could feel his eyes on me. Perhaps he was looking up my skirt as I squatted on my haunches.

'Good Lord. How amazing! I say, I do believe we've met before.'

I stared at him, giving him an ice maiden special. Was this the line that launched a thousand passes? Who did this guy think he was? OK, so I'd cannoned into him, but that didn't give him the right to start propositioning me.

Under my stare he became embarrassed, the jaunty self-assurance slipping away. He laughed uneasily. 'Look, er, it does sound terribly corny, but we really have met before. Harriet Nagelson's, in New York? You are Mary Grapelli, aren't you, unless I've made some terrible mistake? What are you doing over here?'

I was half ready to say, 'Well, yes, you have. My name is Heather Feigenbaum.' Instead, I reluctantly owned up. As he expected me, as men do, to have some extremely good reason for not being where he thought I should be, I admitted I was with McAllister's. In spite of the interrogation, my hormones inevitably dictated that my irritation level went down a couple of points. Now that I really looked closely, the tall figure with the boyish face and dark blond hair did look vaguely familiar, but I couldn't recall a name. Harriet's parties were always full of stray English.

He held out his hand and we shook briefly. 'Geoffrey Reynolds. Odd that we should bump into each other like this, eh?'

It could have been and he obviously expected it to be the prelude to a proper conversation. But I nodded unenthusiastically and glanced pointedly at my watch. 'I really have to dash. I'm terribly late.' As I turned to go, I added insincerely, 'It was nice meeting you again.'

As I settled myself in the cab with mirror and comb, the encounter was already fading, a loose end in life's pattern, I thought.

He called me in the office the next day and asked me to have dinner with him the following evening. I was amazed to find when I had put the phone down not only that I had agreed, but that I was excited by the prospect.

Thank God he didn't try to be clever and take me to an Italian restaurant. I can't stand them. All that fake bonhomie and real lousy wine. The place he chose was French, in a not very fashionable bit of Kensington. I must have looked a bit askance when we got out of the cab, but he laughed. 'Don't worry. You'll like it.'

I did. I knew straight away from the white walls, the clean linen and quiet intentness of the other mainly non-English clientele that it was a place for serious eating. I knew also from the first mouthful of Puligny-Montrachet that Geoffrey knew how to choose wine. As I watched him through the evening, I saw that he knew how to drink it too. He didn't mess about sniffing it or rolling it around his mouth as if he were going to spit it out. He glugged it down and kept on pouring.

He seemed to be able to hold it, though. And so could I. We worked our way through crudités, turbot, a venison en croûte, ending up with a magnificent platter of cheese adorned with fresh vine leaves with which we savoured the second bottle of Hermitage.

We had started off, naturally enough, talking about food and wine, in the course of which I confessed my hatred of Italian restaurants. Geoffrey had found this immensely amusing. 'But you must be Italian, aren't you, somewhere along the line?'

I explained that my father's family, though settled in New York for a couple of generations, never forgot that they were Lombards. I had inherited their contempt for the Mezzogiorno and all its works, nowadays typified by cardboard pizzas and Mafia chic.

'Garibaldi and Co. had a lot to answer for, putting us all into the same country, my grandfather used to say.'

He liked this, and laughed.

It was a nice laugh, unforced and warm. It pleased me. It pleased me too that unlike most men he had not immediately launched into some monopolizing account of his own views on life. He encouraged me and listened attentively while I talked. Not that I needed much encouragement. I love conversation. It must be hereditary, or maybe ex-Catholics never lose the taste for confession. I found myself telling him the whole-life bit in its not particularly gory detail.

About how Francis Grapelli, commercial lawyer and younger son of a clan of Italian-American garment manufacturers, had met whilst on secondment to a law firm in London a pretty young English secretary. To the relief of his family, she had turned out to be a good Catholic girl. The marriage, however, took place at a registry office without dynastic splendour as the English side was, to put it mildly, not pleased by the prospect of, as they put it, a dago son-in-law. I was born soon afterwards at Queen Charlotte's. My names – Maria Eleanor – reflected this clash of cultures. Of course, to my mother I was always, in the English way, Maria as in Black Maria and not the heroine of *West Side Story*.

'In the end, I solved the problem and became Mary.'

'When did you do that?' His eyes crinkled at the edges in anticipation of the answer.

'When I lost my virginity, of course.'

He laughed aloud, this time a fruity, Rabelaisian sound which rang out even above the animated conversation of the other diners.

'Hang on, we'd just got you born. How long did you stay here?'

'We went back to New York when I was about eight. I liked the Big Apple at once, but poor mother was never really happy there.'

' "Was". Is she . . .?'

'Yes. She's dead. They both are. They were killed together in an auto wreck – I should say car crash. I was thirteen years old. A bad time to lose your parents, if there's ever a good one.'

'I'm sorry.' His concern was swift and unfeigned. Instinctively his hand had reached out to grasp mine in a warm squeeze. I smiled my appreciation: how infrequently Englishmen understood the need for non-sexual physical contact.

I gently disengaged. 'Oh, well. It was a long time ago – twenty-five years nearly. See what an old hag I am.'

He poured more wine into my nearly empty glass and looked at me levelly and appraisingly. 'Thou hast kept the best till last,' he said.

There was no question of my returning to England. My mother's family had never shown much interest in me. I loved America and hated the thought of England. I had no wish to settle amongst distant unknown cousins. I was absorbed into the warm but suffocatingly close family life of the Grapellis.

But as time went on, I realized that sadly but inevitably there would be a drawing apart. The future that had been mapped out for me – marriage to the distant cousin who had been marked down for me almost at birth so I could endure a life of domesticity and child bearing – was not the one I had in mind for myself. After endless family arguments and tantrums, I had got my way. I stopped going to Mass and went to study literature at the City

University. It was there that I ceased to be the virgin Maria and became the liberated Mary. It was there also I met Frank Lieberman, who had a bad case of not wanting to be Jewish. He was tailor-made to upset and alienate my family and I was the classically unsuitable bride for his.

For a couple of years we had relished our differences and fought with them spectacularly in bed and out. Then it fell apart. He was making his way in the groves of academe, and got the chance of tenure at Colorado State University. I was already set on a career in publishing and was dogsbodying at Scribner's waiting for the next rung on the ladder. I loved New York. I had no intention, having already escaped once, of throwing it all away to be a campus wife in the Mid West. We separated and eventually got our divorce. It was all, unsurprisingly, amicable as we had neither money nor kids to argue about.

A few months after we split up I landed my breakthrough job at Hiram and Hartstein, the doyen of New York publishers – in its own humble opinion. I moved to a better apartment on the East Side a few blocks from the Park. For the next few years I never looked back. Until about two years ago.

Here I paused and took another reflective swig of wine. Geoffrey said, 'I must have met you at Harriet's around then. What made you come to London?'

I shrugged. 'The usual thing in a big corporation. Orders from on high. And at H and H they don't come any higher than Max Vincent. Even God has to make an appointment. The company had just taken over a British publishing house. After surveying what he had bought at McAllister's, particularly the character of the chief executive, Max decided he wanted someone on the editorial side he could trust to civilize the list and clear away the managerial dead wood. So he told me to volunteer and made it pretty clear I'd be back writing blurbs and making coffee if I didn't. Sensibly, I regarded it as a promotion. But I still cried when the jumbo flew out of Kennedy. I couldn't imagine life on the outside, particularly not among a load of stuffy Brits, their horrible food and their miserable climate.'

'And now?'

I laughed. 'I guess I got used to the climate.' I pointed at my plate. 'And the food's improving.'

'We don't have climate, you know, we have weather.'

I said, 'I like Jack Benny too.' Then I was almost sorry for my sharpness when I saw his disappointed, rueful expression. He grinned disarmingly. 'You're right. I'll try to be original next time.'

'You do that.' I liked the way he had taken the swipe. Here was a guy who could maybe even laugh at himself. I found myself thinking, What else can he do?

I said, 'Hey, this evening's not supposed to be all me. How about you? What were you doing in New York that time?'

'That time I failed to make much of an impression?'

'Yeah, that one.'

'I was the American correspondent of the *Hobbesian*. I had to do things like keeping tabs on the American budget deficit. I sat in on endless briefings from the men at the Fed.'

'It sounds really fascinating.'

'Well it was, up to a point. I had an advantage over most of my journalist colleagues in that I did know about economics. A great deal, as a matter of fact. I have to say that. I suppose it sounds slightly immodest.'

'Not to a New Yorker. But if you're that good an economist, why did you go into journalism?'

'Pure chance, really. When I left Cambridge I went to work for Hazenbach's, the merchant bankers, in their economic forecasting department. I used to write the odd article in my spare time in learned journals and they were quite well received. I liked doing that. Though I jogged along there for a number of years, I didn't actually care much for working in banking. Most of my colleagues seemed to be using it as a platform to become Tory MPs. That is if they weren't Tory MPs already.'

'So you left?'

'Not quite just like that. I had a comfortable billet. Anyway, as you can see' – he waved his arm at the restaurant – 'I've got expensive tastes. What happened was that the bank took on as clients a bunch of characters, journalists, who had this stupid idea that they were going to start a daily newspaper, a quality to rival *The Times* and the *Telegraph*. Everyone in the City thought they were quite mad, but the bank didn't and succeeded against all the odds in raising the capital. I thought this was the most terrific thing, real David and Goliath. So, after a few glasses of celebratory champagne, Taittinger I think it was, and a good year, I offered my services as economics correspondent. And for some unknown reason they accepted. The rest is history. The *Quotidian* went from strength to strength. It made my name, such as it is. I left only because the *Hobbesian* made me an offer I couldn't refuse.'

'And that was New York? How long did you stay?'

'I was there for three years. Till a couple of months ago, in fact. Then the mag wanted me back here as associate editor to start a new section. To broaden its appeal out of technical economics. They'd been advertising on the tube and all over the place and didn't want their new readers to be disappointed. I suppose it was partly my idea. I thought of it after I wrote the book.'

'Book. You write books?'

'Don't look so surprised. It wasn't a novel or anything. I can't do stories, I'm afraid. No, it came out of my meeting a chap in the States. An extraordinary man. Inherited millions from his father and turned them into billions. From computers. Or rather computer programs. Software. I'd always been fascinated by the machines. The book was about their future: how computers could be made to do everything. How they'll make all current social and economic systems obsolete. It's a bit out of date even now, of course.'

A vague bell was ringing. I had it. I was amazed my publisher's instinct had let me down thus far. I didn't know a damn thing about computers, but I remembered a good seller right enough. 'You're that Geoffrey Reynolds! *The Digital Universe*, Random House in the States, Century over here,' I said.

'That's it. Well done. Did not so badly. Of course, everyone thought I'd made a mint and I jolly well didn't. Authors don't, do they?'

I made a face. 'Sometimes. But never as much as they think they should. What was it that interested the magazine?'

'They liked the idea of being able to predict the future shape of society. Not just computers, but new trends, new kinds of behaviour. Everything we do comes down to money in the end. So anyone who's ahead of the game either makes more money or hangs on to what he's already got. And we aim to keep our readers ahead.'

'I guess it could involve almost anything.'

'That's right. I'm looking for what may be a key element in the future. It brings me into all kinds of places. The day before yesterday, when I bumped into you, I was on my way to see your boss. About trends in publishing. Videos, audiotapes and competing media generally.'

'And did you get what you wanted?'

'Sorry, you'll have to read the article. I didn't ask you to have dinner with me so I could bang on about my work. I'm awfully boring about it when I get carried away.'

'You're not. Why did you ask me?' I spoke lightly but the answer suddenly seemed important.

He hesitated. 'This is going to sound silly.'

'So be silly.'

'Well, when we bumped into each other in your awful offices it seemed, sort of, meant. Extraordinarily apt, anyway. You see; I'd been thinking of you earlier that day. I was scrolling over some work I had done in New York, and Harriet's party and you just popped into my mind.'

'Synchronicity, isn't it called – a sort of déjà vu in the future? But, why me, for God's sake? It's very flattering but I can't believe I could have made that much of an impact. What was I doing at Harriet's? Swinging naked from the chandeliers?'

We both laughed. The idea of there being such things to swing from in Harriet's dingy low-ceilinged walk-up was ludicrous.

'You weren't doing anything. You were just yourself. Vibrant, energetic, sexy, clever. You seemed to sum up New York for me. Remember I was new there. I was in love with it all. It was so different from the stuffy male world I had left behind in London, where women like you simply didn't figure.'

'Wow! That's the first time anyone's made me a symbol. You didn't do anything to investigate the reality, though.'

He turned down the corners of his mouth. 'I know. More fool me. I was going to, then got buried in my work. Then I thought it was too late. Come to think of it, you must have left just after we met. I didn't know that, but I knew there was bound to be someone else anyway.'

'But you think there isn't now?'

'I hope there isn't. I had to find out. You can't pass up second chances. Is there?'

I thought about that while I cut myself a piece of ripe Pont L'Eveque. Then I said casually, 'You haven't told me about yourself. Aren't you married, or are you too busy in the future?'

'No, I'm not married. I've never been married.'

Looking back on it, there was a depth of melancholy about the way he said this, as if briefly a door had been opened into a dark and secret room. But at the time I merely thought it a little strange, and although I hadn't said anything as always my face said it for me.

'Ah, no. You don't have to worry – or, rather, you do have to worry. Despite public school and Cambridge, I haven't succumbed to the *vice anglais*.' His eyes dropped to watch his forefinger trace the embossed pattern in the thick material of the tablecloth. 'Oh, there have been relationships, but I've never met anyone I wanted to . . . Not since . . . But that's the past and that's a country I don't care to dwell in. The future, though. That's a different matter.' Abruptly his mood changed. He raised his eyes and looked me full in the face, smiling, challenging. 'You didn't answer my question.'

'Didn't I? As a matter of fact, there isn't.'

In the gently vibrating silence, we drank up the last of the wine. It was getting late. And it was decision time.

The waiter, who had been hovering with gradually decreasing discretion, went with alacrity to get the check on Geoffrey's signal.

17

He looked up from his wine glass and again reached out his hand to clasp mine. This time I returned the pressure.

He said, 'Will you come home with me?'

I was surprised and excited at the nervousness, the uncertainty in his voice. I smiled, a sudden warmth flooding my chest. 'Yes,' I said.

I somehow expected that he would be a considerate lover.

In my time, I'd lost enough expensive lingerie from types who thought that the only way to express maculinity was to tear a girl's clothes off, and then tear into her as well. 'All prick and no performance' was how a friend used to put it. Guys who simply wanted you as the anonymous object of some retarded adolescent sex fantasy, who, so to speak, shrank into insignificance in bed, no matter how promising they seemed before they got there.

Since I'd been living in London, apart from one or two fiascos, I'd anyway more or less given up on men. I had my job, my new apartment and a whole new way of life to discover. I told myself I didn't need the creeps. I certainly didn't need anyone to sweep me off my feet. It was because Geoffrey seemed such a tentative, decent fellow that I went back with him.

I wasn't, though, expecting much passion. But I was dead wrong.

His apartment was in Limehouse. He'd been there, he told me in the cab, long before it got fashionable and the office blocks mushroomed and the admen moved in. It was over a scruffy newsagent's by Limehouse Reach.

We climbed a dark cramped staircase and emerged into a tiny foyer. He pushed open a door and ushered me into a long narrow room littered with books and papers. 'Just concentrate on the view,' he said apologetically.

He slid open the big French window at the end and we walked out on to a balcony. Around us on our side all was dark. The river could be heard rather than seen sluicing against the embankment wall twenty feet below. On the south bank there were spots of light from offices and apartment blocks which glittered in tiny reflections on the heaving swell of the mid-channel as the tide ran strongly upstream. There was a cool breeze carrying with it a cocktail of river smells. Over us arched the London sky, flushed at the horizon, like the warm flanks of a great beast, dark only at its highest point where glinted a few cold stars.

We stood there in silence for several minutes. I sipped from my glass of whisky, then drank it down. He put his arms around me and we kissed, gently but with a hint of longing.

'Let's go inside now,' he said.

He showed me the bedroom and the bathroom adjoining, then left me alone. I undressed quickly and slipped under the quilt. There was a subdued light from the lamp on the bedside cabinet. He came into the room quietly. He was naked, the gleam of his pale body shadowed at its centre. He slipped into the bed beside me. For a few moments, we lay apart. I felt his warmth filling the bed and heard his breathing.

I reached out and pulled him close, feeling my full breasts squeezed against his chest and the hardness of his erection against my thigh. We kissed again but with more urgency, our tongues reaching deeper and deeper. I lay back, pushing his head down, showing him what I wanted. Gently he sucked at my nipples, teasing them into life with his tongue. Then he kissed all around my breasts, covering them with warm saliva then blowing the wetness into tingling coolness. His hands cupped and caressed them, valuing and nurturing them.

I held him tight against me, stroking his head. I felt myself gradually growing moist and open as my desire grew. I parted my thighs wide and pushed him further down. He did not hurry, but seemed to read my mood, seemed to know my pattern of arousal. His fingertips continued to play gently with my now swollen nipples, softly tweaking and plucking them. I heard myself moaning quietly with pleasure.

He kissed my stomach, moving gradually, tantalizingly, downwards. Then at last I felt his tongue there, moving with exquisite sensitivity up and down and around the centre of my being. I felt myself swelling, and beginning to dance to an irresistible rhythm. I felt his hands warmly clasping my hips and moulding my buttocks, his tongue now moving in response to me. My body tingled, then grew warm as if washed over by the slow regular sweep of waves on a tropical beach. My breathing quickened and I felt my spine arch upwards. I reached down again to feel his head, stroking his hair gently, pulling him closer and closer. Then the waves were hot and surging, whirling me out into the boundless ocean. I cried out, again and again. His hands tightened on my hips as I heaved and shuddered, and his tongue urged me on and on.

Finally it was over. I sank back into the bed as if I were a pool of feathers. My limbs seemed molten. He lay by my side. His hand swept my hair back across my sweat-beaded forehead. He gently kissed my parted lips.

I reached out and hugged him close. I could feel him against me, still hard.

'What about you?' I whispered.

He nibbled my ear, then said softly, 'Ladies first, now it's my turn.'

But, I was pleased to discover, it was mine again.

He stayed in Hampstead the following weekend. We made love with ever-increasing passion, talked long into the night and on the Sunday morning, after a late breakfast of quails' eggs and champagne, walked miles over the Heath, hand in hand, in the brilliance of spring.

That night, at dinner, we spoke little, lost in our thoughts. Then, our glasses charged with the last of the wine, we drank a silent toast.

He said, 'Monday tomorrow. It's late. Time to go home.'

'So, go.' Then I added, 'But make the hell sure you come back.'

He reached out and our hands clasped, fingers intertwined.

Looking back, it seems like a fairy story. Even more so when a month or so after he'd moved into my apartment, the prince asked the princess to marry him.

And she said, 'For God's sake, what the hell do you want to do that for?'

'I just do. It seems right, somehow.'

'I've been married. I don't see the point.'

'Well, I haven't and I do.'

'But why? Aren't you happy the way things are?'

'Of course I am, but I suppose I'm a conventional type at heart. I need security, commitment. I also love you very much. Please say you will.'

And he gave me that little-boy-lost look I found impossible to refuse.

I went over and kissed him. 'Believe it or not, I also love you very much. So I will.'

He was a very determined guy when he wanted to be, as this country cottage business showed.

We met Hugh Robinson as Geoffrey had arranged in the saloon bar of the Royal Baltic Hotel in Queen's Hythe. The place was already filling up with post-church, pre-lunch drinkers, but he was not hard to recognize from type, a tall heavily built fortyish man, his brown hair shot through with grey in a lovat tweed suit and those heavy brown shoes, all toecap and little holes, that only English country gentlemen – or at any rate people who want to look like English country gentlemen – wear.

We must have been recognizable from type too, because he was already rising from his chair and putting out his hand in greeting.

Geoffrey got the drinks and Hugh Robinson started that discreet mixture of friendly chat and socio-economic interrogation with which salesmen, even upper-class estate agents, prepare their pitches. Having had a whole heap of contact with the breed recently, I knew that all the while he would be tailoring his description of the property to fit what we wanted.

'Forest House,' he said finally. 'It's a very special place. It's not really the sort of property for most people round here.' He gestured vaguely at the crowd. 'It's definitely for a more sophisticated buyer. As I said in the advert, it's a bit off the beaten track. If you're looking for peace and quiet, you've got it. But let's go there now and I'll tell you about it on the way. We can go in my car.'

The car turned out to be a Range Rover. Geoffrey looked suspicious. Hugh caught the look and interpreted it. 'Don't worry, old boy. Not essential. There's a perfectly good track – used to be a big highway in the Middle Ages or Roman times or something. You'll see. It's not exactly mountainous in this part of the world.'

We drove out of town on the main road. I looked out at empty fields, newly ploughed, whiskery stalks of old stubble sticking out from the turned clay, and leafless trees and hedgerows. Despite the agent's careful presentation, I could see this Forest House turning out to be another waste of time. I had gotten cynical in the weeks we had spent tramping around tacky barn conversions, little rural slums and derelict dog kennels which smart-ass young men in suits tried to persuade me were going to be a rest cure from my quiet, warm, comfortable Hampstead apartment. And what I had tried for Geoffrey's sake to kid myself was at least partly pleasurable in a late fall that was unusually warm and sunny was now in the back end of winter a drag de la drags. I couldn't wait to get the viewing over and hurry back to a hot bath and a good book.

Hugh, having given us his prepared tutorial on the history of the place, was lecturing Geoffrey about electricity. Geoffrey knew hardly anything about the subject but this put him at only a slight disadvantage. He nodded sagely with the appearance of total understanding. I supposed this was the journalistic training.

'It's a low-voltage overhead system. Everywhere in the country-side is the same. It's jolly lucky it has a supply at all. There are a few places around here that don't, you know. It would cost a fortune to put one in now. The same supply serves a couple of farms about two miles off.'

'Sounds just the ticket. I say, can I use the word processor?'

'Absolutely. Of course, being on sticks out in the open, it can be a teeny bit vulnerable if there's a really bad storm, but that doesn't happen very often, does it?'

We had left the main road. On either side, there were lines of dark pine trees and then prairie fields stretching away to the horizon. It had started to rain steadily out of a leaden sky.

The car slowed and then negotiated a sharp turn. 'Right. This is the famous track. There's about half a mile to go now,' said Hugh. 'From where we turned off at the crossroads it's about three miles into the village. Barton St Margaret. There's a shop there, and a good pub.'

'Quite the café society,' I remarked half to myself, but got a nasty look from Geoffrey anyway.

We bumped along in silence. I must have dozed off because the next thing I heard was Hugh saying, 'This is it.'

He stopped the car and we clambered out.

The first thing I was aware of was an amazing stillness. The rain had stopped and the chilly wind had died away. The car stood on a small gravelled driveway in front of a plain yellow brick house. All around was a forest, but the house itself stood alone on a patch of green turf, slightly raised from the level of the track.

It was, I suppose, as a house unremarkable, no more than a decent cottage. According to Hugh Robinson, it had been built for the overseer of the farm workers on this part of what had once been a great estate. The workers' cottages themselves, which had gathered around forming a small hamlet, had long since tumbled into decay. Their bramble and nettle-choked ruins could be discerned a little way off, half hidden under the eaves of the forest.

I marvelled that it had somehow survived through the long period of neglect which attended the decline of the estate. The land had lost fertility and the armies of men who had once laboured at the harvest had themselves fallen before the scythe in the Great War. Broken by the Depression and the collapse of farmland values, the estate had been sold to the Forestry Commission. Its magic wand had waved into being a great plantation of fir and Corsican pine. This now swept around the house on either side leaving it poised as if between the paws of a great animal. The track we had been on continued past the house, plunging again into the shelter of the great trees, to emerge again only when they retreated before the salt marsh and sand dunes of the coast.

But a physical description hardly conveys the quality of peace which surrounded the place, a peace which drew itself from the silence of the forest, the grandeur of the overarching sky and the sense of isolation. For though it was but half a mile from the public road, it seemed, in the midst of that sparsely populated country, remote almost in the American way, in a way in which I had not thought anything other than a farm or the grandest mansion could be remote in the densely peopled mass of southern England.

And there was the forest. As I looked around at its dark mass, I felt I could be in Vermont or Maine, except that here the threatening sense of total wilderness was absent. It was comforting to know that instead of trackless wastes merging into the vaster emptiness of the Canadian Arctic, there was only a mile or two away the dull domesticity of an English village. Here the postman would call if anyone chose to write, and, oh glory, milk could be delivered.

I felt, with some amazement, a rising sense of excitement, of exultation, almost, even, an epiphany. The cynicism with which I had set out was dissolving like the nasty taste of a childhood medicine, leaving only a sense of well-being. All the accumulated sense of weariness and bitterness fell away. This was what we had been looking for. This would be our retreat, a place just to be, out of the mental treadmill of the city. It would be the still centre at the hub of our turning world. And for me, the product of an uneasy alliance of different cultures and further split between two nations which were, as the man said, divided by the same language, it might be somewhere to call home.

After these highfalutin ponderings, I had no energy for the mere detail. I left Geoffrey to walk around, listening to yet more lectures from Hugh on septic tanks and water bores and rights of way. I sat alone in the big kitchen, occasionally hearing their heavy feet clumping on the bare boards upstairs and their loud male voices. Despite the dirt and the smell of damp and the dull weather outside, I could see it bright and clean and warm.

When they came back, I thought that even Geoffrey had been struck by what I was beginning to accept was simply the magic of the place.

I wondered that anyone would want to sell such a place. Why

would they want to leave? Who had lived there? I asked Hugh. He hesitated slightly before replying.

'It's a trust. None of the beneficiaries want the place – they're all abroad – so the trustees decided to sell. Took them a while to make the decision. That's why it's been empty.'

I hardly noticed at the time that he didn't say exactly who had been living there. I put this evasiveness down to the incorrigible habit of the real estate salesman. It didn't then seem to matter anyway.

Neither of us spoke for some time after Hugh dropped us back at the car. Then Geoffrey said, 'I don't think it's worth an offer, do you?'

I couldn't believe my ears. 'Listen, bud. You tell that guy you'll pay whatever it takes to buy that place. And you make sure you do buy it.'

'You didn't really like it, did you?'

'Geoffrey!' I turned to him in anger, but I saw he was laughing. The goddamned British sense of humour.

2

Well, he did buy it. Geoffrey insisted he deal with the legal side of things. I seemed to spend about half my time in the office arguing about the minutiae of contracts, something which, even though I was pretty good at it, I really hated. I was too allergic to anything to do with the law to want to have that kind of extra hassle in my domestic life as well, so I was more than happy to leave him to get on with it. Maybe that was my first mistake.

Of course, every now and again I would ask what was happening – in a mild and unthreatening sort of way, seeing that it was his money and not mine. He would mutter something about searches, or requisitions on title or some goddamn thing or other. He seemed quite happy with the lawyer he had, some guy in Queen's Hythe whom Hugh Robinson had recommended. He said the usual firm he went to in the City, where an old school friend was a partner, had gotten too expensive and high powered for small potatoes like Norfolk cottages. I thought at the time that Geoffrey's casualness about the transaction and the length of time it seemed to me to take arose from the indulgence felt by his kind of Englishmen towards their law. They regard it as part of their heritage, requiring conservation, not demolition, like something run by the National Trust, its extreme and evident decrepitude being part of its charm.

As a result, it wasn't until April – closing, or rather I should say the completion date was on the first, so maybe the law did have a sense of humour – that we could move in.

I waited eagerly for the coming weekend. We would leave first thing on Friday morning. I was intending to stay there for the rest of the following week to get things organized, although part of the deal with Michael Underdown-Metcalfe, the Chief Executive of McAllister's, was that I would work on a typescript while I was there, just to make him feel happier about this unreasonable request for unseasonable leave so soon after Easter. Geoffrey had to be back for a meeting first thing on Monday and had a full schedule the rest of the week, so he would get the Sunday afternoon train to Liverpool Street from Queen's Hythe, returning the same way the following Friday.

The early start ended up a late start. Geoffrey had flown back from Lisbon only on the Thursday evening, later than he'd promised. He had been in Portugal for a couple of days, looking at the future of the wine industry there as part of a larger study of the whole European drinks market, a subject close to his heart. He was still recovering from the final piece of research when he staggered into the flat at midnight. The next morning he refused to get out of bed at the appointed time. When he eventually did get up, he breakfasted only on paracetamol, then exhausted by the effort slumped back into an armchair with the morning paper. I had to load the car, no easy job from the third floor with no lift.

There was a lot of stuff. Bedding, towels, crockery, cutlery, all the things you take for granted at home and miss like hell when you've not got them. During the week, I had bought what we needed and spent evenings getting everything ready. I had made a list and ticked things off as I carefully packed them into cartons from the supermarket and big plastic dustbin liners.

I hoped Geoffrey's airy confidence that the items of furniture which were included in the deal – the place had been bought more or less as it stood – were actually there when we arrived. Otherwise it was going to feel even more like camping out. I regretted not being more insistent that there should be an inventory or something, but Geoffrey had waved away my suggestion with the assurance that that was not the way of these things, and country solicitors wouldn't understand my metropolitan-American obsession with contractual minutiae.

Finally we were ready. I did the driving, of course, and Geoffrey continued sleeping off the wine research. The result of all this was that it was early afternoon by the time I turned off on to the track at the little crossroads.

It was still a glorious day. In London it's easy to forget that there are such things as seasons. There's not much scenery in the tube. But today even my citified eyes could scarcely avoid noticing that everywhere there were blobs, tufts and swathes of greenery. As we hit the ruts Geoffrey groaned. This had happened intermittently throughout the drive. It had been like driving an ambulance.

He woke up completely when we hit the particularly rough bit at the beginning of the forest. I mouthed his familiar opening words to myself. 'The trouble with women is that they've got no idea about machines. This is a car, not a tank, woman.'

We swung off the track on to the driveway. I stopped the engine and just sat there taking in the peace. In the afternoon sun the old handmade bricks of the façade glowed the colour of country butter and clotted cream. For the first time in my life I was beginning to feel I had come home.

I climbed out of the car while Geoffrey yawned and stretched. Hugh Robinson had left the key in an envelope under the front door mat. It was suitably large and old-fashioned looking. With excitement, I fitted it into the lock, turned it and pushed open the plank door. Inside it smelt musty, the result of long unoccupation. Dust motes hung in the beams of sunlight streaming in through the stairway window. I looked up at the cobwebs on the cracked ceiling and then down at the uncarpeted floorboards, shrunken with age and showing at their edges the honeycomb evidence of woodworm. I didn't care. It was our house and soon it would be beautiful.

We unpacked the car. Or rather I unpacked it. Geoffrey gently carried in a couple of extra special bottles of Dão and busied himself with the complex task of opening one of them. I had brought plenty of groceries. I suspected that the shop in Barton St Margaret, if it were up to the usual village standard, would be handy only for such British delicacies as baked beans and fizzy lemonade. We could drive into Breckenham or Queen's Hythe for anything else we needed the next day. I wanted to lose no more time that day. We had to get the place straight first.

I dumped everything in the hall and went into the kitchen. This faced south-west over the garden. The afternoon sun flooded through the small casement windows. There was a huge old pine table with a top once no doubt snowy white with scrubbing but now, like everything else, coated with a thick layer of grey dust. Geoffrey, with his unerring instinct for his own well-being, was sitting at one of the wheelback chairs drinking a glass of wine. He looked thoroughly at ease.

'You sure you're comfortable?'

He made his Cheshire Cat face. 'Lovely day, eh? How about a spot of lunch?'

'OK, but then we work. You want to sleep on the floor tonight?'

'You Yanks. You're always so damned energetic.'

'Oh, yeah. Isn't that just as well?'

We ate some bread and cheese, drank some wine. I refused to make coffee, and prodded Geoffrey out of his chair. I forced him like some reluctant beast of burden to carry stuff up the stairs.

The main bedroom was at the front of the house. It was light and airy. On the bare floorboards stood a double-size iron bedstead of the kind that Florence Nightingale probably took to the Crimea. The aged mattress had black and white striped ticking given visual interest by those stains which mattresses seem to attract. There was a chest of drawers in ugly brown veneer and a matching wardrobe which smelt of naphtha.

I flung up the bottom pane of the sash window and leaned out. The cool breeze wafted the scent of pine into the room. When I turned round, Geoffrey was lying on the bed.

'You idle mensch! Get off that bed right now!' I darted over and started to roll him off.

'I say, you fellows, yaroo!' he protested in his Billy Bunter voice, rolling back and pulling me down on the bed with him.

'You horrible British pig! You stink of wine and Gorgonzola and garlic and . . .'

His full lips met mine hungrily, our tongues joyously consorting. I felt my breasts tingling and my body aching with desire. I reached out and felt the fullness of his erection. I spread and raised my thighs, crossing my legs over his buttocks to hold him tight against me. The bed creaked like a windjammer in a hurricane in protest at our gyrations. For a glorious hour there was no one but us in the whole wide world.

The thing about married sex is that when it's over you still have the dishes to clear. Or in this particular instance, you have a whole neglected dirty house to clean.

The first thing I saw when I opened my eyes after a delicious nap was a small scaly insect making its way towards me over the mattress. I yelped. 'Geoffrey, it's a flea!'

He grunted and leaned over me, his hand resting on my stomach. 'No it's not. It's a woodlouse. Harmless. Likes damp. How are you feeling?' His hand started to move downwards.

I squirmed away, giggling. 'No, you sex maniac. No more. We've got to get on. We can't leave the house to the insect world.' I slid off the bed and stood up. The breeze was cold on my naked skin. Shivering, I shut the window and went in search of the bathroom.

When I came out, I had my plan of campaign. 'Geoffrey, you've got the bathroom. I refuse to use it again until it's clean. It has green mould in the tub and the toilet is stained bright orange. When you've done that, sweep out and dust the bedroom and shake out and turn the mattress. Then clean the stairs and the hall.'

Somewhat to my surprise, he got on with it. I gave myself the kitchen. At home I never did any real housework. We had a cleaner, despite my American reservations about servants, a couple of times a week. The idea of taking any pleasure in such drudgery would have seemed ridiculous. Here it felt different. It felt like a challenge to get the place feeling like a home. I responded to challenges.

So for the rest of the afternoon and into the evening I worked hard physically in a way I never did in London. I scrubbed the floor of the kitchen which had been covered in apparently age-old grime, revealing the warm russet glow of the handmade bricks. I washed down the powdery distemper of the walls and, perilously perched on a chair on top of the table, swept the cobwebs and dust from the massive beams of the roof. I scoured the butler sink and the wooden drainer and polished the brass faucets till they shone. I wiped out the shelves and cupboards. I removed the encrusted mould from the inside of the small, old and basic refrigerator. I was surprised and relieved when it shuddered into life when I switched it on.

Most of one side of the kitchen was taken up by a vast fireplace which contained a huge cream-enamelled wood-burning range. I remembered Hugh Robinson had said that it heated water and kept the whole place warm as well as cooking so I steeled myself to getting the hang of it. The fire compartment was choked with a mass of black flaky ash. It looked as if the last user had burned a ton of newspaper in there. I shovelled it into a cardboard supermarket carton and put it in the woodshed out in the yard by the back door. I dumped the rest of the trash on top of it in a plastic refuse sack. Hugh Robinson had been a bit vague about what happened to the garbage. I was sure it would be down to me to find out and do the necessary.

I had already looked in the shed and seen that we had inherited a goodly supply of wood. I came back bearing pine logs hither and some dry twigs for kindling. Using one of Geoffrey's newspapers – the *Telegraph* seemed suitably inflammatory and he would be kept too busy to read it – I got a fire going in the stove, and also laid and lit one in the sitting room grate to cheer up that dingy room.

Outside it was dusk. The only sounds were the crackling of the burning logs and the occasional metallic gongling as the heat dispersed through the range and into the plumbing. I collapsed into a chair and found to my surprise that doing real practical things, even dirty, messy, unpleasant things, did me a whole lot of good. I was completely exhausted, but I felt as relaxed and happy as at the beginning of a vacation.

Geoffrey stuck his head round the door. For the last hour or so I had heard no sounds of activity from his direction. He had obviously been loafing. 'Any chance of supper, Molly?'

He dodged back laughing as I threw a duster at him.

Later, we ate the cold chicken and salad I had brought with us. I was too exhausted to try to start learning how to cook on the range. Then we sat on the sofa by the fire in the otherwise dark sitting room and drank big glasses of port.

I looked over at Geoffrey, his face fitfully illumined by the embers. He was staring at the fire, his eyes seemingly focused on something far in the distance. I picked a log from the pile beside the hearth, leaned over and tossed it gently on to the glowing ash. There was a crackle as new flames engulfed the tinder-dry wood.

He came out of his reverie and our eyes met.

I smiled. '"Whenever you look up, there I shall be. And whenever I look up, there shall you be,"' I quoted, doing my best to sound rustic.

'What?'

'Hardy. Don't you recognize it? *Far from the Madding Crowd*. Gabriel Oak to his Bathsheba. That ad was quite appropriate really, wasn't it? Funny that that Robinson guy didn't have what you might call the feel of a literary man.'

'Was it? I imagine he could read. Yes, I do recognize it now you remind me. I should have said it to you, though.'

'You will, Oscar, you will.'

He chuckled comfortably. 'I say, you do really like it here, don't you?'

'I did the first time I clapped eyes on it.'

Then he said something that I suppose I was too tired and too woozy to pick up on fully. 'I knew you would. I hoped you would.'

'Well, I do. But you sound as if you'd already made up your mind before we even came here.'

He turned back to the fire, blinking as if his eyes stung from the occasional spiral of woodsmoke which drifted into the room as the wind moaned softly in the chimney. 'I suppose I did. I mean, I suppose I had a kind of feeling about it. That everything would be all right.'

I had the same feeling. My life had been crowded with husband, lovers, work and the petty rewards of minor success. But there had been a void there. In this place, this place that Geoffrey had found, I felt for the first time in my life the peace of true fulfilment, as if at long last the grey ashy crust of everyday existence had been pierced by the bright flame of a new life.

I clasped his big warm hand. 'Can I risk another quotation? "And all shall be well and all manner of thing shall be well." Julian of Norwich – so she's at home here. My love, you are a funny old stick. You're so English, on the surface all proper and correct. But underneath I think there's an old Romantic poet wanting to get out.'

'That's the first time anyone's ever called me Byronic, Molly.'

'Hang on! Who said anything about Byron? He's not the only Romantic poet.'

'No, don't spoil my pleasure. Byron might be quite appropriate.'

'Why? Are you nursing some dreadful psychic wound, like Childe Harold?'

He shrugged. 'I might be. I could be like the late lord himself – "mad, bad and dangerous to know".'

'Dangerous! Geoffrey, you're the least dangerous person I know. You're so solid, so, well, there. And if I don't know much about you, it's because you don't ever tell me. Remember the big warning sign you hung over our relationship that first time? "The past's a country I don't care to dwell in".'

'God, did I really say that? I must have been pissed. Such flowers of rhetoric I have in my cups.' He was silent for a moment then he said, 'Would it matter if I were . . . sort of different from what you think? If there were things about me you might be surprised about?'

I should have been struck then by the sudden growth of seriousness in his tone. But my euphoric mood carried me on, reckless of what he might be trying to say. I moved close to him, making the battered old sofa creak in protest. 'Geoffrey, I love you. You can tell me or not tell me anything, but I can't believe that there's anything which would stop me loving you.' I leaned over and kissed him. 'Now you're going to say you rob banks.'

He held me close, his chin resting on my shoulder, his face buried in my hair. His muffled voice said, 'I've robbed several banks. I'll tell you about it soon, very soon. Please trust me. Say you do.'

'I do, I do,' I said sleepily. 'Let's go to bed.'

There seemed no need then to spoil the delightful mood. If Geoffrey had something to tell me, he would have all the time in the world to do it.

On Saturday morning he insisted on our going into Breckenham for the market.

'It's a real country market. Come on. We've got to start showing ourselves in the community.'

He had dressed the part. Gone were the double-breasted suit, silk tie and shiny shoes he wore in the weekdays, but instead of the jeans and leather jacket which were his usual Hampstead weekend clobber he wore baggy brown corduroy trousers, a Viyella check shirt and an ancient tweed jacket of generous cut which had belonged to his father. He had also acquired a pair of heavy brogues.

Breckenham on Saturday was transformed. I remembered it only as a dull Sunday town of dark old-fashioned shops and damp back alleys clustering around the huge open expanse of the triangular market-place.

Now a shanty town of tents and stalls had appeared covering the market-place in a tattered blanket of faded green, brown and off-white. And it was teeming with people who spilled out on to the side streets, ignoring the few cars such as ours trying to make their way through.

We were looking for somewhere to park. Geoffrey had ignored

the warning signs of cars on the sidewalks well out of the centre and had pressed on insisting that we should find a space convenient to his needs. We ended up stuck in a mass of jostling humanity. They buffeted and scraped their way alongside and in front of the car without a care for its expensively maintained paintwork. Geoffrey was fretting. He twiddled anxiously with the knobs of the dashboard stereo, increasing the volume of Elgar's Cello Concerto – chosen in celebration of the Englishness of the occasion – to a level which would have made the old boy scream in agony.

After fruitlessly revving the engine a couple of times, he finally honked the horn loudly and savagely. The knot of pedestrians glared back at us over the red hood. One big fellow with long greasy locks and a well-filled khaki jacket leaned forward and banged on the windshield, angrily mouthing words whose meaning was pretty clear despite being drowned in the languorous thunder of the cello. Geoffrey's response was to snap down the central locking button, hoot again even more peremptorily and nudge the car forward threateningly, a rogue male surging into combat in answer to a challenge.

'For God's sake Geoffrey, control yourself!' I yelled. 'This is England not Beirut.'

The crowd sulkily separated to let us pass. Nodding heads followed our progress, no doubt memorizing every detail of our appearance should they chance to meet us again on more nearly equal terms. Geoffrey grinned triumphantly. All the natives needed was a bit of firm handling.

Eventually about three streets away Geoffrey found a parking space just about as long as the car. He made me get out and help. After a session of arm waving and shouting at one another, he was finally satisfied with the result. He was still agitated and made minute and suspicious examination of the bodywork.

'Look, Geoffrey, relax. This is the goddamned country. People move slower here. They take their time. That's one of the reasons you came here. Remember taking time? Once you get in that auto, you're some kind of crazy man.'

'I don't mind their taking time, but why the devil do they have to take it front of my car?'

I sighed. It was a waste of time trying to talk to him in this mood. We walked in silence past redbrick terraces of houses.

Geoffrey did not cheer up when we emerged from the quiet side road back into the market-place. He looked around him and wrinkled his nose at a greasy onion smell which drifted over from a converted single-decker bus whose destination board read 'Josie's Cafe'. A ragged queue was waiting patiently for tea served in white styrofoam cups and for substances libellously alleged on a scrawled blackboard to be burgers and hot dogs. Over some kind of tannoy system the Beatles' 'She Loves You' was being blasted out. I started to laugh.

'Ye olde typical peasant market, full of cheery forelock-tugging country swains holding shepherd's crooks and buxom maidens? The Casterbridge Hiring Fair? Is that what you imagined?'

'God, it's like some kind of awful sixties timewarp.'

'Well it's OK by me. It's British social history. Just the thing for foreign tourists. Why don't you go and have a drink? I want to look round even if you don't. I'll join you later.' I grabbed his arm and shepherded him in the direction of the Golden Lion Hotel.

I wandered around. At one of the fish stalls I bought a couple of nice crabs and at one of the vegetable vendors some local potatoes and a white cabbage for the coleslaw I was going to make. The stallholders were cheerful. They smiled and exchanged pleasantries as they handed out parcels roughly wrapped in old newspaper. Away from Geoffrey's gloom, my own mood lightened. Knowing he wouldn't think of it, I bought myself a big bunch of what the flower man called 'lovely daffs'.

It felt good. Perhaps I was going native. For someone who had spent most of her life jostling along overcrowded sidewalks, fighting for a place at lunch counters, scrambling for seats in taxis, planes and subway trains the bustle of Breckenham Market was a rest cure. And beneath the superficial tackiness of the cheap carpets and the shoddy furniture, the dreadful clothes and the plastic shoes, was something that had disappeared from the Hampsteads of the world, a gentleness and a harmony. I remembered girlhood vacations at small towns on the coast of Connecticut and Massachusetts.

On one stall, displaying cheeses in different shades of yellow and orange but all of the same unyielding texture, there was an old-fashioned wicker basket piled high with huge brown eggs.

'Are those free-range?' I asked the youngish woman serving.

She nodded. Then with a cheeky smile and a half-glance over her shoulder to the back of the stall, she said slyly, 'Not as free-ranging as he is.' She had spoken loudly enough to raise a growl from the grey-haired man unpacking boxes.

To my amazement, I laughed out loud. I was still smiling at the feeble joke as I positioned the egg box carefully in the top of my now full holdall. Perhaps this was what being in the country did to you. Painlessly removed the sophisticated responses that living in the city had painfully beaten into you. Soon I would be sucking a straw and saying 'Eee!' and 'Aah!' with the best of them. What would my colleagues in Bloomsbury – or even better my ex-colleagues in Fifth Avenue – think of me? I remembered Geoffrey. Left by himself in a bar, he was capable of forgetting not only the time but where he was or even who he was. I felt I had earned my snifter.

In my perambulation, I had gotten to the far end of the market-place. I started to make my way back through the crowd to the Golden Lion Hotel, which stood at the top end on the other side of the main highway, its once elegant but now slightly shabby Georgian façade contrasting with the adjacent distinctly less elegant redbrick Victorian Corn Hall, now demoted to a JobCentre.

I was standing opposite the hotel waiting for a gap in the traffic when I caught sight of Geoffrey. He was in the main entrance, at the top of a short flight of steps, shadowed by the pedimented portico and its fat white stucco Doric columns. I called to him and waved. He seemed to hear my voice over the noise of the passing traffic. He looked out and to my surprise I saw what seemed to be an expression of alarm on his face. He turned back into the lobby and from his gesturing arm appeared to be having an animated conversation with someone inside.

A figure, apparently the object of Geoffrey's attention, detached itself from the gloom and emerged into the daylight. It was a woman, dark-haired and slim in a dark blue coat. To my amazement, a hand, presumably Geoffrey's, appeared on her shoulder, apparently trying to restrain her or pull her back inside. She shook it off with an angry twist of her shoulders.

Then the little scene was hidden from view as a large container truck ground and wheezed to a halt slap in front as the traffic lights changed. I hopped with impatience as I waited for the last cars to pass on my side. At last I dashed across the road, but when I emerged on to the pavement in front of the hotel both the woman and Geoffrey had gone.

I looked up and down the street. Perhaps she had changed her mind and gone in again, or slipped into one of the shops on the other side. I was surprised to find myself thinking like this, but Geoffrey had given every indication that he didn't want us to meet. And that was disturbing.

He was in the lounge, poring over the crossword page of the *Guardian* with a bottle of red wine and a glass at his elbow. He seemed not to notice until I plonked myself down on the Windsor chair opposite. Then he looked up, with his usual boyish grin. 'Hello, gorgeous. Care to join me?'

'Why, are you coming apart?' It was one of his favourite routines, but one that he never tired of. He chuckled delightedly.

I hoped he was going to say something convincing about the drama of the steps. Instead he pointed at the wine bottle. 'Shall I get another glass? It's vile stuff, though.' The bottle was three quarters empty. I wondered if she had had some. I shook my head. 'I'd like a Scotch, please, Bell's.'

'I know. No soda, on the rocks, but easy on the ice.' He got up. 'Ain't nobody in Norfolk orders a drink like you, baby.' This was delivered in the accent which he fondly believed was authentic New York cab driver.

While he was at the bar, I swivelled the paper round to see how he was getting on. Geoffrey usually whipped through these things in twenty minutes or so. He hadn't managed a single clue.

When he came back with the drink I said, 'Who was that lady I saw you with just now?'

He met my eyes straight, their unclouded blue as innocent as forget-me-nots. 'Lady? What on earth are you talking about?'

'I saw you just now in the lobby here. I was on the other side of the road. I yelled out and waved. You had a woman with you. Dark, blue coat, your type. You bump into an old flame, Geoffrey?'

He shook his head, the picture of bemusement. 'Sorry, darling. I haven't a clue what you're on about. I've been in the bar for ages. Haven't spoken to anyone except the barman and haven't moved except once to go for a pee. Must have been somebody else you saw. I didn't know you were back until you materialized in front of me.'

I stared at him. I didn't want to believe he was lying. Perhaps I had been mistaken. It had been some distance, and in shadow. What the hell? I tried to push the incident into the file marked 'Bad things I don't want to think about'. I raised my glass, 'Cheers.'

'Slainte.'

'Geoffrey.' I pointed to the bag. 'Have I got a good lunch here. Crab. Fresh as the morning.'

'Lead me to it, me beauty,' he said with a comic leer.

I felt my head swimming. I was being cowardly. I had to say something.

Finally I spoke. 'Remember, after lunch you have to finish the stairs. And no arguing.'

I met his eyes. They were so blue.

I had a real sense of anticipation as we bounced up the track. It was like being on vacation, time didn't seem to matter. As I stopped the car and switched off the engine, the only sound was the swashing of a slight breeze through the pines and the air was faintly spiced with their resin.

I took my bag with the groceries straight through to the kitchen. I was pleased with the effect of my hard work of the day before. It looked and smelt clean. The stove gave out its comforting warmth in here even though the rest of the house still had about it the faint lingering chill of unoccupation. The old table gleamed white from the scrubbing I had given it.

I took out the cabbage and started to slice it for coleslaw. I was so preoccupied that I didn't immediately notice that the kitchen door to the yard at the side of the house was open slightly.

'Geoffrey, have you been through to the yard?'

Having opened a bottle and poured out one glass, he was sitting at the kitchen table engrossed once more in the *Guardian*.

'No. Why?'

'The kitchen door's open.'

'You must have forgotten to shut it.'

Along with everything else of a similar nature the task of ensuring that any place we were staying in was properly locked up when we went out was delegated to me. It was safer that way as Geoffrey had no sense of concern about the state of doors, windows, water, gas or electricity. Although I didn't think I had quite yet tipped over into total obsession, this habit of his had undoubtedly sharpened up my own propensity to check out such things. I was absolutely certain therefore that the kitchen door had not only been properly closed but locked three hours before.

'Geoffrey, you know I don't forget that sort of thing. Geoffrey! Put down that newspaper and listen. Someone has broken into our house.' I was outraged and alarmed at the very idea.

He waved his hand dismissively. 'But there's no sign of a break-in. Burglars these days don't worry even in London about a bit of noise and mess. Out here you could use gelignite and nobody would hear a thing. Not that you'd need to. A child could kick in any of the doors.'

He was right, but I didn't like being reminded of it. I couldn't bear to think of this place being invaded in that way.

I went over to examine the door. The lock, an old tinplate rimlock screwed to the ledge-and-brace door, had been turned back. There was no sign of its having been forced. Whoever had opened it must have picked it. Or used a key.

Geoffrey could see that I was rattled and did his best to reassure me. 'Don't worry. You could have forgotten. Or it could have been that fellow Robinson. He had a key. He might have looked in to see whether things were all right when he was passing. He knew we were coming down this weekend.'

'Oh yes? He doesn't strike me as a guy who would do anyone that kind of favour. Not that it's much of a favour to go round opening people's doors and then leaving them open.'

I had a careful look around the rest of the house. There was nothing out of place. I supposed I could have forgotten. Even though nothing would convince me that I really had, I chose to forget about it. But nevertheless a faint sense of unease lodged itself at the back of my mind, a small cloud in yesterday's empty sky.

That night I woke up suddenly, as if startled by some sound or by a vivid dream. I lay on my back in the darkness. Whatever had dragged me back into consciousness had faded. My mind was at that moment a languorous blank, and there was no noise apart from the gentle rustle of the wind in the trees. Geoffrey slept quietly by my side. I thought then how strange it was that we two very different people had joined our lives together. Till death us do part. Funny how I, who thought myself so modern, so enlightened, fiercely wanted that old-fashioned fidelity. I wanted him and would fight to keep him. Restless with the memory of what I had witnessed that day, I slipped quietly out of bed and went to the window.

Softly I drew aside the curtains, pushed up the window and leaned out. My loosened hair blew across my face and lips. I pushed it back and held its warm scented mass pressed to my cheek. Across the moonlit clearing the wind danced with the trees. I could hear their branches creaking as they swayed in its embrace. Above me the clouds swirled, offering ragged glimpses of stars a thousand times brighter than those seen dimly against the orange sky of London. I seemed to be watching from the bridge of a ship across a dark and heaving sea. I closed the window and returned to the bed.

To my eyes, the darkness had become a pearly grey. I raised the corner of the quilt and looked down at Geoffrey's sleeping form. He lay towards me on his side, his knees bent and his hands clasped to his lips like a child. I slid back under the quilt, feeling the warmth from his body. Gently I reached out and my fingers found the cord of the pyjama waistband. I pulled and the knot fell open. Slowly I slithered down the bed until my head was level with his thighs, then moving inwards my lips found and closed over the head of his limp penis.

At the first caress of my tongue, he stirred and woke, the stifled groan of protest swiftly becoming one of pleasure. As I slowly moved my head, I felt him stiffening, growing, filling my mouth, feeling my saliva flowing over him. I ran my tongue around the ridged edge of his glans and massaged the gently pulsing shaft. His hand stroked my face and neck, then reached down for my breasts. I withdrew, and still holding him with one hand and with the other on his stomach, pushed him over on to his back so I was kneeling between his open thighs. I whispered, 'Relax, my love, this is for you.'

Then with my mouth wide, I bent down to him once more.

3

On Monday I slept late. In London the multifarious noises of the urban morning: milkmen, traffic, kids going to school would rouse me at seven, my usual time. Here in the middle of the forest such things were only a memory. So it was about eight when I came to. The bed felt big and empty. It always did these days when Geoffrey was away. I had finally gotten used to not being alone. That was what marriage did to you.

I had taken Geoffrey to the train station the previous afternoon. He hated to hang around on platforms waiting for connections and had insisted on going early to catch the last through train to Liverpool Street.

I had done some more pottering around when I had got back, had a supper of leftovers, then sat reading by the fire in the sitting room until way after midnight.

Before going up, I had stood in the front porch looking across the clearing, hearing the rustle of the breeze in the trees, the occasional squawk and clatter of a roosting bird, and further off the staccato barking of what must have been a fox. I felt suddenly out of normal space and time, as if I were on the edge of some enormous other universe, one that began where the dark border of the pine trees met the paler star-illuminated sky.

I hauled myself out of bed, yawning and stretching mightily, my body after my recent exertions aching with the reappearance of muscles and sinews I thought had been lost. I opened the curtains, flung up the sash window and leaned out, resting my bosom on the window sill, the air flowing deliciously cool down the front of my nightdress.

The view still grabbed me by the throat. I felt I would never tire of it. The bedroom faced north-east. The trees fell away from the slight eminence of the clearing in great rolling waves. To the north, they stretched clear to the horizon, an uninterrupted dark green expanse, as humpy and uneven as a bed quilt. Couched on its rise in this country of undulating plains and gentle slopes the house had a mountain's eye.

This morning the sky was an infinitely pale milky blue at the horizon. The sun was yellow like the yolk of a newly poached egg. Already the chill air of the night was warming, and from the dew-soaked grasses of the clearing arose a faint steam. There was only a slight breeze wafting the sharp, sweet scent of the forest into the room.

I bathed quickly in the off-white but now clean tub. I put on a simple Donegal tweed skirt, a honey blouse and a tan-coloured V-necked sweater, the most country things I could find in my wardrobe. I never wore trousers. I always felt women were enough at a disadvantage without covering up too much of what they indisputably had. I knew I had nice legs.

Downstairs, I told myself there was no way I was going to stay inside on such a day. I took a chair and table out through the sitting room French windows on to the terrace at the back of the house and drank my coffee and ate my toast in the sunshine. Then I settled down with my task, a mile-high pile of photostat type-script called *The Thought Stealers*, alleged to be the world of science fiction's answer to *War and Peace*.

I had to finish the editing this tome. The author and the contract for it had been acquired by Michael, who had by some no doubt devious means lured the guy away from his previous publishers. He had volunteered as a sweetener that the editorial director herself, who being an American was a science fiction fan by birthright, had personally demanded to be the editor. This was a complete fabrication, of course. But I had been told to go along with it and who was I, a mere woman, to argue when the profits of McAllister's and hence the genitalia of Michael Underdown-Metcalfe were on the line?

I scribbled a few notes as I went along and actually made a good deal of concentrated progress for about two hours before I surfaced for a breather. The sunlight was intense for so early in the year. I shielded my eyes from the glare. With this partially obscured vision the garden looked almost respectable. There was a big area of tall grass, buttercups and sprouting clumps of cow parsley which ran down the slope to a broken-down post and rail fence. This must at one time have been the lawn. Beyond the fence was an area of scrub and beyond that loomed the first great trees of the forest. Huddled to the side there were some ragged fruit trees of indeterminate variety. A cold frame from which all the panes of glass were missing indicated the possible former presence of a vegetable garden. A few shrubs, up to their middles in last year's dead nettles like reapers in a cornfield, completed the assets of this horticultural disaster area. And the massive growth spurt of the spring had only just begun.

I ruefully contemplated the weeds already thrusting their way through the frost-damaged bricks of the terrace. A huge effort would have to be made outside. It would certainly test the resolution of two new country dwellers. I sighed and shifted my gaze back hastily to the sunlight and the trees.

It was then that I saw something moving at the edge of the forest.

It was too far away to see quite what it was. It was the quality of the movement which caught my attention. It was not the scuttling run of the pheasants which were as common as sparrows round about. It was an odd spasmodic slow crawl by something dark coloured and much larger than a pheasant. There were intervals of several minutes in which whatever it was seemed to rest, to gather strength for the next push. I was reminded of those war films of infantry moving forward on knees and elbows, rifles held in the crooks of their arms, shuffling from cover to cover. As I watched, I saw that this reaction was not so fanciful. The object appeared to have a purpose and a direction. It was moving in a roughly straight line away from the shelter of the trees across the open clearing. There could be no doubt about it. It was headed for the house.

I stared at it, a dry tightness gripping my throat. I pushed back the chair and stood up, somehow compelled to meet this visitation halfway. The long, still-wet encumbering grass and tall weeds soaked my pumps and the hem of my skirt as I ran down to the fence. It felt as if I were wading thigh-deep through the shallows of a lake.

I stepped on to the bottom rail to get a better look. The rough wood under the palms of my hands seemed reassuring. I could now hear the rustling noise of the moving thing. There were other sounds. A sort of panting and a whinnying kind of whimper, the distress note common to animals and to humans. Then the sounds were level with the fence. A few feet further down a patch of dry grass parted and the muzzle of a large dog pushed under the rail. I felt the fence tremble slightly. Or maybe it was I who was trembling.

It was a black and white dog with longish hair, a type of collie. Its head was resting on the ground, the ears pressed flat against its head. It was whimpering in pain. It rolled its eyes towards me. They were wide in distress and entreaty, the whites showing clear all round the pupils. We stared at each other for some moments. And then with a gesture of what I was amazed to think of as impatient disappointment, the dog turned its eyes back towards the house and uttered a series of yelping barks. It made me jump. I felt the skin tighten at the back of my neck. The barks died away into mumbling growls and then, as if the animal was exhausted with the effort, they reverted to the whimpers. It continued its agonizingly slow stubborn crawl along the ground towards the house.

I watched it, shocked and terrified, and with a kind of fascination. I do not like dogs. In fact I am afraid of them and this fear held me back from rushing towards this one immediately in the way that someone might have who loved and trusted them. It was dragging itself along with its forelegs alone. I saw the reason for this as it emerged from its cover.

It was horribly crippled. Its hindquarters were coated with a reddish-black sticky mass of semi-congealed blood, which had matted its hair and attracted a further accretion of pine needles and dried grass from its crawl through the forest. Its back legs trailed limp and broken behind it. Its tail was nothing more than a pathetic stump, from which hung tatters of bloody skin and hair. Some extraordinary animal will seemed to be driving it on. Despite its injury, it had already moved several yards away from where I stood. I could see the effort in the straining muscles of its forequarters, and hear the rasping pant of its breath. Its tongue lolled from its mouth and there were flecks of dried foam on the corners of its black lips, curled back from its yellow teeth in a rictus of agony.

The poor thing had been shot. I stood appalled as it crawled nearer and nearer to the house. I hadn't any idea as to what to do. I watched numb with indecision as its broad back rested for a minute before continuing its mindless insistent shuffle, flattening the grass with a red smear as it went.

I had finally started to move towards it, and had caught it up in a few strides, when a huge voice yelled from behind me, 'Stop!'

I turned sharply. A man big enough to match the voice was running towards me. He was carrying a single-barrelled shotgun the size of a cannon.

'Don't go near him!' he shouted. 'He's half-savage.'

I stared at him, fury welling up inside me. 'You shot him.'

Suddenly I hated this man with his big red face and his bristling grey moustache. He was now standing between me and the dog which had stopped moving and lay with its head in its paws whimpering pathetically.

'He's been taking my pheasants. I saw him a few days ago and loosed off a couple of barrels. Obviously hit him, but he got away into the undergrowth and I couldn't finish him off. Then just now, as I was passing, I saw the blighter again. Stand back.' He took a few steps towards me and almost involuntarily I retreated a similar distance. He was obviously a man who expected people to do what they were told.

He turned back to the dog, and before I realized what he

intended he casually pushed the shotgun down almost into the ear of the dog and pulled the trigger.

The blast made my ears ring. The dog's head had been blown apart. Digusting lumps of glistening greyish brains and bloody flesh littered the grass.

I hung my head aside, a bitter taste rising in my throat.

'Sorry about that. Had to do it. Put the thing out of its misery. It was half-dead anyway. Couldn't do anything kinder to him.' He prodded the body with his foot. 'Look how thin he is. Must have been living wild for some time. I thought it was a fox at first getting into the pheasant run. Then my keeper saw him and we kept a watch out.'

He suddenly seemed to take proper notice of me, and a less brusque note entered his voice. 'A bit upsetting I expect, if you're not used to these things. I say, you're new, aren't you – at the house? Staying here for a few days, what?'

'It's our weekend place. We've just moved in.'

'Is that so? I'm sorry about the mess.' He waved his hand to indicate the remains of the dog. 'I'll get one of my men to come along and clear it up. Don't want to ruin your view.' He gazed at the dog again as if he were reminded of something. 'That's jolly odd.' He spoke more to himself than to me. He bent down and reached unconcernedly into the bloodied fur where the dog's neck had been. His fingers hooked around something and tugged. 'Aha, hey presto!' he exclaimed in boyish triumph. He held up in his red-stained hand part of a leather strap from which dangled a small round metal disc.

'I thought so. It came to me that I'd seen this dog before – but not recently. And I was right. Here.'

He thrust the identity disc towards me. Despite the blackish encrustation I could read the words engraved on it. 'Ruff. Forest House.'

I stared at him in astonishment. 'Whose dog is this?'

His pale blue eyes stared back at me. He seemed relieved I wasn't going to have hysterics. For a moment, his brow furrowed slightly and the eyes narrowed. Then he said, 'Chap used to live here. Dog was his. Funny chap. Sort of boffin, I believe. University man. Didn't know him, or see him about. I remember the dog, though, and there may have been a child, I think. But they went, maybe a year or more ago. Place has been empty since. Cartwright, my agent, never said it was for sale. Usually I rely on him to know that kind of thing. Might have been interested myself: shooting box, perhaps. London agent, was it?'

Despite the casualness of the question, I sensed his keen interest. What cheek, I thought, after the way he had barged in here. He would be asking the price next. I was damned if I was going to be interrogated in my own backyard.

I shook my head and said, deliberately curtly, 'Queen's Hythe. Robinson's.'

'Robinson's? Never heard of them. Still, they're here today gone tomorrow, those people nowadays.'

That seemed to close the matter. He looked down at the dog again. 'I wonder where you've been all this time, Ruff old fellow. But wherever it was, it seems you decided it was time to come home.'

He eyed me appraisingly for a moment, and I felt oddly uncomfortable under that gaze. 'Well. Must be going. Work to do. Good Lord! Never introduced myself. Funny time to do it. How do you do? James Edwardes. Barton House. Too messy to shake hands, I'm afraid.' He held up his large hand for me to see the blood.

'I'm Mary Reynolds.'

He grunted by way of acknowledgement and farewell, striding off down the slope and back into the forest, the shotgun tucked like a toy under his huge shoulder.

I felt I had to get out. The business of the dog had left me rattled. There was something queer as well as just shocking about the incident.

Anyway I couldn't carry on working with Ruff's pathetic corpse lying out on the lawn. I needed a change of scene. A drink. I remembered that Hugh Robinson had said there was a pub in Barton St Margaret. I had never been there. I would go there now.

I got into the car and started it up. With a rush of what seemed like anger, I slammed it into gear and roared off down the track. I don't usually drive fast but that day I hurled the car round the bends recklessly. I could feel the suspension bottoming as it hit the deeper potholes. A good thing Geoffrey wasn't here to purse his lips and tut tut. I would have pushed him out.

I was so intent on the sensation of violent movement that I completely failed to stop at the junction with the road. The car bounced heavily as it hit the edge of the tarmac and I hurled it into a skidding right-hand turn. For a moment I thought I had lost control completely as the big machine slid back across the road with a howl from the tyres. It bumped hard against the grass verge then mercifully responded to my frantic wrestling with the wheel before we ended up in the deep roadside ditch.

The road was empty of traffic. No one had seen my half-hearted attempt to kill myself. The shot of adrenalin from the near accident cleared my head. What the hell did I think I was doing? I slowed down. I grew calmer as I drove along the monotonous pine-edged road. After a mile or so, a black on white sign announced that I had arrived in Barton St Margaret. I would hardly have noticed otherwise. There were a few cottages set back from the road with long front gardens full of young broad bean and cabbage plants. People obviously didn't waste precious grow-ing space on lawns and flower beds in this part of the world. Then the road bent right in a sharp turn and there were more cottages and a pretty green with trees and beyond a church tower. By the side of the green was a tall white-painted post with a swinging sign board in an iron frame. There was a picture of a clownish man doing something effortful to a barrel. I had found the Cooper's Arms.

I turned the car into the gravelled parking lot beside a low-built whitewashed building with a curvy pantiled roof. There were a few other cars, clearly belonging to locals. Cortinas, Japanese pickups and a couple of drab-coloured Land Rovers, all liberally splashed with mud. I examined myself in the mirror, combed my hair and rubbed my moist eyes with a tissue. When I climbed out I felt rather shaky. I pushed open the heavy wooden door and let it bang behind me.

There was a small lobby with a cigarette machine and two doors. I didn't feel up to the public bar and I wasn't too sure of the reception a woman on her own would get in there. Maybe it would be too friendly. I didn't think I could handle that at that moment.

The lounge bar was empty. It seemed rather homey and welcoming despite that. It was more like a front parlour than a bar, with comfortable armchairs and a real wood fire burning in the small grate. From the public side of the bar at the end of the room I could hear sounds of laughter and male voices.

I perched myself on one of the fake-leather-topped padded bar stools. A chunky man in a red sweat shirt with grey crew-cut hair came through from the public bar. He gave me a thorough but not unfriendly once-over. I said from sheer force of metropolitan habit, 'Scotch please. Bell's. A double. On the rocks, but easy on the ice. No soda.' It was one of the few things I said which still sounded American.

'Right away, lady.'

I glanced at him sharply, taken aback. He grinned at me and raised a quizzical eyebrow.

'You're a long ways from Fifth Avenue,' he said as he turned to fiddle with the optic measure on a whisky bottle.

'And you're a long way from' – I thought quickly – 'Des Moines?'

He grinned again and placed the drink on the bar. He bent over on his. thickly haired forearms like a bartender in a Western. 'Pretty close. Well, maybe not that close. Gary, Indiana.'

'Like the song,' I said rather foolishly. 'In *The Music Man.*'

'Yup. Sure made us real famous.' His voice was heavy with irony.

At least he wasn't the sort of guy who wanted to fall on my neck and reminisce like down-home folks. Why, we weren't even on a first name basis yet. Perhaps living here had had an effect on him as well. I glanced around again, taking in the detail of the room. Over the mantel was a framed colour photograph of some kind of warplane, a jet, camouflaged. In front was a slightly younger version of the landlord.

He had followed my gaze. 'Flll. My plane.'

'You liked it here.'

'That's right. I was at Lakewaters. Royal Air Force Lakewaters they call it but it's as American as momma's apple pie. I had no particular reason to go back Stateside at the end of my tour, so I sank my gratuity here. It's a nice life.'

He went away in response to a call from the public. I drank the Scotch down in one. People sometimes say it's the idea of the drink rather than the reality which brings comfort. This is bullshit. The liquor burned my throat. I felt easier to be away from the house and the mess in the garden.

The landlord returned. I was obviously a change from the ploughboys.

'Are you visiting around here?'

'We have a sort of weekend and holiday place.' I thought I'd get the 'we' in somewhere.

'In the village?'

I bit back the remark which rose to my lips. If this had been London, I wouldn't be spending time chatting up the bartender. But in the country you did, apparently.

'No. On the edge of the forest. A couple of miles away.'

He stopped wiping the glass in his hand and looked up with interest.

A voice from the public called out, 'Ross, 'bor, never mind your new girlfriend. Have you forgotten about the regulars?' It was followed by a chorus of rustic guffawing.

I gave a thin smile.

He went into the public and I heard more laughter then a lot of murmuring. I didn't have to guess the subject.

When he came back, he had the grace to be slightly shamefaced. He shrugged. 'Seems like old Norman knows about you. Or at least about your house. There isn't much round here that Norman doesn't get to hear about. Forest House, he said.'

I nodded.

'Country people, well they kind of take an interest. Specially foreigners. Still, everyone who's been here less than twenty years is a foreigner. After that, you're just new. I've only been here two years or so. That means I haven't really even properly moved in.'

'And what does old Norman know?'

'The previous owners. A guy and his daughter. He used to do handyman stuff for them. I can't say I ever knew the guy. He never came in here. Not a sociable type, according to Norman.'

'Where did they go? Why did they leave?'

'According to Norman, it's all a bit of a mystery. Left suddenly. No one's seen them since.'

There was another shout from the public. 'I got to go. Thirsty men in there.' He pointed questioningly at my empty glass.

I glanced at my watch. 'Thanks for the talk. I have to be getting back.'

The sun had gone in. Grey clouds swirled, promising rain. I was getting into the car when a small man in a shabby raincoat and long black wellingtons came hurrying out of the pub and waved at me. He came alongside the open door. Bloodshot blue eyes set in a wind-scoured face bored into mine.

'You're the new lady at Forest House. It's a queer thing. I didn't let on in there but I never heard about it being sold till him what reads the electric meters said t'other week.' He seemed put out not to have been consulted in the matter.

I nodded. 'Is that so? I'm Mary Reynolds. And you must be Norman.'

'Norman Fincham is the name,' he admitted. 'I did general work for Mr Mallen. Gardening, and that.' He paused meaningfully.

'Well, Norman, if you've a mind I might just have some gardening for you myself.'

'I might be interested. But it's a long way for me and I'm not getting no younger.'

I wasn't fooled by this elaborate show of indifference.

'OK. You think about it and let me know. I'm here all this week.'

He grinned, showing broken yellow teeth. 'OK, missus.'

I assumed our little interview was over and started to shut the car door, but he didn't move away. Instead he bent over and poked his head inside. I could smell the booze on his breath. He hadn't shaved and his cheeks and chin were covered in white sprouts of bristle. 'He came back then,' he said.

'What?' For a moment I didn't get it.

'The dog. Her dog.'

'How did you know that?'

The yellow teeth appeared again. 'Like he told you, I get to know things. One of his men were in there. But I knew he would.'

I was getting bewildered by the pronouns. I seized on the last. 'What do you mean, you knew?'

'That dog. He were clever. He found his way home. You couldn't keep him away for ever. Faithful, dogs are.'

'Faithful?'

'To their owners, of course. He came looking for her.'

'Who? Mrs Mallen?'

'No, not Mrs Mallen.' He seemed amazed at the idea. 'The little girl. Lucy she were called.'

The image of Ruff with his head blown to pieces came forcefully back into my mind and with it the feeling of nausea I thought I had got rid of. 'It's a good job she wasn't there to see it,' I almost shouted as I slammed the door and turned the ignition key. Norman's reply if there were one was drowned by the roar of the engine as I revved it furiously and drove away in a spray of flying gravel. In the rear view mirror I saw Norman staring after me.

I still didn't feel ready to go home. Instead of turning right towards the road back to Forest House, I turned left and drove along the side of the green towards the church. This stood on a slight rise, set back from the road and almost hidden by a grove of tall beech trees. I stopped the car on a pull-in outside the oak lich gate. Opposite was a row of tiny cottages in the same yellow brick as that of Forest House. Their latticed windows were opaque with net curtaining. The only clue as to whether anyone was at home was the smoke rising out of a couple of the chimneys and the accompanying acrid whiff of burning coal in the windless air.

I closed the gate quietly behind me. I like churches. Being raised a Catholic tends to cure you of religious feelings, but churches always have the effect of somehow calming me down. I don't go in with my usual bang and clatter, so it was with almost reverently slow tread that I walked the slippery paved path through the churchyard towards the door in the south porch.

It was a big church, surprisingly so for that small village. There was a squat tower at the west end, the pale stonework meticulously panelled with squared-off polished flints which glinted in the sunlight. There was more flintwork on the interstices between the big windows of the nave. The churchyard, although large, was well filled with old gravestones, blotched with white, grey and orange lichens and almost sunk in the waves of coarse unmown grass.

I stopped in front of the wire netting cage that covered the opening of the porch and prevented birds from getting in. Despite the sunlight and the warmth, there was an air of dampness hanging about the place. I opened the metal-framed gate and stepped through into the darkness of the porch. The gate was on an unusually strong spring. It twisted out of my hand, slamming behind me with a clang which made me jump and rang in the silence.

So much for good intentions. Slightly ashamed, I was more careful with the massive door into the church. The Suffolk latch operated soundlessly and the door pivoted on well-oiled hinges.

Inside it was chilly, with the usual musty smell of old prayer-books and mice. The odour of sanctity. Despite the bright day outside, the solemn colours of the Victorian stained glass maintained a suitably religious gloom. I went over to the end of the nave, under the tower, and looked back to the altar. The body of the church was filled with high-backed pews, the ends by the aisles elaborately carved with poppyheads, strange faces and even farm-yard animals. I was intrigued to see such richness, but this was nothing to the shock I had when I looked up into the roof.

I gasped out loud with astonishment. Instead of the plain vaulting I had expected was something wonderful. Angels.

I stood transfixed, my head thrown back so far it was painful, gazing at them as they hovered in the gloom, their wings outstretched, almost fluttering against the confinement of their wooden prison.

Gradually, as my eyes became accustomed to the darkness, I saw that they had faces, serene faces, faces no doubt of comely village lads and lasses of how many centuries before – six, or seven? The carvers' hands had given them nevertheless a strange androgynous beauty which transcended his models. They truly seemed beyond the dirt and disease, the squalor and the sex of human life. I had read of these amazing works of medieval craftsmanship but never seen one before. It was a double hammerbeam roof, the weight of the whole structure being supported at intervals on two conjoined arches, which rested not on cross members but on jutting piers of wood and stone, the so-called hammers. At the end of each of these piers was a carved angel, so that a double rank of figures seemed to float in the void, a heavenly host indeed.

I gazed up until the crick in my neck became unbearable, then I lay full length on a convenient pew so I could continue to revel in this aerial sculpture gallery. I don't know how long I lay like that. It was ages since I had taken such pleasure in a work of art, and all the more welcome that I had found it by serendipity and could view it alone and not jostling and struggling with sharp-elbowed strangers in a London gallery. I felt myself transported from the nastiness of the morning and the depression it had generated.

Then from the end of the pew I was lying on, I heard someone cough.

Startled, I sat up. As I did so, I became aware that while I had been engrossed with the angels I had been displaying some sights of my own. My skirt had fallen down my raised thighs, revealing just about all there was to reveal of my pants. As they were white cotton, and neither very transparent nor that skimpy, I didn't think they would be much of a turn-on, but you couldn't be too sure these days. Back from the pinnacles of the human spirit, realism reasserted itself. I was alone in an ill-lit remote building with a coughing person, and from the sound of it a coughing male person. Although my heartbeat count was up quite a few points, I rearranged myself in what I hoped was a calm and unhurried manner, praying that the subdued light would conceal both my blushes and the pallor that had quickly succeeded them. I didn't want to give the creep the satisfaction of seeing my embarrassment and alarm on top of everything else. Then he spoke.

'You been looking at the angels.'

I could see him clearly now. He had come round the end of the pew in front and sat sideways in it, turned back to face me, his right arm hanging down, the hand resting on the prayer book shelf in front of me.

I smiled in what I imagined was a self-possessed, polite but unencouraging way. 'Yes. They're wonderful.'

The fingers of the hand on the shelf stirred slightly, like something in a rock pool. He seemed pleased by this conventional remark. Behind the thick lenses of the NHS glasses, his eyes seemed to swim. His mouth pursed as if he was considering something of no little moment. Then he said, 'Being as you like the angels, I could show you the Devil.'

4

AT LAST BRO BEN-ATTAMAN RESTED. The graves stretched in a line along the verdant bottom of the valley. No more would the hordes of Kar-Enrop disturb the minds of the People of the Path. They were vanquished utterly.

And as Bro Ben-Attaman rested on the smooth stone, still holding the worn shaft of the spade, a shadow fell on the earth before him. Looking up and shading his eyes against the brightness of the noonday sun, he saw the lithe body, smiling face and laughing eyes of Minadorca. She held out to him the teasing fingers of her right hand.

'Come with me,' she commanded.

Behind her, he saw the smoke rising from the hearth fires of the village where the feast was being prepared.

He rose to his feet and hand in hand they descended the path together.

THE END

Gratefully, I turned the typewritten page over and added it face down to the stack on the table beside me. So much for *The Thought Stealers.* I scribbled a few final notes. Really, the Miltonics of the last sentence were a bit blatant, but the readers probably wouldn't notice, nor would they care two hoots if they did. What the hell. It felt good that I had finished the job, the more so having regard to the other distractions of the day.

When I had gotten back from Barton St Margaret I was surprised to see on the mat when I pushed open the front door a cream–coloured envelope addressed to 'Mrs Reynolds, Forest House. By Hand.'

I tore it open. There was a sheet of the same cream–coloured writing paper headed 'Barton House, Barton St Margaret, Norfolk.' The letter was in fountain pen in a strong, clear hand: 'Dear Mrs Reynolds, Sorry again about all the fuss. I hope the men have cleared the mess properly. You might like to have this. Yours sincerely, James Edwardes.'

'This' was in the envelope. It was the dog tag, mercifully cleaned and shiny. I dropped it and the letter into my purse. It seemed significant, somehow. Proof that the whole thing had happened. In the garden there was only a line of flattened blood-stained grass which came to an abrupt halt in the middle of the lawn. All around the vegetation was trampled down. Ruff's pathetic corpse had gone. James Edwardes had kept his word like a gentleman.

But the strangeness of the business could not be cleared out of my mind so easily.

The room felt cold. The fire in the sitting room grate had gone out. In my concentration, I had not noticed the passing of time. It was almost sunset. Through the sitting room window, dark grey clouds edged with reddish gold promised another shower by nightfall.

I went into the kitchen to make some tea. It was warm in there, the range was behaving itself impeccably. I opened the firedoor and fed it a log or two. I drank the tea, warming my chilled hands around the mug. I felt the need to talk. I wished Geoffrey were here. It was annoying there was no news about the phone installation. It was amazing that the mysterious Mallens hadn't had one. Perhaps they hadn't gotten round to it. Perhaps they hated telephones. There were some weird people who did. I felt lost without it. Geoffrey said I was a phone junkie. Coming from a journalist, that was quite something.

The need to talk to Geoffrey was stronger by the minute. The nearest public phone was probably in Barton St Margaret, but I didn't fancy wandering around by myself in the dark looking for it in view of what had happened. That left Breckenham. I pulled on a jacket and locked the front door behind me. I stood for a few moments staring across the clearing. The gathering clouds drained the colour out of the landscape. A strong, cold wind carried drops of rain. I remembered the bright sun of the morning and shivered.

I parked in the now empty tarmac expanse of Breckenham market-place. The shops had long since shut and the only sign of life was at the Golden Lion Hotel where they were probably serving early dinners to the double-glazing reps and life-insurance salesmen who were, no doubt, its main customers. 'Oh to be in England!' I muttered to myself as I fumbled with stiff fingers at the car door. I huddled the jacket more closely round me in the scything wind as I crossed the road.

There was a phone booth outside the post office. It seemed to have been used as a lavatory recently, but was otherwise operational. Wrinkling my nose, I shoved in the phone card and dialled the number. It took a while for him to answer.

Jealously, I saw my sitting room with its Liberty print drapes, crowded bookshelves, thick carpet and cosy sofa, bathed in the soft yellow glow of the lamps. No doubt Geoffrey was already well into a bottle of Pouilly-Fumé, waiting for one of the meals I had thoughtfully prepared and left for him in the freezer to heat up. Perhaps he was thinking of me, perhaps a little worried that I was OK.

Finally he answered.

'Hi. Missing me?'

'No. Should I be? It was only yesterday afternoon.' He could be irritatingly matter-of-fact sometimes.

'It seems like a month to me. I'm missing you. I've had the most beastly day you can imagine.'

'Oh?'

'You don't have to sound so interested. I mean, after all, you don't care that I'm stuck here while various country bumpkins go round blasting dogs with shotguns and trying to rape me.'

'What on earth are you talking about?'

I told him.

'I don't see what you're so upset about. OK, the dog thing was a bit messy.'

I was disappointed in him. The messiness wasn't the upsetting part, but he obviously didn't see that.

'And I hardly think your encounter with what sounds like the village idiot qualifies for a narrow escape from the Boston Strangler.'

'Well, it seemed like it at the time. I was pretty glad to get out of there. This guy followed me all the way through the churchyard saying, "Please, miss, come and see the Devil." What was I supposed to think?'

'Darling, I'm sorry. I thought you'd be having a lovely time. I thought the weekend was super. Particularly our Sunday morning special.'

'Mmm. Mind you, don't get too used to that. The succubus doesn't come to order.'

'Succubus. What a lovely word that is! I'll come any time for her.'

I sighed down the phone line. 'I'm going to miss you tonight. Perhaps I should come home tomorrow.'

'Is this the woman who coped single-handed for years in the urban jungle? Is this the toughest operator in publishing talking? I thought you had all kinds of things you wanted to do there to make it nice for us.'

He was beginning to make me feel rather silly. It was the first time in our relationship that I had felt this power men seem to have over even the most astute woman. And, of course, I succumbed to it.

'You're right. Till the weekend, huh?'

We said our farewells and I put the phone down. I didn't know why I was so thrown by what had happened. I guess it was because I was somehow out of context in a world I didn't yet know how to handle. Perhaps Geoffrey was right. I had to put it out of my head. There was work to do. Tomorrow, having got *The Thought Stealers* out of the way, I could get on with some more work on the house.

★

It was nearly dark as I drove back along the narrow lanes with their overhanging trees. The headlamps lit up the undersides of their branches so that it was like driving along the endless nave of some fantastic cathedral.

Despite my resolution, my mind kept returning to the business of the dog. Why had poor Ruff decided to come home? If the animal really had been looking for the girl Lucy Mallen, as Norman had said, then where had she gone?

By this time I had left the road and was bumping along the track. There were only the last vestiges of light in the western sky. As I came in sight of Forest House, a cheery welcoming yellow glow came from the curtained front window of the sitting room.

Then I remembered that I had left no lights switched on.

As I slewed the car on to the driveway and slammed on the brakes, my heart pounding, the light went out.

There was no denying I was scared but, let's get it straight, it wasn't the dark or spooks I was afraid of at that moment. Broad daylight in Central Park, particularly at that wooded bit by the Japanese bridge, is far more terrifying to me than the forest around Forest House, even on a moonless night with the wind howling in the trees, for a very good reason: like the creeps that hang around there.

As I sat in the car looking at the now darkened front of the house, I wasn't worrying about things that go bump in the night. They were bullshit. I was worrying about what really scares me. People.

It's people who go round robbing, raping and murdering. I always thought how odd it was that the occult forces of evil got such a bad press from just doing a bit of green slime, making with the weird noises and maybe throwing a few pots and pans. If you want real evil, then you go to those serial killers that the States produces so effectively. I hadn't heard any of them were ghosts.

I was thinking about the guy in the church. Maybe he wasn't as harmlessly loony as Geoffrey so kindly and with his enveloping masculinity reassured me on the basis of no evidence whatsoever. Maybe he had come back for another look at me. And there was the unlocked kitchen door. Someone seemed to have a key.

Whatever, I wasn't going to spend the night in the car, nor was I going to hare back to some police station to have a bunch of hairy males laugh their heads off at my typical female cowardice. I wasn't going to be scared out of my house by some faulty wiring or some country bumpkin fooling around looking for a VCR I hadn't got. I got out and slammed the car door extra hard. In the trunk I found the toolkit. I took from it a large screwdriver. With this in one hand and Geoffrey's heavy duty torch in the other, I crunched up the gravel of the front path with as heavy a tread as I could muster.

I stuck the screwdriver in my coat pocket as I unlocked the front door. Just like in the movies, I pushed it back with my foot and shone the torch inside.

The hallway was empty. Keeping my back against the wall, I edged in sideways and found the light switch. I worked my way through the house in the same way. When I had looked into and turned on the lights in every room, I felt pretty sure that there was no one else around. Not only that, but I could find nothing out of place. The kitchen door was still locked. I slid the bolts across, just in case any visitor decided to return. I went and bolted the front door as well.

I felt a good deal calmer after these precautions. I decided to push out of my mind any speculation as to what had happened. There was nothing further I could do at present.

I sat at the kitchen table and poured myself a large glass of whisky which I drank in a couple of swallows. Then I went to bed, leaving all the lights on. As there was no lock on the bedroom door, I jammed a chair under the handle. I kept the torch and the screwdriver on the floor beside me. I'm pleased to say I went to sleep immediately. It felt like it had been a long day.

Looking back on it, I'm surprised I didn't think to check the attic. It never occurred to me.

I rose early the next morning to a bright day. I felt full of energy, pleased how I had dealt with the fear of the previous night. The tweed skirt was crumpled and covered in grass seeds. I put on a green woollen jersey dress with a broad belt of dark green leather as I was venturing out into civilization. As I drank my coffee, I drew up my shopping list.

I had spotted the DIY warehouse on the outskirts of Queen's Hythe on one of our previous visits. I was always sniffy about such places until I needed decorating stuff, then I tended to head for them rather than hardware stores run by officious and unhelpful men in brown overalls with a million biros clustered in their top pockets. I liked to choose what I wanted without being hassled or patronized.

I've always done my own decorating. In New York, I couldn't afford the prices the best decorators charged so I had had to learn how to do it. I eventually got pretty nifty even at such tricky arts as ragrolling and marbling. People who came to my apartment were impressed. It got so I actually enjoyed doing it. I had done up the Hampstead apartment single–handedly. I didn't see why I shouldn't do the same to Forest House. Geoffrey had given me a free hand, being virtually colour blind and with no manual skills whatever – at least as far as painting and decorating were concerned. I had decided to go along with the character of the place and keep the effects simple.

I spent an enjoyable hour or so choosing paints, wallpapers and tiles, and loading the cart with brushes, rollers and all the paraphernalia necessary. As I drove back I was really excited at the prospect of getting started right away, so when I came in sight of the house I was annoyed to see that I had a visitor. A large boxy vehicle that seemed familiar stood on the drive. As I climbed out of the car, a figure emerged from round the side of the house. It was Hugh Robinson.

He appeared surprised and not exactly pleased to see me at first, then his face assumed a cheerful smile of welcome. He came towards me holding out his hand. 'I wasn't expecting to find you in. I thought you were in London in the week.'

I let my irritation show. 'You're in the habit of calling on people who aren't there?'

His smile became even warmer. 'Good Lord, I suppose that did sound a bit off. No, what I meant was that I had another reason for being here.'

'Really?'

He cheerfully ignored my mood. 'Yes. Bit of a silly business. I was searching for a dog. I don't suppose you've seen it?'

' "The dog it was that died," ' I said.

His eyes narrowed and the bonhomie faded ever so slightly. 'What do you mean?'

I told him. Together we walked round the house. I pointed out the place on the lawn.

He stared down at the ground pursing his lips and rubbing his chin.

'Why on earth were you trying to find the dog?'

He gave his lopsided grin. 'Why don't we go inside and have a cup of coffee? I'll tell you about it. It's no great story.'

We went inside and he sat down at the kitchen table. He waited until the coffee was made before he spoke. He sipped it once, then replaced the mug deliberately on the table, rubbed his clasped hands on the bridge of his nose and leaned back in the chair.

'The dog belonged to Julian Mallen, who lived here. We had been friends for years. His daughter Lucy had looked after Ruff since he was a puppy. He was devoted to her and pined awfully when they left. Julian had asked me to have him put down, but I couldn't do it. I would have had him myself, but my wife wasn't keen.' He drank some more coffee. 'Anyway, in the end I arranged for Ruff to go to some people over in Queen's Hythe. As far as I knew all was well. Then last night they phoned and said that he had gone off a week ago and hadn't come back. They asked me to have a look around Forest House in case he'd turned up at his old home.'

'Which he had.'

He rubbed his nose again. 'Obviously.'

'I don't understand why it took all this time for him to decide to come back.'

He shrugged. 'Who knows how animals think? They're hardly rational in our sense, are they? I don't suppose time has the same meaning for them.'

'Why didn't the Mallens take Ruff with them? Wasn't the little girl upset to leave him?'

'Of course. She was very sad about it. Cried for days when Julian said they were leaving him behind.'

'Couldn't they have taken him? Seems hard on the poor kid.'

'They went to your part of the world. Julian is an academic, a physicist. He got a much better job in the States. He had to find a place to live there. They couldn't take the dog.'

'You didn't say anything about this guy Mallen when we looked at the place.'

'Why should I have? It's not relevant to you, but Julian didn't actually own it. It belonged to a family trust of which he was a beneficiary. When he decided he didn't want to live in it the trust took some time to decide to sell. That was why it was empty for a while.'

'I see. I suppose I just like to know about things like that.'

He didn't reply. Instead he got to his feet. He loomed over me, his dark curly hair almost brushing the bottom of the low beam across the middle of the room. He jerked back his cuff to reveal a heavy gold watch. 'Good Lord, is that the time? I really must be going. A pity about Ruff. Giles and Emma will be sorry, but that's the way of the country. Old Edwardes didn't have any choice. Don't get up. I'll see myself out.'

He strode out of the room. I got up and dashed after him. 'Hang on a minute. There's something else I wanted to ask you.'

He stopped and turned in the narrow hallway, his big rugby player's frame almost filling it. He raised his eyebrows. 'And what was it?'

I hesitated. I wasn't quite sure how to put it. Then I blurted out, 'Do you still have a key? To this house, I mean?'

He looked at me narrowly, then shook his head. 'No, I don't. Why should I have? Why do you ask?'

'Oh, I just wondered. Geoffrey, I mean, wondered if you'd . . . er . . . called by since we moved in.'

'No, of course not. I'd have no reason to. Today was exceptional, as you realize.'

I explained to him about the kitchen door, wishing more and more that I hadn't got into the subject.

'I can see it's disturbing, but I'm not guilty, I'm pleased to say. If you're worried about keys being in the wrong hands, you should get the locks changed.'

He was in a huff, but that was too bad. I felt I'd had to ask.

I watched as he climbed into his car, revved the engine hard and drove off, the big machine making easy work of the rough surface.

So much for Norman's mysterious Mallens. It was all terribly straightforward. So why was it that, for some reason, I had the oddest feeling that what I had heard was not entirely true?

But such a vague feeling was not something I wanted to dwell on. I was keen to get at something uncomplicated after which I could see some real results.

I stripped off my green dress and flung it on the bed. As I rummaged in the wardrobe I caught a glimpse of myself in the spotted silvering of the mirror on the inside of the door.

I couldn't resist standing back to examine the full image. It wasn't all bad, I had to admit. I no longer beat up on myself for not being statuesque, like the golden-haired all-American Wasps I went to school with. I was now comfortable with being five feet five in my bare feet, resigned to being well proportioned, with full breasts which had a tendency to droop in anything but the most expensively engineered bra. I grabbed a handful of the creamy flesh on my hips. There seemed more of it than usual, I had to admit. Marriage to Geoffrey, whose idea of exercise was a stroll from the car to the restaurant, might yet prove terminal to even the modified version of a figure which I had persuaded myself to accept.

I reminded myself that I had, for a change, some physical work to get on with. Hey, perhaps I could persuade McAllister's to go for a title such as *Paint Yourself Slim*. It sounded a neat idea. I turned back to the tangle of old clothes I had thrown into the bottom of the wardrobe when we arrived. I found what I was looking for – an old shirt of Geoffrey's I was going to use as a painting smock.

I had my hand on the doorknob to go downstairs when through the open bedroom window I heard someone banging on the front door.

'Oh, shit,' I muttered. Far from being remote and inaccessible, the place was becoming a bloody circus. Who was it now, Jehovah's Witnesses? I leaned over the window sill and yelled down. 'What do you want?'

Norman Fincham shuffled out of the shelter of the porch and turned his gargoyle face up to mine.

'Afternoon, missus. I thought I'd come to see about that old job.'

'Damn.' My hair had fallen into my eyes again, and my involuntary gesture of sweeping it back with my hand had succeeded in smearing yet more paint into it. I put the paint roller back into its tray and got down from the chair I had been standing on. After wiping my hands on a rag, I took off and retied the old scarf more tightly around my forehead and behind my ears. My right arm ached, and the shirt was generously stippled with dry emulsion paint. I stood back to admire the work I had done.

The small square sitting room was transformed. The ceiling was now brilliant white instead of yellow dinge. Instead of the ghastly shiny green, the colour of an aquarium which hadn't been properly cleaned out, the walls were a delicate cream. A clearly lit space had appeared.

I moved over to the window to see how Norman was getting on. I was pleased to see that he too was making good progress.

Perhaps he was going to be an asset. Certainly the bargain we had struck seemed reasonable to me, but I wasn't up on countryside rates. We were going to need someone and it might as well be Norman. He knew the place and presumably had some idea of what might be hidden under the rampant weeds. I knew nothing about gardening, but I supposed I could learn. Perhaps Geoffrey would actually take an interest.

In one of the outhouses – still unexplored territory – we had found, at Norman's suggestion, some rusty implements, a spade, a fork, a scythe and a thing which Norman said was a mattock. They had apparently been left there by the Mallens and Norman greeted them as old friends. He produced from the folds of his dirty raincoat a well-worn sharpening stone and set to work on the scythe.

Using this, he had already cleared a big area of the lawn. I watched for a while his stubby figure in stained brown corduroy trousers and red lumberjack check shirt methodically sweeping down the knee-high grass and weeds, obliterating in the process the faint tracks which still remained from the death throes of Ruff. The sun had begun to dry the swaths of cuttings and the sweet smell of new-mown hay filled the air.

I made tea for us both and carried it out to the terrace. Norman sat with his back against the house wall, his big gnarled hand wrapped around the mug. He drank gratefully.

'He looks better now,' he said, jerking his head to indicate the lawn. 'There's proper grass there under them weeds, but you'll be needing a lawnmower. Them petrol ones is best.'

'Did Mr Mallen have a lawn mower?'

Norman's yellow teeth appeared momentarily. 'Well, no, now as you mention it, I don't believe he did. He liked me to use that old scythe. Didn't like the noise, he said. 'Course, 'tis hard work for a man who ain't getting no younger.'

'I'll think about it.' I had an idea that motor mowers were a major cost item. Geoffrey would have to dig into the Aunt Edith pot again if he wanted one.

I was becoming curious about the Mallens in a way I never normally was about the previous occupants of other places I had lived in. This house was not an anonymous flat. It had a personality to which its other inhabitants had contributed. I felt conscious of the way in which I was myself contributing to the place.

'Mr Mallen liked the peace and quiet here then?' I primed the pump of what I was sure would be a flow of reminiscence.

'Oh, yes. He did that. Spent all day inside, working at one of they whatsitsnames. He called himself "Doctor" but I heard tell he were one of them scientists a Perfessor at Cambridge. Hardly saw him some times. 'Course, I didn't come every day. Just Thursdays. He'd leave a note if he wanted anything particular. Taters dug or that. He looked after himself. My missus would have done for him if he'd wanted, like she does for several ladies and gentlemen around here, but he didn't want anybody about disturbing his work he said.'

'Wasn't there a Mrs Mallen?'

'Ah now, there must have been, but not in my time. That Lucy, poor little motherless soul she were. She told me once, "My mummy's dead, Norman. She died when I was little. I don't even remember her. Isn't that awful?"'

'It was Lucy who looked after the dog, you said?'

'Yes. When she were here. She weren't here all the time. Only in the holidays. She went to one of them boarding schools, in Cambridge she told me. She liked it better here, she said. Ran wild she did, with that dog. Lonely for a little 'un, my missus said. But not that Lucy. She really loved it here.'

'I suppose she must miss it, in America. The dog missed her.'

'Is that where they went then? America. Well, they didn't never tell me.'

'You mean they didn't tell you where they were going?'

'Why no. 'Twas all a mystery to me. I got this letter from Dr Mallen. He left it at our house. I weren't there but he spoke to the missus. He said in the letter he was moving and wouldn't be requiring my services no more. He left me my week's money. That was all. Five years I worked for him as well, ever since he'd lived here.'

'And you've never heard any more from them?'

'No, not so much as a postcard. Still, maybe if they've gone to America 'tis hard to get such things.'

Norman seemed genuinely sorry at the manner of their parting, not just at the absence of proper severance pay.

'It does seem odd they left like that. They must have known. Didn't Lucy say anything?'

70

He shook his head. 'Now that I think on it, she didn't seem so happy for quite a while before. She weren't her usual self. Quite peaky she looked. I told my missus and she said as how it weren't right for a girl to be so shut away with no friends, and that father of hers. "A right sociable one he is, I don't think," she said. She never had no one from her school to stay, not that I saw. But she never said anything about going away.'

He stared down mournfully into the empty mug. Clambering awkwardly to his feet, he said, 'Best be getting back to work. I'll finish that old grass before I goes.'

I was cleaning out the roller and brushes in the kitchen sink a couple of hours later when Norman tapped on the window. 'I finished him, missus.'

I went out to admire his work. He had raked up the cuttings and piled them out of sight by the side of the outhouse. A green sward now stretched down to the fence, the broken rails of which had been roughly nailed back into place. A pleasing sense of order was emerging.

I walked back with him to the front of the house to where his old black boneshaker was propped against the side of the porch. I paid him what we had agreed and arranged for him to return every Thursday to work in the garden so it looked nice when we arrived for the weekend.

He was wheeling the bike on to the drive when he stopped and turned back to me. I could see something was troubling him.

'Missus, you mustn't mind about the boy. My Tom.'

I looked at him, baffled, but he was staring at the worn rubber footrest of the pedal.

'He's a good boy and he doesn't mean no harm. He takes a powerful interest in the church and the vicar says he's, like, looking after the place. There ain't nothing he can't tell you about its history. 'Course if you don't know he's there he might give you a bit of a turn, but not meaning to.' He raised his eyes up to gauge the response in my eyes.

I understood. I nodded slowly and encouragingly. He seemed relieved.

'I was a bit alarmed, I must admit, when he started talking about the devil,' I said.

'Ah, now, he'd've been trying to show you something interesting that you might have missed. 'Tis a queer carved face. Hundreds of years old. They call it the Barton Devil.'

'How old is your son?'

'He'll be eighteen next birthday. He's our youngest and doctor said it might be that we were both getting on like when we had him that he's the way he is. Sir James at the big house has him do what he can. A real old-fashioned gentleman, Sir James. Always been good to us. The boy's strong but a bit inclined to wander off in a world of his own.'

He swung his leg over the crossbar. Then he said, half to himself, ''Course, you don't want to believe what folks might say about the boy. About that old row he had with the Perfessor.'

'Row?'

'He got really mad and told my Tom he weren't to come and see Lucy no more. They'd been quite pally, even though she were only a little girl.'

'Why did Dr Mallen say that, Norman?'

He didn't answer, but went back to staring down at the pedal.

'Why did he say such an unkind thing?'

'Tom would never have done that, what he said. I don't believe that kind of thing ever enters his head. He wouldn't. Nor that other little girl, either. 'Tisn't in the boy.'

'What isn't, Norman?'

He shook his head. 'Nothing to worry you, missus.'

I watched him slowly but determinedly pedalling off down the track.

'This is very good,' Geoffrey said, wiping a dribble of sauce from the side of his mouth with his napkin. He drank appreciatively from the glass of claret, his full lips making a slight slurping noise. He resumed the attack on his plate and enthusiastically ate another forkful of cassoulet.

I had picked him up from the station in Queen's Hythe. It was a cold wet evening and the train had been an hour late. I had had to sit in the car in the big car park as there was no waiting room, just a sort of open bus shelter of steel and glass in the middle of the concrete platform. The original station buildings had been abandoned and stood on the other side of the tracks, their windows crudely bricked up.

There had been a clutch of other cars waiting in the dusk for the London train. Volvos, Mercedes, Range Rovers. Cars that spoke of solid wealth, country houses and wives that waited patiently at train stations for the bread-winning conquering hero to return to the adoration of his family. It pissed me off that by association at least I was one of those who thus attended.

'I'm glad you're enjoying it.' I sipped a glass of mineral water. I didn't feel like alcohol. I watched Geoffrey chasing a piece of sausage around his plate, spearing it with his fork and then cramming it into his mouth. I pushed away my half-finished plate.

'Not hungry? Golly, I'm starving. I can finish yours. Waste not, want not as my old nanny used to say.'

Geoffrey's old nanny was quite often a guest at dinner. Along with his old French master and the old chap his father had paid to teach him to box.

'Geoffrey!'

The sharp, hurt tone in my voice stopped him in the act of shovelling my uneaten food on to his plate.

'Geoffrey, you're not listening to me.'

'I am. I have been. I just don't see what there is to get so upset about.'

'You might try a little harder, then. I was scared. And whatever you say now, so would you have been.' I stared at him. Tears were starting to come and I blinked them back, furious with myself. I hated to be seen behaving like the little woman and having to be comforted by the big strong man.

Geoffrey reached out his hand and grasped mine. He squeezed it in clumsy reassurance. 'Sorry, darling. It must have a bit of an odd experience.'

I had told him about the light as we drove home.

'It was. I had half a mind to get the cops, if there are any in these parts. I don't like the idea of someone hanging around.'

'It was probably the dodgy electricity supply. We can have it checked if you want.'

'OK.' I sighed. 'It doesn't seem quite as peaceful here as I thought. Not this week anyway.'

'Is it the business with the dog?'

'It's not the only thing.' I told him what Norman had said about the Mallens. 'The whole thing feels wrong to me.'

'I don't see why it should. That Robinson fellow told you about the dog and the whatstheirnames, Mallens. They moved away. The family trust sold the house to me. That's all there is to it.' His hand tightened on mine again for a moment, then he let go and gave it a pat.

'But you're a journalist. Doesn't it awaken any professional curiosity?' I fiddled with my upturned pudding spoon. My disembodied face, bloated in the convex mirror of the bowl, stared out at me.

'It doesn't, actually. I don't work for the *News of the World*. I deal with facts and ideas, not feelings. You're the storybook person.'

'So you think I'm imagining it. Perhaps you think I read too many novels.'

Geoffrey carefully laid down his knife and fork. Picking up the wine glass, he tilted it so the candlelight glittered harshly on the crystal facets. He pursed his lips then put down the glass again deliberately without drinking. He stared at me quizzically but not unkindly. 'I never said that. In fact, you're usually pretty down to earth. All I mean is that the fact the Mallens left apparently in a bit of a hurry doesn't in my mind add up to anything. People in real life do do odd things, unplanned things, muddled things. This fellow was an academic, wasn't he? They're always a bit dozy about practicalities.' He grinned ruefully. 'After all, I should know.'

'I suppose you're right. I have just have this funny feeling sometimes that there's more to it.' I shrugged. 'Perhaps it's being on my own here. My imagination may be running riot.'

5

It already seemed strange being back in London. In a matter of a few days at the cottage I had gotten used to the quiet. Away from it I was at once far more aware of the incessant noise. I seemed to hear more clearly the constant roar of the traffic up and down Rosslyn Hill, the continual hee-hawing of the police sirens and the intermittent muffled drone of the jumbo jets. I noticed too the dirt: the grime condensed out of the air which coated the outside paintwork of the flat when I pushed up the bedroom window on that dull Monday morning.

I stood shivering in the cold urban air as I smelt petrol fumes instead of the resin of the pines. I looked gratefully at the big plane tree in the street outside, its bark as mottled and multicoloured as an Impressionist painter's palette. New green leaves were bursting from their buds in a way which I never remembered noticing before. I thought of the wheat thrusting from the warming earth of Norfolk. At home, I was beginning to be homesick.

'Shut the window! It's bloody freezing!' I turned to see Geoffrey stripping off his red striped pyjamas and putting on shorts and singlet. He vanished into the bathroom, where I heard the whirr of the exercise bicycle. I had bought him this as a birthday hint a couple of months back. So far the novelty had not worn off. Neither had the middle-aged spread.

I went through to the kitchen to make coffee. The mail was on the mat in the hallway. Amongst the usual bills and circulars was a letter for Geoffrey in a handwriting I didn't recognize. It was heavy, good quality stationery. I noticed that it had a Norwich postmark and was dated the previous Saturday. I weighed it thoughtfully in my hand, the memory of a dark-haired woman in a blue coat flickering in my mind. Irritated at this speculation – it was probably something to do with the house purchase – I shoved the letter in the rest of Geoffrey's pile and left it on the kitchen table.

He barely glanced at it when he came into the kitchen, merely scooping up the pile and stuffing it in his briefcase. He was dressed to go out. He never had breakfast at home on a weekday, preferring to go to one of several haunts in the City where he could catch up on the overnight financial news.

He bent down to kiss me, pulling me to him with his usual passion.

I responded, and I clung to him for a moment, wishing that the figure in the blue coat would get out of my head. ''Bye, Geoffrey,' I said. 'I'm going to be late tonight. Got a dinner. Don't wait up.'

'You shouldn't wear yourself out. You're wasted at that place, you know. Working for that fellow. He's a megalomaniac. Maybe you should get out before he does a Samson on you – or before someone does it to him.'

I stared at him. This was one of several hints he had given out lately. 'Hey, what is this? Do you know something I don't?'

He shrugged. 'You know the City. Always gossiping. Think on, though, as they say. Besides, you might like to spend more time at home, now we've got the cottage.' Before I could respond he bent down, kissed me again and was gone.

I heard the front door slam, then his heavy tread on the stairs.

As I drank my coffee, I puzzled over what he had said. What was he talking about? That I should leave McAllister's before disaster struck? But how could it, since H and H had taken over? And what would I do then? 'Spend more time at home'? Doing what? Ironing his shirts? Making jam? Running coffee mornings? What the hell was this?

I looked at my watch. Good grief, I was running late. I would have to bend his ear about it at the next opportunity.

★

That day the office was as frantic as usual.

In the morning the phone never stopped. One of my authors was freaking out about the lousy treatment she had had on her publicity tour and threatening to go elsewhere with her next. I had to find out the truth from publicity and then calm her down. Another was raging about her latest royalty statement, which she claimed was better fiction than hers. She was absolutely right as the accounts department readily admitted. I was bidding for a blockbuster in an auction run by an agent with whom I had previously crossed swords and who was therefore trying to change the rules every time it looked as if I was winning. My in-tray was crammed to overflowing with mail, as if I had been away a year not a week. My secretary didn't show but considerately phoned in halfway through the morning to say she had had a row with her boyfriend and was too emotional to work and she was sure as a woman I would understand. Worst of all I had to see Michael.

For various reasons, he and I did not get along.

Michael Underdown–Metcalfe, chairman and chief executive of McAllister's Publishers plc, known to all and sundry behind his back as Mighty Underhand Methods, is hard to describe in a few words. In fact he's pretty hard to describe whatever number you allocate. He's one of those characters often described by people who don't have to work with them as 'larger than life'. And, yes, he is big. If you can imagine Michelangelo's David gone to seed with a big paunch and bags under the eyes, wearing a Savile Row double-breasted chalkstripe, then you're somewhere near.

I thought I knew about Michael and the link up with H and H before I joined the company. Max Vincent gave me a thorough briefing and let me see the file the private detective agency had prepared on him. Max liked to know with whom he was dealing. He wasn't known at H and H as the Godfather for nothing.

I continued to think that I was in possession of privileged information for a long time. It wouldn't be until later that I would realize I had been unknowingly playing one of women's traditional roles: I had been had.

According to Max's private eyes, Michael liked to present himself as a Scottish gentleman who also happened to be a successful entrepreneur. But despite the double-barrelled name – unrecorded in any almanac of notable families – and his carefully cultivated fruity public school accent, it was obvious that he hailed from somewhere a good deal further east. Where he had originally come from, however, was something that even the gumshoes hadn't figured. It was a sensitive topic: any public suggestion that Michael's background was more Old Estonian than Old Etonian met with a torrent of lawyer's Latin. Michael used the legal system as his own personal security service.

And of course he had that most useful of protections when it came to anyone sniffing too close. He was not only rich and successful, but he was the boss of one of the largest publishing houses in the UK. Nothing is as seductive to a potential critic as the prospect of his great thoughts finding a willing publisher: Michael was an expert on vanity.

The publishing success was undeniable. When Michael turned up in Edinburgh in the late forties in his new civvy suit and the rest of his worldly goods in a paper valise, McAllister's was a small-scale Scottish printer. Every so often it produced a tome of local interest, such as *The Flora of Midlothian* or *The Dominie's Jest Book*. This hardly constituted publishing even by British post-war standards.

Michael, through his gift of the gab, had himself installed as sales manager. He persuaded the honest scions of the original McAllister, a son of the manse whose idea of investment had been to buy a new set of Es for the printing press when the old ones wore out, to branch out into the real world of books. Somehow he had spotted the market for cheap textbooks for the new schools which were being opened in response to the booming post-war birth-rate.

Encouraged by the ample profits from this source, McAllister's went into general book publishing, expanding the printing side for its own books as well as those of other publishers. At some stage in the sixties, Michael managed to buy out the original family interests, ending up in sole charge of what was by then by publishing standards a sizeable empire.

It didn't last, however. When the recession hit in the early eighties, the company ran into trouble. That was when, as Max put it, he made the famous phonecall. As he told it, H and H had been looking for a foothold in the UK market for some time. 'Such an opportunity, baby, it was begging me to take it.' As he didn't say, like all sharks he could scent blood from across an ocean.

The negotations were what you might call lively, like two bull elephants discussing the same piece of savannah. It must have stuck in Michael's craw to have to do a deal. He was essentially an independent seat-of-the-pants flyer, not a corporate airline pilot like Max. In the end, however, Hiram and Hartstein walked away with what they wanted, a position in the increasingly lucrative British and therefore EC market without the need for the expensive and time-consuming business of building a list.

The main condition was that they had to keep Michael as chief executive, still with his own minority interest in the business. Max agreed to this in the hope that, in the words of LBJ, Michael was better on the inside of the tent pissing out than on the outside pissing in. Nevertheless, as he didn't 'trust that limey sonofabitch a fucking millimetre', he needed someone of unimpeachable loyalty to tell him what was going on that the balance sheet didn't. That was where I came in.

Max persuaded me to take it in his usual ingratiating way. 'I see this as your big chance, baby. Don't do anything disrespectful like turning it down, huh?'

I asked if I could think it over. He passed me an envelope. 'Think while you open this.'

It contained a twenty thousand dollar cheque made out to cash 'for removal expenses' and a TWA ticket to London for the following Monday. One way.

I was pretty sure that Michael knew or suspected my special brief from the American senior partner, and this gave our encounters a definite spice. They could have had an even more remarkable spice if I had wanted.

After a month or so in the job, after having seen Michael only in formal meetings in the company of others, he invited me to the executive suite on the top floor for an evening meeting, apologizing that his busy schedule hadn't permitted him to get to know me more informally until then. As Michael's appetite for women was legendary even in New York, I had a pretty shrewd idea what to expect.

I had to think hard how to play it. I knew, of course, that being screwed by your boss could be merely an addition to the ways you were already being screwed by his company. That was why I had so far resisted such entanglements. But I must have had a bit of a devil in me that day. Perhaps I had also reached the age when that kind of attention can be flattering, not just irritating. Because at least part of me wanted him to find me desirable.

And I have to say that although Michael might have lost his youth and gained some flab, I had seen already that he could be amusing and even charming when he wanted. Most importantly he undeniably had that indefinable charisma of the wealthy. The aphrodisiac of power, didn't someone call it? As Scott Fitzgerald said, 'the rich are different'.

So I concluded that it would do my ego no harm if he did want to have an affair. But it would remain my choice. My ability to choose was the only power I had. If I did decide it was what I wanted, it would have to be on my terms. Anyway, I told myself, he couldn't sack me like the secretaries who occasionally demurred. I could play the game, and I could win.

What I didn't realize, though, was that Michael didn't stick to the rules.

He was at his desk scribbling comments on a report at the same time as dictating into a machine – the busy executive touch – when I opened the heavy panelled door in response to his grunt of welcome. He put down the gold fountain pen and came round to greet me, his great bear paw outstretched. 'Mary, how absolutely lovely to see you. And how, er, lovely you do look.'

I smiled warmly. 'Michael, I've been so looking forward to our chat.' I extended a languid hand, the scarlet fingernails matching my lipstick, my only concession to the occasion apart from an extra dab of Rive Gauche behind my ears.

He looked me up and down as he ushered me to the buttoned leather club sofa and got me a Scotch. I wore one of my usual office dresses, elegant but unfussy, with a high collar closed with a rather good sapphire brooch. I suppose it was sexy in an understated way. And the hem was, as usual, above my knees, which were nice and not things I wanted to hide. But I deliberately didn't want to look obvious. If he were interested, then it wouldn't be because I was got up like a hooker.

I leaned back on the slippery cushions and crossed my legs, causing the dress to slide higher up my thighs. I sipped the Scotch and gazed around. 'This is really nice.'

It was ghastly. Michael had no taste, and didn't have the sense to leave the decor to people who had. It was full of heavy oak panelling, fake beams and dark wine colours. I suppose he was aiming at the upper-class gentleman's club look, but he'd succeeded only in creating the kind of ye olde Englishe pubbe you see in airports around the world. In the context of the high-tech building in which it was ensconced it was pathetic.

He sat down beside me, and we chatted about New York, about H and H, and what high recommendations I had come over with.

Then he said, 'I do hope we're going to have a rewarding relationship.'

I stared at him. He was even cornier than I'd thought.

'I'm sure we will. When I heard about the merger' – that sounded less wounding to the ego than takeover – 'I was so very anxious to come and work here with you. You've quite a reputation in the Big Apple.'

He gave his crocodile grin. 'If you say so. But nothing like the reputation I'm going to have.'

Something about the way he said this made me sit up mentally, although physically I remained nearly horizontal. I noticed that the dress had slipped even further and hastily tugged it down. I murmured noncommittally.

He got up to refill my glass. As he handed it back to me, much fuller than it had been the first time, his fingers brushed mine. 'You're a very attractive woman.'

'Why, thank you. At my age you appreciate compliments, particularly from someone of known . . . discernment.'

He laughed. 'You shouldn't worry about your age. A beautiful woman is beautiful at any age. She's forever at her peak. When I was fifteen, I loved a woman who was seventy. She was a woman of power and she had a sexual energy to match mine. And I was insatiable. I am still.'

He let that sink in, then said, 'I suppose you've heard stories about me and women. They're all true. I love beautiful things. I love to possess them. But once in a while I meet a woman who is not just beautiful, but intelligent, successful, independent. Like you. That's a powerful combination.'

I inclined my head in acknowledgement, and took a small sip at the whisky.

He lowered himself carefully down on to the sofa. 'You've probably noticed that you're not only the sole woman on the board, but also that there are no other women in even middle management in the company. Have you thought why that is?'

I had noticed, and I could think of several reasons. I smiled sweetly and said, 'You tell me.'

'Rarity. We don't seem to make women like you in this country. Women who can remain feminine and yet beat men at their own game. From what I've seen of your work so far, I'm very impressed. The Somerset deal was good. There's no limit to the success someone with your talent could have in this company, my dear.'

I nodded, pleased despite my intention to keep a cool head. Jane Somerset was indeed a coup. To snatch one of the country's best-selling romantic authors away from her publisher of fifteen years, in the teeth of opposition from her agent, for a four-book series had at a stroke re-established McAllister's as a force in this market, and done no harm at all to my reputation on the canapé circuit. I said, 'Yes, it was a good deal. And not as expensive as it could have been.' I didn't rub in the fact that it was only since H and H had appeared on the scene that McAllister's bankers would have trusted them with the kind of money that had been needed.

Michael grinned his reptilian grin. 'We'll have to see about the long-term profit, of course, but you seem to have got a grip on editorial staff costs as well.'

'Guy resigned of his own free will,' I said somewhat defensively.

'Precisely. We wouldn't want to have had to pay him off, would we?'

'I know he was one of the old McAllister hands, but he couldn't adapt to the changing market.'

Michael gave his booming laugh. 'He couldn't adapt to you, my dear. He was an old queen who'd gone way past his sell-by date. Been trying to get rid of him for years. He wouldn't leave and I couldn't fire him – too expensive and cause far too much of a stink in the business. Now he's left us gratis. He might bitch a bit but no one will take any notice. He's quite eclipsed. You're to be congratulated.'

He shifted his bulk round and faced me. I stared at him, aware close up of the bloodshot hooded eyes, heavy jowls and the hairy eyebrows. Inside this bloated carcass was the slim, handsome young man who had taken the old Scottish worthies by storm all those years ago. Until that moment, I had been tempted. It might have been fun. I might even have, against the odds, got some advantage by it. Probably just long enough for me to lose my credibility with Max Vincent.

I gave a lazy smile and drank more whisky, but a sick feeling was gathering in my stomach. I was getting stupid in my old age. Forget the build-up and the flattery. The only thing special about me was that I was an obstacle to Michael's absolute rule. An irritant that the oyster wanted to be rid of before it became too much of a pearl.

He leaned closer. I could smell the designer aftershave. 'You are so damned sensual,' he said. His hand reached up to my cheek. 'You have such beautiful skin.' The hand dropped to my shoulder and began to draw me towards his lips, his eyelids lifting and his eyes now burning into mine.

I disengaged myself from the encircling arm and sat upright, still facing him. I looked at him directly. 'You're also a very attractive man, Michael. I'm very flattered. But we're both grown-ups. It wouldn't work out, our working together and having another relationship. I can't mix them like that. I'm sorry.'

I saw immediately he didn't like it. As in many powerful men, a little boy lurked below the surface. A petulant, spoilt, wilful little boy who wanted his own way. And when thwarted a nasty, even dangerous, little boy.

'You didn't have that difficulty with Max Vincent, I believe.'

I almost slapped him. 'That's a damned lie.'

'If you say so, my dear. Please, let's not fight. Let's not let our business relationship colour the rest of our lives.' He replaced the arm and said in a wheedling tone: 'You don't really mean you don't want me, Mary darling. You may say you don't now, but I know you really want me. And by God I want you.'

Why is it men always say that women don't know their own minds? Is it to justify the fact that they're often bullied into changing them?

I made light of it. 'Michael, you're terribly persuasive. But believe me, I really don't want to have an affair with you.'

'Who said anything about an affair? As you said, we're both grown-ups. It doesn't have to be anything complicated, does it?' His arm dropped to my waist and began to draw me to him.

The presumption of it made me wild. 'Oh, I see. This is just a rite of passage for the new woman in the company, is it? Your *droit de seigneur*, is that it? Thanks a lot.'

His grip tightened angrily. His voice lost its polish and became coarse and hard. 'Now don't play the injured innocent. You're no blushing village maiden.'

I wriggled out of the arm again. 'I've had it with this conversation.'

84

I stood up, grabbed my purse and headed for the door. I was even feeling elated by the row. It would do the bastard good to get a poke in the eye occasionally.

Then before I reached the door, he leapt to his feet and caught up with me. I was surprised by the speed of the movement. He grabbed my wrist painfully hard and wrenched me violently round to face him.

His voice had become even harsher. 'I see. You really like it the hard way, do you? You can yell as much as you like, by the way. No one will hear you.'

My elation collapsed like a badly made soufflé. This was the sort of trouble you expected in singles bars, with men whose eyebrows met in the middle. I cursed my naïve misreading of his character. Another sonofabitch with the caveman complex. I tried to get free but his big hand held crushingly firm to my wrist.

'You let go of me right now. And get this straight. I do not, repeat not, want to be fucked by you, now or ever, OK? *Capisce?*'

He didn't slacken his grip but threw his other arm round me, drawing me into a bear hug. I struggled but he was so strong. I kicked out at his shins, making him grunt with pain, then my shoe came off.

We wrestled like this for a little while, then he tripped me and I fell heavily to the thick pile carpet, dragging him with me. He hung on to my wrist, twisting it round and pinning my arm to the floor. He did the same to my other arm. He lay across my legs to stop me kicking out, his pelvis digging into my crotch. I squirmed furiously but I couldn't get free. Then I stopped and tried to think.

Panting with exertion, we both lay there for a few silent moments. I could feel his hot moist breath on my face. His eyes, underlined by heavily incised purplish bags, gazed down into mine. I tried to read their expression. Was this a bluff, a game? If it was, it wasn't very amusing. Was he really going to force me? The hell he was!

I took a deep breath. 'Michael, you hear this and hear it good. If you do not let me get up and walk out of here, then you are going to be in serious trouble. Maybe you are stronger. But I'll fight you. I'll hurt you. I'll really hurt you. And when it's over I'll go to the cops. If I walk, we can forget it ever happened, OK?'

The fierceness in my voice surprised even me. He didn't think long. He let go and rolled off me. He lay there on his back staring at the ceiling.

I scrambled to my feet and grabbed my shoe, my loosened hair tumbling across my face. I rushed lopsidedly to the door and pulled it open before he could change his mind.

As I slammed it, I heard him say, 'You'll regret this, bitch.'

'On the Greek kalends,' I muttered to myself. He wouldn't have understood.

I got out of the building fast, and luckily managed to flag down a cab right away. I sat on the cold vinyl seat, trembling all over. With anger as well as relief. But I calmed down gradually. I vowed to myself: don't get mad. Get even.

Of course, after that, we had to see each other frequently, sometimes in private meetings. I found it difficult to be relaxed, but he always behaved himself. I never told anyone about the incident. Gradually the memory faded as other concerns took its place, but I always made sure I wasn't alone with him in the building again.

As to his making me regret it, there were few enough signs. I could never quite pin down whether his attitude to me reflected that threat muttered in anger and humiliation. He was an absolute bastard to work for, that was true. It was also true that I was not the only one who felt that way. His mercurial management style, which veered from dictatorial to paternalistic to indulgent, sometimes in the course of a single day, was endured by everyone at McAllister's.

It was quite a pain. He would personally vet all expenses claims, sending me little notes scribbled on scraps of paper niggling about minor items. This was a big joke, because his own expenditure charged on the company – the executive flat, the massive entertainment bills, the limos – made mine look like nothing more than change. He signed every cheque for everything, from the latest advance to the janitor's wages.

He quibbled about the details of deals and contracts for the most petty reasons, throwing out those I had thought were totally uncontroversial. Then, he would cavalierly wave through a recommendation about a new deal involving a big commitment, backing my judgement against those of sales or the accountants. There wasn't any system to this. I felt frequently disorientated. H and H were by contrast almost a bureaucracy, with procedures which had to be gone through. Max would hardly ever step in on matters which he thought beneath him. Michael intervened in or tried to control everything that went on with what amounted to almost a mania.

Most particularly, he liked to wrongfoot me by buying in stuff and doing deals without my knowledge. He had done this several times. They were sometimes absolute stumers, like the series on the great houses of England edited by some society woman he was screwing. Michael, like so many of dubious social antecedents, loved a lord or, more particularly, a lady.

Sometimes, though, they were deals of considerable acumen. He liked to filch authors, by charm or bribery or even less respectable methods, just before they had their breakthrough book. He had a way with him, I had to admit. He also had connections all over the place – at the universities, in Parliament, in foreign governments. These brought in material which no one else could have. Michael regarded it as a huge game, and himself as a piratical entrepreneur, blasting the opposition out of the water, revelling in the opprobrium he garnered to himself in the process.

But I can't claim he behaved like this simply to spite me. He would have done it no matter who was the editorial director. I guess I should have felt undermined and resigned in protest, but that would have hurt no one but me. I would have ended up with no job here, and no prospect of returning to my old one in New York. Max wouldn't have had any sympathy: he had put me here for a purpose and he was totally ruthless when it came to what he regarded as failure. So I stuck it out.

I not only stuck it out. In my own opinion, I made out.

The fiction list when I arrived had consisted of a few lousy thrillers and several series of utter dross, though admittedly profitable dross. Most of these I quietly strangled. To replace them I brought in some good fiction. Not over-literary. I wouldn't say I had the most refined intellectual taste, having trouble with novels in which guys are having trouble writing novels, or which deal sensitively and poetically with necrophilia. It was solid reading for an intelligent audience. OK, so it was mainly a female audience, but that only serves to emphasize the intelligence.

Michael sometimes backed me. More often he didn't. He had gotten so used to easy profits from junk that he mostly regarded anything with a pay-off longer than the following afternoon as financial suicide. As I've said, it was mainly the big deals that caught his imagination. He could understand telephone number advances. The steady unspectacular investment in real and eventually rewarding talent was something he had trouble with.

The problem for me was that his preference for the big-ticket items had an added wrinkle. He couldn't bear that anyone was better at making these deals than he was.

I had soon realized that my early coup with Jane Somerset had paradoxically done me no good. It was too much like the way he operated, so it made him jealous. It was too much unlike the way I normally operated so I couldn't hope to repeat it. In fact, it was a genuine piece of serendipity on my part, having known Jane from way back and having discovered quite by accident that she was pissed off with her present publisher. She had welcomed the idea of working with me, and had overcome her agent's reluctance to have anything to do with McAllister's.

The result was that it was thrown back in my face whenever Michael felt like putting the knife into the performance of my department. This had happened quite frequently of late.

Moreover, although I didn't know then, the Somerset deal would later have other consequences.

So it was with no pleasure that I contemplated our meeting.

As usual, he kept me waiting. I sat for half an hour in the outer office watching his latest secretary – they didn't last long – feeding a succession of letters into the fax machine. Michael loved sending faxes. He liked anything instantaneous. A fax, he would say, sent overnight is like a dawn raid by the police. Clearly something was afoot. No doubt I would be the last to know.

I had the usual frisson as I crossed the place in the carpet where we had trysted three years earlier.

Michael was in a jovial mood, and started by allowing himself the pleasure of some minor humiliation.

'What's this about your going to Shropshire next Wednesday?'

I put my papers slowly down on the table. Fending off such attacks was to be approached carefully.

'I think you'll recall it's to see Tom Charleson, Michael.'

'And who the hell's he?'

I sighed, fairly audibly. 'I told you about him at our last meeting. He's a poet. A well-known poet. He wants to place his memoirs. I know him slightly. It's a small deal, but lots of prestige.'

'Why can't the bugger come to London?'

'Michael, he's very frail. He's over eighty, for God's sake.'

'I've never even heard of him. I certainly don't remember your mentioning him. I don't want to waste money on unsaleable crap like that. You should look at this month's figures.'

'I have. They're on budget.'

'I want better than budget. You know you haven't done a really decent deal since that Somerset woman. How many years ago was that? I've brought in umpteen big books since then. You can't run this company by farting around with superannuated poets.'

'But Michael, the deal was approved. It's not unsaleable. It's been properly costed –'

He cut in. 'I've just unapproved it. Forget poetry. Let's talk about a real book, whatyoumacallit, *Thought Stealers.*'

I bit back my anger and told him what I thought of it, which was basically that it was nasty, brutish and long, but would probably sell hugely to the mental incompetents who loved this stuff and seemed to number about half the population.

'Good, good. I'm glad we agree about something.' He smiled patronizingly. 'You always have to remember, as they say, no one went bust underestimating the public taste. And by the way, don't worry about the contract, he'll sign anything. I know something the tax men don't.'

We discussed some of the detailed work we would need. I would meet with publicity to agree the campaign. We would both have lunch with the author. Michael thought the combination of threat and flattery would work well.

'Arrange it for next Wednesday, will you? I think you're free then?'

There were a few other outstanding matters of a less controversial nature which helped me recover my temper.

I was gathering my papers together when he said, 'And how is Geoffrey?'

'Geoffrey?' I was astonished. I thought for a moment he must mean someone else.

'Yes, Geoffrey. Your Geoffrey.'

'He's very well.'

I was surprised at Michael showing such polite interest. But there was more.

'I thought he looked very fit. He tells me the cottage is going to be a great success.'

I was completely taken aback and unusually with Michael I blurted out without thinking, 'You mean you've seen him? Recently? I didn't know you knew him.'

'Oh, you'd be surprised whom I know, my dear. Geoffrey and I are very good friends.'

Michael never volunteered things like that without some ulterior motive, usually an unpleasant one. I saw him watching me, gauging the effect. I tried hard not to show that I was deeply disturbed, not only that Michael and Geoffrey were well acquainted – that was bad enough – but that I had had to learn it from Michael, and make it obvious to him that I hadn't known.

As this ball had obviously been served inviting a return, I should have disappointed him and refused to play. But an anxious curiosity overcame me.

'How come you know him?'

Michael smiled wolfishly. I had taken the bait. He could now enjoy his little game. I was more than ever convinced that I would hear something calculated to annoy or hurt me.

'He interviewed me a year or so ago for that magazine he works for. A boring old rag, but I liked his style and read some more of his stuff. It was good. Now he does some freelance stuff for me. Oh, nothing to do with McAllister's. Some of my other interests. I'm surprised he hasn't mentioned it.'

How could I have forgotten about Geoffrey's interviewing him? On that day of all days? Perhaps that was why. I didn't want to associate the best thing in my life with the worst. Now it turned out that they had gotten associated anyway.

'Perhaps he did. I must have forgotten.'

'How unlike you to forget, my dear. Geoffrey is such a splendid chap, isn't he? I've been very pleased with what he's been doing. You can tell him I said that.'

'And what has he been doing?' I didn't care any longer about not playing. I just wanted to know.

'I'm sorry, my dear. That I can't tell you.' He put his forefinger to his fat red lips. 'Trade secret.'

I got up to go. He had had his fun. But he hadn't quite finished. 'You know, my dear, I've become famous as a publisher, but one day I shall be even more famous, maybe for something else. You should remember this conversation.'

The day did not improve. I had a lunch with a very boring potential author, an ex-politician who couldn't decide whether to go ahead with the memoirs or await recall, and who tried rather feebly to grope me after the pudding.

The afternoon was spent in a meeting with men from finance about figures, about which I know nothing, as opposed to money, about which I know a great deal. Men, I find, are the other way about.

When I came out of the meeting, I found that Geoffrey had called and left a message. I thought it curious at the time, but I had no opportunity to reflect upon its significance until much later. The girl at reception had taken it in the absence of my secretary. It read: 'Change of plan, darling. Got a rush job on. Going back to the country for peace and quiet. Will ring tomorrow.' That was all. I called the flat at Limehouse, which he had kept on and used as a workbase. I got no answer.

Then I pushed my sense of annoyance and disappointment to one side and concentrated on my in-tray, constantly interrupted by yet more calls. At six I packed it in and rushed off to Covent Garden accompanied by a girl from publicity. There was a launch party for one of my books, the autobiography of an ancient acting knight, being held at the Theatre Museum – publicity specialized in such wittily apt venues for these junkets – followed by dinner at the Groucho with the author, an egotistical pain in the ass who took the first cab and left me in Greek Street being propositioned by a crowd of drunk Scotsmen. When I eventually got a taxi, the driver, hearing my accent, tried to persuade me that the best way to Hampstead was via Heathrow Airport. By the time I had straightened out the sonofabitch and we were rattling up Belsize Road at an almost illegal speed, it was nearly one a.m.

I paid off the cab, and thought twice about not tipping him. I had had enough hassle for one day.

I stopped at the top of the marble entrance stairs of the apartment block to look down on the lights of London. I often did this. It gave me a feeling of space and freedom, as if I were perched high in some eyrie. It consoled me that I had conquered the day.

I had not the least premonition then that there would be no more normal days to conquer.

6

It was no good. I couldn't sleep. I dragged my hair out of my eyes and stared at the illuminated digits of the clock. Two thirty-three a.m. I had been tossing and turning, burying my head in the pillow, pounding the mattress with my fists, trying to drown out the noises inside my head for well over an hour.

Normally I sank into unconsciousness a few moments after I hit the sack. Even after a busy day, I slept like a log no matter what. I prided myself on not taking my work to bed with me. But now I felt terrible. But it wasn't work. It was Geoffrey.

During the activity of the day, I had had no time for the questions his behaviour had prompted. Now, in the long hours before dawn, they whispered to me insistently, demanding attention.

I sat up in the bed, feeling the emptiness beside me. Free from the muffling duvet, I became aware of sounds other than those in my mind. There was a low moaning noise outside. For an instant, I felt a prickle of alarm. Then I realized it was only the wind.

I lay there, trying to imagine that I was back at Forest House, that Geoffrey filled the space beside me, that the nagging questions were silent and that all was well. But here in London there was no comforting blanket of darkness: the room, despite the heavy curtains, was filled with an eerie orange glow from the street lights.

The sound of the wind seemed much louder. There had been a stiff breeze blowing when I got out of the cab. That wasn't unusual on the comparatively lofty heights of Hampstead, but the sashes of the tall bedroom window were rattling distinctly and the moan had risen to a high-pitched keening. I got out of bed and went over to make sure the window catch was properly fastened.

The bedroom overlooks the side of the apartment block, facing towards Hampstead Village. I pulled back the curtain and peered out into the street. Even as I stood watching, what had been just a high wind was turning into a howling gale. The trees shading the sidewalk twisted and turned, their branches almost bending double against the onslaught. Sheets of newspaper and packaging lofted into the air and zoomed around aimlessly like huge white moths.

I pulled the curtains firmly closed again. I couldn't go back to bed. The row outside added to my anxiety. I needed a drink. I pulled on my robe, went through to the sitting room and got myself a whisky from the drinks cupboard. I sat down in the fireside chair and downed the shot in one. Then I poured another. I hadn't been drinking that day – I never did when I was supposed to be working, and that alone made me about twice as effective as most of my male colleagues – so the alcohol quickly fired me up, letting loose my anger and frustration.

How could he have gone to work for Michael, of all people, and not told me? Was this part of his journalist's code, to keep such things secret even from me? I didn't believe that. OK; so he didn't need to tell me what he was working on if it were commercially sensitive, but he could have, ought to have, mentioned the bare fact of the arrangement. To leave me to find out from Michael in circumstances which made it pretty clear that we had secrets in our relationship seemed to me hard to forgive. He knew how I felt about the guy – even if I hadn't revealed all the reasons – and his working for him without telling me in spite of that seemed pretty much like a betrayal. It made me question the whole nature of our trust. To cap it all there was what he had said only that morning about his attitude to McAllister's and its boss. If he felt like that, why also had he taken the job, whatever it was?

Trust was a sensitive issue ever since I had seen him with the strange woman in Breckenham. I had bottled up my suspicions there, partly out of a desire not to spoil the rural idyll right there and then with a row, but partly out of fear of what might be revealed.

I was deeply unhappy about his precipitate departure for Norfolk. It didn't make sense that he should do that after only one night back. Particularly as we had been apart the previous week. It wasn't that I resented our being away from each other. We both had commitments that meant we spent a good deal of our time in different locations. We weren't Darby and Joan. We needed time to ourselves.

Our separations were, though, always planned or at least known about in advance. Geoffrey wasn't the kind of journalist who disappeared into the world's trouble spots at a moment's notice. It wasn't like him to go off like this. I was also puzzled by the reason he had given. What could he possibly be doing that required him to be in Norfolk? Peace and quiet? But the work Geoffrey did required a phone and all the backup of the books and materials he had stored in Limehouse. It was because there wasn't a room for him to keep his stuff in the apartment that he had kept on his old place as a workbase. He could have spent time there if he'd wanted to be alone. There was still a bed and the basics of existence.

I was driven to the conclusion that it wasn't just that he wanted to get away from me in order to concentrate on work but that he specially wanted to be in Norfolk for a reason he hadn't disclosed. And I didn't like that feeling. The woman in the blue coat, dark-haired and oddly sophisticated in appearance in that workaday country town, bothered me. If I had seen what I thought I had seen, Geoffrey had been lying. And the only reason for him to lie was that it was not an innocent encounter of two old friends. It had much more significance. Perhaps he had gone back to see her.

If he was two-timing me, then he was going to be sorry indeed, very sorry. Almost as sorry as I was. I poured another drink and slumped back in the chair. The tears were already pricking my eyes. I really thought I had at last a man I could trust, who wouldn't cheat and lie and deceive. I wanted to think that he remained what I had thought him to be, a straightforward, slightly indolent, old-fashioned honourable Englishman. It was this image of him that had stopped me so far from trying to drag the truth out of him. And also there was part of me which didn't want the truth: I could hold him anyway by what was special about me. I remembered how I had caressed him, how I wanted him to think no one could love him in the way I could.

I looked at my wristwatch. Three-thirty a.m. He was snug in bed probably by now, after a bottle of decent claret. In bed. Perhaps with her, whoever the hell she was. I poured myself another drink. I stared angrily at the phone. If only the phone had been put in when it had been promised instead of being held up by allegedly difficult engineering conditions and problems with equipment suppliers. And if only Geoffrey hadn't had an unreasonable prejudice against mobile phones, his or anyone else's. 'I'm not some yuppie who wants to make calls on the bog,' he had said. Given the means, I would have called him late as it was to tell him . . . to tell him – what? To tell him I loved him, the bastard.

I poured out yet another drink, hoping it would calm the turbulence in my mind.

The wind now shrieked past the outside of the windows, slamming and banging them in their runners as if it were trying to yank them out bodily. It bellowed in the sitting room chimney like a banshee. In front of the fireplace the cream carpet was speckled with the soot which had been dislodged. I parted the drapes to look out again into the street. The sound reminded me of a sales conference I was at in Florida. But that was a hurricane. In England there weren't such things, were there? I wasn't the only one who was beginning to think it wasn't normal.

Lights were coming on in the houses on the other side of the street. The noise of the gale had woken up the neighbours. Not that I knew who they were. They might as well have lived on the other side of London for all the contact we had. We stared at each other out of our ordinary suburban living rooms while outside the roar of the elements made us think we were in the mid-Atlantic.

Then through the noise of the storm, I heard another. A straining, splitting, cracking of wood. Staring out across the street, I saw something unbelievable. One of those vast London planes, a tree nailed down to the sidewalk by a network of twisted roots, was moving. Very slowly, it was leaning forward. Chivvied and goaded by the wind, the speed of its fall quickened and it began to topple over. Instinctively, I flinched away from the window as the crown swept forward. The lower branches on the underside of the almost horizontal tree hit the road surface, cracked and broke off. The crown smashed down directly on to one of the parked cars on my side of the street. There was an explosive sound of glass as the windscreen fragmented under the buckled roof. Then there was only the wind.

It had happened so quickly and yet I seemed to have had infinite time to watch every stage. I felt afraid. This was indeed no ordinary storm. That tree had weathered maybe more than a hundred years of London storms. In the street outside, I heard the sound of voices. Front doors were open. Someone – presumably the owner of the car – was standing on the sidewalk as the now vertical branches of the fallen tree whipped and thrashed in the wind.

I turned away from the window. I was sick with anger and frustration, miserable and rejected, my nerves ragged with the nagging clamour of the gale. With no hope of sleep I went to bed.

But eventually I did sleep, the dizzying roller-coaster sleep of alcohol-assisted exhaustion.

The piercing buzz of the unforgiving alarm dragged me out of my slumber at the usual time. I lay in bed not quite aware of where I was. I could have been in Norfolk, for there was an odd silence in the room. The wind had gone, and so had the usual sound of commuter cars churning down the hill into town. Looking blearily out of my window, I saw why. The tree blocking the highway and the crushed car were still there. I had somehow imagined that, like the debris of a party, someone would have gotten up early to clear them away. A group of boys and girls in school uniforms hung around the wreck. One boy was walking precariously the length of the trunk up into the branches of the crown. A helmeted policeman was standing watching, but apparently with no other purpose. I shrugged. That was England. I felt groggy and hungover, but my black mood of earlier had dispersed. I had a cold shower to wake myself up. Feeling slightly fresher, I made coffee and switched on the radio for the seven o'clock news bulletin. I listened with amazement.

The newscaster was saying in the usual neutral tone with which the BBC reports disasters that last night's storm had indeed been of unusual violence. Winds of almost hurricane force had hit not only London but had torn their way across the whole of southern and eastern England. Norfolk and Suffolk were particularly badly affected.

Last night it simply hadn't occurred to me that the terrible weather had hit anywhere but Hampstead. I forgot that England was so tiny. Events which in the States were merely local would spread here over whole counties.

As I heard the reports of trees down, of roads blocked, of power supplies disrupted, of damage to property, of injuries and deaths, I forgot temporarily all about the anger and hurt I had felt over Geoffrey's absence. My thoughts were of his safety. I saw the trees crashing around and on top of the house. Or the chimney collapsing into the bedroom, or the wayward electricity supply bursting into flames. I felt selfish at not having thought of this before. While I was erecting a whole edifice of deceit purely out of my interpretation of a few trivial incidents, I hadn't once reflected that he might be injured or in danger.

I knew then I couldn't go through the whole day not knowing how he was. Anything could have happened there and no one would call to see. I thought of him lying hurt in that lonely house. I had to get there to find out.

Even in the midst of my concern I couldn't help reflecting that my unannounced appearance would also help to resolve some of those other doubts that nagged at me.

I gulped down the remains of the coffee and dressed hurriedly. It was too early to call the office. I would stop on the road and do that later.

There was a car-hire office in Pond Square. I ran virtually all the way. I had to dodge my way round a knot of rubber-neckers in Heath Street. An entire scaffolded building had collapsed and the road was littered with rubble and splintered wooden boards. A few workmen in orange dayglo jackets rooted aimlessly in the wreckage. The inevitable spectating policeman held back the too curious. It must have been like this in the war: a constant sense of unreal excitement and a legitimate reason to be late for work, or to take the day off.

The hire company office was open, an oasis of transatlantic purpose in the zombie-like atmosphere that seemed evident everywhere else. They had a car, thank God. Please let it really be a nice day.

It took me an age to get out of town. Roads everywhere were blocked by fallen trees, and there were few signs of anyone unfalling them. I made endless detours through the rat runs in Finchley and Hendon. It had the effect of keeping me busy and concentrated. I was on the Barnet bypass before I had time to reflect maturely on exactly what the hell I thought I was doing.

I had to have gone nuts. Geoffrey would tell me that right away. He was in absolutely no danger, I could see that. Right now he was probably frying up some bacon and eggs, perking coffee and generally feeling all was right with the world. It would take more than a storm to disturb Geoffrey Reynolds' legendary ability to secure his own well-being. I had panicked like a hysterical woman, over-emotional, not thinking things through.

At the next exit sign, I almost chickened out and turned back. But whatever the rational basis for what I was doing I felt I had to go through with it. I pressed my foot down harder on the gas. OK, so Geoffrey would think I was crazy. But I cared about him and I didn't mind letting it show.

And behind that was still the intense curiosity, the compulsion if you like, to find out just what the hell he was doing there. The corrosive jealousy would have to be flushed out sooner or later. Why not sooner?

I stopped in Baldock to call the office. I needn't have bothered. No one was expecting me. One girl on reception had made it, but only because she lived round the corner in Queen Square. The Northern Line had, as you might expect, packed in without a struggle. Michael hadn't got in. Unusually, he had gone home to Guildford the previous evening to pay his wife and family a rare visit. Fallen trees had jammed the traffic on the London Road and he was stuck somewhere in his company limo with only the chauffeur and his car phone for company. Tough.

I told the girl on the desk to find my diary and cancel my appointments, those that hadn't already cancelled themselves. The British were good in a crisis. I began to feel better. The sun was out and I was playing hookey.

There were no holdups on the road, although on every side there were signs of the violence of the gale: missing chimney stacks, flattened fences, smashed greenhouses. One thatched cottage had been stripped of its roof and sat forlornly in its debris like a plucked fowl amidst its own feathers. By Thetford I was feeling peckish and pleased there were only a few miles to go. I hoped Geoffrey had something good for lunch. A fresh plump pigeon perhaps. I had been stupid to worry. He would be alone surrounded by work. There was nothing more sinister to be concerned about.

I slowed down, looking for the sign to Barton St Margaret. On the minor road, there were more signs of the storm. The verges were littered with twigs and branches, but the forest had been planted back from the road, keeping it clear. By now the sun was strong in a cloudless blue sky. I rolled down the window and breathed in the familiar strong resinous scent of the forest.

I still was not too good at spotting the entrance to the lane so I overshot the first time and had to turn round in the road. There was no other traffic. I swung the wheel hard over on to the track to the cottage. The tyres rumbled on the rocks of the lane. In a few moments I would see Geoffrey and all would be well, all manner of things would be well.

It was about halfway along, where the lane begins to climb into the forest proper, that I saw the BMW.

It was facing me, off the track, skewed round slightly, nose against a small tree, the front fender and nearside wing crumpled by the impact. I stamped on the brake pedal. The hire car skidded on the loose surface, stalled and stopped a few yards away from Geoffrey's car.

It was very quiet. I heard only the faint ticking sound from the engine as it cooled, and the sound of my breath rasping into my tension-stiffened chest. I sat bolt upright, gripping the steering wheel tightly with both hands, staring through the fly-spattered windshield. The sun glinted on the shiny red paintwork of the BMW, turning its windows into opaque silver. For some moments I sat like this, as if I were hoping that I was witnessing some strange trick of the light or a mirage.

Then my hand, out of sheer force of habit, reached out and turned off the ignition. The red warning light in front of me blinked out. The small familiar gesture roused me. What I could see was entirely real.

I pushed down the handle and kicked the door wide.

The car was empty. I wrenched the driver's door wide open. It had not been fully closed, the lock not engaged, as if it had swung to on its counterweight. The key was in the ignition, on his RAC keyring. I leaned in. There were none of his things on the seats. And, thank God, no blood. Just the faint smell of leather.

I leaned against the side of the car, resting my forehead on the sun-warmed metal of the roof. I felt a nausea rising in my stomach. What on earth had gone on here? Then my numbed brain began to function again. He must have abandoned the car after the accident. He must have been shocked. He had gone back to the house until he felt well enough to get help. He must be there now.

My heart hammering in my chest with relief, I ran to my car, reversed it on to the track and, gunning the engine until the wheels flung up a cloud of dust, drove past the crippled BMW like a lunatic to the cottage. It looked very peaceful as I once more jerked the car to a standstill. This time I leapt out right away.

The front door was open. There was no sound from inside. I ran up the stairs two at a time and burst into the bedroom. The bed was undisturbed. On the floor by the wardrobe was the soft leather valise that Geoffrey used on his trips. It was unzipped and I could see glimpses of shorts, part of a shirt. Some mounting sense of horror made me shrink from touching it.

I flew back down the stairs. In the sitting room, there were signs of him – empty glasses, newspapers, books, magazines strewn over chairs and on the floor. In the kitchen, there were dirty plates in the sink. A half-full bottle of Burgundy stood on the table in the midst of the purplish red stain left by spilt wine. How many times had I told him to use a coaster? There was a wholemeal loaf with several slices cut from it on the breadboard and a platter with a selection of cheeses, still in their clingwrap.

He must have been near the end of his evening meal. The chair was pushed a long way back from the table as if he had got up suddenly. Then for some reason, he had gotten into the car and driven off down the track. He must have skidded in the dark, crashed into the tree. But where was he now? What had happened here last night? I felt helpless and confused, overwhelmed by the sense of absence the traces of him radiated.

I ran out of the front door and stood on the driveway, the shingle pressing hard into my feet through the thin soles of my city shoes. I gazed around at the dark impassive trees, then back at the house with its blank windows. The warm sun and the cloudless sky seemed to mock the darkness in my mind.

I called out 'Geoffrey!' Or rather I screamed it over and over again till the clearing rang with it. There was a noisy clattering of birds from the trees, and further off came the harsh call of a pheasant. But there was no human reply, though I strained my ears to catch the least sound as the silence flooded back.

I ran to the car and once again roared off down the track to where the BMW lay like a scarlet insect among the trees.

I got out and stared about me once more. I forced my mind to think. Where would he go? Was he injured or just dazed or shocked? Perhaps he had got as far as the road, flagged down a passing car and was even now in hospital, or a bar. I seized on this thread of hope eagerly. I had been overreacting, panicking. I needed to get to a phone, call the police, get someone to phone the hospitals, get a search going.

Then by the side of the track in front of the crumpled nose of the BMW I found a shoe.

A black elastic-sided shoe, slightly scuffed and worn, but with the heavy solid look of the handmade article. Geoffrey's.

It was jammed under a fallen branch or small tree trunk which lay half overgrown with grass and brambles. In the dark, he must have tripped over it and wrenched off the shoe. He had not retrieved it because he could not find it in the dark. He had gone on.

The shoe pointed into the forest. The fallen branch lay parallel with the track. Therefore, he had been crossing the obstacle when he lost his shoe. For some reason which I could not fathom, he had been heading into the forest.

I leapt over the branch, oblivious of the briars snaking around it which tore at my skirt and scratched my bare legs.

The trees there were planted close. The light of day hardly penetrated. I trod the thick mat of needles, stretching my hands before my face to avoid the sharp spurs of broken branches which stuck out into my path from the pale fissured trunks of the firs.

Then a few yards away, where the sun slashed bars of yellow light through gaps in the dense canopy into the gloom of the wood, I saw at the foot of a massive fir what looked like a bundle of clothing.

Half stumbling over roots and broken branches sunk in the deep drifts of pine needles, I ran to him, as if my urgency now could make up for the hours I had missed. My heart was pumping at such a rate I felt sick and dizzy.

He was slumped forward on his hands and knees, his face pressed against the base of the trunk. For a fleeting second, I thought he had fallen asleep in this childlike pose. I reached out to grasp his shoulder and shake him gently awake. But where there should have been warm, familiar, yielding flesh under the grey wool fabric of his jacket, there was something hard and cold and alien. Then I felt him move under my touch.

Held in that posture only by the stiffness of death, he toppled over on to his back, his legs drawn up against his chest, his arms thrown up beside his head. I let out a scream which came from the very pit of my being and left me drained and shaking. Then I sank down on my knees beside him clasping him in my arms, pressing against his icy lips my own soft warmth as if I could breathe the life back into him, hugging him close and stroking his hair and saying his name over and over again.

I wept, and was blinded by tears. But I could not shut out the vision in my mind of his face, his staring eyes and his mouth open in agony.

When finally I raised my head, the sun no longer shone down through the branches. In the gloom, there was the scent of pine.

Part Two

7

'Doesn't anyone know where the bitch has gone? What about that agent of hers? She told me she didn't.'

'Vanessa? She says not to me as well. She says all she knows is that she's in France, probably the south.'

'That narrows it down a lot. Is she being straight with us? How does she know that much?'

'She had a couple of postcards. No address, but postmarked from different parts of Provence. She read them to me. They were full of *Je ne regrette rien*, and no sign that she was coming back. I believe what Vanessa says, actually. I don't think she wants to fall out with us. If she knew any more, she'd tell. She doesn't want to get a reputation for colluding with absconding authors. According to her, she last saw her about six months ago when she came in to talk about the outline for *This Spider Love*. Everything sounded fine. She seemed on top of the world.'

'How bloody nice for her. She's left us with a fine fucking mess: The expensive advance publicity for the new series, not to mention the contract money. We end up with one book and a lot of egg on our faces. I don't like the company looking so bloody inept. I've a good mind to get someone to track her down. I used to know a man in the Sûreté.'

'I think France has changed a bit since *The Day of the Jackal*, Michael. Even if you found her, you can't force her to write the books. It'd be quite hard even to get the money back.'

'There are ways.' He spoke casually, but the words left a chill in the air.

I didn't reply, but stood up from the low chair reserved for the recipient in what Michael called bollocking sessions.

He remained slumped in the outsize captain's chair, twiddling the fat gold fountain pen in his thick fingers. 'Hey, where are you going? I'm expecting you to come up with some suggestions. It was your deal. I thought she was a big pal of yours, anyway. You quite sure you haven't heard?'

I took a deep breath. 'I wouldn't at present call her a friend of mine,' I said carefully, 'and I hope you're not suggesting, Michael, that I'd conceal information or do anything to undermine the company's interest even if she were.'

He waved it away with a sardonic leer. 'Of course not, my dear. You can go away. But have a good think about how we get out of this one. It'll be in all our interests, won't it? Especially yours.'

This meeting showed that as far as the company was concerned I was back in business after my little local difficulty, or rather, as Michael had put it at the beginning, that I sodding well ought to be by now. I had accordingly been hurled into the chilly waters of the very deepest end, into what was being referred to by the men in suits on the fifth floor as the Jane Somerset disaster.

The Somerset deal, that darling first child of those early thrusting days with McAllister's, was falling apart. She had contracted for four blockbuster historical romances to be delivered at annual intervals. The first one, *A Bracelet of Bright Hair* had just been published, to bad reviews but good sales, the way round that publishers like to see it. This was terrific. Readers were already thirsting for the next volume in the series. What was not terrific was that the chances of there being even one sequel, leave alone three, were just about zero.

Jane Somerset, or Jane Fucking-Somerset as she had been double-barrelled by Michael, had disappeared, taking with her a large payment which had been made in advance for the unwritten novels. It seemed unlikely that she would either volunteer to return it or give value for it in terms of completing her contract.

Michael had been, by all accounts, incandescent when this state of affairs became evident. Vanessa Wordsworth had done me the kindness of telling him first and bore the brunt of his volcanic rage. Now the object of his wrath in the absence of La Somerset was, unsurprisingly, me. Widowhood would no longer protect me.

As I sat that evening over the remains of my supper, a half-empty whisky bottle at my elbow, I reflected on the events which had occurred during the time that had passed since that terrible day when I had lain against Geoffrey's cold body in the damp drift of brown pine needles. I could still summon up at will their disinfectant odour. It had been, what, a few months? Three, actually. Ninety-two days, actually. Long enough, of course. I ought to be doffing the widow's weeds a little bit, now I was 'over the shock'. What concern there had been had noticeably begun to evaporate. The hushed whispers and the worried glances were replaced by the cheery greetings of normal times. Off-colour humour was once again permitted in my presence in the mail room. I had come through. My rent cheeks and my ash-covered hair no longer spoiled the atmosphere.

I didn't get used to this, but I wasn't so surprised by it any more. And of course it is true – all clichés are true up to a point – that the only healer is time. I had indeed in those few short months struggled to come to terms with grief and loss. I was reconciled to their everyday presence. They were like half-grown children, sometimes leaving me alone, sometimes demanding instant and total attention. But I could not yet begin to reconcile myself to the new element which had compounded these terrible but clear feelings into a turgid devil's brew. Doubt.

I had gone back to the office the day after the funeral. It seemed the only home I had left. People said I should get away, but I couldn't see the point. The only thing I wanted to get away from and couldn't leave behind was me. Besides, I couldn't cope with going alone, and there was no one around I could go with. I saw how much I had neglected friendship since my marriage. I had lost touch with so many people. The friends I had left in London were the sort of people who had commitments – jobs, husbands, lovers, children – which I could hardly expect them to drop for the chance to spend a miserable time with a sad case like me. I hoped that under the influence of the working routine, the ache, the resentment, the anger and the hurt would leave me alone for a few hours. To some extent they did.

But I knew I was not the same. My concentration was very limited. I would find myself in the middle of dictating a letter staring at the wall or out of the window. At inconvenient times, I would feel the tears start to my eyes and I would have to leave the meeting or break off the telephone call.

To begin with, everyone I encountered at such times was kind, but the kindness took the form of pretending that my grief was an illness arising from some impersonal source such as a virus. It was the kindness one extends to someone convalescing from a minor operation. There had been flowers from people in publishing I had hardly given the time of day to, with warm messages of condolence. Young men opened doors for me with elaborate courtesy as if I had been overwhelmed by a sudden physical frailty.

Colleagues in a meeting would carry on politely as if nothing had happened when I gathered up my papers and fled the room, weeping, much as they might have done if an elderly relative of infirm body and feeble mind had vomited or been incontinent. By their lights, they were being very understanding. But they did not realize that grieving is an endless process of rehearsal and repetition. The last thing you want is to deny the grief and the source of the grief. I suppose I had not known this, having gone through adult life until then without suffering the consequences of unlooked-for loss.

No one seemed to realize that I wanted to talk about him, and about what had happened. But no one ever did talk to me about Geoffrey. His death had made a taboo. Even people I thought were my close friends would only make a few brief and tentative remarks about 'how I was feeling?', at which I had to say that I was feeling fine or much better, not that I was completely bloody devastated and how the hell did they think they would feel if the person closest to them had just dropped down dead? Against my better judgement, I went to a dinner party at which everyone had quite clearly been briefed by my hostess that I was still shaky and that they should stay off any sensitive topics from love to the price of funerals. I sat numb and tongue-tied, drank too much and left before the pudding. No doubt the story would be around town before morning. Mary was taking it very badly. In fact, just between ourselves, the poor thing has quite gone to pieces. She always liked her drink, but now she's really hitting the bottle.

A few days after his death, I had summoned up the courage to look through the few newspaper accounts which someone I knew in a PR company had collected together and sent me. The story in the *Quotidian* was fairly typical:

JOURNALIST FOUND DEAD AFTER STORM

Geoffrey Reynolds, the journalist, was found dead early yesterday near the woodland track leading to his isolated weekend cottage two miles from the Norfolk village of Barton St Margaret.

The body was discovered by his wife, Mary, a senior executive with McAllister's, the publishing conglomerate run by flamboyant tycoon Michael Underdown-Metcalfe, when she arrived at the cottage by car from London. It is believed that Mr Reynolds (42) had felt unwell in the night and had gone to summon assistance, but suffered a fatal heart attack only minutes after setting out in his red BMW car which was found abandoned nearby. A police spokesman said that foul play was not suspected, and that the hurricane-force winds which had battered the area the previous evening – see our page 1 story for details – did not appear to have contributed significantly to the tragedy.

Mrs Reynolds, who was too distressed to talk to our reporter, is thought to be resting at her Hampstead flat. Friends said that the recently married couple had only just moved into their country retreat.

Mr Reynolds was for several years this newspaper's economics correspondent, where his laconic but incisive and provocative articles enjoyed a wide following, even among those he criticized. He was also a former North America correspondent of the *Hobbesian*, the economic and financial journal, and its former associate editor. The dead man's colleagues today paid tribute to his intelligence, good humour and professionalism and his love of the good things of life.

I had read such accounts on countless occasions, brief notices of someone else's tragedies. Now they were mine.

At least if you worked for a newspaper, they took care of their own and sent you out with a pat on the back. Mind you, on that basis, even the assistant printing room cat would merit a paragraph. It wasn't much, but it was better than I would manage unless I happened to get raped and murdered. So that was my husband, lover of the good things of life. Did that include me, I wondered?

They had even got the details basically right, for a change. No doubt the astute reader – if there were such things – might wonder precisely what the hell had really been going on. But at least they had spared me the imputation of lunacy or second sight or both. Nor had they bothered me. Geoffrey just wasn't important enough, when it came to it, to anyone but me.

As I read the piece again, I pulled up at the last paragraph. Annoyed, I read it again, carefully. Yes, there it was. 'Former associate editor' of the *Hobbesian*. Now that wasn't right. He hadn't been former but current. Give the man his due. Even the printer's cat would get that.

I picked up the phone and rang the news desk of the *Quotidian*. Fortunately I got someone who recognized me, and they put me on to the fellow who had subbed the item about Geoffrey. He was sympathetic but not apologetic. 'We did check that with the *Hobbesian*. We do with that sort of thing. They told us he was non-current. Sorry, but there it is.'

Even more annoyed at being made to look a fool at the *Quotidian* because they or the *Hobbesian* had got their facts wrong, I put in a call to the editor of the *Hobbesian*.

He rang me back in minutes. 'Mary, I was so sorry to hear about Geoffrey. I would have come to the funeral, but I had to be in Brussels. I hope the flowers were OK. Poor Geoffrey, I know he would have preferred Taittinger.'

'They were fine, thanks. It was kind of you. As for the drinking, I think his friends made an extra effort on his behalf afterwards. I'm ringing because of this silly mistake in the *Quotidian*'s piece about Geoffrey. They say he was your former associate editor. That's not true, is it?'

There was a pause at the other end, then a slightly nervous cough. Charles Waterson wasn't the type of journalist who was used to dealing with grieving widows, only bleeding economies. Then he said, 'Yes, that's correct. Geoffrey left us, oh, about six months ago.'

'What?'

'It was perfectly amicable. Said he'd got something he wanted to follow up himself, something outside the *Hobbesian*'s interests. Something about a book. I thought you'd know. I mean I thought he would have –'

'It's all right, Charles. It's not your fault. I'm not going to go hysterical on you. He must have forgotten to mention it. We led very busy lives.'

'Of course.' He accepted my feeble piece of face-saving gratefully. 'Well, if that's all I can do . . .'

'He didn't say what this thing was?'

'Other than to stress that it was nothing that would conflict with the *Hobbesian*'s interests, he didn't as they say reveal his sources. He was a stickler for etiquette, but he was still a journalist.'

I replaced the phone, my head swimming. What on earth had Geoffrey been up to? Six months ago, he had packed in a perfectly good, well-paid job for the vaguest of reasons and to cap it all he hadn't bothered even to mention it to me. I felt hurt and sick. I wouldn't even have contemplated doing such a thing without talking to him, but Geoffrey had kept it from me. Why? Six months ago. I cast my mind back. He hadn't seemed in the least bit different. Only in one respect had our life changed, and that was obviously completely irrelevant to this matter. The coincidence stuck in my mind, though.

It had been about six months ago that we had started to look for a cottage in Norfolk.

The other thing I had had to deal with at this time was Geoffrey's will. Geoffrey and I had, at my suggestion, not to say insistence, made wills when we married. Neither of us had done such a thing before. He had left everything to me, and I had left everything to him. We had made them as a gesture for the present rather than the future. All my worldly goods, etc., etc. The event they presupposed seemed then too massive and far-off compared to the wonderful delirium of the present. We were young enough, or perhaps just irresponsible enough, not to worry overmuch about what Geoffrey called the Big D.

This insouciance had merely paralleled the carefreeness – some might say carelesness – of our lives. We were both independent people when we married, and to a large extent we remained that way. We kept our own bank accounts and managed our own financial affairs. I had bought the Hampstead apartment quite cheaply when I had first come over. I paid the mortgage. We had a joint account for household bills. We each paid into this by standing order every month. I paid the bills and managed this account, investing the monthly surplus in a building society to meet the big annual cheques. As I think I already said, Geoffrey was not a practical man. He was hardly unique in this respect, of course. Forest House would have been an additional factor in this arrangement, but we hadn't gotten around to thinking about that in such coldly practical terms. We had been like children with a new toy.

Geoffrey's death revealed how little I really knew about his finances. I didn't know how much he earned as we avoided discussing money as much as other people avoided discussing sex. Like such people, I assumed we each got about the same. Until the day he told me about the aunt's legacy, I never had the impression that there was any capital tucked away. Although he lived well, apart from his liking for fine wine, he had no major extravagances.

It was only because I was wanly doing the expected thing that I summoned up the energy a fortnight or so after Geoffrey's death and wrote to his solicitor informing him, in case he hadn't already heard, of Geoffrey's death and asking for an appointment to discuss his client's affairs. He was a partner in a middle-ranking City firm. Geoffrey had been at school with him, and I gathered they had maintained contact over the years. He and I were the executors. I had never actually met him, but I was slightly surprised he had not found the time to come to the funeral.

I had a call from a snooty secretary in reply who gave me a date and time when it would be convenient for him to see me. I gave her the date and time when it would be convenient for me to see him. After a bit of Sloaney humming and ha-ing, I got my way.

I made the mistake of being punctual, forgetting the games such people liked to play, games which they had picked up from dealing with clients such as Michael. Accordingly, I kicked my heels for half an hour or so in the reception area of Warrender Pearsons' expensive offices near Guildhall. Finally, I was ushered into the presence by the snooty one – all blonde tresses and silk knickers. God, these people gave themselves airs.

Peter Goodman rose to greet me. He was tall and thin, in a clinically correct dark suit, white shirt and a tie whose insignia would mean something to the right person. He was almost certainly younger than he looked, but assurance and a big fee income add their own gravitas to relative youth.

'Mrs Reynolds, how nice to meet you. Please accept my condolences for your recent bereavement.'

'Thank you, and it's Mary, please. I do hope I haven't interrupted a busy schedule,' I said, giving him a charming smile.

'I don't want to waste your time, so let's come straight to the point.'

He didn't want to waste his time, he meant. He'd already wasted mine. I smiled again.

'You wrote to me to discuss the position relating to your late husband's will. I have to say at the outset that as far this firm is concerned, Mr Reynolds did not actually make a will.'

'What? But he came to see you. I know he did. I had my secretary make the appointment for him. He told me about it.'

'Please, I didn't say that he did not do so. Yes, he consulted me about a will. I have here the attendance note I made at the time.' He pointed at the thin manila file on the blotter in front of him. 'As you would expect, I asked him about his assets. Mr Reynolds said he had no private means, only his income from journalism. Presumably you know about any bank and building society accounts, investments, insurance? I'm afraid I have no records of those things here. Also his tax position. I asked him if he had an accountant. He said he didn't: he handled his tax affairs himself. There may be some income tax due if he was self-employed. There usually is, I'm afraid. I then advised him about the consequences and advantages of making a will: certainty of beneficiary and so on. I'm sure he was aware of that. It was agreed that I should draft a will naming you as the executor and sole beneficiary. I did so. Here is the draft.' He held up a couple of sheets of paper. 'I sent him a copy, asked him to confirm that it was in accordance with his instructions, and if so I would have it engrossed for execution. I have no record that he did so confirm. I certainly never prepared the engrossment, nor does it appear that a bill was sent or requested. Of course he may have gone elsewhere, or he may simply have changed his mind. That happens. The process is not one that everyone wants to think about, as you can imagine.'

'Yes, of course. But he certainly led me to believe that he had done it. Perhaps he was going to but took fright as you say. As far as his financial affairs are concerned – tax and so on – I don't have a clue. It seems silly I know, but we kept things separate. Old habits die hard. We hadn't been married long. Does there not being a will make that much difference?'

'If there is no will, then the intestacy rules apply, which bring in new classes of potential beneficiaries. Broadly speaking, as his widow, instead of the whole estate you get only a lump sum and an interest in the residue. What kind of interest depends on whether there are issue, or if not whether there are other close relatives, parents and brothers and sisters.' He looked down at the file. 'It appears I did explain this to your husband. I have a note that he asked me about the legal meaning of issue.'

'And what is it?'

'Basically it's descendants: children and their children.' He hesitated. 'We touched on another matter. I have to say that he asked me whether the definition included, er, all children, whenever or however born. Which it has for many years.'

I was beginning to feel weak with all this. I had also the insidious beginnings of a migraine. 'So what is there to do?'

'Well, it would certainly be advisable to sort out the tax situation. You could write to the Revenue as a potential administrator of the intestacy to find out the position. Frankly, there'll be less of a bill from us if you do that. If there is a big tax bill and no assets then it could mean the estate is technically insolvent and that can make things a lot less straightforward.'

I raised my eyebrows. 'He couldn't possibly be insolvent. He'd had a considerable legacy from an aunt. Didn't he mention that? He'd used some of it to buy the cottage in Norfolk.'

'A legacy? As I indicated earlier, he said nothing to me of any substantial capital sum of that nature. Perhaps it came to him after he gave me instructions on the will.'

I stared at him. 'It can't have. He said he inherited before we were married. Anyway, he said he'd bumped into you somewhere and discussed buying the cottage. You recommended he get a local firm. You said it wouldn't be worth London prices for that sort of property.'

He stared back. 'That might well have been the advice I would have given, but I don't recollect actually doing anything of the sort, I'm afraid. In Norfolk, did you say? Nothing at all like that. I really didn't know your husband so it couldn't have been on a social occasion.'

'But you were at school with him!' I burst out in amazed irritation.

It was his turn to look amazed. He tried to make light of it, unconsciously fingering the tie as he spoke. 'Oh, no. I never had that pleasure. I would certainly have remembered. I met him only once – on the occasion I've discussed. I don't recall his consulting the firm otherwise, not in my time. He came to me through a colleague who retired. You see we don't do much private client work any more. Only for very long-standing connections or members of staff. Virtually all our work is commercial these days.'

I didn't know what to say. I suddenly had the feeling that I had stepped off the top step of a stairway which turned out not to be there. Like Alice, I looked around with interest at the things I saw when I fell, then landed with a bump. I felt quite dazed. So much so that I felt I had missed something.

'So Geoffrey never asked you about buying in Norfolk? You never recommended a Norfolk solicitor?'

He was starting to look surreptitiously at his watch. 'Quite so. Mrs Reynolds, I'm afraid I have another appointment in a few minutes.' He gave a slightly warmer smile. 'Why don't you go through his papers? I expect the details are there. I'm terribly sorry I'm unable to be of more help.'

'Thanks. I guess I'm still in shock. I must have misunderstood what he said. You're right. I'll have to go through his papers. I haven't steeled myself to do that yet.'

He nodded. 'Yes, of course. I do understand.'

I was at the door when something he had said struck me. 'You said he came to you from a retired colleague. Would it be possible to speak to him?'

He shook his head gently. 'Ah, no. You see he died a year or so ago. He was a great City character, our Mr Venables, the last hereabouts of what we call general practitioners. We took over his practice, such as it was, about ten years ago when he finally retired, although he continued to wander in for some time as a consultant. He must have been over eighty. His name lives on, though.' He picked up a piece of headed notepaper. Underneath the main heading could be read in very small print 'Incorporating Venables & Co'. 'Now I think of it, Mr Reynolds did say that Mr

Venables had originally acted for him when he took the lease of a flat. I believe the connection was made between them not at public school, but in Balls Brothers.'

I nodded casually, trying not to show how much my brain was reeling. 'A wine bar,' I said, 'How very appropriate.'

As I rode down alone in the lift, I gazed at myself in the mirrored wall. I didn't look different, but inside I felt about a hundred years old, too aged and weary to put together the information I had gathered in this brief meeting and bowed down in anticipation of its weight. For I knew intuitively that all I had known of the man I had been married to was somehow under question. I wondered what else there would be to discover. It was not long before I found out.

At ten a.m. on the Saturday following the visit to the lawyer I had been sitting in my dressing gown at the kitchen table with a half-drunk cup of cold coffee deep in dismal thoughts, facing another weekend of roaming about on the Heath, mooning about the apartment, TV and drink. That was all my energy level had allowed me for the three weeks or so since his death. I lived on ready meals and junk food from the supermarket. I hadn't read one book in that time. I had to make a huge effort to wade through the very few authors' typescripts I had in the office and which I hadn't felt able to delegate. I hadn't gotten around to doing what the lawyer had more or less told me what was my duty as an executor to do – go through Geoffrey's papers to establish his financial position. And also to solve the puzzle about which lawyer had the title deeds of the cottage. That particular problem was also connected with the recent file I had had to open labelled 'Lies Geoffrey told me'.

Were they really lies? How far along the scale of mendacity did you rank such matters as whether you were an old school friend of a prominent City solicitor, when the truth appeared to be you had been a chance connection of the partner of a predecessor firm? Why had he told me about consulting the alleged friend about the cottage when he hadn't? If not, to whom had he gone for the legal work on the cottage?

But more than that, if Geoffrey had not attended the same school as Peter Goodman, where had he gone? If he had not told me the truth about so many matters, how well had I really known him? Did I know anything about the man I had married? One thing of which I had always been ignorant now seemed strikingly significant.

It might have seemed peculiar to anyone who has had what you might call a standard model marriage – assuming there are such things – in which you meet the guy, meet the folks, do the business, live happily ever after with a widening circle of offspring and grandparents, that I knew nothing whatever of Geoffrey's background. I had never met his parents. He never spoke of them. But it has to be understood that we had met when we were both as it were fully formed. We had gone through lots of living, and childhood was a long way away.

Even so, I had told him at length about my multicultural childhood. I had shared with him that devastating moment when Sister Bernadette Concepta, the principal of the College of the Holy Blood, called me in from basketball class in the gymnasium and told me of the auto wreck on the Taconic State Parkway – God, how bathetic the name sounded then, sounds now – which had wiped out the lives of my father and mother. I had stood there in a short navy skirt and white aertex blouse, shivering as the perspiration dried cold on my forehead, staring down at my sneakers, the parquet pattern of the floor whirling in sickening spirals and finally flying apart to reveal only blackness beneath.

I had thought that was, had to be, the worst life could offer. I knew differently now.

I had shared that with him and he had listened, but he had shared nothing of his own in return. Then I had been a little hurt, puzzled even, that he could not reciprocate in the least degree. I had not pressed him, however. What was preventing him might have been a loss as deep as my own, or some pain long buried into which even I would not intrude uninvited. There was anyway, I had consoled myself, all the time in the world for such matters to emerge in their own season. I did not know then those livelong minutes really would be all that heaven allowed.

The more I thought about these things the more the possibility arose that Geoffrey's parents were still alive. Plenty of people his age had parents living. I felt a pang of guilt that I had not thought of this before. I had been preoccupied with my own feelings. I had let Geoffrey go into the dark without any blood relative by him. Whatever had happened in the past would surely be cancelled out by death. I owed it to him to do my utmost to find a mother or a father and allow them to grieve. But where were they?

I stacked the breakfast things into the dishwasher, noted that it was full to overflowing with greasy crocks, and dragged my mind around to finding the detergent and filling the compartment. I slammed the door and broke a fingernail as I pushed the 'on' button. Yet one more thing I couldn't seem to do properly these days.

Of course, in the case of a living person the answer to these questions could be sought and discussed. With Geoffrey, there were no such answers. Death left questions that would forever be unanswered, loose ends, puzzlement, dissatisfaction. If I wanted answers then I should have to find them myself from what remained. And that meant summoning up the courage and making the effort. That meant also that I should have to go at last to the flat in Limehouse where Geoffrey kept his papers. Only there was there the documentation that every citizen of the twentieth century willy nilly accumulates. To the extent that my questions had answers, they would be there.

He had never fully moved into my apartment. Sure, he had some things here. The bathroom was littered with used razors, a couple of bottles of aftershave which I had given him – umpteen worn and flattened toothbrushes, a couple of skeletal shaving brushes, a toothpaste tube squeezed in the middle and a pile of washcloths so old they were transparent. These grubby male articles had always seemed a bit of an intrusion in my beautiful space while he was living here: Geoffrey had inherited from either school or home a reluctance to waste money on anything other than the most basic hygiene equipment.

As I sat on the cork-topped stool, draped in one of my biggest and fluffiest American towels – how I scorned the mean-sized and coarse-textured British kind – drying my toes after a long hot shower, I felt an almost physical judder as I looked around, as if a motor had suddenly started up again. I couldn't stand this junk while he was alive. I was damned if I was going to have it when he was dead. He wasn't a saint and I wasn't living in his shrine. It was time for a clearing out. It was a day for action.

I dumped his bits and bobs into the wastebasket, then tied up the plastic liner and put it by the front door to go out to the trash.

I got dressed in old skirt and sweater, then made my plan of campaign. I would go to Limehouse and make an inventory of what was there, deciding what had to be kept and what could be sold. I would also go through whatever personal papers were there to give the lawyer the lowdown on the money side. This weekend I would also sort out his clothes and other belongings which until then I had utterly shrunk from. That had been feeble and pathetic. It was pointless being sentimental about things, particularly mundane, everyday things like shoes or stupid male garments like suits and shirts.

I had slummed about in my misery for quite long enough. I would continue to grieve, but I would not sink under it. Geoffrey was dead. Nothing would change that. I was alive. That was also a fact to be recognized and remembered.

Trembling a little, I slid the Yale key into the lock and pushed open the door. A pile of post behind jammed underneath it and made it stick halfway. I managed to squeeze through the gap into the dark hallway at the foot of the stairs. I groped for the light switch.

I hadn't been here for months. I hadn't had whilst he was alive usually any reason to go there. It was, since our marriage, his workbase, his private place. On the odd occasion, I had gone there to change if we were going to a play at the Barbican or to one of the City functions which Geoffrey attended and which sounded interesting enough to tag along to.

Because of that first time, I had always had a soft spot for the old place. It was so much a part of what I had in spite of myself begun to think of as 'us'. As a result, since his death, I had dreaded having to go there again.

I felt in my purse for my handkerchief, dabbed my eyes and blew my nose. Then I went up the stairs. The sunlight streamed in through the huge window in the living room. Beyond the railing of the balcony I could see the river, running full and strong, its brown swell flecked with flashes of silver and gold. I dumped the armful of mail on a chair and sat down on the sofa. It looked as if he had just stepped out for a minute, down to the Grapes for a lunchtime drink before returning to work on the latest piece for the *Hobbesian* or for the other journals to which he was a regular contributor. Newspapers and magazines were strewn around on the chairs and floor. On the sofa a couple of books lay open spine up. How often had I told him it cracked the binding to do that?

It had always been a bachelor apartment, severely masculine and functional in its decoration and furnishing. I had had no hand in it at all. The walls were white-painted unplastered brick. The floor was uncarpeted, the floorboards sanded and stained dark brown. There were a couple of monochrome wool rugs, a long steel and glass coffee table, its lower shelf loaded with magazines and papers, a couple of Charles Eames chairs, and the long sofa covered in charcoal corduroy. It was uncosy, stripped for action, impersonal. Even the pictures and prints on the walls told you little about the man: some old theatre posters in cheap glass clip-together frames, a few decent drawings he had picked up over the years, nude figures mainly, and an oil portrait of John Maynard Keynes by some hanger-on of the Bloomsbury Group. It was not the room of a man with a highly developed visual sense.

To see what made him tick, you had to turn to the right-hand wall. This was entirely taken up by a huge built-in white-painted bookcase with an extra-wide shelf running the whole length which he used as his desk. Conventional desks he scorned as hopelessly small for the papers he needed to spread around and the piles of cuttings and other paraphernalia with which he liked to surround himself. There was an elaborate high chair of the kind that architects and draughtsmen use, but he often worked standing up at the unit as at a kitchen work surface.

The shelves above groaned with his enormous collection of books on every topic vaguely connected with economic and political theory. Underneath there were box files no doubt stuffed with other papers which he had collected over the years. This stuff might be useful to somebody. Perhaps his old colleges? But then nowadays they tended to look such gift horses in the mouth, unless they were also garlanded with cash in the form of an endowment to pay people to sift through and catalogue it. That was out of the question, given what I had learned about the state of Geoffrey's finances, even supposing they wanted it anyway. He hadn't been famous, really, not even well known, except to a few experts and maybe even these impressive-looking tomes were run of the mill to the savants of the wealth of nations. I hadn't a clue. Despite being married to an economist, I knew no more of the subject than I had beforehand, and that was only enough to enable me to understand the news headlines.

Just looking at the titles made my head reel: General Theories of this and that; Studies of price fluctuations and capital accumulations; a whole shelf of Debt, Deficit and Recession. Not for nothing was it called the 'Dismal Science'.

It still amazed me somewhat that Geoffrey had had the mental application to be familiar with all this, given that he was, apparently, quite incapable of doing the simplest things, such as making toast that wasn't burnt or an egg that wasn't hard boiled, or finding a pair of socks that matched or a clean handkerchief. Like so many intellectual men, his brain seemed set up to handle only the most abstract matters – or that was the impression he had liked to give me. I strongly suspected that he, like most men, when push came to shove, could shift for himself quite well if there wasn't a woman around to clean the house and pick up the laundry. He had managed it for years before I happened along, hadn't he? And even when I was around he had been fairly effective when he wanted to be. Over the purchase of the cottage, for instance. He'd positively discouraged me from getting involved there.

It was a class act, of course, the helpless male, a whizz when it came to dealing with international finance, but hopeless at keeping enough money in his pocket to pay his cab fares. I guess we, I guess I, encouraged this dependency. Women had to be all things: as well as high-powered, high-earning executives, we had to be nurse, lover, cook-housekeeper and accountant. It was a kind of power, having this dependency on one. I suppose I had enjoyed it, to an extent, while it lasted. And in the end it hadn't lasted long enough for me to tire of it, had it, my darling?

I sat for a good while staring at the books in their dark blue and dark grey cloth bindings, like men's business suits, in a way I had never done before. They were an aspect of Geoffrey I had never come to grips with. Now I never would.

As I stared thus at the shelves, I noticed a collection I hadn't registered on my previous visits. Some of the books were old, obviously secondhand. Some, however, mainly paperbacks, although well cracked along the spine seemed fairly new. This wasn't what had caught my eye. It was the subject matter.

They were, as far as I could see, on cosmology, nuclear and astro-physics. I knew even less about these subjects than I did about economics, skipping over the science pages in the newspaper even quicker than I did the business and financial. But I did know about books and some of the titles, particularly the more recently published ones, were familiar. It was my job to know what was selling, so I recognized some of the names of the authors: Capra, Davies, Hawking, Bohm, Ferris. And on racking my brains, such names on the older tomes as Heisenberg, Niels Bohr and Max Born brought memories of the science classes at the College of the Holy Blood, wherein it had been whispered by a too-radical young science teacher, dismissed soon after, that maybe Genesis Chapter One did not have the whole story.

But I had never suspected Geoffrey of an interest in such other-worldliness. As far as I was aware, his scientific knowledge extended only to such earth-bound tools as computers. I had never seen him star gazing, something which even I as the most sceptical of sceptics was guilty of. Speculatively, I ran my finger along the shelf. It came away covered in dust.

Then I noticed some papers poking out of the top of one of the big battered tomes. I'm always endlessly curious about what people stuff absentmindedly into books they have been reading. So what was it? I pulled down the copy of *Quantum Theory and Beyond* and extracted the crumpled sheets of photostat. Judging from the closely printed double columns and the number of mathematical formulae it was from a very learned journal. I flicked through the stiff papers to find the title page. Then I had it.

I stared at it. The author of 'Some numerical features in biology re-examined in the light of new developments in quantum theory' was a Dr Julian Mallen, FRS, Fellow of St Saviour's College, Cambridge, England.

How very strange. I recalled my conversation with Hugh Robinson. He'd said he was a physicist. It had to be the same man. He must have done this article before he'd moved to the States. I wondered if Geoffrey had made the connection. He'd never said anything to indicate he had. It must have been one of those weird coincidences that one sometimes heard about.

Judging from the title and the provenance, Geoffrey must have been quite deeply into the subject. You wouldn't read a thing like that for amusement. Just glancing at it and its pages of algebraic notation made my head spin. I had never heard of this Julian Mallen as a scientist. I was pretty sure he wasn't even halfway famous like the authors of many of the other books, although being an FRS he was presumably quite eminent. What was Geoffrey doing with such obscure lore?

Then I noticed that stapled to the corner of the sheaf of photocopies was a small square of paper which looked as if it had been torn from a scribbling block. It had been folded down over the back of the pages so that I hadn't seen it at first. I turned it back and smoothed it out to read the ballpoint scrawl.

Reynolds. Here's the early thing of mine we discussed. It treats of some quite extraordinary correlations. It could form the basis of Ch. 8. Regarding the draft Ch. 4 you sent, it's clear you've diverged considerably from my actual position, but that in the circumstances is your privilege, I suppose. I've arranged for the rest of the material you wanted to be sent to you. M.

What the hell was this about? M? Presumably Mallen himself as he referred to the article as 'mine'? And Ch. 4 and Ch. 8? Presumably chapters of a book. But what book? Geoffrey had sent a draft chapter. That sounded as if he had written it, particularly as Mallen didn't sound too pleased with it. But that was Geoffrey's 'privilege'. Mallen was sending material, so they must have been collaborating in at least some respects. But what on earth was Geoffrey doing writing a book with a physicist? Particularly an eminent one. He was an economist. It didn't make sense. Moreover, how come he was calling the shots on the writing? And if he were on good enough terms to write books with this man and go on to buy a house from him, why hadn't he ever introduced us or even mentioned any of the business to me?

How many more of these little surprises had Geoffrey got in store for me? My head was buzzing already and I hadn't even begun to do what I had come here for. I stuffed the sheaf of papers into my coat pocket. They would have to wait.

First I had to find the papers I needed for the lawyer.

I had always known that Geoffrey had been fairly poor at personal record keeping. The effort of organizing his professional life seemed to exhaust his powers of administration. Occasionally he would leave bills and other pieces of correspondence lying about in Hampstead. They were invariably printed in red or couched in threatening terms. If I ever mentioned this, however, he would merely growl that it was his business and that he had managed to run these things well enough when I hadn't been around and that he didn't need my help now that I was. He would go on to rationalize his inefficiency by coming up with some theory of the amount he saved by never paying bills until the last possible moment. To me it seemed a waste of time and energy. I tended to pay bills when I got them to get them out of the way. But then I wasn't an economist.

I had, then, no very lively hopes that what I needed would be filed in an orderly way.

I sat on my heels in front of the bottom shelf of the bookcase hopefully and methodically going through the big box files of papers. Bad luck. They contained nothing but professional stuff: cuttings, printouts, extracts from journals and notes of interviews in what seemed a remarkably organized state.

I stood up to massage my aching calves and wandered over to stare out of the window at the river. It didn't help. Ol' man river, he don't know nothin'. I felt the same. Nowhere in any of the stuff I had looked at was there anything which might be regarded as pertinent to Geoffrey's existence as a citizen of the United Kingdom. What had the silly man done with it?

I stared hopefully around the room, then back at the work shelf. There were a couple of big cardboard supermarket cartons tucked almost out of sight by the side of one of the oversized hi-fi speakers near the window. I groaned to myself as I pulled one open. Here it was. The Reynolds archive. What a bloody awful mess!

There were papers and correspondence of every conceivable kind: bank statements, credit card bills, tax assessments, invoices, dry-cleaning and laundry bills, tube tickets, restaurant checks, wine merchants' accounts, bundles of old cheque books bound together with rubber bands. And none of it was in any kind of order or chronology. It was as if he had stirred it around periodically to prevent the mass crystallizing into a spontaneous structure of its own. For God's sake, it would take weeks to delve through this stuff. How could you do this to me?

God, I was so sick of all this. I ran my hands through my hair in frustration. For a few moments I felt like picking up the spilling cartons and throwing them into the Thames. Gradually I calmed down. I would sort out them out, but later. I had to decide about the other contents of the flat.

From my holdall I took out the clipboard I had brought with me, the top sheet of the sheaf of blank paper headed 'Inventory of G's flat'. I wrote on it 'Books, files, etc. To store'. That at least dealt with the matter for the moment.

The other problem confronting me on the desk was the computer. It stared at me with an intimidatingly blank eye. No wonder they call them monitors. I was one of those people whose knowledge of such machines began and ended with HAL in *2001*. They terrified and confused me. I had gradually got used to my basic and idiot–proof word processor, but Geoffrey's state of the art gubbins was, I knew from his futile attempts to explain how it worked, completely beyond me. It was the only time I had ever seen him really angry with me, that afternoon here in the early days of our marriage. 'I don't see how an intelligent woman can be so bloody stupid!' he had raged. 'Darling, you're so beautiful when you're angry,' I had said to him before collapsing in helplessly hysterical laughter. I was a little drunk then, I remembered, but even sober I wasn't going to turn into a queen of the electronic keyboard.

It seemed a waste, though, to consign it to the saleroom where it would realize only a fraction of its cost. I patted its grey top. 'Shall I keep you to play games, as a toy-boy?' I asked it. Was that what they meant by being user-friendly?

It said nothing, but sat there enigmatically, clean and shiny. Suddenly surprised by something about it, I peered closer. It was awfully clean and shiny. In fact it looked almost brand new. I thought back to when I had last seen it. It had been grubby with constant use. I remembered that and remarked on it to Geoffrey. Its keyboard had been quite off-puttingly grimy, smeared with the kind of greasy film that office equipment manages to attract, particularly when handled by a fairly slobby character like Geoffrey. Perhaps he'd cleaned it. Never. I sniffed at it. It had that indefinable taint of newness, of being just out of the box. I'd always been able to detect that on electrical equipment. Perhaps it was some stuff they put in the factory to preserve it in some way. I ran my finger over the casing of the monitor. It came away with a tiny piece of white substance sticking to it. A fragment of the sort of polystyrene packaging material this kind of thing was always packed in. That could mean only one thing. It had only recently been unpacked. It was new.

Why should Geoffrey have gone to the expense of buying a new computer? He'd not long bought the last one, he said. And it was the same make, as far as I remembered from my fraught afternoon trying to learn its intricacies.

As I gazed around, at a loss with this latest piece of puzzlement, something else struck me. There was no sign of any of the disks which he'd used on the thing. There'd been a whole box of them, right there by the machine. They weren't there any more. I distinctly remembered them from my abortive lesson in computer technology.

I sat down on the sofa, totally bemused. What had he been doing? I shrugged my shoulders. How well I had thought I had known this man! That started to make me feel weepy all over again, so to distract myself I picked up the pile of mail I had brought up from the street door and leafed through it.

If I'd been hoping for anything personal, I'd have been disappointed. It was the kind of post you don't have to open: the printed heading on the envelope says everything. Junk mail, free offers, magazine subscription reminders, an electricity bill. I threw it down beside me in irritation and the envelopes flopped one by one to the floor. Out of habit I knelt to pile them up again. As I collected the last one up, a big white packet with details of concerts at the South Bank, I noticed the smudge of dirt on the back. Not just a smudge, though. It was a footprint. A large, male, featureless leather or crepe sole.

It might have been made by a clumsy postman dropping and treading on it before he pushed it into the box. But what if it hadn't? What if it had been made after the mail had come through the door? The only person who could by rights have trodden on it was me. And one of my peculiarities was not size ten feet. That meant someone else had been in. Someone who had carefully removed Geoffrey's computer and replaced it with an identical model to hide the theft. Someone who had removed the box of disks.

I looked back at the shelves. After I had glanced through the box files, I had replaced them. But now there was a gap on the shelf which I would swear hadn't been there before. As if the files had been rearranged to conceal the fact that some had been removed. I got up and looked at the date on the back of the last file. It was over a year ago. The notes for work in progress for the last year or so were missing. There would surely have been such materials: Geoffrey's work patterns showed the steady organization that was missing elsewhere. I could see no reason why Geoffrey would have removed them. The someone who took the computer stuff must have taken those as well.

I imagined him pushing through the front door as I had against the wedging spill of mail. In the dark, he had trodden on it, leaving his mark. Perhaps it had been raining. He had shoved the whole lot back when he left, probably after going through it.

I stopped myself. What on earth was I doing? Was I losing my grip on reality? Geoffrey could have removed the disks himself. He could have replaced the computer – perhaps it had been faulty. As for the missing files, I couldn't be absolutely certain that they had ever existed. How could I then assume that someone other than Geoffrey had removed them?

Perhaps I was going crazy. Why would anyone want to break in, take a computer which they immediately replaced and the worthless paperwork of a dead journalist? It didn't make sense. I could imagine what anyone else would say. A man, that is. How could I explain to your average London plod about a burglary that might not have taken place? I could hear it. 'How long is it you've been a widow, Mrs Reynolds? I expect you've been feeling very, well, stressed.' Oh yes. They were bloody social workers now, weren't they?

Yet again I ran frustrated hands through my hair. I could definitely feel the beginnings of a period pain. Christ, that was what I really needed. Maybe I should retire to bed.

But I had come here to do a job. I had to get on with that. Try to forget for the moment the complications Geoffrey had left behind.

I glanced around the room again, scribbling notes on the pad. I would have the computer taken to Hampstead. I might learn to use it. I didn't want any of the furniture. The pictures I would keep. That was the living room done.

Oh well, I sighed. I couldn't put it off any longer. I took a deep breath and went through the hall to the bedroom door.

I paused there for a moment. This was where it had started. What was that phrase of Yeats's in 'Leda and the Swan'? 'A shudder in the loins engenders . . .' In the poem, it was the Trojan war. What would it be for me? I had still to find out.

It was a small room, with one tiny window which looked over the alleyway at the side of the building. The blind was down and I ran it up to let in some feeble light. The extra-large bed with the bold black and white striped duvet cover almost filled the space. One wall was taken up with a clutch of built-in laminate wardrobes. There was a hanger with one of his dark suits. He kept a change of clothes here, for when he had to stay overnight. A rack of wire clothes baskets contained underwear – the tasteless virulently coloured boxer shorts he favoured – a few pairs of socks, shirts, a sweater. I opened the big plastic shopping holdall I had brought with me, and stuffed the clothing in. The Hampstead branch of Oxfam was going to get lucky.

I grabbed the duvet and started to bundle it up. I would take this with me too. As I did so, I caught my knuckles on the sharp edge of the bedside table, which had been covered by the overhanging quilt. I stanched the blood welling from the wound with a tissue, then went into the bathroom to fix it properly.

I opened the mirror-fronted door of the medicine cabinet on the wall over the basin, hoping to find a Band-aid. I was annoyed to be confronted on the glass shelves by similar rubbish to the stuff I had just thrown out of my apartment: an ancient tube of athlete's foot ointment leaking gunge, a cluster of brown glass pill bottles, aerosols of deodorant and shaving foam, some more horrible flattened toothbrushes. I riffled through it, but there was no sticking plaster.

Then, pushed to the back of the cabinet, I found a small glass phial with a round gold-plated top half-full of clear liquid. With a sick feeling in my stomach I picked it up and turned it round. The label read in small gold lettering, 'Essence of Genuine Norfolk Lavender'. It wasn't mine. I'd always hated the old-fashioned perfume, redolent of linen cupboards. But some women liked it. Some woman had liked it.

A bottle of scent. It's strange how objects insignificant in themselves take on a history from their surroundings.

I sat down heavily on the bathroom stool, holding it in my hand. It could have been here for ages, left behind by some long extinct old flame. But it was the word 'Norfolk' which burned in my mind. That and the image of the woman in blue I had seen with Geoffrey in Breckenham. That exchange seemed to indicate a current relationship. And now I knew that she must have been here. But when?

I didn't dare look at my reflection in the mirror. I plunged my hot face into the cold water, then rubbed it vigorously on a towel. That done I went into the kitchen. There was a jar of instant coffee and some dried milk powder. As I drank the sour-tasting brew, I leaned against the Formica counter, its hard edge a physical equivalent of my need for something to hold on to, something that would stop me drowning in a pool of swirling emotion.

At that moment, I felt doubly bereaved. Not only had I lost the man I had loved, but I seemed to be losing the man I had thought him to be. What did lie underneath the superficial charm? A faithless lover, perhaps. The worst of it was that now my trust was breaking, my suspicions would be aroused and my anxiety would seize on every little detail of our life together to hold it up to the light of criticism.

I threw the cold dregs of the coffee into the sink and rinsed the mug. I wiped my brimming eyes and blew my nose. For the first time, I dared to cast my mind back to the night of the storm, when I had also been consumed with suspicion. Perhaps it had been that as much as anxious love which had forced me to Norfolk? I had been thinking then as well of the woman I had seen at the Golden Lion.

And I knew that unless I discovered the truth of what had happened, of the kind of man I had been married to, then no matter what efforts I made to the contrary such suspicions would recur to torment me over and over again. I should grow obsessed and bitter, my life consumed and condemned to a future of sterile negativity. I had to know. I should find no peace until I did.

How much worse is the betrayed widow than the betrayed wife! For me there was no chance of reconciliation, no comforting explanation, no tearful excuses, no joyous luxury of forgiveness. No prospect, really, of anything other than more pain, more disillusion. But with that knowledge, there would surely come some understanding at least, some recompense for the fierce love that still remained. For if I did not love him, why did I feel so injured by him? Yes, I did love him, whatever he had done, whatever I discovered. I would cling to that. I saw quite clearly then that I had nothing else to cling to.

Even though it had been over two months ago the thought of Limehouse made me shudder. I drank up the last of the whisky from the tumbler. The bottle was empty. I looked at the kitchen clock. Time to go to bed, thank God. Tomorrow, it was back to the company store. What did I get? Another day older and deeper in ... I stood up a little unsteadily, grabbing the side of the refrigerator for support. Thanks ol' pal.

Then the phone rang. I stared at it. Who the hell could it be at this time? Probably an author. One of those bastards. They never knew what time it was, never slept. Always thinking about themselves and their precious bloody books. Probably wanting to know why I hadn't got back to them on their latest masterpiece. They were calling all the time since my mourning period had been deemed expired. They were great at describing other people's feelings, but damned bad at empathizing with them in real life.

It went on ringing. Whoever it was was persistent. Perhaps it was a double-glazing salesman or the Avon lady. Only one way to find out. I picked up the phone and then nearly dropped it again in astonishment.

It was Anna. My so-called friend Anna whom I hadn't seen for months. Anna whom I hadn't expected to hear from ever again.

Anna who should by rights have been lying as low as a spider's ankle. Dear, sweet, infuriating, irresponsible Anna. Shameless, treacherous Anna. Anna Caroline Dalton, only daughter of Sir Richard Dalton Bt, of Woldingham in the county of North Yorkshire. Novelist. Under countless pseudonyms. One of which was Jane Somerset, now aka Jane Fucking-Somerset.

'Anna,' I said. 'Anna!'

'Oh God, Mary, you must hate me. I've really messed things up this time, haven't I? Are you ever going to forgive me? You can't hate me more than I hate me. I'm a rat. No. Worse. Just think of what's worse than a rat. That's me.'

'Don't be silly, Anna. I don't hate you, though I must say I've felt like giving you a bloody good spanking lately. I've had a hard time at the office about you. Where the hell are you? Where have you been since you er . . .?'

'Vamoosed? It's a long story. I've been in France, but now I'm back in London, thank God. I can imagine how bloody it must have been at McAllister's. God, I feel so horribly guilty as well as horribly stupid. You've no idea what's been happening to me.'

'That's certainly true.'

'There. You see you're angry. You do hate me. I knew it was going to be a mistake, mixing up our friendship with dreadful contracts and deadlines and that sort of nonsense. Now that's gone, I've lost everything.'

'Join the club.'

'Oh Mary, darling, what do you mean? Surely that awful boss of yours isn't going to sack you because of me? That would be dreadful.'

'No. It isn't that. Not yet. Much worse.' I heard my voice breaking, and tears pricked my eyes.

'Mary, what's the matter? Do tell me, please.' Her soft warm voice was full of genuine concern.

I had forgotten how the strength of her generous emotions could break through even the tinny confines of a telephone line. Hearing her made me realize why I had been so upset at her disappearance. It wasn't anything to do with Michael and the stupid contract. I had missed having her around. Missed her like hell. I told her the brief facts about Geoffrey.

For a moment there was silence. Then she said, 'My God, Mary. To think I've been going on about me all this time. You poor thing. Do let's get together to have a proper talk. I feel terrible that I've left you to go through this on your own. What about the weekend?'

Of course I was free at the weekend. Then I had an idea. It came to me so suddenly that it might almost have been at the back of my mind waiting for an opportunity to come out. All it had needed was the right person.

'Anna, say immediately if you don't want to, but I would really like to go away for a few days if you would come with me. I want to go back to Forest House. I think I've been wanting to for a while, but I haven't been able to admit it to myself. I don't have the courage to go alone, but there are things I need to do there.'

To my relief, she said without hesitation, 'Of course I'll come with you. When? How do we get there?'

8

I backed the BMW a little nervously out of the lock-up. It was the first time I had driven it or anything else since it had been repaired and brought back by the garage in Queen's Hythe.

As I swivelled my head over my shoulder, I half expected to see Geoffrey framed in the rear window waving his arms in ineffective hand signals and hear his anguished voice beseeching me not to scratch the paintwork, as he always did when he was over the limit and I had to get out of the tight corner he had gotten into when he was sober. Grief has funny ways and even odder times when it sneaks up and hits you over the head. These scenes which irritated the hell out of me at the time now seemed unbearably poignant. I stopped the car on the forecourt and wept briefly into my handkerchief.

I drove to Cricklewood to collect Anna from her old nanny's sister's house where she was, she had told me, camping for a while until she managed to get somewhere more suitable sorted out. I followed Anna's surprisingly cogent directions through a maze of identical streets.

I parked outside 14 Cressida Gardens, squeezing into a space between an old Cortina with no wheels propped up on piles of bricks and the front part of an articulated lorry. One of the neighbours obviously brought his work home. The rusty wrought iron gate which covered the somewhat diminished gap in the rampant golden privet hedge squealed as I forced it open. I made my way gingerly up a concrete front path cracked and upheaved as if the victim of a minor and extremely localized earthquake.

Was this the place? If so, it was a bit of a comedown from the lovely flat she used to have in Hornton Street.

In confirmation, the maroon-painted front door with a leaded light panel apparently made out of winegums opened and Anna appeared in a flowing pink silk dressing gown.

'Mary, darling. You poor, poor thing.'

We hugged warmly, she stooping a little to allow for the difference in height. She swept me into the sitting room. 'Welcome, me lass. Nobbut the front parlour'll do for thee.'

The old nanny's sister was in a home, and the little semi-detached already showed more signs of Anna than her. The drably proper furnishings had been overlaid with the paraphernalia of Anna's eclectic taste. Hardback novels – Anna was one of the few people who bought new books the minute they were published – not to mention slews of shiny paperbacks on her myriad interests: as well as fiction, there were philosophy, cookery, the occult, ecology and poetry. There were *Vogue*, *Vanity Fair* and umpteen more glossy magazines. There were clothes in Anna's preferred rainbow colours scattered over every chair, some still in wrappings of tissue paper or poking out of carrier bags with exclusive names. On a side table was all manner of spirituous liquors. A vast box of chocolates glinted at me richly on the coffee table. The room smelled strongly of coffee, tobacco and expensive perfume.

Anna laughed when she saw me gawping at this magnificence. 'I've been overdosing on shopping since I got back. The most exotic store in my Provençal *bidonville* was the *quincaillerie*. I hadn't bought a book for yonks. Anyway French books look so ugly.'

'I thought you said you were broke.'

'I'm not broke broke. Not broke enough not to have a few goodies to cheer myself up. Just broke enough to have to shack up here instead of the Savoy. Anyway, must get on. I know what a worry wart you are about time. Relax a bit, eh?'

This meant that she was nowhere near ready. In all probability the process of packing had not even begun. I sat drinking a cup of Anna's delicious coffee and reading the newspaper on the sofa next to a very large and somewhat mangy marmalade tom cat, which, Anna said, had wandered in a couple of days before and now seemed very much at home. I didn't mind waiting and I hadn't expected anything else. Ever since I had known her Anna had never disgraced herself by being remotely on time for an appointment. So far, in her professional life as romantic novelist, her eccentricity and unpunctuality were not only forgiven but positively expected. Sooner or later I would have to tell her that things had changed a bit, but that was business and could wait.

Business. I gave a wry smile as I reflected what Michael's reaction would be if he found out I had been having cosy chats with Public Enemy Number One instead of serving her with a writ. I had told him I was taking a long weekend. He had nodded and asked whether he would know the difference. Perhaps he would change his tune if I brought back the straying ewe-lamb. I wasn't counting on that, however.

No, I was beginning not to care two hoots about McAllister's. I was enjoying being in the company of a real friend, someone with whom, no matter what the time gap and the problems, I could relate without pretence or artifice. I was glad she had come back.

I had forgotten how relaxing I found being around her was. For the past months I had been hardly able to sit still. I had not even glanced at anything as mundane as a newspaper and had consciously avoided the TV news programmes. Now suddenly I felt a hunger to know about something other than myself and my own grief and misery. Yes, later I would talk to Anna about Geoffrey and she would listen, but for the present I was content to sit there in the small stuffy room, next to the smelly cat, reading about upheavals in foreign countries which seemed to have blown up to major proportions in the period of time I had been preoccupied with my own emotions.

As I sat there, I could hear Anna upstairs pounding about and muffled exclamations of annoyance from time to time until finally, about an hour after I had arrived, she burst into the room and announced, 'Ready!'

She had on what I assumed was her country gear: chic designer jeans, a purple fisherman's knit sweater and knee-length white patent leather boots. Her long blonde hair was caught up in a white polka dot silk bandanna.

'You look terrific. Just the thing for muckspreading.'

In the hall were piled Anna's things: a bulging zip-up suitcase, a makeup case, a sports holdall and a whole mass of plastic carrier bags. It seemed a lot but then Anna was never one to run the risk of being less than amply provided.

Seeing my amusement, she became more serious. 'You'll be grateful when you get there. I've been up since six putting some food together. And I went shopping. I bet you didn't even think of that. Were we going to live on fish and chips or something?'

I nodded limply. I had had the vague idea that I ought do something about food, but somehow I couldn't get up the energy. I had told myself we could stop and get supplies somewhere on the way. I felt overwhelmingly grateful for Anna's thoughtful practicality. It reminded me that under the zaniness was the respect for basics of a Yorkshire upbringing.

'So Geoffrey had had a heart attack?' Anna's voice was unselfconsciously full of curiosity. For the last hour I had told her the full details of the events leading up to Geoffrey's death. The front passenger seat of the car was pushed back and Anna's long legs rested on the dashboard. In an old, stained ivory holder she smoked one of the extra kingsized cigarettes she currently favoured. Last time it had been cheroots. She was hard to keep up with.

I paused before I answered, looking for the Norwich exit from the Newmarket bypass. I remembered the last time I had driven here in the hired car and shivered. I was a different person then.

'Yes, there was a post-mortem. It was quite clear. The surgeon said that Geoffrey had been what he called "a man of intemperate habits who frequently drank to excess". That was true enough, I suppose. He concluded that he'd had a heart attack whilst driving. After he'd hit the tree, although he wasn't injured, he would have been dazed and confused. He wandered away into the forest and then had another more massive coronary which killed him. QED.

It was so open and shut there was no need for an inquest. Myocardial infarction. Sounds harmless like that, doesn't it? Just another piece of science jargon like titration or oxidation.'

'Do you ever wonder what really happened that night?'

'Of course I wonder. I wonder over and over again. I wonder what might have happened if I'd been there. I wonder what I might have been able to do if I'd gone there that night instead of waiting for the morning. I never stop wondering.' My voice must have sounded strained and fierce because Anna laid her hand lightly on my arm, tensed from my mood and from gripping the big steering wheel.

'I know you do. And there's no point in saying that you've absolutely nothing to reproach yourself about. Death doesn't leave us with tidy emotional edges. There's always unfinished business. I know that. But I meant the question in a much more basic, objective way. Geoffrey could have had the heart attack at any time. But what was the particular reason he had it then?'

'He was exerting himself. He'd hurried out of the house. Bumped the car in the dark. The strain of that was what set it off.'

'But why did he go out into such a night?'

The doubts and questions I had been trying to suppress came surging back. 'I don't know, Anna. I don't know and I wish I did.'

'You said he was in the middle of a meal. Not like Geoffrey, was it, to abandon his dinner − and a decent claret, I shouldn't wonder.'

'Burgundy, actually. I know, I know. But none of it was like him really. Bolting off to the country like that. He said he was working on a project, but there weren't any papers there. Just a few clothes in his grip.'

'So he's only been there a few hours, gets all warm and comfortable, a meal in front of him, and then he dashes out into the night. Was there any sign that anyone else had been there? Anyone who might have gone to see him? Was there any sign of, well, a disturbance?'

'Anna, for God's sake, what can you be talking about? This isn't one of your novels. Who would come calling at that hour in that place? Are you saying he might have been assaulted? By whom? Who would want to do that to Geoffrey? And there was no sign of anything like that. He had a heart attack, that's all.' I rammed my foot down on the gas pedal making the engine roar and the car jerk. Anna's cigarette dropped ash on her jeans and she brushed it crossly away.

'Hey! Mind my bike! I don't know why you're getting annoyed with me. I thought you wanted to talk about it. I'm just saying what occurs to me. I suppose I have a different point of view, that's all. I'm not being deliberately callous.'

'I'm sorry. What you said brought up something I haven't mentioned.' I told her about the woman in Breckenham, and how Geoffrey had lied about her.

'So you think she might have been the caller, if there was one?'

'I don't see how she could have been. Geoffrey would never have tried to get away from her.'

'But he might, then, have been getting away from someone? There could have been another car, couldn't there? There was no one to see or hear anything.'

'Yes, I suppose you're right. Someone could have driven up and away again. It hadn't been raining so there would have been no tracks, and after I'd ripped up and down like a dragster a couple of times, not to mention the police cars and the ambulance, there wouldn't be any way of distinguishing them. But where does that get us? Geoffrey still died of a heart attack – natural causes. The police didn't think anything of it.'

'The police! Come on, it's only on TV that they solve crimes. Mainly it's obvious there's been a crime, so they arrest one of their usual suspects for that kind of thing and beat a confession out of him. Here they must have been glad to write "closed" on the file rather than get involved in something that might turn out to be nothing.'

As I listened to her clipped upper-class voice, the doubts and uncertainties I had shovelled away into the packet labelled 'Things about Geoffrey's death that don't make sense but I want to forget about' came spilling out. 'Please, Anna, you're probably right, but

I have to have time to think it out a bit more. Let's leave it for the moment, shall we? Whatever the reason, it's the sheer fact of his death that's so awful. Getting to the bottom of it doesn't have a high priority when all the time I can see his body lying there at the foot of the tree amongst the pine needles . . .' I could feel the tears start to flow. I took my left hand off the wheel and fumbled in my purse for a hanky.

'God, it must have been ghastly for you. What on earth did you do afterwards?'

'I closed his eyes,' I said. 'It's strange, isn't it? All the times I've read about it or seen it in the movies. I used to think I couldn't do anything like that. Not with a corpse. Then I did it. They were open, staring. I couldn't leave him that way. But, he wasn't a corpse. He was Geoffrey.'

'The Greeks put coins on the eyes, to pay the ferryman.'

'That wouldn't do for Geoffrey. He never paid cash for anything. I hope Charon took American Express. "That'll do nicely,"' I intoned sepulchrally. Then I giggled, something between a giggle and a sob. 'You must think I'm terrible making a joke about it.'

'You have to cope somehow. You have to go on living. But after you found him, how did you get help? Were the neighbours around?'

'No neighbours, not for a couple of miles. I had to drive into Breckenham. I don't know how I made it in one piece. Everything was a blur. I went to the police station. I managed to explain the situation sufficiently calmly, then it was like watching a slow-motion film. There was an elderly police constable at the desk and he seemed to be hardly moving, noting down the details in a log book and only after what seemed like hours arranging on the radio for a patrol and the police doctor to go to the house. He wanted me to stay at the station and drink tea but I had to go back. Then it was all admin. Removing the body. The post-mortem. Where did I want the funeral? Death notices. Letters of condolence. It seemed to go on for weeks.'

'I'm sorry I wasn't there for you, particularly the funeral.'

'You weren't to know. I'm sure there was nothing in *Le Monde*.

143

The funeral helped. A necessary end. I felt there had to be a ceremony of some sort, a point at which I could look back and say, "That's when it was over." It was a cremation. Geoffrey always hated burial grounds, that slow mouldering. He couldn't stand the idea of it. We had to go to some place in North London, miles away. There's a chapel but I didn't have a service. Imagine what he would have said if a priest had been involved! There were a surprising number of people there. From the *Quotidian*, the *Hobbesian*, the bank where he'd worked. We stood there in silence. I didn't want a lot of words. There were a couple of reports – the sort of two–paragraph jobs journalists get in their own papers. Outside, I thanked them for coming. I wish I'd felt like talking to them properly. I got asked to the Flask where they were all going afterwards. Any excuse for a piss-up, as one of them said. But I just got a cab home. Next morning I went back to work.'

We had been quiet for a while. Outside the landscape was darkened under heavy clouds. In the end, as it was so late, we had stayed behind for lunch. We had stopped on the way for tea. Time was irrelevant. All sense of being in a hurry had left me. I felt secure in the womb-like enclosure of the car. I felt I could have driven like this for ever.

Beside me, Anna, smoking yet another cigarette, stared through the side window. I slowed the car for the bend in the road, looking out for the familiar sign, 'Barton St Margaret 3m'.

'Nearly there,' I said.

'Quelle place!' Anna stood by the open car door staring up at the house.

It was back lit by one of those stormy skies which make you feel as if you are on the edge of another world. Above the black fretted line of the pines, in a clear, lemon-yellow lake floated immense islands of dark grey cloud. A breeze moaned gently through the trees, and there was the uneasy clattering of pigeons disturbed by the noise of our arrival. I paused in the front porch, the heavy key in my hand, reluctant now to step into a dimension of the past, a part of my life I had been trying to brick up into oblivion. But memory will not be denied. I turned the key and pushed into the little hallway.

It smelt a bit damp, but in every other way it was as if I was just returning from a trip to Breckenham.

Before I went back to London, I had arranged for Norman Fincham's wife, the lady who did, to clean it up so that when I eventually did come back I wouldn't be faced immediately with the mess of Geoffrey's brief occupation. I couldn't bear to do it myself then. So everything in the kitchen was tidy, the plates, mugs and glasses neatly replaced in the dresser, and the refrigerator switched off, emptied, cleaned and left ajar. On the table was a scrap of paper with a message laboriously inscribed on it:

Dear Mrs Reynolds, I was so sorry to hear that poor Mr
Reynolds had passed away. I hope you find evrything here
as you would want it. Happy to oblige.
   Yours sincerely, E. Fincham (Mrs)
PS. I'm sorry I couldn't get up the paint in the little room. It
had gone all hard.

There was a banging from the hall. Anna staggered through the door, almost hidden by festoons of plastic carrier bags which she plonked down on the table, then flopped into a chair.

I started to laugh, tears in my eyes. I threw the letter over to Anna, who read it and then stared at me in a puzzled fashion. 'I don't see what's funny.' She looked at it again. 'Oh I see. "Evry-thing as you would want it." Hardly, in the circumstances.'

'Good old Mrs F. I know what she means. I must thank her properly.' I stopped laughing and got out a handkerchief to wipe my eyes. 'I'm sorry. I'm a bit hysterical, I think, being here.'

'I'm not surprised,' said Anna lightly, bending down to unpack various goodies from the bags. 'What's that about the paint?'

'I did some painting in the sitting room when I was here before . . . I mean just after we moved in. I suppose there must have been a few splashes on the floor I didn't notice.'

'But she says the little room, not the sitting room.'

I looked at the note again. 'So she does. I hadn't noticed. And I'm supposed to be the sharp-eyed editor. How odd. What is she talking about? Let's go and see.'

The smallest bedroom of the four – the little room – had in daylight a view over the garden and the forest beyond. I hadn't been in it since the day we had moved in. I'd had no reason to: it was empty of furniture and with the same dingy style of decor as the rest of the house.

I pushed open the door. Anna was peering over my shoulder. I could feel her warm breath on my neck.

'My God,' she said. 'You must have hired Jackson Pollock as your decorator.'

No wonder Mrs Fincham had been defeated. The bare wooden floorboards were encrusted with an impasto of dried emulsion paint: whorls, blotches and great serrated-edged splashes of it. The perpetrator of this mess had also surprisingly managed to apply paint to places for which it was intended. It sagged and curtained in thick uneven layers on the walls, running down over the skirting boards in thick veins to end in little dried pools. It dripped from the ceiling where it hung in gelatinous globules like emergent stalactites.

If it were not for the telltale evidence of a paint tray containing a brush and a roller brick-hard with old paint together with a bundle of familiar paint-streaked clothes by the door, I would have imagined that the effect could have been achieved only by a vandal or by standing in the middle of the room and hurling an open paint pot around.

For a moment I was too astonished to say anything. Then leaning weakly against the door jamb I said, 'Geoffrey. He's ruined those trousers. But why?'

'He wanted to surprise you. Poor man. Not a dab hand at DIY, was he? The colour's nice though. Quite a subtle pink. A nice washed-out style to go with this place.'

'I chose that, for God's sake. To go in our bedroom. What on earth did he think he was doing, the chump? Why this room?' I couldn't take any more. I slammed the door and pulled Anna towards the stairs. "Come on. I need a drink.'

I was halfway down, but she hesitated on the top landing, looking back at the closed door. 'It is odd, isn't it? It's almost as if he were trying in his cackhanded way to get it ready for someone.'

Downstairs, I poured out a whisky with a shaking hand and downed it in one. I was trembling uncontrollably, my teeth chattering.

Anna shivered as she helped herself from the same bottle. 'Not very warm, is it? What do we do, rub sticks together?'

'Of c-c-course,' I said.

'Mmm . . .' I stretched out luxuriously on the sofa. In the hearth blazed a huge log fire. The curtains were drawn on the wet and windy evening. I could hear the rattle of the raindrops and the window gently bumping loosely in the frame.

We had had the boeuf Bourguignon from one of Anna's big orange iron pots, and drunk with it the contents of two unlabelled black bottles of red wine which had travelled with her from France. It made Cahors taste like cherryade. On the low table in front of me, within handy reach as I reclined like a Roman, was a cup of coffee and glass of cognac from one of the bottles left here by Geoffrey. For the first time in ages, I felt that life might yet have something to say for it.

Anna, curled up in the big armchair by the fireside, had a similarly contented look, despite the fact that I had been quite shamelessly talking nonstop all through dinner about myself and Geoffrey. She must have known the whole story of our life together as well as I did. It had been so good to indulge what I had been denied so long, to unburden my feelings to someone who would listen and not look impatient or stand in judgement.

We were in a companionable pause. I felt I had for the moment talked myself out. Somewhat guiltily I said, 'Well that's me, for starters anyway. But I haven't let you get a word in about you. I'm absolutely dying to hear. And whatever you say will not be taken down in evidence. I'm not your editor at this moment, I'm a friend. Of course, if you don't want to . . .'

She uncurled her long slim legs, freed from the amazing boots, and stuck them out in front of her, staring fixedly at the slender ankles and narrow bare feet, their toenails splashed with vermilion.

She sighed. 'Well, if you really want to know about me. It's not a pretty story. I'm a mess. That's what I am. I'm a laughing stock. Why? *Cherchez l'homme*, don't you know? I meet this French guy, at a party, a private view at this gallery owned by an old mate. The guy, he's the artist. He's young, but not that young. Keep those eyebrows of yours down and listen! He's gorgeous and I fall head over heels. It's the real thing, a union of minds as well as bodies, though the union of bodies, is, *magnifique* too. Like Cézanne, he says 'e needs ze sunshine. Wizout *le soleil*, 'is art it cannot flourish. So, what do I do? I sell my nice flat in Ken, and run off to France, to Provence with him. I forget everything – writing, my contract with McAllister's, my dear friends, everything. I tell you I was mad, a crazy woman. We – or rather I – buy a wonderful old château with vineyards, lakes, you name it. We spend the first six months in bed fucking each other deliriously, interspersing the fucks with incandescent rows which led to more fucks. It was great. Then I wake one morning to find I've not only been fucked but screwed. The bastard has cleaned out our joint bank accounts and scarpered. I'm left with a crumbling ruin in the middle of nowhere and a few hectares of rotgut-producing vines. It's worth about half what I paid, but no one wants to buy it anyway. In the process of this fiasco, I've spent the money I got for the McAllister's series. As I don't need to remind you, the delivery date for the manuscript is about two months past and I haven't written a word of it and I don't believe I ever will. I'm getting old, my hair's falling out and my tits are shrivelling. I've alienated my friends by my stupidity. I shall end up in a cardboard box at Charing Cross.' She took a hearty swig of brandy. 'And I drink. Look at me. Completely smashed.'

I did look at her. I caught her eye and grinned. 'Well, Anna, if that isn't the most awful load of garbage. To listen to you, you wouldn't think you were one of the most successful popular novelists around. Of course you can still write. Remember when I first met you you were churning out fifty thousand-word weepies for the Women's Afternoon Library in less than three weeks. And I'll bet your recent experience has given you about six new plot lines. You'll do it. I know you will. And what's all this about alienating your friends? I'm not alienated. I've never been more delighted to hear from anyone. I feel more alive now than I've felt for months. You're the Life Force, Anna. Don't you know that?' It might have been the drink but I really felt that. I felt suddenly as if a whole weight of dark emotional stuff was slipping away from me leaving me clean and naked.

I yawned uninhibitedly. The booze, the rich food and the fire were having their effect.

Anna swallowed the remains of her cognac, tipping up the wine glass – Geoffrey scorned the balloon brandy snifter as unutterably naff – so that it covered the tip of her slightly snub nose, her pink tongue emerging like a greedy animal to lap the last drops of the liquor. 'You look like I feel. Just point me at the bedroom.'

'Straight up the stairs. It's the big room at the front. You can't miss it. It's the only one with a bed.' I giggled a little drunkenly.

'What do you mean "the only one with a bed"? Where are you going to sleep?'

I pointed at the sofa. 'Here, I'll be fine.'

'You can't sleep on that dreadful thing. I won't put you out of your own bed. I'll have the sofa.'

'Don't be silly, Anna. You're much too tall. Your legs will stick out the end.' As I said this, I started to laugh. The more I thought of Anna's elegant form uncomfortably couched with her legs dangling over the moth-eaten arms, the more I laughed. I leaned over, weak with mirth. Gradually the fit subsided and I stood up straight to see Anna with her hands on her hips looking at me solicitously.

'I'll bet you haven't laughed like that for ages. It shows things are getting better. Anyway, as you think that my sleeping on this mouldy old item is so ridiculous I'm not going to.' She waved her arm as if it held a magic wand. 'Dada! I pronounce with the wisdom of Solomon. We'll share the bed.'

We staggered upstairs with our cases. I took a deep breath and pushed open the bedroom door. Here if anywhere in the house lay preserved the living essence of my brief time with Geoffrey. But it felt the same as any other room, with only the slight chill of disuse. The bed was stripped bare, as I had left it when I went home the day Geoffrey . . .

'Grab hold of this end.' Anna peremptorily interrupted my reverie by chucking a sheet at me. We spread it on the bed and tucked it in untidily. With a further amount of disproportinate effort we managed to stuff the quilt crookedly inside its cover. We had another tussle with the pillows and finally we both collapsed on top of the puffed-up duvet gasping for breath after these exertions.

I had started feeling distinctly woozy, in a pleasant sort of way. I rolled off the bed and headed for the bathroom where I used the john and brushed my teeth. I stared at my flushed face and tangled hair in the cracked mirror over the basin. I felt slightly ashamed, larking about in our room so soon. What right had I to carry on with life when he was dead? But something old and fierce in me replied: I had every right because I was still alive. Grief has to have troughs as well as peaks. It's as if the mind knows that the highest intensity of loss and longing cannot be indefinitely sustained for it would crack under the strain. We have to build up strength from joy to survive the next bolt of grief which will hurl us back into the pit from which we thought we had emerged. I undid the buttons of my blouse, I splashed cold water over my face and neck and ran a comb through my hair. My eyes looked back at me from the glass, bright with unshed tears.

9

'God, quel dump!' Anna, standing wrapped in a padded burgundy ski jacket and holding her white cashmere hat to her head in the strong and unseasonably cold wind, surveyed the centre of Queen's Hythe. 'I thought this was supposed to be a wonderful medieval town. Hanse merchants and the Baltic trade and what have you.'

'There are some nicer parts,' I said, feeling for old time's sake that I had to defend the place, albeit weakly. 'We used to come here a good deal when we were house-hunting. Geoffrey . . .'

'OK. I know. Let's find Robinson's and get that over. Where did you say it was?'

I tried to remember. 'Geoffrey said it was down by the church.'

'So let's hit the church. This way?'

I nodded, a little uncertainly. She strode off purposefully, her tall slim figure, long legs encased in the white leather boots, looking exotic and even outlandish amongst the pale overweight women and short, furtive-seeming men. I struggled along in her wake, past the seedy cut-rate chain stores that lined the long pedestrianized High Street.

This had been Anna's idea, I reminded myself. I didn't want to spend my day off interrogating Hugh Robinson. But I had to admit there was a kind of inevitability about it, given our conversation the previous day.

We had started off with the kind of leisurely Sunday breakfast that lasts the entire morning. Being Norfolk, there were no croissants, but, thanks to Anna, there was good coarse bread from the Cypriot bakery near the house in Cricklewood, scrambled eggs, French preserves and more of the divine coffee.

We sat at opposite ends of the kitchen table, alternately feasting and talking. The sun streamed through the windows and the range beamed its comforting heat towards us over the russet brick floor. Under Anna's unobtrusive yet incisive prompting, I had told her the whole story of what had happened after the funeral. Now I had done so, I felt strangely cleansed. All the doubts and suspicions were out in the open as if after harvest I had laid the fruits on the sunlight-whitened pine of the tabletop.

Anna nodded sagely. She was wearing a full-length greeny-blue silk robe with a wide belt gathered into a huge bow at her waist. She looked poised and almost Oriental with her oval face and ever so slightly slanting eyes. Like a cat's, her eyes had the power to dilate at will and they did so then, her gaze penetrating and full, the colour of the exotic gown.

'Listening to you, I'm pleased I've never married,' she said. 'To go through what you've gone through, and then to find out that half of what he told you was lies. I think it's amazing you can enjoy anything. You must be made of sterling stuff, Mary Reynolds.'

'That's quite a compliment, coming from you. You're hardly a delicate flower yourself. And anyway, what about Pierre? Didn't you fall for him?'

'It wasn't the same. OK, I didn't imagine that he'd actually swindle me, but deep down I think I knew from the start it would never have lasted. I suppose every time I hope this one will be different, but really the only difference this time was how I was so recklessly stupid in pursuit of it. But you and Geoffrey. It was meant to be for keeps, wasn't it?'

I poured more coffee to get time for the answer. 'As far as I was concerned, yes it was. I thought he felt the same. Until –'

'Until you saw him with the mysterious lady in blue.'

'That was the start, I suppose. But at the time I tried to push it out of the way. I pretended I had imagined it. But since he died it's all come flooding back. And there are the other things I've just told you about.'

'The lies, you mean.'

'Yes, I suppose they were lies. Concealments, deceptions anyway. They're so hurtful. And yet . . .'

'And yet, despite everything, you're still in love with him, aren't you?'

'Of course I am. That's the worst part of it. These questions to ask and no one to ask them of. How can I believe the worst of him now? There's always some explanation, even one that is good enough to want to believe it.'

'Well then, why don't you find it?'

'What do you mean?' I frowned at her, irritated in advance by what I knew she was going to say.

'The explanation, of course. Tease out these anomalies, mysteries, curiosities. Why did he throw in his job? Who was the woman you saw him with? Was she really his mistress? Why did he suddenly get the urge to buy a country cottage? Why should anyone steal his personal papers? Why can't you find the deeds, or any trace of the lawyer who acted for him? As you're here, why not start with that one? That agent fellow: why not go and see him? Find out what he knows. I'll help you. Why don't we go tomorrow, to where is it? Queen's Hythe?'

Anna in this mood was a force of nature. Helplessly I had agreed. Which was why I was panting along, my peasant legs struggling to keep pace with her patrician stride.

We had arrived at the church, a great sprawling barn of a place set in a small market square. I looked around, glad of an opportunity to catch my breath.

'That's it, I think.' I pointed to a narrow cobbled lane branching off the square on its far side. There were pale brick eighteenth-century houses with steps up to raised front doors and handsome carved white doorcases. They bore brass plates by their sides. Solid, respectable plates, worn with repeated polishing. Solicitors, accountants, architects, insurance companies. The houses were succeeded by a small parade of period shopfronts, a couple of building societies, a bank, an antique dealer, a place selling furnishing fabrics. And at last a hanging sign which read 'Estate Agents'.

'Aha!' said Anna as we stood outside.

I shook my head. 'This can't be the place. It doesn't look right.' It was a branch of one of those national chains. From the coloured photographs of their stock in the window, it specialized in cheap modern boxes on housing estates.

'Well, let's ask.' Anna thrust her way in through the plate-glass door. Inside, it was all soft grey carpet and splashy scarlet fittings. Not the sort of thing Hugh Robinson would have been at home with.

A carefully groomed young woman rose from behind her grey laminate-topped desk. 'Good afternoon. I'm Sharon. How may I help you?' I repressed a snort. US business manners had spread to deepest Norfolk.

Anna said, 'We're trying to find an estate agents called Robinson's. They're supposed to have an office round here.'

Sharon smiled vacantly. The company training manual had not provided the answering formula for this sort of enquiry. Finally she said in a less carefully modulated voice, 'I dunno. I haven't ever heard of them.' She turned to a young man in the desk behind who had just put down the phone with a flourish he had obviously been practising. 'Dave, lady here says have we ever heard of Robinson's?'

Dave jumped out of his desk and bounced over to us. His red outdoor face and bulky figure did not go with the dark chalkstripe suit. 'Robinson's? You sure that's the name?'

I decided it was time I took over. 'Yes. The guy I dealt with was called Hugh Robinson.'

'No firm in this town of that name,' Dave said. 'Here you get to know all the other people in the business. No one I know called Hugh Robinson. Must be somewhere else.'

'Of course it's not.' I heard myself beginning to sound irritated, with even a note of hysteria. It seemed to happen often these days. 'I met him. He must be here someplace.'

Dave glanced sharply at Anna, as if to say 'take this loony away'. I held up my hands. 'OK, I'm sorry. I must have got it wrong. Thanks anyway.'

In the street, Anna put her arm round my shoulder. 'This was a bad idea. It's my fault. It must stir up a lot of memories.'

I shrugged angrily out of the hug. 'You don't think that. You think I'm going crazy. You think I invented this guy.'

'Of course I don't, you great silly. You're bound to be affected by what happened. Maybe you don't remember things as well as you think. It takes time to get back to normal.'

'But Geoffrey definitely said it was a place down by the church. Why would he get it wrong?'

She gave me an old-fashioned look.

'OK, so this is another of Geoffrey's inaccuracies. But why on earth would he lie about the estate agent's office?'

She merely shrugged in reply.

We had been walking on as we talked, not noticing that the street was a dead end. The sidewalk stopped abruptly at a set of steel railings. Beyond and below was a newly constructed dual carriageway road which had sliced across the old street, leaving the rest of it truncated on the other side, the flanks of its half-demolished buildings supported by concrete buttresses. There was a raw unfinished feel about the unpainted railings, the ragged broken edge of the sidewalk and the damaged tarmac of the roadway. There was no way but back. We leaned for a moment together against the barrier looking silently at the traffic on the road. There were traffic lights further down to the left and the stream of cars, trucks and buses on our side slowed and then stopped as they changed.

One large boxy vehicle with dark green paintwork towards the front of the queue, in the middle of the stream of traffic, seemed vaguely familiar. I stared at it. It was only fifty yards away. I could see the back of the driver's head and his dark curly hair. It was Hugh Robinson.

My feeling of lassitude and defeatism suddenly fell away at this apparition. I was consumed with the desire to have it out with this fellow. He must know the answers to some of the questions which had been bothering me. He had to be confronted.

The traffic lights showed red and amber and the waiting vehicles revved their engines in typical macho anticipation as if they were on the starting grid of a race. I vaulted over the railings and hit the tarmac on the other side running. The lights changed to green as, panting, I drew level with the Range Rover. There was no mistaking the slightly hawkish profile and the full curling lips.

I dodged through a gap between two vans, grabbed the passenger door handle of Hugh Robinson's car and wrenched it open. 'Hi, Hugh. Surprise, surprise. Can we have a word?'

He looked down at me from the height of the driver's seat. For a brief moment, an expression of alarm crossed his broad face, then it was replaced by one of fury. 'What the devil do you think you're doing?'

The cars in the inside lane to my rear were moving over the junction. Behind the stationary Range Rover I could hear horns honking as the other drivers frustratedly realized that they were losing a few seconds of their valuable time.

I knew that if I could hold him there a minute longer the lights would change again. I put my foot on the doorsill and started to climb aboard. He must have realized the same thing. He shot out his long arm, his big hand bunched into a fist, and thumped me in the solar plexus.

The blow knocked me backwards against the swinging door. It saved me from a somersault. Instead I slid out and down between it and the wheel arch, landing on my hands and knees on the rough road surface. Above me I heard the door slam and the engine roaring. The lights were at amber. I scrambled to my feet to see the Range Rover halfway across the junction. I was vaguely aware of voices shouting and cars hooting. I could feel the sting of pain from the scrapes on my palms and kneecaps. I shuddered with tearful anger. The bastard. He wouldn't get away with this. Unthinking I ran after him over the junction.

The lights on the crossing had just changed to green. I charged across, making a lorry swerve to avoid me, its tyres squealing and its driver hurling abuse. I jinked between the oncoming cars and finally made it to the pavement on the other side. Breathless but exhilarated, I might have been back in New York.

I ran along beside the road, a harsh pain flooding my chest and my legs aching. The traffic, moving only sluggishly, was already slowing for another set of lights. I squinted anxiously for the Range Rover, impatiently shoving the hair out of my eyes.

Then I saw it, again in the middle lane, only ten yards away. I started to wave and yell, 'Hey, you. Stop! Wait for me!' I saw his anxious face, white with tension and anger, turn to meet mine. I stepped off the pavement. The stream of vehicles was still moving but the Range Rover was well back in the queue for the lights. This time he wouldn't get away.

Then a heavy hand grabbed my sleeve and a voice said, 'In a bit of a hurry, aren't we? I should cross at the crossing if I were you, madam.'

I stared at the chubby red face beneath the blue helmet. I could smell the cheap deodorant. 'You don't understand, constable. I have to talk to that man in the Range Rover. Please let me go.' I wriggled, but the young policeman's restraining hand held firmly to my cuff. As I stood there, the traffic began to move more swiftly. Then I saw the Range Rover turn right and disappear round a bend.

'You can't go walking out into the road like that. You'll get yourself killed. Now please calm down, madam. Is everything all right?'

I sighed with frustration. Why was there always a cop around just when you didn't need one? I became aware that I must have looked a bit of a fright. My skirt was muddied at the hem, my tights were ripped and my knees were bleeding. My hair was mussed up. By the usual standards of the Norfolk constabulary, I might be turning into an interesting case.

'I'm sorry, I'm fine. I kind of tripped over back there. There was someone I wanted to talk to in that car, but I guess they didn't —'

'Why, honey, what in tarnation are y'all doing?'

We both turned sharply at this interjection. It was Anna,

slightly out of breath but fetchingly pink-cheeked, radiating sexual glamour like heat from a nuclear reactor and seemingly possessed by the spirit of Scarlett O'Hara.

I was beginning to feel faint again now that the burst of energy was leaking away. Oh God, I had gone and got myself arrested.

'You silly little baggage!' she chided, enfolding me in a hug. 'Have you been a bothering this fine young officer of the law? Officer, I gotta tell you, my friend she ain't feeling herself. Her poor dear husband recently departed this earth, and the poor darling has been just mortified. Don't you trouble no more. I can take care of her. But thank you, you dear man!' She held up her slim hand and I thought for a moment that the mesmerized young fellow was actually going to kiss it.

Instead, relieved to be freed of the burden of one or possibly two well-heeled but raving lunatics, he brushed his helmet in the ghost of a salute. 'If everything's all right then, madam, I'll be on my way.' He looked at me narrowly. 'No more running out in the road, please.' He strode off with a heavy and purposeful tread.

Anna's embrace tightened. She swung me round and practically frogmarched me in the opposite direction. 'You stupid fool! What on earth did you think you were doing?'

'Hey, look. I thought I'd given the cops the slip. No more third degree, please.'

'Well, talk about gratitude! Who got you out of a hole, then? And you're lucky you're still alive. When you jumped over those railings I thought you'd gone completely potty. I was worried, blast you. Next time I won't bother.' She dropped her encircling arm and quickened her pace.

I had to trot to keep up with her. 'Oh come on, Anna. Slow down. I am grateful. And I don't think I'm even partly potty. Let's go and get a drink.' I looked at my watch. 'Well, tea or something.'

She stopped and grinned, shaking her head gently at me. We hugged briefly. 'Where's the best hotel in this burg?' she said.

'So that was Hugh Robinson?' she mumbled, inelegantly, through a mouthful of toasted teacake. 'Really bowls a girl over, doesn't he?'

The lounge of the Royal Baltic Hotel was full of large floral chintz-covered furniture, a goodly proportion of it occupied by the ample bottoms of the Queen's Hythe tea-taking classes, archetypal matrons wearing on top of elaborate perms the kinds of hats in which could be discerned the glint of hat pins.

We had secured a low table by the showy Victorian marble fireplace although it contained nothing more warming than a display of dried flowers. I had bought new tights and sticking plaster on the way there and cleaned myself up in the loo, but heads had still turned at our appearance. From time to time, there was an inquisitive glance in our direction. At this rate, we would be in the local paper.

'That's what's bothering me. I mean, really bothering me. The guy is pretty smooth, has been up to now anyway. Why does he suddenly react like that? I can still feel it where he hit me. I only wanted to talk to him, for God's sake.'

Anna put down the china teacup and shrugged. 'He didn't want to talk to you. Perhaps he thought you'd found dry rot.'

I shook my head. 'No, he seemed too scared for something like that. He behaved instinctively, pushing me out. He really didn't want to talk to me. But whatever could he possibly want to avoid talking to me about so much?'

'It is odd, I have to admit. Whatever else he is, he doesn't seem to be the typical estate agent – or even an estate agent at all. If he is, where's his office?'

'That must be why we met in here that time.' I shuddered at the memory, a sudden vision of Geoffrey's tall figure bearing a tray of drinks,· Geoffrey smiling, the world before him. I got out my handkerchief and blew my nose.

Anna put out her hand. 'I'm sorry. We should have gone somewhere else.'

I put the handkerchief back in my purse. 'No, these things have to be faced. It's not that they're bad memories. It's good to have them. It's good to talk about them. It's just that they are upsetting as well.' I got the handkerchief out again. 'I am a tearful fool today, aren't I?'

'Nonsense. It's good for you. You just said so. I say, I've got an idea. Let's go and call on our Mr Robinson. About time he got pushed around.'

'What do you mean? We don't know where he lives. He might not even be called Robinson,'

Anna waved her arm airily. 'Details. We can find out. Don't you remember I used to write detective stories? Esmeralda Pym Investigates. They were great. Paid the rent, at least.'

'OK, Esmeralda. Go on. Where do we start?'

She drained her cup and replaced it carefully on the saucer. Her eyes narrowed in thought. For a moment or two, as her smile faded in her concentration, she seemed older. Then she said, 'Let's start with what we know. You can't assume anything. It's certainly a waste of time ploughing through the phone book looking for Robinsons. Even if he is called that, it's a terribly common name. If he is scared of something, he would be on his guard when he answers the telephone. And what do we ask? Are you the naughty boy who's been pretending to be an estate agent? Forget that. So what do we actually know about him?'

'Put like that, not very much.'

'Go on. Think.'

'You look as if you've already done that. But I don't know anything about the man, objectively. Only his appearance and manner, and what he told me. If you discount that as being put on or invented, I don't think there was anything I really knew. What does one know about most people, come to that?'

'What indeed?' said Anna drily.

I wasn't in the mood for ironies, particularly ones that were raising issues I didn't want to let myself think about. 'All right, Esmeralda. Tell. What has your sleuth brain come up with?'

'The car, of course.'

'What do you mean, the car? So he had a car. Where does that get us?'

'A long way, maybe. I don't suppose you got the number?'

I shook my head. 'I didn't have my I-Spy book with me. Didn't you? You're supposed to be the detective.'

'No, dammit. I was too busy watching out for you. That would have been a bonus. We may still get there without it.'

'You've lost me, I'm afraid.'

'Don't go away.' She got up and strode off in the direction of the lobby. The behatted ones broke off their chats to follow her with their eyes.

She came back a few moments later with the fat volume of Yellow Pages under her arm. She thumbed through it. 'Here. Range Rover dealers. There's only one in Queen's Hythe. After that the nearest one's in Norwich. They're relatively unusual, expensive cars. That's what gave me the idea. Even if he didn't buy it there, there's a good chance he has it serviced there. Do you fancy a trip to' – she squinted down at the printed advertisement – 'Water Lane?'

There are times when events seem to take on their own momentum. You go with the flow. Since Geoffrey's death these times seemed to be happening more frequently. It felt good to let things happen. Let other people take decisions. I would go along with it. So it was that I found myself standing in a biting easterly wind on the forecourt of Fenland Motors. At the end of the narrow street there was a glimpse of grey river on which the sunlight glinted fitfully. Around us were the warehouses and sheds of the port of Queen's Hythe.

'They're probably closed,' I had said as we sat in the car gazing at the plate-glass windows of the showroom. I actually hoped they would be. Despite my lethargy, I felt some deep-seated reluctance to start on the business of tracking down the man who might or might not be Hugh Robinson. The incident earlier had made me suspect that the stakes had somehow been raised enormously. Otherwise, why had he reacted as he had? At some level I suppose I hoped that whatever Anna had in mind would not work. That we were wasting our time. But in my heart of hearts, I feared the consequences of what we seemed blithely to be embarking upon. As if we would be stirring the mud at the bottom of what until now seemed a crystalline pool. Who knew what might be lurking at the bottom? And who knew how deep it might be?

'Nonsense. There are lights on.' Anna had pulled down the sun visor and was reapplying her bright scarlet lipstick. Wrinkling her mouth, she studied the effect, then ran a comb through her hair, making it wilder. She rummaged in her bag again and found a scent atomizer. She puffed a little of the heady stuff around her neck and ears. Then she unzipped the ski jacket and undid another button of the lemony blouse she was wearing under the orange V-neck sweater.

'What on earth are you doing?'

She turned and flashed me a smile. 'Preparing to treat with the enemy. You stay in the car. With that expression, you'll spoil the effect. If I'm not out in five minutes, you'll know I'm having a good time.'

She climbed out and sauntered across the tarmac to the double entrance doors. Was there a hint of a wiggle in her hips? For God's sake, what did she think she was up to?

I looked at my watch. She had been gone half an hour. I started pacing up and down impatiently. Perhaps she would see me and hurry up. I thought of Geoffrey. 'What do you women bloody well do in there?' was one of his catchphrases.

I had just decided to go in and drag her out when she reappeared at the door attended by a young man in a shiny blue suit. They shook hands and Anna actually patted him on the cheek. I heard her say, '*Au revoir*, Charley dear – and thanks.'

She trotted up, a broad grin on her face. I saw that in her hand she held a sheaf of glossy sales literature.

'OK, baby, let's go,' she said climbing into the car. I followed wonderingly.

'Where?'

'Drive back into town. We need the Norwich road. Follow the signs. No questions till you've found it.' She threw the brochures into the back without a glance.

For the next few minutes I did as I was told, concentrating my attention on following the complexities of the Queen's Hythe ring road. Once I had found the right direction and was heading out of town, I was free to ask the question I had been bursting with:

'Will you please tell me what's going on?'

She giggled. 'I might, if you're nice to me. Stop looking so gloomy. I've found the fox. We're on his trail. His name's Henry Massingham, by the way. He isn't an estate agent, he's a doctor and he lives in a place called South Benham. Not to be confused with North Benham.'

'What? Are you sure? How did you get all that?'

'Esmeralda Pym is never wrong. It was dead easy really. Men are so gullible, aren't they? They'll fall for any feeble yarn if it comes from a bit of skirt. Like randy little dogs, a whiff of sex and they're anybody's. Particularly when they're also a young car salesman anxious to pull off a deal.'

'A deal?'

'Yes. I told him I wanted to buy one of those thingummies. Range Rovers. I sat in one and twiddled the knobs. Very comfy. Better than this old thing. Of course I had to avoid the test drive. As I can't, you know. I said I'd come back tomorrow.'

'Anna, you're infuriating. How did you find out about this man? Please stop tantalizing me.'

'Oh, all right. After a bit, Charley and I got pally. I must say he was getting quite interested, despite the fact that I'm old enough to be his, well, elder sister. I said to him I'd got the idea of getting one of these things from his firm because of the very high recommendation I'd got from a man I'd met at a friend's party who'd showed me his. A lovely green one. Car, that is. Quite new. He was such a nice chap. Perhaps it'd be nice if they mentioned their grateful thanks to him next time he came in? Of course, silly me, I couldn't remember his name, but he was tall and dark etc. Well, he was a good salesman because he remembered his customers. "That must be Dr Massingham," he said straight away. He even told me his address, so I could look him up when I'd "got my new motor".'

I shook my head. 'Anna, you've got the most amazing nerve.'

She tugged my sleeve, 'See that sign? South Benham, a mile and a half. You can show some nerve yourself in a minute.'

I turned off the main street and parked at the side of the small village green. There was, as is common in Norfolk, a carved and painted wooden sign on a post. Below the representation of a round grey tower and a gaudily coloured tree in full leaf, gilded letters confirmed, if I had been in any doubt, that we were in South Benham. In front could be seen the originals: a flint and brick church and a huge copper beech.

'That must be the house,' said Anna, pointing to the Queen Anne brick building which adjoined the churchyard on the far side. 'The Old Rectory. I'll bet the new rector lives in a modern box on an estate, probably the one we passed just now. The church flogged its nice old houses to nouveaux riches, like your friend Massingham.'

I wasn't in the mood for a lecture on sociology. I felt nervous and slightly sick. 'He's not my friend, as you well know, Anna. I'm not sure we should take this any further. I've nothing to go on really.'

'According to what you told me last night, there's plenty to go on. He pretended to be an estate agent called Hugh Robinson. He sold Geoffrey a house. You can't find any evidence of the transaction or the title deeds in Geoffrey's papers. He snoops around telling you some story about a dog. When you see him today, he behaves as if you were infected with the plague. What more do you want? As Geoffrey's not around to do it, you're perfectly entitled to ask for an explanation.'

'That's just it. It's no one's story but mine. He could simply deny it. I don't think I could stand that. I already feel a bit crazy.'

She took my arm. 'Listen to me! Don't be stupid! Of course it's your story. It did actually happen. Hold on to that. If he denies it, then that's more evidence there is something to find out.'

Her grip on my arm was painful. 'Stop shaking me like that, Anna. You look so goddamn fierce. Evidence of what, though, for God's sake? OK, OK, you're right. I started it today and I have to finish it. I'm going, I'm going.'

I got out. Anna put her feet up on the dash and started to read a paperback she'd fished out of her bag. She looked up briefly and grinned, giving me a thumbs-up sign.

I rang the brass door bell, hastily patting some wayward hair back into place and straightening my jacket. From inside, there was a sound of footsteps.

The white-painted panelled door opened. A woman stood there. I stared at her. She was tall, slender, her dark hair cut short and layered close to her head, forming scarcely a frame to the pale oval of her face. She had high cheekbones and huge dark eyes fringed with heavy black lashes. Her mouth with its pastel lipstick was pursed in enquiry, her plucked and pencilled eyebrows delicately raised.

I felt suddenly as if the old worn paving slab beneath my feet had leapt under the force of some subterranean explosion, so quickly did my knees buckle beneath me. I reached out to grab the side of the doorcase to steady myself, my head swimming.

She had started backwards in surprise, then a more generous instinct prevailed as she reached out a steadying arm.

'Are you all right?'

'Yes. I'm sorry. I don't know what came over me.' I stood upright, my heart pounding.

'What can I do for you?' Her voice had relapsed into cold enquiry.

'I'd like to speak with Dr Massingham, if he's at home.'

'My husband's not here. Are you a patient?'

'No. It's a personal matter. May I come in for a moment? I have something to ask you.'

She stared at me, hard, perhaps weighing up whether I was likely either to pass out or try to strangle her. Then she stood aside to usher me inside.

I sat on the edge of the offered armchair in the sitting room. It was a beautiful room, full of the understated and slightly shabby elegance that spoke of long-accustomed wealth. If these people were nouveau as Anna had cattily suggested, then they had done their homework.

She sat opposite, lounging back, relaxed, but observing me closely through eyes that were now slightly narrowed. She waited for me to speak.

'My name is Mary Reynolds,' I said. There was no reaction. The smooth face remained impassive.

She leaned over to take a long filter cigarette from the battered silver box on the coffee table. Putting it to her full lips, she lit it from a small gold lighter. She inhaled deeply like a man, gulping down the smoke and blowing from her nostrils.

I breathed in deeply myself. 'I believe you knew my husband.'

There was a pause. Then she gave a minimal shake of the head. 'I'm sorry, I don't believe I do. I'm afraid you're mistaken.'

'Geoffrey Reynolds,' I persisted. 'He was a financial journalist.'

'No, I don't know anyone of that name. Why exactly have you come here? You said you wanted to talk to my husband. Now you say I know your husband.'

'Not know, knew. He's dead. He died three months ago. Not so far from here.' I ploughed on wildly, even though I could see the mounting alarm in her face as well, perhaps, as something else. 'Your husband showed us the house. He said he was an estate agent. I saw him today and he refused to talk to me. He pushed me out of his car. I want to know why. I must talk to him . . .'

She was on her feet now, clearly agitated. 'I don't know what you're talking about, Mrs Reynolds. Everything you've said is utterly preposterous. Please leave immediately or I shall call the police. If this is some way of gaining access to my husband's services, then it's a very poor one.'

She held open the door into the hallway. I could see black and white checkerboard tiles and a mahogany coat stand.

It was my turn to be bewildered. 'Services, what do you mean? I don't need a doctor.'

She wrenched open the front door and pushed me through it. 'You may not need a doctor, Mrs Reynolds, but I think you definitely are in urgent need of a psychiatrist.'

The door slammed behind me.

I walked slowly down the path. In the distance I could hear the voices of children at play. I had dried my tears by the time I got to the car.

Anna was still reading. I opened the door and slumped into the driver's seat.

'Well?'

'I blew it. You should have been there. I raved on like a loony. The woman said I was nuts and threw me out. I was great.' I started crying again.

She put her arm round my shoulder. 'What woman?'

I stopped blubbing and blew my nose. 'Massingham's wife, mistress, whatever. But I'm right. She did know Geoffrey. By God she knew him. She may be fantastic at concealing it, but I know. I'm not crazy but I wish I knew what the hell was going on.'

Anna was shaking me again. 'Oh, you are irritating. I'm dying to know what happened and all I get is riddles! Explain, for goodness' sake!'

'She was the woman I saw with Geoffrey at the Golden Lion in Breckenham that first weekend. The one he denied being with. I knew it as soon as she opened the door. I nearly flaked out when I saw her.'

'Are you sure? Really sure?'

'Of course I'm sure. I'd know that face and figure anywhere. She's amazing, like a model. And I saw the coat. The blue coat she was wearing that day. It was hanging on the hall stand. Oh, it was her all right.'

I looked up to see Anna staring at me. 'And I know she was the woman he had in Limehouse. I smelt her perfume. Lavender. Underneath, she must be an old-fashioned girl.'

IO

Waiting on the doormat when I returned to London had been a letter from Peter Goodman, confirming in careful lawyerese that I had agreed to obtain all the necessary documentation relating to the deceased's financial affairs. I was then to contact him with further instructions, if I wished, regarding the determination of the solvency or otherwise of the estate. That was his careful way of justifying his doing nothing.

I wrote him a brief acknowledgement, saying I was making progress. I was, in a way. I had done what I could with Geoffrey's affairs. I had given notice on Limehouse and paid the arrears of rent. A letter from the landlord expressed sorrow at the death of so long-standing a tenant; in fact the old bastard would be delighted as he had been trying to put the rent up to a modern level for years. I had had the flat emptied and the contents, as I had determined, variously sent to auction, put into store or delivered to Hampstead, where several cardboard boxes, including one containing the dreaded computer, were dumped in the spare bedroom. Seeing them there was yet another concrete reminder of how my life had changed.

The documents from Limehouse occupied a couple of those boxes. I gritted my teeth one evening and trawled through them.

My first impression at the apartment – that Geoffrey had never thrown anything away, but dumped it in the boxes – was depressingly correct. It was, therefore, even more puzzling that there was nothing in either of them about Forest House.

It was as if his dealings with it had vanished, as if they had never been. Where were the letters from the solicitor, where for good-ness' sake were the deeds? And what about the mysterious Henry Massingham, in his role as estate agent to the gentry? And where did Mallen fit in? I could only suppose he must have gone off to the States, leaving his chum Massingham to sell the house to Geoffrey. Even if it had been one of those cosy deals men got up to amongst themselves, surely Geoffrey would have had the sense to get something on paper. He wasn't a fool, after all. Or was he?

The whole business seemed set to drive me mad. I couldn't cope with it, so I shut the boxes up again and closed the door on them.

There were other things, however, I was relieved to find out, that I could really get to grips with once more. I threw myself back into my work. I read typescripts and wrote long letters of detailed criticism to authors. I lunched. I browsed around book-shops. I went to launch parties. I attended meetings. Yes, I said to myself. I am now back in the swing of the arduous life of the modern publishing executive.

My only regret at this time was that Anna, bored with Crickle-wood, had yet again gone off, this time to see her family in Yorkshire, or rather, in her words, 'to sponge off the aged Ps'. I was irritated by this. Anna was behaving more like a perpetual adolescent than a middle-aged woman. But then – I could talk. I was myself as lonely and as peevish about her absence as any adolescent. I hadn't been able to raise with her the matter of the book. All I got whenever I looked as if I were within a mile of the subject was, 'Please, please, don't mention that now. I'm going to see Vanessa very soon. Promise.'

Michael had meanwhile been ominously silent on the subject. It wouldn't last. Already addicted readers were asking bookshops about the publication date of *This Spider Love*. We were going to look very silly when it didn't appear. I knew the day of reckoning for Anna was fast approaching. What I hadn't in my new-found appetite for my job appreciated was that that day had actually arrived for me.

It came on Monday morning a fortnight after I had returned from Norfolk. I had sensed something was up the moment I had got into the office. My in-tray wasn't as full as it had been. When I looked more closely, I found that several things which had been in there – submissions from agents for new projects which I was thinking over – had been removed. I asked Melanie my secretary for an explanation.

She put down my cup of coffee with a shaking hand. 'David told me. I mean, I heard him say he was going to through it at the weekend. You know he quite often comes in then. I don't know why . . . I mean he didn't say and I didn't feel I could –'

I waved a hand, indicating nonchalance I didn't feel. 'OK, OK. Ask him to pop in when he's free, would you?' I felt like throwing the coffee over her. Thanks for the loyalty, Melanie.

David Henderson was my number two, a bright spark fairly fresh out of Oxford, who had worked in the mail room in the vacations and who had then seemed to me too intelligent to let go into advertising or the city. Since then he had developed so fast it was unnerving. He had already a level of self-confidence that I had long ago given up even aspiring to. He could tap effortlessly into that modern culture which wove together semiotics, deconstructionism, electronics, videos, music, drugs and fashion and which to me, brought up believing T.S. Eliot was a modern poet, seemed impossibly remote and savage, like the South Sea islands to Captain Cook. He came up with an endless stream of ideas, some good, some appalling, all fluently presented and flawed only by his apparent inability to tell the difference. He was able to dismiss the significance of the last thousand years of European culture as a result of being largely ignorant of it. Not surprisingly, he got on well with Michael. He made me feel like Frankenstein.

He stuck his head round the door. 'Wanted me?'

I laid down my pen and ostentatiously shuffled the pages of the typescript on my desk before replying. It was a trick I had learned from Max Vincent. 'Look as if whatever you're doing is more important than them, baby. Make 'em wait.'

It might have worked if you were Max: his aura of power to subordinates was such that they would have been terrified if he'd dealt with them with his pants down on the john. It didn't work for me. In the interval, David had slid into the chair opposite, grabbed another pile of typescript from the desk and started flipping through it, apparently engrossed.

'Yes,' I said.

He looked up. 'Right. I thought you would. It's about the stuff I pinched out of your tray. Orders from on high, you know. Michael told me to do a dawn raid – a Sunday one, anyway. See what you were hanging on to. His words, not mine.'

'Did he have any particular reason to want to do that?'

He shrugged. 'You know Michael. I'd rather you asked him.'

'I intend to. He's in a meeting at present. I thought I should grill you first.' Some hope. David looked as ungrilled as anybody could be.

'If you must.'

'What did Michael say?'

'I'm not sure I should tell you that.'

'That sort of remark makes me even more determined you should. Come on, David. There's no bloody Official Secrets Act here. What did he say?'

'It was only because I didn't want to upset you. He asked me whether I thought the running of the department had got even worse lately.'

'And?'

'I had to say that I thought you weren't quite as on top of things as you used to be before . . . er . . .'

'Before Geoffrey died. You can use plain English, you know.'

'Right. I actually thought it was a bastard of a question for a colleague. A sort of when did you stop beating your wife question. But you know what he's like. I had to answer it. Mind you, I did also say that you had seemed a lot better in the last few days.'

'Thanks. That's typical of Michael. Move in when you're weakest. You're lucky, David. You get the poisoned chalice next. The heir apparently.' Looking at his slim figure in the loose trousers and T-shirt, his fashionable short haircut, his air of insouciant confidence made me feel like the Fighting Téméraire on the way to be scrapped.

171

'Hang on, now, Mary. I think you're jumping to conclusions. Everybody knows things will get better. This is a bad patch for you. He wouldn't fire you. You're too valuable.'

I shook my head. 'No, I know Michael. He's sharpening the axe even as we speak.'

He didn't get the chance to reply. The internal phone buzzed. It was Michael's secretary. He was free now and he wanted to see me.

I smiled wryly at David. 'So long, partner. I'm heading for the I'm not OK Corral.'

I was right, of course.

I was in the low chair again. It didn't take long. Editorial was being restructured to reflect the growth of the list. The editorial department was being split into non-fiction and fiction. David Henderson would be asked to take the fiction. In the meantime, Michael said, he would take over the non-fiction. In the circumstances there wasn't any longer a place for an editorial director of my seniority. A package of compensation had been prepared which I would find generous. If I dissented I should deal with the company's lawyers, not him.

'In case you should be inclined to complain to what you think is higher authority about the philosophy behind this, don't waste your time. I've faxed the details to Max and he approves entirely. And by the way, your external phone has been cut off. If you do want to sob on the great man's shoulder, then it will have to be at your own expense.'

Rook to King four. Checkmate. I stood up to go. 'Is that all?'

'My dear Mary, you've no idea how it upsets me to do this. It's a tribute to your hard work that the restructuring is necessary. We'll make that clear in the press announcement,'

'That makes me feel a whole lot better.'

'I think in the circumstances you might want to leave quite soon, don't you? Before lunch, perhaps?'

'Try and stop me,' I said.

It took me only half an hour or so to sling the personal bits and pieces I had in the office into a couple of cardboard cartons and have them left at reception. In need of fresh air, I walked in the bright sunshine to Russell Square, where I tried to eat a sandwich and ended up feeding most of it to the pigeons.

Then I went back for the last time to the McAllister's building, picked up my stuff and took a cab back to Hampstead.

Over the next few days I called the Cricklewood number several times, without success. Then finally, after a week, she called me.

'Hello, Anna. How was Yorkshire?'

'Stormy. I had rows with my father about my money, and with my mother about my morals. Apart from that it was great. What about you?'

'Nothing much. Oh yes, I got fired last week.'

'You're joking.'

'Not this time. *Finita la commedia*. No husband and now no job.'

'How bloody. But you're so good. Michael's stupid. He's bound to change his mind.'

'Well, I shan't. I've got decent compensation which will last a while. I'm sure I can get another job.'

'Jobs, ugh. I had a job once. I wouldn't get one again. Who'd employ a washed-up ageing romantic novelist with a block?'

'Anna, you're not washed up. You have to be positive about getting down to work again.' But I could tell she wasn't listening.

'Listen. I've had some good news about the château. I had a letter today from my *agence immobilière* – sounds like something to do with constipation, doesn't it? – down there. He begs to report that someone has been stupid enough to make me a halfway decent offer. I shall accept. It means that I can get back some of the cash I've squandered.'

'But that's marvellous. Doesn't it make you feel better?'

'If it happens. It means I have to go to France to sort it out. In fact, I'm booked on a flight to Montpellier the day after tomorrow. You're not doing anything else. You could come too.' She said this lightly, but I could hear she was really anxious that I should.

I hesitated. It sounded nice. Then I said, 'I'm sorry, Anna. I

173

can't. I've got my own real estate problem. I have to go down to Norfolk to sort out the cottage. I've decided I have to sell. I can't afford to belong to the second-home set, not in my reduced circumstances. I have to tidy it up for sale – I can't reckon on finding two more people as blind to its faults as Geoffrey and I were. And most important, I have to find out what on earth Geoffrey did with the deeds. I can't actually put it on the market without tracking them down. I've been through the papers he left in his apartment. They're not there. I suppose I'll have to screw up the courage to have another go at the mysterious Dr Massingham. I'm convinced he knows the answer.'

I heard her sigh of disappointment. 'I see. Well, you can't really leave such a whopping big loose end can you? You know, I've been thinking about our friend Massingham. There's something doesn't add up.'

'You can say that again. I'm beginning to think Geoffrey may have been swindled.'

'Really? I hadn't thought of it that way. Let me think it through again and I'll write to you. Sometimes these things come out better on paper.'

'Anna, you're maddening in this sort of mood. I suppose it'll be Esmeralda Pym who takes the pen.'

She laughed, and said in the tone of her cockney landlady heroine, 'Right you are, dearie!'

I decided to leave for Norfolk the next day. There was nothing to keep me in London.

It took me only an hour or so to pack a bag that evening. I would go to bed early and leave first thing in the morning. I was just collecting together a few personal things from my desk which I didn't like to leave in the flat whilst I was away for more than a day or so: my passport, my building society pass book, some photographs of my parents, the few letters Geoffrey had written me, when I came across a brown official-looking envelope I had until then completely forgotten about. It was another of the might-have-beens.

Our long projected trip to Central Asia. He had wanted to travel the Golden Road to Samarkand, but had never got round to doing anything about it. It was I who had suggested it as a kind of delayed honeymoon. We had never had the time for a proper one after we were married – apart from a couple of days in Paris, where I had inevitably ended up doing the rounds of the French publishers and he had had an interview with the Minister of Finance.

As usual the organization of the trip had fallen on me, including the obtaining of the necessary visas. I remembered at the time that Geoffrey had, in typical journalist fashion, handed over his completed form at the last minute together with supporting documents. I hadn't bothered to look at them. Then we had had to call the trip off. Michael had changed his mind and refused to let me have the necessary three weeks off at the time we wanted – a typical piece of ungenerous cavilling on his part. So I had cancelled the application for the visa and asked the Russian Embassy to return the papers. I had put the whole lot in the desk on the offchance that we might be able to go on another occasion.

I tipped out its contents on to the desk. A sheaf of official forms in triplicate printed in English and Russian on that cheap paper rough with woodpulp which they use there for everything from Tolstoy to loo rolls. A letter from an MP – left-wing Labour – confirming that Mr Reynolds was known to the writer and was eminently respectable. And Geoffrey's worn blue passport.

I picked it up gently, feeling somehow close to him, as if his essence had in some way penetrated the thick leatherette-covered cardboard. The photograph within I had never properly looked at before but, given the limitations of the coin-in-the slot booth in which it had been taken, it was not a bad likeness of the man I had loved. The thick, dark blond untidy hair flopping over the broad brow. The clear blue eyes, free of bags and shadows, the unlined slightly chubby face and the full lips curved as ever in a smile. The straight nose which started off aquiline but gave out in a snub, and which imparted that indefinable look of mischief: Just William grown up.

The pages were crowded with the stamps and visas of a busy travelling life. Geoffrey loved travel, the buzzing activity of airports, the smell of kerosene, the ever-present sense of danger cunningly concealed by the aping of military precision – the smart uniforms and the clipped accents. How sad he would have been to know that the trip to Portugal would be his last.

As I mused thus, I had another of those dizzying disorienting thoughts that came so frequently when I thought of him. If the passport had been here in the desk, what had he travelled on to Portugal? He would hardly have removed it from the envelope and then replaced it.

No. The answer had to be that he had never gone to Portugal that time. It was another entry for the file labelled 'Lies Geoffrey told me'. He had been somewhere else, clearly. With someone else. Perhaps that explained the scent bottle in the Limehouse flat. How dumb I had been! I had trusted him, and he had abused that trust. How little I seemed to know him. I stared at the small photograph, tears in my eyes. What a fool I had been.

I threw the passport back on to the desk and gathered up the papers. As I did so, I saw that there was another item I had overlooked folded into the application forms.

I took the yellowing piece of paper from the envelope and spread it out. The red printed form gave off the slightly musty smell common to all old papers which are left undisturbed for long periods. It was Geoffrey's birth certificate. In the old-fashioned copperplate handwriting of the registration clerk – I could almost hear the squeak of the steel nib – were the brief details of the emergence into the world of Geoffrey Alan Reynolds. Alan! He had certainly kept that quiet.

The other details were news to me. They didn't at all suggest the kind of background that Geoffrey had hinted at. But then that wasn't, given my recent experience, very surprising. I sat back in the chair, dabbing at my eyes with a handkerchief.

I looked again at the slightly crooked block printing of the registration district. I had never known he came from there.

I dug out my road atlas. It was a longish detour, but that didn't matter. It wasn't the Golden Road to Samarkand, but it would do for starters.

I rechecked the address I had written down. Fifty-four Telford Street. This was definitely the place. I walked back down the street. The small, low, terraced houses were of smoke-blackened brick, bay-windowed with vestigial front gardens hedged with dark privet or laurel, looking as stiff and unyielding as if made of painted cast iron.

There was no mistake. The last house in the street was 42. Where 54 and its adjacent properties should have been was part of the car park surrounding a supermarket.

I had left early, full of anticipation that the nagging anxieties would at last be stilled by real information. Anything would be better than the gaping hole that seemed to have opened up in my relationship with Geoffrey. The more I found out that set what I thought I had known slipping and sliding as if on the surface of an ice-covered pond, the more I was convinced that I had to go back to the beginning. To the part of his life before the lies and the duplicity started. Then and only then would I find out who was the Geoffrey Reynolds I had been married to. The child is father to the man. That's what I would find out.

I made good time. It was only just after eleven a.m. when I left the approach motorway to the city. A sign, nearly obliterated by road dirt, read 'Welcome to Coventry'. I stopped at a newsagent's on the arterial road to ask the way.

I had never been to the city and had never expected to. I inspected my slim file labelled 'Things I know about Coventry'. George Eliot had lived here, hadn't she? The Midlands she had chronicled were, it appeared as I stared through the windshield, long buried beneath the housing estates and factories. I had a vague picture of a cathedral ravaged by wartime bombing, a replacement that was considered avant garde when it had been put up in the wave of confident rebuilding – misplaced as it turned out – that had swept the country in the fifties and early sixties. I knew also that it had been the heartland of the British motor industry in the days when there had been one. It seemed odd that Geoffrey had originated here. He was a man without corners, effortless and smooth, owing nothing, apparently, to the hard world of metal bashing and foundries.

I saw that my ignorance of who he was and where he came from might not be accidental. He had deliberately shared nothing of his childhood, as if he had wanted to pretend it never existed. He had shown me no photographs of mother or father. Until he mentioned the aunt who had left him the money which he had used to buy the cottage, he had seemed a man without forebears, as if he had sprung, like Athena, fully formed from Cambridge. Cambridge had been the first fixed clear point in his life, that was evident. Everything before was missing.

As I stood at a loss looking over to the store, with its damp-stained, graffiti-covered concrete walls, a bunker stranded in the urban no man's land of the parking lot, its plate-glass windows garishly obscured by dayglo orange and green stickers advertising the latest bargains, the wind rustling the discarded cartons and wrapping papers in the gutter, I was sick with disappointment. The more so because I saw how my hope had been built on such romantic, unreasonable foundations.

Had I expected to find the Reynolds family home intact, with elderly father and mother weeping when I told them the news of the loss of their son? At some level I had hoped for some such reunion, some sharing, some unloading of the grief I felt. And, as well, some completion of the intolerable blanks. Had I hoped for a cosy sitting room, a display cabinet full of mementoes of their lost son, cups he had won, and photographs? Did I imagine that my loss could find an equivalent in an estranged family, that in some way I could complete not only my grieving but restore to them the son that had left, in death if not in life? How bitterly I then reproached myself with my negligence. How could I have shared the most intimate moments with this man and yet at some level left him a stranger? Had there been no openings when the right questions could have been asked? I had told him everything there was to know about me. That had perhaps been the trouble. I had been more intent on talking than listening. Now the talking had ceased, but I still needed the answers.

I looked back to Number 42. Whilst I had been standing there lost in these reflections, an elderly woman had appeared at the front door fumbling in a vast black handbag, presumably for keys, at her feet a plastic carrier bag of groceries. A measure of hope revived. It would be feeble to go without asking.

I stood by the rotting wooden gate. The small stocky figure in a brown coat was still rummaging in the bag and grumbling to herself.

'Excuse me, please,' I called out softly.

Despite my best endeavours, I startled her. She dropped the bag, and its meagre contents spilled on to the shiny tiled surface of the front path.

She turned to face me angrily. 'What are you doing, young woman? Sneaking up behind a person like that? Made me jump. Look at my bits, all over the shop.'

I opened the gate. 'I'm awfully sorry. Let me help you.' I squatted down and quickly gathered up a shabby purse, a comb and a bunch of keys. She opened the bag and I dropped them in, except the keys which I handed to her. She was suspicious, staring at me with unclouded blue eyes.

'Can I have a word with you, please? Mrs . . . er . . .?' I asked.

The stare hardened. 'Mrs Beecroft, since you're asking. Are you the social?'

'No. My name is Mary Reynolds. I'm looking for a family that used to live in this street. They were called Reynolds too. Did you know them?'

'What's it to you? Can't be no debts, can it? Not that they were the type for that.'

'No, it's nothing like that. It's personal. But you did know them?'

'Them days you knew everybody in the street and they knew you. Not like nowadays. That telly programme's out of date. Folks don't live in each other's pockets like they used to. You'd better come in. You look respectable, not that you can tell these days.'

179

She turned the key in the Yale lock and opened the door. I picked up the bag of shopping and followed her into the house.

'I suppose you want some tea?'

'Yes, please. I mean if it's no –'

'It's no trouble. I can still do that. Sit yourself down in there. I'll have that now, thank you.' She grabbed the shopping bag and pushed open the door of the front room. It smelt of cat or old lady or both. A big clock in a round-shouldered mahogany case with Roman numerals ticked loudly on the mantelpiece. I stood staring at myself in the sunburst mirror above it. What on earth was I doing here?

She returned with a tray, its contents jingling as her hands shook. The early signs of Parkinson's.

'Go on, sit down. The settee'll stand it.'

Rebuked, I did so.

For a few moments, we sipped the hot strong tea. Then she put down her cup. 'Well, what is it you want to know about the Reynoldses and why should I tell you?'

'I was married to Geoffrey. He died recently. As he wasn't in touch with his family, I thought I should find them. Let them know.'

'Dead, eh? It makes you think, doesn't it? I remember them. They were a nice family. Respectable.'

I nodded. This was obviously high praise.

'The lad, he were bright. He went to the grammar, the posh one, miles away. He had to get two buses, his mam said. She were that pleased. Funny to think of him dead before me, and him just a lad. Drink your tea. It'll get cold.'

I obeyed. 'Are they still alive, his parents?'

She shook her head. 'No. He died years ago. Heart. He was in the office at what used to be Rootes, the car firm, you know. Then it was them Americans. Lord knows who it is at the minute. Shut down, anyway, most of it. Well he got that redundancy, and a pension. But he didn't last to enjoy it. Happens quite a bit.'

'Geoffrey had a heart attack.'

'He did? They say it runs in families. Smoke like his dad, did he?'

'Not when I knew him. I think he had, though.'

'Terrible thing, those cigs. My Reg smoked, but not in the house. "You go outside if you want to kill yourself," I used to say.'

I had the feeling that the flood gates of reminiscence were about to be opened. It was probably some time since she had had a captive audience. I had to keep her on the point.

'What was Mrs Reynolds like?'

'Never heard anyone say a word against her. She kept that house spotless. And she had a job too. Worked on the counter at the chemist's that used to be round the corner. That's gone, of course. Knocked it down when they built the super. She lived for her children. She always wanted the best for them.'

'Children? How many?'

'Don't you know? There was a girl besides Geoff. Bit older. Couple of years between them, that's all. 'Course with children it makes all the difference, doesn't it?'

'You mean they were jealous?'

'You know how it is with brother and sister. Fight like cat and dog sometimes. And they were so different. Lizzie weren't a scholar. They tried with her, but compared to Geoff she were a bit of a dunce.'

'Where did she go?'

'Now you're asking. She got married, moved away. She used to work for the council one bit. You could try there.'

'What was her married name?'

She shook her head. 'It was a long time ago. Hang on, though, wasn't he called Johnson? That was it. Derek Johnson. Lorry driver, he were.'

'And what happened to Mrs Reynolds? When did she die?'

'When the council bought the houses from the landlord — and I could tell you a few palms that got greased in that little saga — about ten years ago, she went to live over in Ryton. They gave her a flat in what they call sheltered accommodation. You have a buzzer so they know whether you're alive or not. She passed on a couple of years after that. I don't think she ever liked it there. I went once or twice, but it was a bit difficult with the buses and my walking's not what it was.'

'Did Geoffrey ever see them? I mean after he left school?'

'He might have. I don't remember. We weren't that close, you know, just neighbours. Them days, it were different.'

She stopped, her eyes far away. She seemed suddenly old and frail and tired.

I drank the tea. It had gone cold. Despite the summer outside, there was a chill in the room which seemed to have seeped into my bones.

I had parked the car further back along the street. As I approached I saw that a bunch of kids were hanging around it: lanky loose-limbed boys in trainers and gaudy nylon shell suits. Their pale faces looked bored and discontented.

One of them was leaning against the hood. The rest gathered around as I rooted in my purse for the keys. I felt a tremor of fear as I felt their closeness. I could hear then exchanging crude sexual remarks in muttered undertones. I told myself they were just kids; it was broad daylight; they wouldn't dare do anything, would they? I finally found the bunch of keys, and refastened the clasp of the purse, ramming it tightly under my arm.

I got the door open and scrambled in, the unavoidable flash of leg and thigh as I swung myself into the seat provoking more obscene commentary. I slammed the door shut extra hard and flicked down the central locking button. They were probably harmless but who could tell these days? I wasn't even sure how old they were, as if that mattered. I was angry at myself. A few months ago I would have toughed it out. A few months ago I would never have come here.

Hearing the engine fire, the one on the hood slid off slickly and disappeared below my line of vision. A few seconds later his grinning face and protruding tongue, horribly flattened and dis-torted by the glass, materialized at the side window. It was a trick he had no doubt honed to perfection after much practice.

I revved the engine loudly and wrenched the wheel round,

driving out of the parking space with a screech of tyres. I could hear catcalls and laughter as I drove away down the dismal street.

I had certainly got a picture of Geoffrey's youth. How different it was from what he had, I realized now, so subtly implied by his occasional revelations. He had always implied a fairly privileged upbringing by his occasional references: to his nanny, to his public school. That was a snobbish distortion of the truth. I felt wounded by the concealment. As if I, who shared none of the petty social categorizing of the British middle class, had cared two hoots about where he had been educated! But Geoffrey clearly had. And it came to me that what he must have wanted was to seem like someone wilfully disregarding social niceties, rather than to be a grammar school boy who might be expected never to have known the right thing in the first place. How could he appear déclassé without having the class? But to do that required the concealment of his true origins.

That explained a great deal: his chameleon quality, his appetite for gossip, his close study of style and presentation. He had fooled me, certainly. But then I was beginning to think that I who thought myself so clever was in fact extremely easily fooled.

He had never mentioned a sister. She would almost certainly, unless she were a social-climbing carbon copy of him, have given the game away. So I'd never been allowed even to suspect her existence. No, that wasn't right. I hadn't ever wanted her to exist. I hadn't wanted anyone else to exist. I had been quite content that they didn't.

All I had wanted was Geoffrey. We were complete as we were. Two individuals who lived together and shared parts of our lives. There was no question about our having the sort of marriage where we had spent our time visiting elderly relatives, having tea with aged aunts, entertaining widowed uncles, taking nephews and nieces to the cinema. We had got beyond all that. I realized it was a relief that Geoffrey was a man without the impedimenta of a family. Like me, he was a free-standing individual.

But now he was dead, I had this desire, this compulsion almost, to find out his family history. His sister had her significance because she was, however remotely, a part of the man I had loved. Yes, I had loved him. She was now the only part of him left. I expected no reincarnation, but nevertheless hoped for some shadow of the life that had gone.

'Mrs Johnson? Do you know what department she's in?'

I shook my head. 'Sorry, I don't.'

The girl at the sapele veneer desk waved a thick wad of typescript at me. 'This is the Council Internal Phone Book. See these names? Hundreds, there are. Listed by department. And then they're not even in alphabetical order.'

'I could search through it. It is important.'

'Oh, no. I couldn't let you do that. Confidential, this is. Personal matter, isn't it?'

'Yes,' I admitted.

'Well, then. You could be anyone.'

'I'm not anyone,' I said, my irritation level rising. God, how I hated dealing with these bureaucratic tangles. Keep calm, I told myself. The one sure way not to get what you want is to get nasty. I smiled ingratiatingly. 'Please, Ms . . . er' –

I glanced quickly down at the nameplate – 'Ms Williamson. I do need to talk to Mrs Johnson, Elizabeth. She's a relative. I have something important to tell her. Here's my card. I'm really quite harmless.' I gave her what I hoped was a winning, woman-to-woman smile.

She examined the card I had given her. 'London,' she said. For some reason this seemed to boost my credentials. 'I'll have a word with Sue in personnel. If you'd like to have a seat?' She pointed at a grimy pvc sofa sandwiched between a potted palm and a chrome steel column ashtray.

I heard her talking on the phone, then she beckoned me back.

'There is a Mrs Elizabeth Johnson. City Engineers. Do you want me to find out if she's in?'

'I nodded, suddenly nervous. I heard her say, 'Mrs Johnson? Carol, Central Reception. There's a lady here wants to speak to you. She says she's a relative. From London. All right?'

She waved the instrument in my direction. I took a deep breath before cradling it on my shoulder.

I bought the drinks. A whisky for me. A lager shandy for her.

She had suggested the pub. It was near the council offices, concrete outside, fake Victoriana within. She hadn't finished until five so I had had to hang around for several hours in the soulless shopping precinct of which the city centre consisted.

She sat on the velour banquette. I sat opposite on the reproduction wheelback chair. She didn't look at all like him. She was a small, dark-haired woman, her face pale, her eyes deeply shadowed, her cheeks hollow. She wore a green, cheap-looking waterproof jacket over a thick blue cardigan, a white blouse and a navy polyester skirt.

We sipped our drinks. Finally she broke the tense silence. 'So Geoff's dead, then. Funny that, really. He could have been dead for years as far as I was concerned. Now he is, I can't take it in.'

'That's the feeling I had, still have sometimes. Of not quite believing it.' I had had to tell her straight away in the lobby of the office where she worked, surrounded by notices about roadworks and garbage collection. She would never otherwise have come with me to talk.

'You must think me a bit callous, but I don't think I'm going to go home and weep buckets. We weren't close. The last time I saw Geoff was at Mam's funeral. He turned up in a big flashy car, stayed for the service in the crematorium and went straight after. He didn't even come home for the reception. I suppose he thought it wouldn't be up to his standards. You don't have to say anything. I can see he never mentioned me, did he? He would have been ashamed to, I bet.'

'We weren't married for very long. We didn't talk much about the past.'

'How did you know how to find me?'

I told her about Mrs Beecroft. 'It wasn't as difficult as I thought it would be.'

'So she's still alive, then. The nosy old cow. You couldn't walk down the street without she was twitching her nets or opening the front door. I really hated that place. I hated it even more when I saw how it was Geoff who was going to get away. He was the one who passed his eleven plus, the one who won the scholarship to Casaubon Grammar. They wouldn't even buy me a decent dress to get married in. And a fat lot of flipping good that did me.'

'Marriage, you mean?'

'That's right. Now I'm on my own again. Except I've got two kids at school to feed and clothe on the pittance the council pay me. He's out of work and never gives me a penny piece.' She looked up at me, her dark eyes burning fiercely in her pinched, lined face. 'I don't suppose you know about that kind of thing. Look at that outfit you're wearing. You're not short, are you?'

I was stung into a response. 'Everything I have I earned, through bloody hard work. And you might like to know I'm now out of a job, so you're one up on me there, at any rate.'

'Don't give me that. Geoff was always flush. I expect you've got it all. I haven't heard any of it was coming my way.'

I shook my head. I didn't want to get into a quarrel with this bitter, dissatisfied woman. I said gently, 'That's not the case. Geoffrey spent what he earned, and more. He left nothing but debts, apart from the cottage – and that he bought from the money his aunt left him.' Then I said, 'If there is anything left when I've sorted his affairs out, I'll gladly share it with you.' No, I didn't feel magnanimous. It wasn't really my money anyway.

She crumpled. 'I'm sorry. I wasn't asking for anything. I don't want his money. You're his wife. And it was generous of you. I'm not really horrible. I suppose no matter what I said, it is a shock. Things keep flashing into my mind. Little things – you know, when we were kids together. Going to the park, a day at the seaside.' She wiped her tears with a crumpled used tissue from her jacket pocket. 'Are you really out of work?' I nodded, and drank up the whisky. I was feeling like crying myself.

'I'm sorry you've got that on top of everything,' she said. 'Debts, are there? Even as a lad, he always wanted the best of everything. It was Mam and Dad's fault. They pandered to it.

Spoiled him rotten.' She drank some more shandy. 'But what were you saying about a cottage?'

'It's in Norfolk, in a forest. Quite small and secret. It was going to be our own special place. Just the two of us.' I could see it before me as I spoke.

'It sounds nice. But what I meant was you said he bought it with money he got left.'

'Yes. An aunt. Aunt Edith. He didn't say any more about it, only that she died before we met.'

She was agitated again. 'He can't have. It must have been quite a lot of money. No one in our family had two ha'pennies to rub together. And more to the point, Mam had a sister but she was killed by a bomb in the war, and Dad's sister died when we were kids, years ago. And neither of them were called Edith. Wherever that money came from, it wasn't from our family.'

It was my turn to be agitated. 'But that's what he said. Why would he make up a thing like that? And if the money didn't come from Aunt Edith, where did it come from?'

She laughed. 'It sounds like him. Even when he was a kid he used to make things up. About himself, where he lived. Sometimes I used to think he actually believed his stories. I remember once when we were on holiday – I suppose it was Skegness, it usually was – he told some old couple that he was on holiday from Eton and his family owned the pier. He even offered to show them round. They believed him until they saw me laughing my head off and I told them it was my kid brother having them on. But to him, it wasn't just a laugh. He really seemed to believe it for a time. That was why he was so convincing. He could do the voice. He could drop the Midlands accent just like that when he wanted.'

As I listened something was screaming, It isn't true! The man I married was everything he appeared to be. He was real. But underneath the scream, another voice was growing in volume, a voice that said: who was it you really knew? Who was it? Who?

11

'Hi, Norman,' I shouted. He was at the end of his back garden, bent over, digging potatoes. He looked up, and unhurriedly stuck the fork into the ground. Wiping his hands on the sides of his brown corduroys, he ambled to where I stood leaning on the garden wall.

'Mornin', missus. Not seeing you, I never got the chance to say how sorry I was, like, about your husband. 'Twas a terrible thing.'

I nodded in acknowledgement. 'Thanks, Norman.'

Ritual pleasantries over, he waited, his china blue eyes narrowed in anticipation, his chin as ever covered with two or three days' growth of white stubble.

'I've come to ask you whether you couldn't do an extra day at the cottage. It's much better now, thanks to you, but I think it does need a bit more time. You see, I want it looking good. I've decided to sell.'

'Ah.' There was a flash of yellow teeth. 'Two days that would be.' I could almost see the wheels turning as if I were watching one of those primitive mechanical computers. ''Twouldn't be easy. 'Tis a busy time now, what with harvest and all.'

'I'd pay a bit more for the extra.'

'A bit more, eh?'

I mentioned a figure.

His features remained impassive. Then, with an intake of breath and a sucking of yellow ivory, 'If you could see your way to maybe' – he mentioned a slightly higher amount – 'then it might be worth my while. 'Tis a bit of a way, and I'm not getting no younger.'

I sighed with feigned reluctance. It was still a good deal. 'OK,' I said. I stuck out my hand.

Norman wiped his crusted paw again before he gingerly shook mine.

Negotiations concluded to mutual satisfaction, he became affable. 'I got some good new taters. Maybe you'd like a few?'

'Why, thank you Norman, that would be very nice.'

He wandered back down to the potato patch, calling out as he passed the back door, 'Tom, you there, boy. Get us one of them old carrier bags. Your mam don't like me coming in with boots on.'

In a few moments the slightly hunched, shuffling figure of his son emerged from the house and followed him carrying a crumpled Tesco's bag.

They walked back together up the path, Norman squat and brown, white tufts of matted hair poking out of the open neck of the red checked lumberjack shirt, looking like something out of the Wind in the Willows; Tom, slender, tall, head bowed and eyes occluded behind the pebble-thick spectacles. It was the first time I had seen him since the business in the church, which might as well have been centuries ago. I was amazed at my fear then. In the warm sunlight, he was just a boy.

Norman handed over the bulging bag. I made a move to my purse, but he munificently waved away any payment. 'Now you're here, Tom, you should tell the missus you're sorry for frightening her that time. Go on, boy.' He gave him a sharp nudge of encouragement.

Tom glanced up, his eyes not meeting mine, then looked away again. He blushed and mumbled.

'Speak up, boy, the missus can't hear you.'

'Sorry, missus.' He blushed even deeper.

I could see how much of a child he was, and probably always would be. How stupid I had been. But that was metropolitan conditioning for you.

'It's all right, Tom. I tell you what.' The idea suddenly came to me. 'Why don't you show me the famous Barton Devil now, if you'd like.'

189

Tom blushed, and turned to his father.

Norman gave him a playful shove. 'There, now. 'Course you'd like. Go on then, boy.'

After the warmth outside, the interior of the church seemed dank and chilly, except where the shafts of sunlight carved tunnels through the gloom, swirling with dustmotes. Where they hit the worn flagstones, there were splashes of colour from the panels of stained glass, blue, purple and blood red.

I shivered. I had on only a thin cotton summer dress, my shoulders bare.

Tom held open the heavy door for me to enter, then closed it softly behind him. He beckoned to me, then loped off along the side aisle in the direction of the altar. I followed slowly down the nave, glancing up again at the magnificent roof where the angels spread their wings.

He had stopped at the aisle side of the last pillar of the nave and I joined him there. The pillar was fully illuminated by the blaze of sunlight which fell on it directly through the grisaille window opposite.

He stood aside as I came up. 'There he is, missus.' He pointed to the top of the pillar, several feet above our heads.

Despite the sunlight, I could see nothing, not knowing quite what I should be looking for along the line of his pointing finger. Then as I stood on tiptoe and craned my neck, I saw it.

On the projecting rim of cream-coloured stone which formed the lowest part of the capital was a face. It was so lightly incised that in certain lights it would have seemed merely an unevenness in the ashlar. It was a face which seemed to grow from the grain of the stone, angled slightly so as to peer down from its height, smoothly youthful, but without definite gender, just a suggestion of a brow, of eye sockets, a nose. It was only the lower part that was given definition, a sharp pointed chin, and a full-lipped smiling mouth. But not a pleasant smile; a supercilious, disdainful, mocking smile, a cruel smile and, it was hard to avoid the word, an evil smile.

I shuddered, but this time it was not with cold for the warm sun lay on my back. I was clearly not the first to use such a word. Why else was it called the Barton Devil? Generations of villagers had looked upon this face and had had from it the same tremor, the same apprehension of strangeness, the feeling that a small corner of the ordinary world had been turned over to reveal the grinning terror beneath.

At my elbow, Tom said, 'He's a queer one, ain't he? Seems to be looking right through you. Seems like he's saying, I know you, boy, I know what you've a-done, and smiling to himself about it, about what'll happen.'

'Yes,' I said. I thought of other strange smiles, those smiles which Leonardo created. Their enigma was that they too had more than a hint of the diabolic. Whoever created this one would have surely recognized them. Poor Tom, to feel his childish misdeeds were being perceived by this medieval mason's prankish tour de force.

To lighten the mood, I said playfully, 'And what have you done, Tom? Have you been a bad boy?'

He whirled away from me as if I had waved a red-hot iron in his face. 'Nothing. I ain't done nothing. What do you know anyways? You don't know.' He cowered back against the wall opposite, his arms spread and his fingers digging into the scarred uneven stonework. His eyes were wide and staring, magnified by the thick spectacle lenses.

I took a step towards him and then stopped. I cursed my stupidity. The kind of repartee that crackled in Bloomsbury was quite inappropriate here with this overgrown child and I should have known it. He was obviously badly frightened. 'Tom, listen to me. I wasn't accusing you of anything. I'm sure you haven't done anything bad. You're right. I don't know anything. I was making a silly joke.'

He continued to stare, but the hands gripping the stone appeared to relax. His head dropped towards his chest in his familiar hunch. He mumbled something I couldn't catch.

'Are you saying something, Tom? Tom, I really am sorry I upset you.'

'It's always me, getting the blame. I didn't do nothing, I tell you.'

I could see that in an odd sort of way there was something bothering him which he didn't want to tell me and yet which he was feeling driven to confess. What was it? Scrumping apples? Pinching from the shop?

'I'm not blaming you, Tom. I know you're a good boy. Whatever it is, I won't blame you.'

He slithered down the wall and sat in a heap on the flagstones, his knees up and his face buried in his thighs. I sat down beside him, my back resting on the cold stone.

Then, his face still hidden and his voice muffled, he said, 'He said I did, but I never. I wouldn't do anything to hurt her. But he told my dad. And then afterwards she got took away. All because of me. I don't have no one to talk to any more.'

I had the oddest feeling then that I was hearing something very important, without having a clue as to why or what it was. 'Who said you did, Tom? Who was it?'

He raised his head. Tears were bright in his eyes and smeared his cheeks. 'The Perfessor. What dad worked for. What lived where you live.'

'Dr Mallen, you mean?'

He nodded. 'Him. He was real mad. He said I touched her, but I never. I wouldn't. He sent her away.'

'Is it Lucy you're talking about, Tom? Is that who it is?'

''Course it is. There weren't none but them two. He told me I had to stay away from her. I couldn't go there no more. But I had to.' He turned to me, his eyes huge with entreaty. 'I had to see she were all right.'

'Of course you did, Tom. So you went back and what happened?'

'I went back. It was on a night. I saw her get taken away. It was because of me. But I never touched her, never, honest.'

'I know, Tom, I know. What happened? Who took her away?'

'Some men, or maybe one of them were a woman. The man carried her out. She were all limp like an old rabbit in a trap. They had a big car. They put her in it. I was watching. They didn't see me.'

'Where did they take her, Tom?'

'Don't know. It were a bit after that that Dad said the Perfessor had gone away too. She would have stayed if it hadn't been for me.'

I took a deep breath. I looked at my hands and saw that they were clenched tight, the knuckles bone-white. 'Did you ever tell anyone this, Tom? About Lucy's being sent away?'

He became frightened again. 'No I never. I daresn't. Dad told me not to go bothering them again. Said he'd lose a nice bit of work. He was really mad when the Perfessor went. I never said nothing about them again. You won't tell him, will you?'

'No, Tom. I won't tell. I'll keep your secret. But I don't think your dad ever thought you were bad. You ought to believe that. Let's keep it between us, shall we?' I checked my watch. 'Goodness me. I have to be going.'

We got up. I felt stiff, and my bare back was like ice. Before I walked away, I looked up again at the Barton Devil and his ghost of a smile.

I slumped down on a stack of cut-down tree trunks, out of breath. It had been quite a pull up the long, surprisingly steep forest track and I wasn't used to the exertion. Ahead of me was a clearing where a whole block of trees had been felled, apparently quite recently. Their stumps could be seen amid the tangle of briars and weeds that had, freed from the deadening shade of the canopy, sprung into rampant growth. Eventually I supposed the area would be bulldozed and replanted with young trees, starting their forty-year cycle on the way to the sawmills. The mud of the track was deeply imprinted by the tyres of the loggers' trucks and littered with sawdust and small branches. This was a working forest. No nonsense about the tranquillity of unspoilt nature here. Yet there was peace despite the signs of human activity.

No one was working in this section today and the only sound was the quiet moaning of the wind in the topmost branches. The birds were silent. Perhaps the recent activity had frightened them away.

I had come out to get rid of the stale feeling I had woken up with. The cool, fresh day with a hint of rain in the breeze cleared the dull ache in my head better than any analgesic. I wasn't really a great country walker. I mainly regarded rambling as another recreation of people who concocted homemade wines, something they did when they weren't train spotting or morris dancing. But on that day, once I had put on a raincoat and my long leather boots – I still hadn't gotten round to buying wellingtons – for the first time I had felt like exploring the immediate surroundings of the forest. After all, the next few days might be the last I spent here.

From the cottage the track plunged straight into the trees, gently switchbacking across what had been, before the forest had come, the undulating heathland of the Breck. This was the Roman road or packhorse way that the man who said he was Hugh Robinson had told us about. On one side, the cottage side, Norman had told me, was the block of land owned by the Barton Hall estate, where Sir James Edwardes had his pheasant coverts. The other side was owned by the Forestry Commission where the conifers grew thick in solid phalanxes.

I had been walking for about half an hour before I rested on the logs. I had it vaguely in mind to go down one of the open fire-breaks or vehicle access ways which I had noticed crossed the main track at fairly regular intervals and which presumably divided the forest into blocks. I would in this fashion, I estimated, eventually come upon the cottage from the opposite side, thus avoiding having to retrace my steps.

I had grown pleasantly warm, so I unbuttoned the coat and loosened the scarf at my throat. I leaned back against the rough bark of the trunks. The furry grey-green lichen or moss which covered them tickled my ears. I stretched out my legs and closed my eyes, feeling the sun on my face for the first time since I had set out.

I must have lain like this for about ten minutes, then the warmth faded as the sun went behind a cloud. I hauled myself upright and stepped back on to the sandy flint-strewn surface of the track. In front of me I was surprised to see a figure standing by the side of the track about two hundred yards away. Whoever it was – it looked like a man – hadn't passed me so he must have come from the opposite direction.

As I drew nearer, the man – I could now see the dark beard and the flash of mirrored sunglasses – remained standing there, apparently gazing in my direction. It appeared as if he were waiting for me.

He was dressed in a waxed jacket, corduroy trousers, and a wide tweed cap. On his feet he wore walking boots. Around his neck was a pair of binoculars. It was the standard countryside rambling garb affected by the types I had seen pass the cottage going this way. For some reason, though, I felt a tremor of apprehension. Something in me wasn't convinced that this was the usual redundant schoolmaster or early retired postman on a hike. My senses and my suspicions suddenly went on red alert, the way they had one time when I had been foolish enough to stay almost too long in Central Park on a winter's afternoon. I noticed that a vagrant uncoiled from a bench as I passed and started plodding after me. Then there had been plenty of people about to deter an immediate attack or whatever he had had in mind and I had jumped into a cab the moment I hit Fifth Avenue, leaving him gazing at me from the sidewalk.

This guy was not a vagrant. He was tall, his jacket filled out with muscle and no sign of middle-aged spread. But it wasn't a crime to be fit. It wasn't necessarily the sign of a psychopath that he stopped a while to get back his breath as I had. I wasn't in the middle of New York City either. I wasn't literally within shouting distance of anybody.

I saw that without consciously doing so I had slowed my pace, so the gap between us had hardly diminished. He seemed to recognize my hesitation because he raised a hand in cheery male greeting then continued walking along the path ahead of me in the same direction.

I breathed a quiet sigh of relief, then reverted to my normal walking speed. He didn't seem a fast walker himself, because even though he had been well ahead, I was gaining on him. Then the alarm bells in my head rang again. I had read enough espionage thrillers to recognize that you didn't have to be behind somebody to follow them. You didn't have to chase somebody to get near to them. Why had he walked back in the direction he must have come? He had seen my hesitation and feared I would turn tail and run. OK, so he was just a tired pedestrian. He wouldn't mind if I peeled off at a convenient side track.

Unfortunately there wouldn't be one. I would have caught up with him long before any escape route presented itself. I had seen the last one just before the pile of logs. On either side there were only the closely spaced trunks of the pines. I wouldn't get ten yards.

I suddenly didn't care whether I looked like an idiot to some innocent countryside lover. If I saw him again I could always say some typically daffy feminine thing like I'd remembered I'd left the iron on at home.

I turned and ran back down the track as fast as I could go. As I hurtled along, my clumsy boots slithering on the loose surface, I glanced back over my shoulder. I saw that he had stopped and was apparently observing my flight with cool interest. My breath was burning in my windpipe. I was hot and my scarf had worked its way under my ear. Still running, I sneaked another look behind. The man, whoever he was, had gone.

I turned my head back and saw with astonishment a green-clad figure emerge from the forest in front of me. But this time he was carrying a gun.

I stopped dead, an ice-cold wave passed through me. Then the man turned towards me and waved an arm in greeting.

It was not, and, cursing my stupidity, could not have been the man I had run away from. It was James Edwardes.

'I hadn't got you down as a jogger, I must say.'

'We city types, we need to get our exercise.' I was out of breath so this didn't come out with quite the heartiness I had intended.

'Do you ride? Good country for a horse, this. Miles of forest tracks.'

I shook my head. 'If nature had intended me for a horsewoman she'd have given me longer legs. Jodhpurs don't suit me.' I thought this would sound better than I was scared stiff of horses.

He gave his booming laugh. 'You should see the types who get on nags at the local horse trials, my dear lady. You should have no such inhibitions.' But seeing the face I made, thankfully he dropped the subject and said hastily, 'Jogging, though, is just as good. Whatever, I've never been able to stay indoors for long, rain or shine. I've roamed these woods for fifty years, and watched them grow, since I was a boy.'

'I guess you know them well?'

'No one better. Every inch of them. My mother disapproved. Said I was more like a forester's boy than my father's heir. Sometimes feel I would have liked that. Spending every day under the greenwood tree. Hate it when they cut them, though. Has to be done, but they get to be old friends, trees. There's your place now. Bit like the gingerbread house in the fairy story, what?'

We had been walking as we talked and were in sight of the cottage.

'Am I the wicked witch, then?'

'Good Lord, didn't mean that. Said it without thinking. Clumsy of me.'

I smiled at his confusion. 'That's all right.'

'By the way, I'm glad I bumped into you. I . . . Dottie and I have been meaning to ask you if you might like to come round for a spot of dinner one evening. Must be a bit lonely for you, eh? Day after tomorrow any good?'

I was a little surprised by the invitation. Somehow I hadn't thought we were going to be on such terms. But I thanked him and said that my social calendar was quite free tomorrow evening.

'We dine at eight,' he said as he strode off down the track. 'We'll see you at about seven-thirty.'

★

I stuffed the key into the front door with hands that were shaking as much with anger at myself as residual fright. I must be going crazy. What did I think I was doing, turning tail and running at the sight of some perfectly ordinary stranger walking in the woods? Had James Edwardes witnessed more than he had let on? But if he thought I was crazy he'd hardly have invited me to dinner.

Forget it, I said to myself as I washed the dishes from breakfast and the previous night's supper. I had a right to be nervy and jumpy after everything that had happened. In any case, I'd rather look an idiot than run the risk of having some lonely nutcase get friendly in the middle of nowhere. The woman's right to choose, wasn't it?

I made some coffee and sat on the sofa in the sitting room. The fresh paint made it bright and cheerful. I could see how it would improve the rest of the house if only I could get around to it. I had come here with a detailed plan of everything I had to do and a list of the things I had to buy and arrange. So far, I had ticked off only one item. 'Fix Norman re garden.' Once here I found myself irresistibly slowed down.

Suddenly everything seemed as if it could wait. For the first time for as long as I could remember, there were no deadlines to meet, no typescripts to read, no authors to cajole and cosset. My enforced leisure had made time seem almost infinitely extendable. OK, so I had come here to deal with the matter of the elusive deeds and make the place presentable to a more perceptive buyer than Geoffrey and I. But now I was here, I didn't feel the urgency. No one was on my back, no one was in the driving seat but me. If it took longer, who cared? If I wanted to walk in the woods once in a while, no one was going to ask me why I hadn't been at my desk. No one would page me for calls from New York.

I wouldn't be able to carry on in this insouciant jobless fashion for long, but whilst I was phone-less down here there was nothing I could do about it. Besides, no job offers, not even one as a filing clerk, had winged my way since the word had gone out that having parted company with McAllister's I was waiting anxiously for a call.

I felt a twinge of guilt at my idleness. I should at least try to do something from the list of 'Things to do at the house' I had prepared. Something not too strenuous to make me feel I had spent part of the day in useful activity. How about this? 'Sweep yard and tidy woodshed and outhouse'?

It turned out not to be a soft option. The brick surface of the rear yard hadn't been swept in an age. The fine old bricks, similar to those on the kitchen floor, were covered in an accretion of slimy lichen and encroaching weeds. I did my best with a brush then switched to scraping with a spade, which was much quicker. I soon had a wheelbarrow full which I dumped on Norman's makeshift compost heap.

I was perspiring freely when I had finished. I sat on a kitchen chair in the sun to survey my work. I quickly saw with irritation that I had missed a mouldering cardboard box peeping out of the open woodshed door.

It was soaked by rain and full of garbage. I then remembered what it was. Of course, the debris from the range and other trash. I had stuck it in the shed on the very day we had moved in and forgotten to clear it away. That day when I had also spent my time sweeping and cleaning. It had been here ever since, an untouched icon of a happier time. But not any longer.

I brought a black plastic garbage sack from indoors and laid it open-mouthed on the floor. Then I picked up the box, which was heavier than it had been since its soaking. As I lifted it, the soggy cardboard sheets forming the bottom opened and the contents fell out in a blackened mass, missing the open sack but spreading themselves freely all over the clean, swept bricks.

'Hell and damnation!' Bits of charred paper scattered everywhere like damp black leaves, crumbling instantly to granular dust. I grabbed the broom and began sweeping again vigorously, feeling like the sorcerer's apprentice as my workload increased exponentially despite my best efforts.

I got the loose flakes into the sack with my hands, together with the ruins of the box. The main part of the contents had remained where they had fallen in a dense clump. I gingerly picked it up, hoping it would stay in one piece, and quickly dumped it into the sack where it immediately separated into its component sheets.

I noticed with idle curiosity that some of the paper at the centre of the bundle had not been wholly burned. It was browned by the fierce heat and the edges were fretted and blackened, but it was quite recognizable for what it was: wide, lined paper covered in writing in blue ink. Big, round handwriting. The handwriting of a child.

Finding it disturbed me. If I were the sort to believe in premonitions, I would now say that it struck a chill into my heart. It was the fact of finding it there, amidst a charred pile, itself partially consumed by the same fire.

I knew next to nothing about children or the process of bringing them up, other than having gone through it myself, an experience which had made me not want to repeat it with any of my own. But what I did know was that the loving parent treasured the offspring's every production, from childish scrawl to graduation dissertation. They did not throw them into the flames like so much trash. Even someone with such ill-developed maternal instincts as I could not imagine doing such a thing.

I spread out newspaper on the kitchen table and carefully separated the unburnt paper from the flakes of ash. It was obviously the remains of a school exercise book. Judging from the dates at the head of one or two of the pages, it was a couple of years old. I reckoned that the writer was probably then about nine or ten. There were spelling exercises – 9/10, very good; 10/10, excellent – underlined. There was part of an essay about a country walk: 'I set off down the track that leads to the village from our house. It was a bright sunny day. A robin redbreast perched on the gate and chirruped as I went past.' It was all familiar. It could have been my own. I could even see her: a bright, confident little girl, head bent over her page in concentration, her pink tongue sticking from the corner of her mouth as she formed the letters. Why would anyone want to destroy such charming memories?

I found the tears pricking my eyes as I came to the end of the pile. The last unburnt sheet was stiff blue paper, part of the cover of the book. In the centre, against the printed words 'Child's Name', the same immature hand had written, 'Lucy Angela Mallen, Class III'.

I picked it up. At the top, the flames had burned away most of the school name printed there. But the bottom of a few letters remained, sufficient to spell out 'The Grove Girls' Preparatory School'. The rest of the address had burned away. I remembered Norman had said she had gone to school in Cambridge. Without quite knowing why I did it, I took a clear polythene bag from a drawer, put the unburnt pages into it then put it back in the drawer. The blue cover sheet I placed in my pocketbook. I took the black plastic garbage sack containing the remains of the box and the ash outside and stowed it at the back of the woodshed.

I washed my hands at the sink, watching the water swirl away down the drain, grey and speckled with tiny black fragments of ash. Why had these things been burned? I thought of Tom's half-incoherent account of her departure. Was that true? If so where had she gone? Why had the man who called himself Hugh Robinson lied to me?

For no reason that I could justify, a hard core of anxiety about the girl refused to be dispersed. I felt somehow as if I held the key to a puzzle which it was my responsibility to unravel. I had to know where she had gone, to be sure she was safe. But where could I start? Not with the man Massingham or his chilly wife. There was no truth to be had in that quarter, not yet. The school. They might have some information. They might not tell me on the telephone, but if I went there I might be able to wheedle it out of them. Anyway, I told myself, it would be a day out in Cambridge. A treat. Just the thing for someone with time on their hands and nothing more pressing to do.

12

The next morning I thought carefully what I was going to do. I should learn from my experience at South Benham not to go barging in. There had to be a reason. That was why I drove into Breckenham and, after getting the number from Directory Enquiries, telephoned the headmistress of the Grove Girls' School. I said I was looking for a school for my daughter Emma, and would like to meet her and look around the Grove. Would she be free sometime tomorrow morning, when I would be in Cambridge? As I had to fly back to Hong Kong at the end of the week, unfortunately that was the only time I had available. This did the trick. The appointment was duly made. Clearly the Grove School was not so popular as to turn away prospective customers.

I had only been to Cambridge once before. Then it had been some shindig at the University Press, their thousandth anniversary or so, I think. The Grove School was in a quiet tree-lined street off the Trumpington Road. Two large Victorian Gothic villas had been linked by an Early Metal Windows structure and surrounded by undulating tarmac. I couldn't imagine aesthetics as part of the curriculum.

The wide gloomy hall smelt of furniture polish. Not surprisingly as every available surface from the creaky pitchpine floorboards to the mahogany balusters and handrail of the cantilevered staircase up to the twinkling brass chandelier was burnished and polished to a state of military perfection. On the wall was a huge pinboard stuck with neatly labelled notices – class lists, dormitory lists, house lists, tennis practice lists. On a side table was a cut-glass vase of fresh flowers and a pile of shiny leaflets headed 'Paying for School fees the Normal Life Endowment Way'. I shuddered. I was in a world I had long ago decided I had no wish to enter. So why exactly was I here? I brushed aside the question as I was ushered by a secretary into the presence of Miss Marian Osborne, Headmistress and Proprietor.

'And how old is your daughter, Mrs Richardson?'

'Emma will be eight next birthday – doesn't time absolutely whizz by? That's next July. James's tour with the bank will be ending next April. We'll have a few months back here to sort things out before we're off again. It's likely to be Brussels this time.'

Miss Osborne nodded eagerly. Her gold-rimmed spectacles sparkled as much as the furniture. 'A bit nearer home, isn't it? But so many of our girls' parents are overseas. We're very experienced at looking after them, I can assure you. A pity it's the hols, and you couldn't see us in action.'

'What you've shown me today is quite delightful,' I gushed. 'Those divine dormitories, so comfortable.' They were, if Devil's Island was your idea of comfort. 'I have no doubt that she will be very happy here. It's so convenient also for leaves. We have a sweet, old rambling house in a dear little Norfolk village which is really quite close. Barton St Margaret. In fact it was because our former neighbour Dr Mallen recommended you so highly that I kept you in mind.'

'Why, of course. Dr Mallen. How kind of him. Lucy was a pupil here for several years. Such a sweet girl.'

'I suppose she must have left by now and gone on to public school. It's some time since we saw them as they've moved away from the village.'

'Poor Lucy. She had very bad luck. She fell ill – glandular fever, I believe – and had to leave before the end of term. I suppose it was about two years ago. I did write to Dr Mallen on a couple of occasions asking after her health but I never received a reply. But that isn't unusual, I'm afraid. He was a busy man and so brilliant, they say. And of course he was a widower.'

I nodded. The lack of such a useful adjunct as a wife would excuse any male discourtesy.

I gathered my things to go. Clutching the glossy brochure I had been given, I assured Miss Osborne that I would discuss the matter with my husband and would contact her with our decision. Meanwhile, would she please reserve a place? I was sure Emma would be very happy there.

I drove out of the gates and away from the school. But my hands were trembling so much that I had to stop in the next street. I stared at my white face in the rear view mirror.

It wasn't the nervous energy employed in my impersonation of the middle-class parent that was making me feel sick at the pit of my stomach. It was fear. A fear I couldn't explain. A fear born out of pure instinct or intuition or whatever. A fear that something had happened to Lucy Mallen.

'So you've decided to sell up, eh? Understandable, but a pity. Pretty woman always welcome in the neighbourhood.'

'James, really! You'll embarrass our guest. Stop talking like something out of the nineteenth century.'

Sitting there in the candlelight, the only other illumination in the room being the soft red glow from the fireplace, that's what it felt like. We could have been back in good Queen Vic's golden days. Absurdly, uniquely in my experience, the Edwardeses dressed formally for dinner at home. Sir James was resplendent in dinner jacket and black tie, around his waist a scarlet cummerbund. His lady – 'Dorothea, but call me Dottie, everybody does' – was gorgeous in a long, warm, peach velvet gown. At her throat was the sparkle of a necklace which contained what I boggled to note were more than a few emeralds among the ice.

As I couldn't imagine they had gone out of their way to awe me with this magnificence, I had to assume it was their normal gear. If you had it, why not flaunt it? Not that the Edwardeses would have recognized any such concept. You wore what you had, probably what your great-grandparents had had. Any idea of doing it to impress was utterly vulgar.

Anyway, I wasn't so socially naïve as to imagine that the Edwardeses' invitation to dinner implied fish fingers in front of the TV, so I had done my best with the limited range of apparel I had brought with me. Luckily, it was force of habit from a lifetime in a business where appearance counted never to be without something passable. I couldn't run to an evening gown but I had got a decorously short cocktail dress in dark blue jersey, its high neck closed by one of my good things, a big amethyst brooch set about with diamonds. With my hair up, I looked quite presentable. Probably my host and hostess were that kind of upper crust who wouldn't have minded if I had turned up in dungarees, but I felt more comfortable that I had on my somewhat lower level responded to the occasion. After all it wasn't every day that the peasants got to dine at the big house.

And, without being Knole or Chatsworth, it was fairly big. I had glimpsed it before from the road, but it was way back at the end of a long drive and the trees of the parkland wrapped it about and partially concealed it, so it wasn't until you came right upon it that you could appreciate it. A classic English country house, Palladian fronted, but preserving behind the façade parts of a much older building: dark oak linenfold panelling and with ceilings crisscrossed with massive beams, the elegance mingled with a heavy practicality.

We had dinner in a room of this period, at a refectory table which could have seated thirty. In a fireplace with a high mantel elaborately carved in the Jacobean manner and surmounted by a medallion carrying a coat of arms, despite the season baulks of timber burned on beautiful iron fire dogs. As we ate, the sun went down spectacularly, its last rays gleaming orange and gold on the leaded lights of the mullioned windows.

I have to say that the food did not quite match the sophistication of the surroundings, but that is the English way. The meat was good if unimaginatively prepared, the vegetables tasted home-grown, but a Frenchman would have found them dull. The wine was another matter. I could imagine Geoffrey's exclamations if he had tasted such a claret. It was of such quality that even he would have hesitated before ordering it at London restaurant prices.

Through the meal we had talked about generalities: London life – I gathered the Edwardeses spent a good deal of time there at their house in Cheyne Walk; the house: James had given me a potted version of its architectural history from the Conquest up to date, and finally, when I was asked about my line of country, publishing. I confessed my involvement in the trade. Dottie contributed that her niece was gainfully employed in an aristocratic art house and it turned out that I knew her slightly. It was when I mentioned McAllister's that James seemed to moderate the bluff archaic country gentleman pose which he had adopted until then and became more engaged. He seemed to be sitting straighter and the watery blue eyes which through dinner had seemed unfocused looked at me sharply from under the bushy brows.

'Isn't that run by that Underdown-Metcalfe fellow? Got a link up with some Americans a while back, didn't he?'

'Yes, in fact I was one of the Americans. I got sent in like the Marines about three years ago.' My expression must have communicated my surprise that the doings of the company were of interest to a country squire, because he was quick to pick up on it. 'I get involved in more than the price of mangelwurzels, you know. Farming's a bit of sideline these days, well, has been since my grandfather's day. You wouldn't keep this place up on farming. Take the Bardolphs – an estate nearly as old as ours. Owned all the land around your place. Look at them now. Land bought by the Forestry Commission after the Great War: knockdown price. My grandfather bought some of it – a wise move on his part as you'd expect. House sold off: offices of some insurance company. Think the earl sells soft drinks in Canada now. Wouldn't suit me.'

'What's your secret of survival?'

He laughed. 'My great-grandfather saw how the wind was blowing. Invested in a banking company. Then he decided that he didn't want to be merely a sleeping partner. Now it's the family business. Mind you, you wouldn't know. Didn't change the name even when he owned the lot. Suppose he wanted to stay a country gentleman at heart. Kept the name of the founder. Hazenbach's. Heard of it?'

'Oh yes,' I said. 'I certainly have. Geoffrey used to work there. Isn't that a coincidence? Perhaps you remember him?'

He was silent for a moment, then he said, 'Geoffrey Reynolds. How odd. Didn't pick up on it, but I suppose it's not unusual as a name. Never saw him here. Yes, I do remember him. Became a financial journalist, I believe. Let me see. Cambridge, of course. Walwyn, wasn't it?'

I nodded.

'Thought so. Got some good people from there over the years. Dottie's brother is a fellow: it's her side of the family which has the intellectuals, of course. A bit pink as a bunch the dons are. Isn't that so, my dear?'.

'Arthur's politics are nothing to do with me, James darling. Anyway, you've always said that the further left they are at Cambridge, the further right they swing when they leave.' She turned to me. 'This is James putting on his High Tory hat to annoy me. You know how men like to have their little games. The fact that my brother has a bit of a reputation in certain political circles hasn't prevented James and the bank from taking his opinions very seriously over the years – and not only about promising undergraduates either. Perhaps your husband spoke of him. He tends to hold the loyalty of his old students.'

'I'm afraid I don't recall his mentioning him. What is your family name?'

'We're Waddington–Smiths, but typically he never uses his full handle. He's called himself A W S for years. Any joy now?'

I shook my head. 'Geoffrey spoke very little of the past. It's one of the things I miss not knowing about him. How he was when he was a very young man.'

'Well, go and see Arthur. He's got a memory like an elephant for such things. He hasn't much to do these days. Practically retired. Give him my love. Tell him he's welcome to come over to make a further assault on the cellar whenever he feels like it.'

'I might well do that, thank you. It would be most interesting.'

There was a pause, the reason for which was not entirely obvious. I wanted James to go on to talk about Geoffrey. I was about to prompt him, when Dottie, growing suddenly restless, said, 'Shall we move to the drawing room? It's become rather chilly in here.'

The candles in their silver holders were burning low and the fire was almost out. Dottie led the way up the great staircase and we paused briefly whilst James pointed out the portraits of his ancestors which hung there, florid gentlemen on overweight horses.

In contrast, the drawing room was brilliantly lit. The chandeliers had been converted to electricity. It was a huge room: the entire cottage would comfortably have fitted within it. Its walls were covered with yellow silk damask. A vast Turkey carpet covered the floor. It was filled casually with the kind of furniture that was usually protected behind velvet ropes and stern notices not to touch. The unobtrusive servant who had orchestrated the arrival of the meal had left a tray with a silver coffee pot on top of a Boulle cabinet.

I sat down gingerly on the Louis Quinze sofa with my fragile porcelain cup and a glass of brandy.

I had expected the conversation to return to Geoffrey, but it didn't. James seemed to have lost interest in the subject. Instead, curiously, he went back to Michael.

'Bit of a buccaneer, isn't he, your boss?'

'Ex-boss, actually, since a week ago. We had what's known as a policy disagreement.'

'I see. Well, strictly between ourselves, you're lucky to be out of it. McAllister's, I mean. There are all kinds of rumours going around.'

'Rumours?'

Then, maddeningly, from somewhere in the room there was the ringing of a telephone. James smoothly set down his glass and went over to the table in front of the curtained window to answer it. I heard him say, 'Nigel, old chap, hello.' Cupping his hand over the old-fashioned black Bakelite receiver, he stage-whispered apologetically, 'Would you ladies mind awfully if I took this call? In the study, of course. It is rather, er . . .'

Dottie turned to me, raising her eyebrows.

'It's OK by me,' I said.

James put the receiver down and went out.

Dottie made a face. 'I do apologize for him. Business. James doesn't like the servants to answer the house telephone. He says the only people who have that number don't want to waste their time on the butler. And he wouldn't hear of one of those machines.'

I nodded. There was a pause, just awkward enough to confirm my feeling that it had been his idea and not hers that I had been invited.

Then she said, 'I was most awfully sorry to hear about your husband's tragic death. He was quite a young man, I believe.'

'Young enough, I suppose.'

'Yes, how silly of me. One is always too young for . . . that. Have you children?'

'No. We had been married only a short time: less than a year. But I can't say that children would ever have been on the agenda. We both had careers. Or rather, I also had a career.'

'I see. I understand.' There was a hint of frost in her voice.

I rushed to make amends. 'Oh, I didn't mean that children aren't thoroughly demanding and fulfilling and . . .' I floundered to a stop.

She was smiling, a little wanly. 'It's quite all right, Mrs . . . Mary. James and I have no children.'

The matter-of-fact words dropped heavily into the quiet room. I realized why she had bridled at that casual dismissal of motherhood by one still on the right side of the menopause. She had clearly desired it both for itself and to perpetuate the Edwardes dynasty. It must have hurt twice as much – to fail the biological imperative and to see five hundred-odd years of history run into the sand. What a stupid thing for me to have said.

Although I said nothing, my face as always let me down.

'Please don't reproach yourself. It's a long time ago. Of course, James was . . . we were both so dreadfully disappointed. For many years, like Abraham's wife, I hoped for a miracle. But in vain. Nowadays, there are so many things they can do. Too late for me, however.'

'I'm sorry. I didn't realize.'

That's quite all right.

There was another pause. I hoped James would reappear to move the conversation on from being stuck in a place which was beginning to embarrass us both. I had the feeling that she had already said far more than usual, and to a complete stranger. I was getting nervous and my mind was gluing up. For God's sake, why couldn't I say something cool and intelligent?

Breeding will out. She smiled brightly and said, 'How sad you have to leave us like this, before you've got to know us properly. Norfolk's a funny old place. Feudal some people call it, but I prefer to think of it as a place where the old English values are still strong. And nowhere more than here. James takes his responsibilities very seriously, always has.'

'Yes. So I've heard. He has quite a fan in old Norman Fincham.'

'Norman's a good example. His family have lived in Barton St Margaret and worked on the estate for generations. James gives him as much light work as he can. Most of the farmers in the county would regard that as sentimental. And the son. Have you seen the boy?'

I nodded.

'He's a very odd one. Strong and a good worker when he wants to be but so unreliable. Goes off for days at a time, when he's not hanging around the church.'

'He was there yesterday. He showed me the Barton Devil.'

She frowned. 'That awful thing. I've been trying to persuade the bishop to have it removed for years. Put it in the County Museum. He says you can't do that. "Would interfere with the architectural and historical integrity" or some such rot. To my mind, in a Christian place of worship it's a monstrosity. It's quite different in kind from other strange carvings you find in churches: gargoyles and so on. And such a contrast with the angel-roof. Who knows how that sort of thing can affect an impressionable mind?'

I was surprised by her vehemence. Perhaps she felt the weird sculpture did not accord with her description of the old rural values, but contradicted her with silent malignity, the serpent at the heart of Eden, the death's-head at the feast: *Et in Arcadia Ego*.

Then to my even greater surprise she said, 'The son, Tom. You should be careful there, I think.'

I looked at her in amazement. 'Tom? He's only a boy. What do you mean?' Even as I said this, however, I thought back to that earlier afternoon in the church when I had not been so confident.

'I don't like to listen to village gossip, but I hear it nevertheless. There was a suggestion that that young man is not as backward, in a certain department, as it may appear. There was some trouble with one of the village girls – quite a little girl as a matter of fact.'

'And they said Tom . . .?'

'Nothing was ever proved and the family moved away. I daresay the girl was as much to blame. They usually are in my experience as a J. P. The community closed ranks, as they often do in such cases. And then Tom was friendly with the Mallen girl, and some fuss went on there. I believe they left quite soon afterwards. The man had no contact with the village, except the Finchams, and we knew him not at all – a most unsociable man, despite his eminence, so there again nothing definite can be said. But the rumours persist, as rumours do. I mention it only for your own protection, alone in that lonely house, a house that the Fincham boy has been seen hanging about even after the Mallens left.'

I didn't reply, but saw from her change of expression, a mixture of pleasure and relief, that James had come back into the room. 'I'm so sorry about that, Mrs Reynolds. My dear. I'm sure, though, that you ladies have found plenty to talk about.'

I smiled, relieved myself to be free from the rather strained conversation. 'Dottie and I have been discussing the village characters.'

'Jolly good. All human life is there. Not unlike the City, what?'

Dottie put down her coffee cup, went over to her husband and kissed him. 'I can see James is dying to carry on where he left off, but it's late for me. I'm going to bed. No, don't get up. You stay and talk to James. He's in his element. He'll stay up all night if you let him.' She swept out.

James got up from the sofa and threw another log on the fire. He stood with his back to the fireplace, broad-shouldered, his heavy-featured face reddened from drink and the open air. He was the image of the squire, straight out of Fielding or Congreve. I was beginning to realize it was just an image.

He'd not lost the thread of the conversation. 'Yes. Rumours about McAllister's. You know how it is in the City? The whole place operates on what you could politely call confidence. In other words, City people get the wind up very easily. The whole place thrives on gossip – except they call it investment analysis. It doesn't matter how well a company is making its widgets or whatever, or even whether it pays a good fat dividend at the end of the year. It has to look as if it's doing it well. It's hardly ever a question of the product, or future plans or investment – whether they've got anything up their sleeves for tomorrow. No one really cares about that. It's more intangible. Management style: do the investors trust the men at the top? Do they think the accounts tally up properly? Does it feel right? Never mind those damned computers. They're glorified adding machines. It's psychology that matters. If they don't like it, they don't buy. If they don't buy, the shares start to fall. And if that happens, they start to sell. Which makes the shares fall even faster. A matter of confidence. Might make a difference if the MD johnny has his hair too long and his ties too wide.'

'Geoffrey used to say much the same. He thought the Cleopatra's nose theory of history applied particularly well to the Stock Market. If her nose were shorter – or was it longer? – her charms would have been less charming and Caesar and Antony would have stayed pals, not rivals. There wouldn't have been the need for a takeover battle.'

'By Jove, exactly! Neatly put. More brandy?'

I nodded and got a generous slug. It was very pale and very smooth and, no doubt, very, very expensive. It was easy to see that the Edwardses didn't pick up their booze with their groceries. 'Are you saying that the City doesn't like the look of McAllister's? That they've lost confidence?'

'I don't think lost is quite the right word. Never had any is more accurate. Don't trust the man.'

'But Hiram and Hartstein took it over. They're blue chip, aren't they?'

'Of course. That's the whole point.'

'What do you mean? You seem very interested in McAllister's. Why?'

'That's quite a story, but if you're really interested . . .'

'How could I not be?' I said.

Although he had already taken enough liquor to lay out the average toper, James Edwardes had poured himself another glass of brandy. Despite – or maybe because of – the booze he appeared altogether more formidable than he had at the start of the evening. The floridity was now not bucolic but choleric. He looked like one of those eighteenth-century squires who were quite at home commanding a man o'war, or running a slave plantation – or fighting pirates on Treasure Island for that matter. I was rapidly coming to the conclusion that the Lord of the Manor of Barton was a very tough egg indeed.

He motioned with the decanter at my glass. I shook my head. He might be able to drink the stuff like water, but I wanted to make sure I kept my mind clear.

'How much do you know about your ex-boss's business dealings?'

'You mean other than McAllister's? Not much in detail. I knew he had interests in other pies. It wasn't a secret. He used to boast about it. "I'm far more important than you realize", "McAllister's is just a sideline as far as I'm concerned" – that kind of thing.'

'Have you ever wondered why such a man allowed himself to get into the situation of being bailed out by a company like Hiram and Hartstein? A bit humiliating, wasn't it?'

'I guess so, but the company was in trouble. Even Michael had to accept that his ego would suffer an even bigger dent if it went bust. A takeover, or merger as we had to call it, was the lesser evil. Of course, everyone knew the real score. A merger is between approximate equals. With H and H and McAllister's we're talking whales merging with herrings.'

He smiled and drank more brandy. 'So when you arrived at the company, did you find things in a mess? Did it look on its uppers? Did Max Vincent send in the accountants? Did he send in anyone but you?'

'No, I was the only one. Max told me that Michael would retain the day-to-day control as chairman and chief executive. He told me to keep an eye on things. And sure there was a great deal of work to do on the list. I brought in a lot of new stuff. So did Michael.'

'Did the stuff you brought in turn the company round? Did it increase its profitability?'

'What are you getting at? I'm sure it did, in the long term. It looks more like a real publishing house now. Authors with real commitment. Customer loyalty. Brand image. Are you saying I don't know my job?'

He held up a large placatory hand. 'Please. I don't want to sound critical of you in particular. You're obviously very good at your job. But what I am saying is that you are not what industry would call a troubleshooter. You didn't, and weren't asked, to shake the place up, change the management systems, go through the books. Underdown-Metcalfe kept the same control over that as he always had, didn't he?'

I pushed my half-full glass to one side and said, 'Come on. Time to come clean. Why are you so keen on pumping me about McAllister's? I don't believe you're just casually interested.'

He picked up a log from the basket and threw it neatly on to the embers. The dry wood crackled as new flames licked up around it. He turned again to face me.

'You're right, of course. There is a reason. But what I'm going to tell you has to remain absolutely and totally confidential. Do you understand me?'

I nodded. He stared at me, the blue eyes no longer watery but narrowed and hard.

'I can keep a secret,' I said. 'Some women can, you know.'

He pursed his lips in acknowledgement. 'All right. As you might expect, Hazenbach's is a bit of a force in the City. I'm not boasting. I don't need to. Anyone in the know will tell you that

Hazenbach's is one hundred per cent copper-bottomed solid. We've never had a bad debt, never been involved in anything remotely, er, dodgy as they used to say. I've made it my business to keep that tradition. I may not be the world's most imaginative banker, but I think I've been around long enough to spot a wrong 'un. And when Mr Underdown-Metcalfe came to me with his so-called partnership deal with Hiram and Hartstein, I showed him the door. All right, he went to a competitor. We lost the business. But I was convinced that it was not all it was cracked up to be.'

'Why on earth did you think that?'

'Partly instinct, partly what I already knew about the man. You see – and I remind you of your agreement – when I'm not running the bank I have another hat as the chairman of a Stock Exchange committee which keeps an eye on trouble which might be developing among our members and which might reflect badly on the Exchange or on the City as a whole. I need hardly say we don't advertise our existence or our proceedings. Officially we don't even exist, so sensitive is the information we have to deal with. There was already a thick file about the activities of Underdown-Metcalfe and his other companies.

'There are dozens of them. The whole thing is so complicated I don't think anyone understands it, probably not even him. They're all ultimately owned by various trusts in every tax haven you can think of. Our information showed that a few years before one of his companies had made a major investment in a media project – the details don't matter – an investment which had caused an extensive international borrowing requirement. Because it was speculative, there weren't any fixed assets – land, buildings – to use as collateral for the loans. But the company did have investments, which were duly pledged against the loans. Do you know what those were?'

I shrugged. 'I've no idea.'

'Shares. Mainly in McAllister's plc. And the loan facility was linked to the value of those shares. The worse those shares perform, the less collateral they provide. If they fall in value the banks start to agitate for repayment. And if they agitate for repayment –'

'Then Michael has a lot of worries. Presumably the original loans have long since been used.'

'Not only that. Our information is that the original speculation was a failure. At that point the whole venture was on a knife edge. Underdown-Metcalfe was threatened with catastrophe. McAllister's shares were not only not increasing in value, they were going down rapidly. For the reason I mentioned earlier: the fact that Underdown-Metcalfe was the chief executive. The shares consistently underperformed, no matter what the profitability of the company. And it was quite profitable, you know, compared with most of its competitors. But the people who held the shares, the institutions, the pension funds and banks, didn't trust him. He was a man from nowhere who might be going back there quickly.'

'And so the merger with H and H came at a very good time.'

'Yes, indeed. It stimulated the market. The connection was perceived to be beneficial by the investing institutions. The share price went up. Then, after all the excitement, the parties involved gave out that the association had been satisfactorily concluded. H and H had become a substantial shareholder in McAllister's and would be closely involved in the day-to-day management of its investment.'

'And that also increased the value of the shares his other companies had used as collateral for their loans? Took the heat off him there?'

'Naturally. All ended happily, what?'

'But as I told you earlier none of that happened. I was the only person who came in from the States. I didn't have any say in the financial management. Max said that was being left to Michael.'

'So?'

I thought carefully, then I said, 'So I think what you're saying is that the so-called merger between H and H and McAllister's didn't happen in the way it appeared. I think you're saying it was a scam.'

'I'm not saying anything, my dear Mrs Reynolds. Merely thinking aloud. It could have happened that way. If Underdown-

Metcalfe could have found a willing collaborator – conspirator is perhaps the more legalistic term – to buy shares on the pretext of a linkage with the company, then it would have been of some benefit to him, got him out of a nasty pickle. Everything else could have been managed, or massaged. Records, registers, what have you. Don't forget, a great deal of what happens in the legal and financial world is done on trust. And trust is always open to abuse.'

'But what was in it for Hiram and Hartstein? Why buy shares at an inflated price in a company they weren't actually going to control?'

'No doubt their shareholders would have the same question. If that had happened knowingly, it might well have been a fraudulent use of the company's funds.'

'So why would Max agree to it? What was in it for him? Money?'

James shrugged. 'Why not? Was he then a rich man? I doubt it. He had an enormous salary and the trappings of a modern corporate chief executive, but that could have gone at any time. Hired, fired. Isn't that the way of American business, any business for that matter? Look at yourself. I think money, enough money, would have been a powerful motive. And my, er, speculations would mean that a great deal of money was at stake. Underdown-Metcalfe's whole fortune, in fact. He would have paid handsomely. There was undoubtedly a great deal of risk for both of them. It is, as I've said, pretty near to being a criminal conspiracy to defraud both companies, not to mention the banks involved. But Underdown-Metcalfe is the sort of fellow who sails close to the wind as second nature. There are plenty of other things he's been up to. Everybody knows that. Between you and me, he's not out of the wood yet.'

He went to the drinks table, picked up the brandy decanter and unasked refilled my glass. He sat down on the sofa opposite and sipped his own drink reflectively before setting it down on the table.

I drank off the snifter he poured in record time. It was a crime to gulp such lovely stuff down. It burned my throat and lit a fire in my stomach. I needed it to handle the mixture of emotions which swept through my mind like tidal waves. Most powerful of these was anger. Anger that I had been somehow, if ever so distantly, part of a shady deal. Anger that I had been so dumb as not to realize my role: not only the token woman, but the token H and H executive. I saw it now. Max, the rotten slimy bastard, had sent the one person he thought was stupid enough – or at best innocent enough of corporate wiles – not to smell a rat. While I was beavering away thinking I had been sent to rescue an ailing company through my editorial expertise, I was just the icing on the cake of some swindle. It exemplified what I had always believed was the male attitude to business – that it was gigantic paper game. That the real lives of the real people concerned counted for nothing against the numbers flashing on the screens of the dealers on the Stock Exchange, or lined up in those glossy annual reports which were better fiction than I had ever published.

My head was beginning to ache. But I hadn't lost track of what he hadn't yet told me.

'How do you know this? What is that stuff about "our information"? And why are you telling me?'

He smiled, and picked up his glass, holding it up to the light as if studying the pale amber liquid. 'A shrewd question, my dear . . . Mary, if I may. I have to confess that at the start of this evening, I had no intention of doing any such thing. However, as the matter of McAllister's and its chairman and chief executive is, so to speak, on my plate at the moment, then the fact that you were formerly well acquainted with the company struck me as being an opportunity not to be missed. Which brings me back to your first question. I've probably said already more than I should. However, on the strict understanding that what I tell you shall go no further than this room, yes, I do have what appears to be "inside information". But it comes from an anonymous source.'

I stared at him. 'Hey, if you're thinking it's to do with me, then you've got the wrong person. I don't know anything about these financial shenanigans, nor do I have any idea whom your info came from.'

'Forgive me if I've been jumping to conclusions. Too much brandy. It just struck me that . . . well, if not yourself, then someone close to you –'

'What?' The word burst out more loudly that I had meant, but I was reeling from the implication. 'You mean Geoffrey?'

He raised his hands in a conciliatory gesture. 'I'm sorry. As I said, it's a rash inference on no evidence. After all, I can't imagine that your husband ever had any contact with Underdown-Metcalfe, other than through you.'

I couldn't stop myself from blurting it out, the wound it had made was still raw. 'Actually, he did. Michael told me he knew him. But that was to do with something else, some other project. One more damn thing I knew nothing about.'

'I see. But might this "other project" have been simply a way of getting close to his subject?'

I shook my head. 'I don't know. I don't know what Geoffrey was doing. It makes my head ache, this business. He never spoke to me of any of it. How can I tell whether what you're saying is true? I was only his wife, for God's sake.'

'Forgive me, my dear. It's late. I've overstepped the mark. Forget what I've said. About Underdown-Metcalfe, and this talk of your late husband. I'm sorry. I won't mention it again. Please.'

He refilled my glass. 'You know, before you leave, you really must see more of the country. That track we met on yesterday: it's an old drove road. Goes all the way to the coast. The Herdsman's Way, they call it. And there's another splendid walk down to the River Gar.'

He seemed suddenly more relaxed. I suppose by then the brandy had done its work. I started to make polite noises about leaving, but he carried on talking.

I suppose even a grandee likes to ramble a little in his cups in front of a compliant – and dare I say attractive? – audience.

'All evening we've been discussing this fellow Underdown-Metcalfe, but who is he? What sort of a name is that anyway? He made it up, I'll be bound. Came from nowhere, didn't he? And that's where he'll end up. Gone without a trace. That's what's wrong with this country, you know, my dear. Too many fellows like that running things. Chaps with no stake. Mushroom men. Now you see 'em, now you don't. We Edwardeses, we've been here in Norfolk since the fourteenth century. Sir Richard Edwardes, the first baronet, was a soldier, a mercenary if you like.' He chuckled. 'A soldier of fortune, a *condottiere*. The Italians called him Il Corvo Bianco, the White Crow. When he came home, he was granted these lands by Richard the Second. He came up by his bootstraps, if you like, but, by God, he started something that lasted. That's what I call a stake in the country. We've held and added to those estates and they've descended in the unbroken male line.'

I said nothing, remembering what Dottie had told me. The fire in under the ornate white stone mantel had burnt away to glowing ash.

'That's finished now. I've got a cousin in Australia, some damned place like Coonawarra, not even on the bloody map. He'll inherit – or his children. They've no stake either. It'll be the end. The estate'll be sold off. The bloody National Trust sniffed at the house. Not quite grand enough for those poofs. Be an hotel or some damn thing. The bank'll go public. The other directors have been pushing me on that already. So in ten, twenty years' time, the best part of six hundred years of history will have gone.' He poured himself another glass of brandy.

I remained silent, not wanting to interrupt his mood, fascinated.

He said nothing for several minutes. He seemed to have sunk in upon himself as he leant forward, his arms upon his knees, even though his massive frame filled the gilded sofa.

He started to talk again and this time his voice was almost a whisper. He seemed to have forgotten I was there. I had to strain my ears to hear him.

'Maybe not. Maybe not. For years I thought like that. I thought my only contribution was to be the last of the Edwardeses. But then I saw that I too could add my brick to history's pile. In the past, it was land. My great-grandfather saw that wasn't going to last. He saw the change, how the world wanted not fields and woods and houses but capital. Free-flowing capital. Capital would define the world of the nineteenth century and the coming world of the twentieth. And he took a risk on his perception, and won handsomely. But what's the word that defines our future? Energy. That's what will drive the world to come. Not land. Not capital. Energy.' His voice faded even lower. 'To harness a source of energy to outlast all others. The race for that would be worth any number of risks.'

13

I was awake. It was still dark: the illuminated figures on the digital alarm clock read two-thirty. As I lay there, I remembered waking with Geoffrey beside me those long months ago. I remembered what I had done, and a feeling of warm and longing tenderness suffused me. I reached out to the empty space beside me, the cool sheet, the undented pillow. Then the feeling faded and the inner emptiness returned, together with another. Fear.

Normally I was a sound sleeper. I had grown used to the night noises both of the city and the country. I had instantly remembered the earlier waking because that too in itself was an unusual and memorable event, not only on account of what had followed. But now I was alone, and my thought was of why I had woken, whether there was some cause which had broken through the solid crust of my sleep. So I lay in the profound blackness of the curtained room, my whole body stiffened and tense and my ears attuned to catch the slightest noise.

I lay like that according to the slowly blinking figures of the clock for ten minutes, gradually relaxing, the darkness growing less impenetrable as my eyes adjusted and the familiar objects in the room resolved into grey phantoms of themselves. I was about to turn over and prepare for sleep again when I heard it. It came not as I had imagined from below, but from above.

It was the sound of crying. A dry, harsh sobbing which rose and fell in pitch, a low murmur of sound which built into an anguished keening before subsiding. I listened with pounding heart and dry mouth, realizing that I was not imagining it, that it was no trick of the wind, my mind struggling to remain in control as a wave of abject atavistic terror rose within, leaving my body ice cold and trembling, the roots of my hair crackling in my scalp as if alive with electricity.

Then, as suddenly as it had begun, it ceased. I willed myself to breathe deeply, flooding my lungs and warming my frozen muscles. My brain functioned at last. It told me again what I had told myself and believed in since early childhood: that the dark of itself held no terrors; that it was only the human mind which conjured spirits from its own deepest recesses. That whatever or whoever was making that noise was animate like myself. I breathed in this knowledge to control my shivering limbs. Gradually reason reasserted itself.

What to do? There was no phone to call the cops, and even if there had been they probably wouldn't have arrived until long after the grisly event, if there were to be one, had taken place. More relevantly, if I were about to be murdered or raped or both I sure as hell wasn't going to lie around waiting for it to happen. I should go down to the car and get the hell out of there.

But I remembered what Sherlock Holmes would have called the curious case of the electric light. Then I had been determined to track down the practical joker, if that's what it was. On this occasion, too, as then, a sense of annoyance was growing. The sound of weeping was not, as things go, very threatening. I was damned if I was going to run away from it.

The decision made, I slid out of bed quietly. I slipped on my robe from the back of the door and then fumbled around for a pair of pumps. I was hardly bullet proof. I was shivering uncontrollably. With cold, I said to myself. I thought desperately whether the contents of the room included anything like a weapon. No, I hadn't gotten round to keeping a shotgun under the bed. I didn't even have a rape alarm, not that anyone would hear it out there. In default of anything else to hand I took a wooden coat hanger out of the wardrobe. I gently turned the knob of the bedroom door, and on tiptoe moved on to the still uncarpeted boards of the landing.

I could see fairly well. Starlight shone through the stairway window, glimmering on the edges of the wooden treads. To my right rose the small winding staircase which gave access to the attic. It was from there that the noise had come.

I'd never given the attic more than a cursory inspection. It was empty of furniture or other objects, dusty and infested with spiders. It had remained quite uncolonized: having nothing to store, I had never even used it for storage. Quite what purpose it was being put to now I would soon discover.

I mounted the first stair, which gave out a protesting wooden groan. I stopped to listen, but from the white-painted door which glowed almost as if phosphorescent at the head of the flight there came no sound. Clutching the coat hanger, I went boldly on.

I paused only momentarily to take a breath before gripping the cold brass of the doorknob, turning it, and throwing open the door.

A blast of colder air, smelling of dust and damp and mould, swept over me. There was a light in there. I registered it as the weak light of a torch before there was a wordless exclamation, a scuffling sound, a click and it was extinguished.

In the dark I was at an advantage. My eyes quickly picked out in the surrounding greyness a darker human shape, crouching low like an animal on the floor in the middle of the room.

My anger broke through my curtain of fear. 'What the hell do you think you're doing?' I yelled. 'And who are you anyway?'

The figure arose from its kneeling position. 'I'm awful sorry, missus, really,' it said. 'Please don't get me sent to prison.'

'You realize you practically frightened me to death,' I said angrily for the umpteenth time. 'What a stupid, selfish thing to do, creeping about like that in the middle of the night.'

Tom was slumped forward at the kitchen table, his head cradled on his arms, the mug of tea I had given him steaming untouched before him. I stood, my arms folded, my robe tightly fastened, my back against the range warming my cold rear end.

'You've done this before, haven't you? It was you fiddling

about with the lights that time just after we moved in. It was you who left the back door open the very first weekend we were here, wasn't it? You've been spying on us, on me, haven't you, ever since we came here? You've been here, in the house, creeping about all the time. What was it? Did you get some kick out of watching us? What are you, some kind of pervert? I've a good mind to get the police in. What would your parents think about all this?'

This last remark finally provoked some response. He raised his head. His eyes were wet behind his dirty spectacles and big tears had gouged runnels of cleanness down his dust-smeared cheeks. His nose was full of yellowish snot. He sniffed hard, and wiped it on his anorak sleeve. 'No, please. It's not like that. Don't tell my mam, or my dad. Please don't. My dad, he'd kill me. And my mam, she couldn't bear it, honest. Please don't tell her. If I got sent to prison, I don't know what she'd do. She'd never speak to me again.' He started crying once more, great gasping, hysterical sobs like a child, burying his face into the crook of his arms.

'Please stop it, Tom. I don't know what to do. What would you do if you found someone roaming about your house in the middle of the night? Wouldn't you think they were at the very least going to burgle you? Am I supposed just to let you go?'

'It isn't like that, I tell you.' His voice was muffled by the thick folds of the anorak. 'I wasn't doing no harm. I wasn't going to take none of your things. You haven't got nothing I want. I wasn't going to hurt you. I didn't try to hurt you or run away when you found me, did I? I could have. I'm dead strong.' His face emerged. There was an odd look in his eyes. A kind of pride seemed to flicker beneath their watery dullness as he said these things. He wasn't quite so cowed any more. He seemed to sense my uncertainty, my lack of natural command in the situation. Someone like James Edwardes would have had him horsewhipped or in a police cell by now, no messing.

The truth was that I was inclined to believe him. Whatever he had been doing in the attic seemed in a queer way not to involve me. He had shown no antagonism towards me as I had ordered him downstairs and sat him in the kitchen. Despite his obvious fear of the police and the family disgrace of prison, I wasn't sure whether what he had been doing was even criminal. It was certainly suspicious, but at that moment I was less concerned to punish him than find out what he had been doing and why he had been doing it. The James Edwardes approach would never have attained that.

I moved away from the range and took a seat opposite him at the kitchen table. 'Drink up your tea,' I said in a more relaxed and kinder tone. 'It'll get cold.' I hoped I sounded like his mother.

He obeyed literally, taking the mug in his brown hands, the skin of which was flaky like the scales of a fish. His fingernails were bitten to the quick and ingrained with dirt. He drank the tea in big anxious gulps, then set the empty mug back on the table. He looked at me, like a dog awaiting his next command, but now with a dog's confidence that he would not be beaten. Not yet, anyway.

'Tom. I'll agree that what happened tonight goes no further. On one condition. That you swear to me you weren't here to rob me or hurt me or spy on me, and that you tell me the truth about what you were doing.'

'You mean you won't tell my mam or dad or get the police on to me?'

'Not if you do what I said. Swear you weren't doing anything bad, and tell me what you were up to. I think I have a right to know.'

He nodded. 'I'll tell you. I swear I weren't up to nothing bad. I weren't going to do no stealing or nothing like that. And I wouldn't hurt you, missus. I wouldn't ever do nothing like that, not to you, not anybody.'

'Cross your heart and hope to die?'

He moved his arms clumsily across his chest. 'Cross my heart and hope to die.'

I nodded, satisfied by the formalities of the oath. He seemed enough of a child to be bound by it. I couldn't be sure he'd ever heard of the Bible, and besides, I didn't have one handy. 'Now, Tom, tell me about it.'

'It's because of Lucy.' His eyes swivelled to the table, apparently engrossed by a study of the wood grain.

'Lucy?' The word leapt out, searing my throat which had all at once gone dry.

'Lucy Mallen, the girl what lived here. We, she and I, used to go up in that attic. She said it were her special place. A secret place. She had her things up there. Dolls and that. She'd play with them. And she'd tell me stories, and she'd read to me. She could read real good. I was never any good at reading. But I like stories.'

'When was this, Tom?'

'In the school holidays. She went away to school somewhere, but when she was home I'd come round.'

'With your dad sometimes, when he came to work?'

'That was when I first got to know her. I thought she was going to make fun of me, because her dad was one of the high-ups and she went to a posh school, but she weren't like that. She weren't like the kids at the school I went to. They were always making mock of me because I were stupid and clumsy, but she just said, "Tom. That's a nice name. I know we're going to be friends."'

'So you used to play dolls in the attic?' I must have sounded slightly incredulous, because he blushed.

'You must think I'm daft. I suppose I am. I liked being there. She were friendly and kind to me. And I liked the stories she told me.' He looked closely at me. 'I know what you're thinking, but it weren't nothing else. Never. She were a little girl. Honestly.'

'OK, Tom. I believe you.'

He became agitated as he had before in the church. 'There weren't anything. No dirty stuff. My mam told me about that and how bad it was. Honest, I swear. That was what he said. I told you I never, but she got took away and because of me.' He started sobbing again.

I leaned over and grabbed his arm, shaking it gently. 'Tom, it's all right. I do believe you. Please.' I didn't know what I believed, though, as I watched this strange half-child, half-man. Eventually he stopped sobbing.

'When she got took away, I kept on coming back. I sort of

pretended she were still here. I'd talk to her just like I used to. I could tell her things I couldn't tell nobody else.'

'But how did you get in?'

'I knew there was a back door key hanging in the woodshed. I used that.' He hoisted up the anorak and fumbled in the pocket of his jeans. 'Here it is. I shan't be needing it no more, shall I?'

I picked up the heavy iron key from the table. 'No, you won't. I don't want you coming here any more uninvited, Tom. Do you understand?'

His eyes were downcast once more, the spark of defiance extinguished. 'I'm sorry, Missus Reynolds. It were only because I liked her, you know. Do you think I'll ever see her again? Dad said you said they went to America. Do you think she might come back and visit?'

'I don't know, Tom. I really don't know, but I hope you will.'

He gave a shy smile, his eyes meeting mine for a brief moment. Then he started mumbling again.

'What was that, Tom?' I leant over the table to hear him better.

'It's about being here, missus. I weren't going to tell you. I haven't told anyone. I were too scared. But seeing as you've let me off, and if you don't say it was me what said anything, then I could tell you if you wanted.'

'Tell me what, Tom?' I was getting tired and felt impatient that this boy was still here. 'Is it something else about Lucy?'

He shook his head. 'I were here that night, the night your husband were here by himself.'

I was so startled I knocked over my half-empty mug of tea. The brown liquid spread out in a thin film on the white scrubbed table top until it reached the crack where the planks butted together. I could hear the steady drip as it splashed through on to the brick floor.

I reached out and gripped the ragged sleeve of his anorak. 'Tom, I do want you to. You must tell me. It's very important. Please.'

'I didn't know he was going to be here. I came after Mam and Dad had gone to bed. They always go about nine o'clock. I saw the car, and the lights on. It were getting real windy then, quite an old storm blowing up. I looked through the window there, and he was here eating his dinner. There wasn't going to be any way I could get in till after he'd gone to bed, so I went round the back to sit in the woodshed a while to wait. I hadn't been there long when I heard the car.'

'Geoffrey's car? Had he gone out?'

'I thought he had, so I came round the side to the door. But it were another car. It stopped in front of the house and didn't have no lights on. I saw Mr Reynolds get up from the table in a bit of a hurry and go into the passage. So I waited a bit and then went round the outside to the front. Mr Reynolds was talking to this bloke from the other car.'

'Who was he? Did you see what he looked like?'

'No, it were too dark. He was big, like your husband, with a dark sort of jacket. That's all I could see.

'Then Mr Reynolds started shouting at him, using bad words. I didn't see what happened then, but I think Mr Reynolds must have pushed the other bloke, because he was on the ground and Mr Reynolds was in his car with his lights on and he revved up the engine and drove off. Then the other bloke got into his car and drove off after him. That's all I saw. I got real scared and ran off home by the back lane through the wood. Then my dad told me at teatime the next day that he'd been found, dead like, and the policeman Dad talked to in the shop said it looked like he had a wonky heart.'

'So you didn't tell the police.'

'No fear, beg pardon, missus. I'd get put in prison, wouldn't I? They wouldn't believe me. They'd say I frightened Mr Reynolds to death. They'd say I was trying to rob him or something. Them old police, make you say anything, they would.'

His words gave me a cold chill. I looked at him as he wiped snot from his nose with the edge of his sleeve, his pale eyes staring at the table, his thick calloused forefinger with its bitten dirt-encrusted nail tracing the raised whorls of the wood grain.

Did I believe him? Did I believe any of it? Oh, I believed he had been here. Why would he invent that? But the rest? Underneath the dim exterior, there was a child's imagination. And if a child felt guilty about what he had done, he would quickly invent a third party to take the blame.

Odd, though, that the story chimed with Anna's version of what might have happened. But neither of them could provide the who or the why. And why should a mysterious interloper cause my husband's death?

I felt suddenly afraid, afraid of having this uncertain being in the same house with me. Afraid and tired and confused. But I couldn't show my fear.

'Thank you for telling me that, Tom. I think it's very important. I want you to go home now and think about whether, in spite of what you said, you'd come to the police station with me tomorrow, to tell them what you've just told me. It would help me a lot, and it couldn't get you into trouble. I'm quite sure you haven't done anything wrong.' I saw his expression become anxious. I held up my hand. 'Don't say anything now. We'll both sleep on it and talk about it tomorrow, eh?' I gave an encouraging smile.

He scrambled to his feet, his haste to be gone apparently as great as mine to be rid of him.

I watched his lanky figure lope across the clearing, now infused with the white mist-laden light of dawn, until he vanished where the track hid him among the looming trees. This time I made sure the doors were bolted as well as locked, and the catches on the windows secured. I looked at my watch. It was four a.m. I went back to my cold bed and finally fell into a restless sleep.

I was awake again at seven with a headache, the sort of headache that seems destined to nag away for the rest of the day. I swallowed paracetamol and drank three cups of coffee. As the warm chemical claws gripped my temples, the pain abandoned my forehead and retreated to its lair at the back of my skull, reminding me by its dully glowering presence that it would soon return.

The key was still in the pocket of my robe. I took it out and tossed it on the kitchen table. Had I done the right thing in the early hours? Was there a right thing? And what else could I have done? Turning Tom over to the police so they could get what they would out of him still seemed a worse option than the one I had chosen: to persuade him voluntarily to tell his story, such as it was. Unless, of course, he had been lying and he was not really a simpleton but a sophisticated criminal deviant who would return to make me regret my leniency. I had taken a chance, it was true. But the whole of life was chance, as I was finding out, since my carefully constructed world had fallen apart.

There was yet another thing about the business with Tom. Something which he hadn't mentioned. Something which I daresay he hoped I hadn't noticed. But I had. I had seen him bending over some object in the attic. It might have been a small box. He hadn't had anything like that with him when he came down the stairs, and it wasn't something he could have concealed in his clothing. Therefore it must be still up there, presumably in a hiding place. Even slow-witted Tom could keep a secret. It wouldn't take me long to find out what it was. I could do that before I went looking for him again.

Again I opened the small white door. The same smell wafted out, but this time the air was warmer from the morning sun which shone in a shaft of light through the small-paned dormer window. Dust motes danced around me. The ridge of the roof was high enough for me to stand upright, but progress at the sides was limited by the massive purlins, more like raw tree trunks than finished timbers, the ancient bark still adhering in places. Everywhere were the pincushion holes of woodworm. I sighed. Yet one more thing Geoffrey and I had not bothered to do anything about in our single-minded pursuit of rural bliss.

It was the ideal den for a child, who could move unhindered under the low beams almost to the eaves, where there were mysterious shadows and hiding places in abundance.

Yes, indeed. But Tom had been crouching in the centre of the room when I had surprised him. I got down on hands and knees and stared hard at the rough boards.

It didn't take long to find it. One of the boards was loose. I prised it up with a knife I fetched from the kitchen. In the recess, on top of the lath and plaster of the bedroom ceiling below, was a cardboard shoe box. I lifted it out.

Inside was Tom's pathetic collection of mementoes. A crayon drawing, crudely done but recognizably of Tom with his arm around a black and white dog. The unfortunate Ruff, presumably. A small doll in some unknown national costume. Some pebbles. A snail shell. A few brownish dry scraps, once flowers. A small leather purse, empty. A girl's shoe, much scuffed, the sole worn through. An imitation silver bracelet, the clasp broken. A red Alice band. And at the very bottom an envelope, unaddressed and unstamped.

I hesitated before opening it. I already felt slightly ashamed of myself, probing amongst these remnants. Why was I doing it? I told myself I was looking for some clue as to what I had begun to feel was a genuine mystery surrounding the whereabouts of Lucy Mallen. But how much of that was generated by my own over-active imagination, fuelled by grief at my loss? Certainly these odds and ends, saved by Tom or which he had found in the empty house after she had left, were of no assistance in that respect, merely conveying an indescribable sense of the inevitable sadness of all human relationships.

I opened the envelope, the flap of which appeared never to have been sealed. She had presumably left it here for him. The note inside was undated and read simply:

Dear Boy,

I can hear them coming for me. I'm sorry not to be able to say goodbye. I can't say any more now. One day I'll come back to see you, promise. Here is a photo I took for you to keep.

Love, Lucy.

It was a small, square, colour photograph, obviously taken by one of those Polaroid cameras. It was rather dark and fuzzy, as if the young photographer's hand had shaken as she pressed the shutter.

Beneath a window with closed curtains was a child's narrow bed, obviously Lucy's. On the red-spotted coverlet sat an assortment of the soft toys you can find in any child's room. I could make out in the shadows a large and rather battered-looking teddy bear, a fluffy red squirrel with beady black eyes, a floppy clown with the stuffing bursting from one arm, a black and orange striped silly-faced Tigger. The animals were positioned in a tableau on either side of a doll lying wrapped closely in a voluminous white lace-trimmed shawl – which might at one time have been a tablecloth – as though paying her court. Arranged in front of the doll on the bed were sprays of some white flower, and on the part of the shawl which covered the doll's head was a small chaplet of blue forget-me-nots.

I stared at the photograph in my hand. What did it mean, this odd and touching arrangement? From what childish fancy had it proceeded? I moved over to hold the photograph in the full light of the sun streaming through the dormer window. As I looked more closely and saw the doll's tiny red face and sleeping eyes, I felt my heart contract within my breast with surprise and shock. For standing there in that dusty attic, it came to me that it was not a doll. It was a baby.

Part Three

14

Loaded down on each side with Sainsbury's carrier bags, I trudged through the drizzle the hundred yards from where I had had to park the car to the entrance to my apartment block. I ought to get rid of the BMW, or at least buy something smaller and cheaper to run. That would be the logical thing to do, but what price were memories, even those enshrined in a lump of painted tin?

Still, even memories had to give way to economic logic at some stage. Doing the shopping reminded me of that. Canned tuna. Cheapo blended butter. Lentils. Lentils, for God's sake! It was like a food parcel from Oxfam. Maybe I was overdoing the austerity thing, but from the day I had been fired the phone had never started ringing.

It wasn't that there hadn't been work around. I had heard of jobs going, but they weren't offered to me. It took a little while before the penny dropped. Not only was I not flavour of the month, I was a banned susbstance. A little bird – actually a big, fat, dirty old crow – had been going around whispering nasty things about me, my competence and my loyalty. Employ this woman at your peril had been the message. And such was his influence that no one had yet dared to risk the wrath to come.

I couldn't prove a thing. And even if I could, what could I do about it? Michael was so well known to the learned friends of the Inner Temple, and had such unlimited resources to set them in motion, that a feeble little threat from me would be doomed from the start. Equality before the law? That was a good joke. What I couldn't figure was why he was doing this. Did he really want to drive me into the gutter? Could it really be because of that scene of yesteryear? It seemed incredible that he would carry that minor humiliation with him still. After all, it was I who was the victim. Or was it something else which I had only now begun to figure out?

Whatever the reason, the campaign had worked so far. Even with reasonably careful housekeeping, the compensation money was not going to last a whole lot longer. Then I would have to scrub floors, or worse.

However, I reflected as I drank a cup of coffee – instant, and supermarket brand at that – it seemed more than likely from what I had heard during the after-dinner conversation at Barton House that the forces of Nemesis might even then be gathering about the head of my ex-boss. I took, forgivably I think, a little schadenfreude in the prospect.

I made myself another cup of the horrible coffee. James Edwardes had more or less told me that Geoffrey had been the anonymous informant – and who better? Geoffrey had the contacts and the skills to tease out that sort of information. Had that been why he had gotten into bed with Michael? It was certainly the implication. I remembered also Geoffrey's cryptic words to me on that last day. It could be interpreted as a warning that the temple was going to come crashing down on top of Samson. But what of the other things I had stumbled on? What about the connection with Julian Mallen? Where was Julian Mallen? Where was Julian Mallen's daughter – and her baby?

I had come back to London to get away from these insistent questions, but try as I might I could not. My mind returned continually to that morning in the dusty attic only a few days before.

I had stared at the photograph for a long time. There was no mistake. The tiny wizened face was human flesh and blood.

There was a point being made to the intended recipient of the photograph. She was saying: look at what has happened. Look at what you're responsible for.

There could be no doubt. There was the letter, addressed to 'Dear Boy', a child's affectionate nickname for the childish young man who spent his time roaming the woods and fields. Whatever Tom had said, whatever I had understood him to have said, he had to be the father of the tiny person in the shawl. Neither he nor Lucy had probably understood what they were about. How strange it was that an act performed thus, not rehearsed and possibly not repeated, could give rise to yet one more human being. A few clumsy fumblings – and here was a person. No skill needed for this piece of creativity. No skill at all.

I laid down the square of glossy paper. I had a queer ache in my bosom and a dryness in my throat. I felt as if I were about to burst into tears. But my tears would be not just for Lucy. They would be for myself.

I had parked the car outside the Finchams' cottage, opened the gate and banged on the peeling paintwork of the front door. There was silence, so I knocked again, harder. This time a net curtain twitched at one of the front windows and after a few moments Norman stood on the threshold. He looked even more rumpled and crumpled than usual, his habitual corduroy trousers bagged and worn at the knees, his check shirt unbuttoned halfway to his belly revealing his extraordinarily luxuriant grey chest hair – fur, one might say – which puffed out of the gap like the coat of a badger. He yawned and, realizing his undress, pulled the shirt together and hastily buttoned it to his chin.

'Beg pardon, missus, I was taking a bit of an old nap. On the settee, like.' His china blue eyes squinted into mine, attempting to read my expression, whether I brought gifts or trouble and no doubt preparing a disavowal if it were the latter. 'Is it about the gardening, then?' he said finally.

'No, there's no problem. I just wanted to have a quick word with Tom. If he's around, that is.'

Norman nodded, as if my having a word with Tom were an everyday occurrence. His big brown paw opened and took hold of his chin, giving it a thorough rub around so that the rasp of the white stubble on his work hardened-palm was quite audible.

'Ah, now, I can't say he is at the present. This being Sat'day, 'twouldn't be his day at the big house so he's usually around hereabouts, but I can't say as I've seed him today. No, I don't believe I have.'

'You mean not since breakfast time?'

He laughed, displaying more than usual of the yellow broken teeth. 'Breakfast time, missus? Like them people on the telly? That's a good one. I'm out long before any breakfast if I'm working. I has my breakfast in the field. If I'm not working, I don't deserve no breakfast.' He laughed again, making me feel like a naïve sociological investigator from a different planet.

I persisted, though, determined not to be diverted by Norman's rustic version of the sort of stuff they taught you on management courses. 'So when is he back, then?'

He shrugged. 'Now you're asking. He goes off sometimes, then he comes back. Always has. Like an old cat, that boy is, sometimes, missus. What you want him for then anyways?' As he said this his eyes narrowed into chips of blue glass.

'Oh, nothing really. I had a couple of questions – about the church. I thought he might be able to help.'

'I'll tell him you was after him, then, shall I, missus? I'll get him to come round, shall I?'

A little too hastily, I said, 'No. Don't bother about that. It's not important. I'll catch him when I'm next in the village.'

His eyes were still boring into mine. Then dropping his gaze, he said, 'Right you are then, missus,' and shuffled back into his house like old Mr Brock.

I was getting into the car when a low-slung fifties-looking sports convertible, the top down, growled up alongside and stopped. A voice I vaguely recognized said: 'Well, hi there.'

I turned to meet the grey eyes of the landlord of the Coopers Arms. He had hoisted himself athletically out of the leather bucket seat without troubling to open the tiny half-door and stood facing me across the open cockpit of his machine. What was his name! 'Hello, er,' I mumbled, closing the door and leaning against the warm metal of the BMW.

'Ross. Ross Earle. I heard about your husband. I'm sorry.'

'Thanks. He would have been a good customer for the pub.'

He nodded, then dropped his eyes as if studying the big chrome-edged dials of his dashboard. 'Maybe you're feeling more up to dropping in some time?'

'I'm afraid not. I'm rather busy at present. I'm here only a few days. I'm putting the house on the market.' I don't know why I volunteered this piece of information. It wasn't any of his business.

'Uhuh. That's a pity, but you being on your own that place is kind of remote. Not everyone would feel comfortable there. Particularly after –'

'That's never bothered me.' I rather snapped this at him. I hated getting the little woman treatment from this guy.

He gave me a big disarming grin. 'No, I guess you're not the nervous type. Me, I'm scared of the dark.'

He stood there a moment more, as if he expected me to say something to continue the conversation.

I said, 'Well, I've got be going. Lots of things to do. Goodbye.' I turned and wrenched open the car door, climbed in and banged it shut.

He didn't move but waited calmly for me to drive off.

I turned the key to start the engine. The starter motor whirred, but nothing else happened. I tried again. Oh, shit. Woman proposes but machine disposes. Once more I flicked the key, grinding my teeth, letting the whirring go on and on.

He came over to stand by the open driver's window.

'Sounds like you've got a problem.'

I turned back the key and looked up at him, blushing furiously.

'Maybe I should take a look?'

'OK . . . Thanks, ' I added belatedly.

He slid into the driver's seat, twiddled with the choke and pushed at the pedals. He briefly fired the starter. Nothing.

'How do you open the hood?'

I stared at him blankly. I wasn't the type who went to women's car-care classes in dungarees. 'I don't know. I guess I've never –'

He ducked down under the dash and poked about, finally finding a lever to pull. The hood gave a click and popped up an inch. 'There she is.'

With the hood up, he pulled and prodded at various bits of the engine. I stood, helplessly looking over his shoulder.

'I think it's due for service but Geoffrey usually . . . and I haven't gotten around . . .' Why was I bleating my excuses as if I hadn't done my homework?

'Why don't I take it over to the pub and have a proper look in the workshop? I don't think it's a big problem.'

'No, really I couldn't expect you to do that. I can call the breakdown service. I mean you must be terribly busy.'

'I don't open till seven. This is my hobby. Believe me. It's OK. I've got a tow line in back of my car.'

I stood in the small kitchen-cum-living room, waiting for the kettle to boil. It was at the back of the pub and through the small window I could see out into the concrete yard. There were plastic crates filled with empty beer and mixer bottles. Stainless steel barrels were stacked up neatly by the side wall. On the other side of the yard was an old open cart shed. I could see scarlet nose of the BMW, shining under the fluorescent lightstrips hung incongruously on the old beams.

Ross had gone into Breckenham to get a new set of spark plugs, having quickly established they were the problem. He had told me to make myself at home in the meantime.

It didn't really seem as if he had even done that himself. The worn furnishings and decor of the living room — floral patterns on everything — had the look of being left over from the previous occupier. There were only a few things which had stamped his own presence on the room. A big mahogany desk cluttered with papers, a year-planner wall chart pinned above it speckled with coloured stickers, no doubt defining such momentous events in the life of the Coopers Arms as the delivery of draught beer. On the other walls were a couple of watercolour paintings: a warplane like the one in the photograph in the bar, a sports car like the one he drove. They were meticulously crafted, more like technical drawings than art. That was how he spent his precious spare time.

One of the ways, at least. There was also a floor-standing shelf unit of varnished softwood – homemade, probably – containing a number of books.

I took my mug of instant coffee to the chair alongside to have a look. I was surprised. Sure, there were paperback novels, thrillers, mostly with a flying theme, and books on motorcar mechanics. But there was a Shakespeare, used-looking, and some well-thumbed Penguin classics: *The Iliad*, *The Aeneid*, Livy, Caesar, Josephus, Thucydides, Xenophon and many others. A lot of war and warriors, but not exactly what I had expected.

I was still looking at the books when the sound of an engine in the yard announced his return. He came in carrying a cardboard package.

'Hi, there. Made yourself coffee? And discovered the library. I guess you expected the *National Geographic*, or "Peanuts"?'

I coloured a little. 'No, of course not. Or rather I mean . . .'

'It's OK. I got the habit on the base. There was a lot of waiting, for a war that never happened. Never could happen, I guess, although we didn't know that at the time. Early on, I really believed that night's duty might be my last. In that situation, you appreciate feeling others have lived through it thousands of years before. The eternal verities, don't they call it?'

'Yes.'

'Well, I'd better get these done for you. It won't take a minute.'

I went out with him to the workshop and watched him fit the new plugs, carefully cleaning the lead of each one before replacing it.

He seemed lean and fit as he leant over the chrome grille, his arms brown against the short-sleeved white sport shirt. I could see the muscles move on his back as he pulled on the spanner.

He slammed the hood and turned to me, grinning. 'All through.'

I smiled in return with genuine warmth. 'Thanks, Ross. I'm really grateful. Now I owe you for the plugs.'

He tried to wave it away.

'Don't be silly. Things like that cost a lot.'

Reluctantly he produced the bill. I gave him some notes and he stuffed them casually in his pocket. I hoped he ran the pub more sensibly.

He handed me into the car and closed the door with old-fashioned courtesy. I wound down the window and looked up at him as he leaned with one hand on the roof. Despite the severely cropped iron grey hair, he had a pleasant open face with copious laughter lines around his mouth. There were finer lines at the tails of his eyes, the eyes of a man with twenty-twenty vision, often crinkled with concentration as he stared into the deep blue of the stratosphere.

'Thanks again, Ross. You've saved me a lot of hassle.'

'My pleasure. Like I told you, it's my hobby. And good luck with the sale. You know, I've been thinking. I could keep an eye on the place while you're away, if you'd like. Drive out that way once in a while. Don't want squatters, do you?'

I laughed. 'That's a kind thought, but you don't need to do that. I can't imagine any trouble there.'

We shook hands briefly and awkwardly. I drove off into what had turned into the late afternoon. He stood at the wooden double gates of the yard, gazing after me.

As I swung the car on to the gravel driveway, I felt all at once sick of the place.

How had I ever loved it so? There it stood, a dull, plain house surrounded by gloomy, oppressive trees. I hated the crushing sense of isolation, the boredom of the wide-open hedgeless fields. I despised the Finchams father and son with their mixture of deviousness and half-wittedness. I loathed the village. I was overwhelmed with the utter pointlessness of my standing there under the big sky with its grey-white clouds like huge fungi. It had been supposed to be a retreat. Now it represented everything I wanted to retreat from.

Ever since I had come here, I had been confronted with things I had rather I hadn't known about Geoffrey. And now there was Lucy Mallen. What did I care about her and her bastard child, or Tom its idiot father? It wasn't any of my business. She was probably looking forward to playing lacrosse next term at public school by now, the child painlessly adopted, the whole thing forgotten about.

But that evening, as I had thrown my suitcase into the trunk and slammed it shut, I looked up at the darkening façade of Forest House and knew that I was not free of it yet. Like it or not, I was somehow woven into the texture of the place. I had my role.

I had shivered as a wind moaned through the trees and blew across the clearing. Perhaps I had no right to ignore these things. For in doing so I might be at the very least refusing help to one who needed it. Help – or justice.

The arrival of the midday post broke into these recollections. There were a couple of brown window envelopes with red print showing, and an airmail letter from France.

I threw the bills to one side and avidly tore open the envelope. There were several pages in Anna's scrawled handwriting. I settled down to decipher it.

Le Château de St Gervais,
382510 St Gervais-les-Eaux,
France

My dear Mary,

You say I never write letters so this is just to prove I can. Anyhow, I don't have any choice at present as the phone has been cut off – some silliness about the bill. Dear Pierre again.

How are you, my dear? It seems ages already. I was quite worried about going off and leaving you like that. You had so much stuff to cope with.

I wish you could be here. It's so lovely and warm, and all around the grapes are ripening. In fact I'm rather beginning to enjoy life here – just as it's nearly over.

The château is sold. I can hardly believe it. I'm waiting only for the notaire to draw up the final sale document. It's sad in a way to see the place go, but it was all part of a fantasy life. From now on I'm going to be a sensible person, be my age.

So I'm clearing up here. Fortunately, the people who have bought the place – a horrid couple from, I think, Birmingham; the Brits seem to be the only buyers here at present – have bought most of the furniture and stuff, so there isn't much to get rid of or ship back. Which is lucky because there isn't at the moment anywhere to ship it to. I had a letter from Nanny Webster the other day. Her sister is compos again and out of the home. She says she would still put me up, but can you imagine? So I haven't got anywhere to lay my head. Could you cope if I can't find anywhere straight away? It wouldn't be for long.

Listen. That's got the begging part out of the way. Since I've been here I've had a certain amount of time to think. About you and your problems. I don't want you to take any of what follows the wrong way. I know I'm into sensitive areas and it's probably going to be upsetting. But it seems to me that if you are really keen to find out what was going on then at the very least some of the less pleasant alternatives have to be considered. So here goes.

What if Geoffrey and this Henry Massingham were actually in cahoots over his being an estate agent? That it wasn't both Geoffrey and you who were being fooled, but only you? Why should Geoffrey want to fool you into believing that he wanted to buy a cottage? I can't answer that. Nor can I say why Massingham got involved. I can only guess that he had some reason for wanting to be there quite often – 'Just nipping down to the cottage, darling' – which he didn't want you to know about. I don't know what that reason was. I think it must have been something to do with his work. Could there have been some secret work that meant he had to be in Norfolk?

Before you dismiss this whole idea as daft, let me tell you how I arrived at it. It really came out of what's been happening here. The more I thought about it, the more I couldn't see how Geoffrey could really have been fooled by such a deception. You see it would have to have been so complicated. I'm always on to the agent here. I ring him up continually. You couldn't do that with someone who didn't have an office. You'd smell a rat instantly. And then there's all the paperwork. You didn't see any of it, but there would have had to have been some. Geoffrey wasn't an idiot – far from it. He couldn't have been taken in by a chap he met only in a pub. He must, on my reckoning, have known about it. And if he knew about it they must have cooked the whole deal up together. QED.

Have I shocked you? You told me yourself that Geoffrey seems to have been a bit of a teller of tall tales on occasions. I'm not saying there's anything sinister about it. He might just have wanted to surprise you with something he had been working on. I won't say any more. Please write to tell me you don't hate me.

God, quelle letter this has been. Haven't I gone on? I must stop to walk down to the PTT, where Madame Defarge behind the counter will with the greatest of reluctance, as if it were one of her own children, sell me *un timbre*.

Love, and take care,

A .

I put the letter down, my head humming. Could she be right? I didn't want to admit it to myself. I had been trying to avoid getting out the bulky file labelled 'All those nasty suspicions about Geoffrey I've been trying not to think about.' Now the contents were spilling out, all over my life.

Henry Massingham. I couldn't go on ducking out of confronting him about it.

But after the disastrous visit to his house, I didn't know how to tackle him. He could simply deny everything. Assaulting me and driving off? Nonsense. It wasn't me. I don't know her from Adam. She's obviously, well, emotional.

Pretending to be an estate agent? Ridiculous. I wasn't even in Queen's Hythe that day. Haven't been in the Royal Baltic for years.

I kicked it around for the rest of that day, but the fact was there was no proof we had ever met. No proof that he had been in any way involved in the sale of Forest House. And without something to tie him into the business – to connect him with Geoffrey or the house in some way – I couldn't see how I could get him to tell me any more about what had been going on.

On Sunday, for the first time since Geoffrey's death, I went out to buy the papers. It was I supposed a further sign of my coming to terms with how things were. Nevertheless, I couldn't avoid being reminded of those quite different Sundays that Geoffrey and I had enjoyed together before the suspicions and the anguish, before, in fact, I had heard of Forest House.

I was flicking indulgently through one of the sections searching for some further juicy item to nibble when I came face to face with the Country Property column.

Oh, the Sundays when we combed this hungrily! Here were the halls, the granges, the lodges, the crofts, the manors, food for a million rural pipe dreams. Here were the umpteen barn conversions, the cottages and the castles that at this very moment had a thousand middle-class, middle-aged couples reaching for their telephones. I smiled to myself, with an edge of patronage. Poor fools, may you at least find your Arcadia.

Then at a sudden piercing memory I froze. The advertisement. Of course. Massingham must have placed the advertisement.

How could I have been so stupid? There was proof – of something. He had either placed the ad himself, or got someone else to do it. In either case, there ought to be some way of tracing it back to him: an address, a credit card number, a cheque. Once I had that, I would have something he wouldn't be able to wriggle away from. I had got the bastard.

First thing the following morning, I called the Classified Advertising department of The *Sunday Times*. I was an irate customer, complaining about one of their ads. Who had placed it? Would they please check their records? I wasn't at all sure it was bona fide. And what was the telephone number again?

They had the answer in seconds – good old computer technology. The advertisement had been placed by a Mr Robinson. And the address? I listened with barely disguised astonishment.

It wasn't Massingham's address. It wasn't even one in Norfolk. It was a London address. One I knew well. An address in E1. Limehouse. Geoffrey's apartment.

I shouldn't have been surprised. It had been staring me in the face right from the beginning. It had Geoffrey written all over it. The knowing jokey allusions – the product of a mind that loved crossword puzzles and brain teasers – the way it was designed to hook me in by playing on my own intellectual vanity. I had been set up, I reflected bitterly. But why? Why go to all that trouble?

Just to double check I punched out the number from the ad the girl had given me. An elderly rural female voice answered.

'Mrs Robinson,' she quavered. 'What do you want?'

I said wrong number and put the phone down. Here's to you, Mrs Robinson. I bet your phone never stopped ringing with queer folks from London. You can thank my late husband for that.

It was obvious that Geoffrey wouldn't have been fooled by a fake estate agent. Only I would have been so stupid, blinded by love or passion or whatever. Geoffrey hadn't been about to turn into a country bumpkin. He was up to something else. But what in heaven's name could it have been? I now saw that Massingham's reaction was instructive. Whatever it was, and for whatever reason he had agreed to collaborate with Geoffrey, he didn't want to be reminded of it one little bit. I shivered. Perhaps the main reason was that Geoffrey was dead.

There was one other small matter. If Geoffrey had not bought the house, then who the hell now owned it?

The answer to that was on the face of it obvious. Mallen must still be the owner. All that stuff about trusts and Mallen's going to America that Massingham had spouted had been a smoke screen, in case I started to get too interested in the deal – and in case I started to get too interested in Mallen. It was, I could see, calculated to make the putative transaction as impersonal as possible. It was a boring old trust selling it after a dull academic had pissed off to the States. It wasn't the family home of a world-famous Cambridge scientist in whom I might have started to get interested.

In fact, I wouldn't even have got this far if Geoffrey had been alive. It had been his play. His death had moved the pieces on the board. A quite different game was in progress and maybe some of the pieces were not very happy with the change in the rules. The King was dead. I smiled grimly to myself. Long live the Queen.

I was in charge of the game and it was my move. And there was one piece whom up to now I had been unable to approach. His presence on the board was shadowy, so shadowy that sometimes I hardly knew he was there. Just what part did Dr Julian Mallen play in this?

All I knew was that he had moved fairly precipitately out of the cottage. Where was he? He had been at Cambridge and Massingham said he had gone to America, but he could be anywhere in the world. I had quickly exhausted my own reference material. He wasn't in *Who's Who,?* which wasn't surprising given what I knew of him. Then something occurred to me. The quickest way to find out the whereabouts of an eminent physicist was to ask another eminent physicist. I dragged out my Filofax and leafed quickly to the right page. Luckily I had kept the number. There he was. Lieberman, Frank J., Physics Department, University of Colorado. I looked at my watch and did a quick calculation. It would be early, but not too early. Presumably Frank was still a workaholic. I punched out the number.

A female voice answered, 'Physical Sciences, Joanie speaking. How may I help you?'

'I'd like to speak to Frank Lieberman please.'

There was a shocked pause at the other end, then the voice of Joanie said sternly, 'I assume you mean Professor Lieberman?'

'He was just good old Frank when I knew him. Listen, honey, this is a transatlantic call. Tell him his ex wants to speak to him urgently.'

'I'll try to connect you.'

There was a pause, then, 'Mary, is that really you?'

'You got any other ex-wives, Frank?'

'What the hell do you want after all this time? I bet the entire campus is buzzing right now. What did you tell the switchboard? Transatlantic?'

'Relax, Frank. It's not a belated alimony suit. I am in London. I called to say hi, and have you heard of a physicist called Julian Mallen?'

'Twelve years and five thousand miles away and you're still trying to drive me insane. Don't tell me you've finally discovered an interest in physics. That I don't believe.'

'Please, Frank. This is important. I'm sorry if I embarrassed your eminence. Have you heard of this man or not?'

'Have I heard of Einstein, have I heard of Niels Bohr, Werner Heisenberg?'

'You mean he's famous?'

'He's the tops, but not in your sense. Only to research physicists. He's not well known even to the average scientifically educated guy. He doesn't do popular stuff. In fact, only a few dozen guys in the whole world – amongst whom I don't count myself – really understand what he's doing. He's way out on the frontier.'

'Frank, I need to contact him. Don't ask why. I gather he's moved to the States. Do you know where?'

'What? That's impossible! Where'd you hear that? When? If it's true, it's news to everyone. I'm not saying that somewhere like Berkeley wouldn't sell its soul for him to go over, but if they had they'd want everyone to know.'

'I see.' But I didn't. 'Then if he's not in the States, where is he?'

'That's easy. You didn't need to make a phone call to Denver to find out. You see, there's another thing he's famous for – for not joining the academic circuit. Visiting professorships, conferences, symposia, gatherings of colleagues. These days we all do that, but not him, not ever. Maybe he doesn't like travel, or maybe it's because he is what they say he is: an arrogant Limey sonofabitch. So he's where he always is: right there on your doorstep in St Saviour's College, Cambridge.'

'St Saviour's College.'

'May I speak to Dr Mallen, please?'

There was a definite hesitation at the other end of the line. Then a male voice, presumably the porter's, said, 'I'm afraid Dr Mallen is not at present in College, madam.'

'When is he expected back?'

Again the hesitation, then: 'I couldn't say, madam.'

'Do you mean he's out? Will he be back this afternoon? For dinner?'

'I can't help you any further I'm afraid, madam.'

'Can I leave a message?'

'If you wish, madam.'

I left my name and telephone number and a request that he call me. But I knew even as I did so that it would be of no use. The voice I had spoken to, for all its polite determination to be unhelpful, was, unintentionally, clear in one respect. Otherwise there would have been more of an attempt at least to find out who I was and what I wanted. Dr Mallen had obviously given instructions that he did not wish to contact nor be contacted by anyone.

What Frank had said had, in cruder terms, merely confirmed what I had already learnt about Mallen. He was a loner to whom communication, either personal or professional, was not important. It explained the absence of a telephone at the cottage even in that remote spot; his brusque, unfriendly treatment of Norman; the unsociability remarked on by Dottie Edwardes.

Mallen was a man who quite clearly liked to remain out of the spotlight. He was certainly not going to respond willingly to a request to speak to him from someone who might possibly be asking extremely awkward questions. They weren't questions you could address to him on a postcard, either.

15

I slid the pale blue envelope with red and dark blue border containing a scribbled note to Anna into the mailbox. I experienced a warm glow as I did so, feeling that by this small action I had made a connection over the distance that separated me from my friend. It would be good to have her around again. I really needed her support, her encouragement. Of course she could stay, I had told her. And I really welcomed her thoughts about Geoffrey and the cottage. In fact she didn't know the half of it, and by the time I saw her there would be much more to tell.

I walked back up Rosslyn Hill from the mailbox. I held tightly on to my umbrella as the rain-soaked wind tried to tug it away. I shivered. Windy days filled me with a nameless dread. I turned down my street and squeezed through a gap in the parked cars preparatory to crossing to the apartment block entrance opposite.

As I waited for a delivery van to pass, I saw a man climb into the driver's seat of a car parked a little way down on my side. People came and went all the time: the street was used by casual visitors to the Hampstead shops, or to the nearby pub. I noticed it only because there were fewer people about than usual, probably because of the vile weather. As I went up the steps to the front door, I looked back into the street. The car that the man had got into was still there. One of those identical small saloons – I hardly knew one make from another: Geoffrey would have, of course. The only thing that registered a faint query in my mind was that I was fairly sure that the man I had seen getting into the car was the same man I had almost bumped into at the postbox. He had been at the box before me, and as he had swung around rather too abruptly he put up his hand in a friendly gesture of apology.

I don't really know why this seemed odd to me. He could have simply stopped here to post his letter. Why hadn't he driven off, then?

From the sitting room window of the apartment I looked down into the street. The car hadn't moved. It was parked almost by the raw hole in the pavement where the great tree had been uprooted in the storm. Because of the angle of view, I couldn't see the face of the occupant of the driving seat, only a pair of hands resting on the steering wheel and part of a dark jacket and trousers.

Perhaps I was getting paranoiac: living alone, not getting out, this brooding over the oddnesses of my life with Geoffrey. Yet as I stared down at the man in the car, I had a tremor of apprehension.

The following morning felt good as soon as I woke up. I knew that my otherwise mainly blank diary had an appointment in it. For the first time in ages I was going out to lunch. Even better, I had been invited. It wasn't business, not strictly anyway. Vanessa Wordsworth and I had been acquaintances for ages, and we had the sort of relationship that was a little warmer than the professional lunchtime friendships cultivated between publishers and literary agents, where after the bonhomie and the gossip, the typescript which had been lurking apparently unregarded under the table would be reluctantly and almost apologetically introduced, rather as one would a slightly dotty aunt.

I had been nevertheless surprised to get the invitation. Vanessa, though kinder and more generous than her reputation allowed, was hardly the sort of person to waste her time with someone even temporarily out of the ball game. The more I thought about it, the more I suspected that our mutual friend, or rather our mutual absent friend, was at the bottom of it. I couldn't quite figure what Vanessa wanted out of me on the subject of Ms Dalton, so I decided to enjoy the lunch and leave her to raise the matter, if indeed that was what it was about.

We met at my hostess's usual restaurant, so habitual to her it was a publishing legend. It was small, French and cheap. An ex-colleague, who had come off worse from an encounter, was of the opinion that this description fitted Vanessa herself. I demurred at the time, even though I could see what she meant. But it was unfair and not even accurate. Vanessa was under medium height, but not much shorter than I. As far as I knew, the Frenchness was a result of upbringing rather than birth: her family had had business interests in Paris and Vanessa was educated and spent a good deal of her early life there. It was this which accounted for the very slight accent. As for the cheapness: well, she was a very tough lady who drove an adamantine bargain, not only for her clients but for herself. Legend had it that she never took cabs, but walked everywhere from her shabby one-room office in Romilly Street. And certainly her clothes − from one of the cheaper chain stores − usually looked as if they had been off the peg for some time. But otherwise the word was quite inapplicable: she was genuinely interested in her clients and in their books, and to my knowledge spent endless time with them, reading and rereading, advising and cajoling until the shapeless bundles of paper turned into crisply presented publishable and saleable works. She was also loyal, intelligent and outspokenly honest. So I was a fan, she liked me, but that didn't mean the lunch date was entirely social.

Nor was it. I had barely taken a mouthful of my vichyssoise when she said, 'All right. Where is she, then?'

'She. Who she?'

Vanessa stuck her head even closer to mine than it already was, owing to the minuteness of the table. 'You know exactly whom I mean. Why do you think I asked you here?'

'I suppose I thought it was something to do with the fact that you considered our acquaintanceship intrinsically worthy of conti-nuity, despite my having −'

'Got the sack,' she interrupted. 'Well, unthink it.'

'Thanks for letting me know. It's a good boost to the ego. It's made my day.'

'For goodness sake, Mary, grow up. You're getting as bad as she is. Pouting adolescence. It must be catching.'

'Look, if all you've got to offer is abuse, I'm going. You can stick your rotten lunch. I don't have to take it any more, remember. There's nothing in it for me any longer. Not that there ever was. I was never on a percentage.'

'More fool you, then. Sit down, Mary, please. I'm sorry. I didn't mean to be quite so abrasive. It's just that Anna and her doings make me angry. It's not your fault. Well, actually in a way it is. If it hadn't been for you, Anna would never have got mixed up with McAllister's and its dreadful boss.'

'You made the deal. It was a good deal. If you feel guilty about it, don't take it out on me. Anyway, it was neither of our faults that Anna met some guy half her age, dropped everything and zoomed off to France.'

Vanessa put down the pâté-covered toast. Her eyes behind the thick plain spectacles went almost squinty with interest. 'Aha! So it was a man. The fool. To throw away a good contract for a fellow.'

'Love makes you do funny things,' I said.

She shrugged. 'Pouf! Love. Well Anna is hardly Cleopatra, is she? All for love, at her age! Has it lasted?'

I shook my head. 'Hasn't she been in touch? I went on and on about at least contacting you.'

'Not since those postcards I told you about. If you know where she is, please tell me. Things are really serious. You know they've cancelled the contract?'

'I didn't. But it doesn't surprise me.'

'And they're talking about suing her for the rest of the advance. The first one did quite well but not well enough to earn it back. They're saying that without the rest of the series it never will. I suppose they have a point, but it's pennies, isn't it, to a company like that?'

'Michael is a man who cares deeply about even pennies. He grudges the loss of them, particularly where he feels he's been had. And I know he does. He told me. I tried to warn Anna but she took no notice.'

'She never does.'

The waiter brought the next course. A steak au poivre for me, poulet véronique for her. We ate in silence for several minutes.

Finally Vanessa said, 'You are going to tell me where she is, aren't you?'

'Actually, no, I'm not.' I held up a hand to forestall the inevitable protest. 'But what I will do is pass a letter on if you send me one. I think Anna does need to be told, but she has to make the decision as to what she wants to do herself. Wouldn't you do the same in my position?'

She sighed. 'Yes. Truly. In fact I've already done just that.'

'What do you mean? Was someone else looking for Anna?'

She nodded. 'I thought it was odd, and when I checked it was even odder. About three weeks ago, a woman rang the office and asked for Anna's address. Said she was a friend of the family and had to contact her urgently. Her father was very ill and asking for her. Well, as I wasn't going to admit to not knowing where on earth one of my authors was, of course I said exactly what you said to me. And something about the story didn't ring true. The woman said I would be responsible for the consequences and put the phone down in a huff. *Mon Dieu*, as if I hadn't been responsible for consequences for as long as I can remember. Well, I rang Anna's parents' house just in case. The maid or whatever who answered said Sir Richard was out shooting grouse, and of course there hasn't been any letter to forward.'

'I have a pretty good suspicion as to who it was, or rather who was behind it.'

'You think so? He wouldn't try anything nasty, would he? He's not a gangster, after all.'

'This is awfully good steak,' I said.

We didn't talk about the matter again for the rest of the meal. I hadn't mentioned the other reason why I thought Michael was being so hard on poor Anna, but I didn't need to. Vanessa wasn't stupid. She would have heard the rumours about my reverse Midas touch. How all my gold had turned to lead.

By the time the coffee came the atmosphere between us had lightened. Vanessa had been bringing me up to date with the latest goings on in the trade, which I listened to, I have to admit, with a certain vicarious enjoyment.

She hadn't mentioned my own situation since her blunt introduction. Then apropos of nothing, she said, 'You're not fixed up yet, are you?'

'No. There doesn't seem to be the right opening at present.'

'A lot of people are being very silly. They can't recognize a first-class editor when they see one. By the way, I'm sorry I was a bit brutal earlier. But put it down to experience. I've been through it myself.'

'You? You mean you used to work for a publisher?'

'Oh, yes. Didn't I ever tell you? It was years ago. I had a very acrimonious departure from Lowell and Fforest. But that's when that fool Tom Fforest was running things. Dead now, I'm pleased to say. Have you ever thought of being an agent?'

The way she said it made me think that the question was not entirely casual. It sounded like the approach to a proposition. 'I hadn't really ever thought about being anything other than a publisher until a few weeks ago.'

'Perhaps you should, in the circumstances. The money's good. You're at the cutting edge. You get to kick publishers around. Well, sometimes. The thing is I'm thinking of winding down a bit. Just a bit, mind. I could do with a partner I could trust. You don't have to say anything straight away. Just think about it.'

'OK,' I said. 'I will.'

When the check came, she said, 'We were going Dutch, weren't we?'

'I don't remember our agreeing that.'

She shrugged and then grinned, carefully counting out notes and coins from an old leather wallet. She scorned credit cards. 'I do think there's an agent in you,' she said.

I left the restaurant feeling more cheerful, my ego boosted. If someone as generally grudging as Vanessa was willing to take me on, then I couldn't be completely useless.

To celebrate, I went into a shop I knew in Neal Street and spent more than I could afford on a nice blouse with bold stripes and real mother-of-pearl buttons. Delicious smells then lured me into a delicatessen off the Covent Garden Piazza where I succumbed to some real Roquefort and a chunk of saucisson de Lyon. To hell with lentils.

By then it was gone five and the pubs had opened.

It was quite some time since I had been to the Wine Vaults, a small, dark pub near the Opera House. I had actually rather avoided going there because it was usually packed with publishing types loudly talking shop. Today my self-imposed exile seemed silly. I wasn't ashamed to show my face, so I would.

I pushed my way in through the crowd. There was already that raucous feeling of a party in full swing which you get amongst the after-work drinks set, even if the place has only been open half an hour. Struggling through to the bar, I collided with a thin young man who had turned away bearing what looked like two gin and tonics. He stared at me, blushing slightly.

'Hello, David,' I said. 'Can I help you with one of those?'

'So how's it going?' I said cheerfully.

David wasn't alone. I had obviously from his less than enthusiastic welcome muscled in on some kind of tête-à-tête. The other tête was a dark, handsome fellow in his twenties with big blue eyes.

His name was Harry Pilbeam. Not surprisingly, it didn't seem significant.

'Really well,' David said in a tone which indicated quite the contrary.

'Come on, David, I wasn't born yesterday. You don't have to do the company PR stuff with me. I worked there, or have you forgotten already?'

'You worked in that shithouse too, did you?' For the first time, Pilbeam spoke. 'It's no good looking at me like that, Dave. I feel truly buggered about.'

I suppressed the obvious response. Instead I asked, 'Do you work there, er, Harry? I don't remember . . .'

He glared at me. 'No, I bloody don't. Worse than that. I turn out the raw material that keeps that fat old bastard in caviare and champagne. Bloody cannon fodder, that's what I am.'

I recognized the self-serving irony immediately. 'Oh, you're an author.'

'That's right. An author who wishes he had never heard of McAllister's.'

He wasn't alone in that, I reflected privately. Pilbeam. With a name like that, he had to use a pseudonym. 'What do you write under, Harry?'

David stepped in. 'Mary's actually very familiar with your work,' he said to soothe his companion's ruffled feathers. 'He's Shelley Birchanger, Mary.'

That definitely rang a bell. '*The Thought Stealers*,' I said automatically. 'SF's answer to *War and Peace*.'

Harry took the remark as a compliment and, mollified, said, 'Right. You read it then.'

'I not only read it, I edited it.'

'So you're the one who wrote the notes. I sort of assumed Dave had done them. Some of them were quite helpful. Why didn't we ever talk?'

David coughed nervously. 'Mary had some personal problems around then which meant that, er . . .'

'My husband died suddenly,' I said. In time to allow Henderson to pinch my work, I thought.

This caused a lull in the conversation.

'What's the problem?' I asked. 'Michael was very keen on the book. We agreed it would be a big hit with the fans of the genre.'

David intervened again. 'Michael's pushed it down the Christmas publication list. It's no longer a lead title. And he's cut the publicity budget to almost nothing. He's just told Harry about it.'

'Bloody right he has, the fat bugger. "Can't waste money on this sort of stuff," he said to my face.'

'What? Why on earth has he done that?' I was genuinely amazed. Even Michael didn't usually throw his weight about so blatantly.

David gulped gin. He looked flushed, as if he had had quite a few. Probably he couldn't take it, either. The booze or the pressure. He suddenly seemed vulnerable, a mere stripling confronting the unpredictable force of his megalomaniac boss. I was beginning to feel like the John Wayne character instructing a greenhorn gunslinger who didn't know one end of a pistol from the other.

He said, 'I shouldn't really be talking to you like this, either of you. You haven't heard me, OK? But Michael's got a big project he's not telling anyone much about. Scheduled for Christmas.'

'So what's new?'

'No. You don't understand, Mary. He's completely over the top since you left. I don't think anyone realized the restraining influence you had. You didn't get along but in an odd way he respected your judgement and the way you stood up to him.'

'He hid it well.' Despite myself I was getting interested. Old habits, old professions die hard. 'What is he up to? He must have dropped a few hints. Michael never could keep anything entirely to himself.'

'Only that it's something really huge. It must be or he wouldn't have messed around with the schedules. Harry's not the only author who's been pissed about. It takes something to want to risk fucking up sure-fire winners like Harry. Something mega-huge. Arnold in production says he's been told to clear the decks for an initial hardback print run of half a million.'

I nearly choked on my gin. 'Sorry. I misheard. I thought you said "half a million".'

'I did.'

'On one title, in hardback? That's insane. What's he going in for, telephone directories?'

'No one's seen the manuscript or knows anything about it. It'll be delivered to the printers at the last possible moment, again according to Arnold. They're having to get one of those firms that do a lot of security stuff.' He lowered his voice and looked around. 'You really haven't heard this, but Michael was a bit tired and emotional the other afternoon. I think one of his horses had come in last. We were talking about some book or other. Then he turned to me, apropos of nothing, and said, "David, my boy, how many books have actually changed the world? Really fucking changed it? I can think of a few. The Bible. The Koran. *Das Kapital*. Mao's Red Book. Well, soon there'll be another. And I'm going to publish it."'

It was quite a good imitation. I laughed. 'He was winding you up. He does that.'

'No, I'm quite sure he wasn't. Why would he go mucking about with bankable titles, upsetting the authors? That's seriously crazy!'

'Wow. Am I glad I'm out of it.' I was, too. Michael was obviously at his most Stalinesque. I was beginning to realize how Trotsky felt.

David drank his gin. He was looking at me in an odd way. Not that sort of way. Not when he had the lovely Pilbeam in tow. No, an uneasy, shifty way.

'There's something I haven't told you, something I've only just put together,' he said.

'Uhuh,' I grunted unhelpfully.

'When he was talking to me, boasting about how he was going to be the most famous publisher in the twentieth century, he added, "Despite some mishaps on the way. Never trust an author, David. If they don't run off, they go and fucking drop dead on you. If you're lucky like me, they've already delivered. But fucking dead – just like that. I never would have believed it. I could have given him fifteen years."'

The noise in the pub seemed to fade. My ears started to hum. I hadn't felt like this since Miss McPherson's ballet class, when I was starving myself to fit a tutu for the school's rendering of highlights from *Swan Lake*. I was going to faint.

I fainted.

When I came to I was kneeling on the floor, my face a couple of inches from the sticky carpet. I could smell the sourness of old spilt beer and ground-in tobacco ash. I raised my head with difficulty. It seemed to have become enormously heavy and twice its normal size. I was surrounded by a crowd of interested faces. Someone was holding me by the shoulders, having obviously administered the traditional cure.

I got to my feet. The same pair of hands held me steady. I had a pain in the butt. I must have bruised myself when I fell off the chair.

The person holding me said in Harry Pilbeam's northern accent, 'Are you OK?'

I nodded. 'Thanks.'

'I'm sorry I didn't manage to catch you before you fell. You must have hurt your bum.'

'Don't worry. It's well padded.'

I went to the ladies', watched most of the way. I splashed water on my face, straightened my hair.

When I came out, the noise level was back to normal and no one took any notice. I was the nine-second wonder. In Norfolk it would have kept them going for a couple of years.

David stood up to greet me. Worry and contrition had made him pale. 'I'm awfully sorry. I didn't realize that it would –'

'I know. It doesn't matter. Thanks for telling me. It's something I ought to know.'

They got me a cab. As I sat on the slippery benchseat, watching the procession of dull streets go by, I knew I hadn't by any means plumbed the depths of Geoffrey's hidden life. But David had told me one astounding aspect of it. Geoffrey had written a book. Not just any book. Something to rival the Koran or the Bible. Geoffrey. The idea was preposterous. Utterly preposterous.

Home sweet home. Was I glad. I clumped up the stairs to the apartment. Mrs Greenbaum's cat unwound itself sinuously from the banisters as I passed and hissed at me. It always did that. It knew I wasn't kosher.

I fumbled for my keys as I climbed the last flight, but as I stood in front of my familiar dark blue front door I saw that I needn't have bothered. It was already open.

★

263

'You don't know yet what's been taken, miss?'

'I'm Mrs Reynolds, actually. No. It's such a mess. It'll take ages to sort through it.'

'Very well, madam. Perhaps you'd ring the station with the missing items as soon as you can. They'll give you a crime reference number. For the insurance.'

'Thanks. I know the system. It's happened before.'

The young policemen weren't interested. I knew the chances of this particular crime being solved were zero. They knew it and they knew that I knew it. We were going through a bureaucratic farce.

I showed them out. They hadn't even had to expend any powers of detection on the means of entry. The door had been simply kicked open. The door frame was splintered where the deadlock mortise had been smashed out by the impact.

I asked around. Nobody had heard anything, seen anything. The flat opposite was empty. It was hardly ever occupied as the people worked abroad. Mrs Greenbaum was sympathetic but almost deaf. Her neighbour had been watching television all afternoon. That left the cat. He was probably the lookout but he wouldn't cough. Not even to the Old Bill.

The emergency lock man came round to fix the door later that evening. At least I would feel safe when I went to sleep. I don't know why, though. Burglars weren't like lightning. They were quite capable of striking twice or even three times.

Strangely I didn't feel any of the things you're supposed to feel, or even as I had when it had happened the first time. Then I had been new to London, and I thought I had left that kind of stuff behind in New York. I remembered I had felt violated, angry, hurt, depressed. Now I seemed to take it in my stride. It was just one more thing. A minor incident in the flow of city life, like being almost run over on a pedestrian crossing or getting an imaginative check in the restaurant: unavoidable in any urban area from Albuquerque to Zaragoza.

I instinctively knew the reason I reacted like that. I had supped full of horrors lately and a smashed front door, a bit of untidiness and the probable loss of a few things I couldn't care less about were way down on the scale of things that upset me. I was still reeling from what I had been told in the bar. That occupied my thoughts even as I drifted into uneasy sleep.

The next morning the fingerprint man came round with his magic powder and soft paint brush. Another component of the Metropolitan Police make-it-look-as-if-something's-being-done machine. When I told him that one set of fingerprints would turn out to belong to Geoffrey, who couldn't be contacted for a comparison, he didn't seem to care.

After he had gone I got down to it. The mess was as bad as it looked. The books had been tumbled from the shelves in the sitting room and lay higgledy-piggledy. Magazines, files and papers from my ransacked desk lay strewn around. In the vestibule, the coat stand had been overturned and the contents of the closet where I kept brooms and cleaning equipment flung about. It was this I had seen when I took my first peek through the door. In the bedroom the dressing table drawers had been pulled out and overturned, and cosmetics and talc had been spilt in a sticky aromatic pool on the glass-covered top. My clothes had been dragged out of the closet and tallboy and scattered around. That would put up the dry-cleaning bill, and some of the more intimate things I wouldn't feel like wearing again. In the kitchen, every container had been opened. There were spillages over the counter and floor. In every room, pictures were pulled awry or yanked off the walls. In places even the fitted carpets had been ripped away from the skirting boards.

It took a long time before I was fully satisfied that I had even made a start on what was needed. I had worked without a break for three hours and it was late afternoon before I was able to sit down at the kitchen table with a cup of coffee and a sandwich made from the sausage I had bought in Covent Garden what seemed like years ago.

I had had a piece of paper to write down a list of stolen items by me while I worked. It was a puzzling list. There was nothing on it. Despite the shambles, I hadn't been able to find a thing missing.

This was odd. I had the usual complement of consumer durables – TV, video, hi-fi – that the burgling classes seemed to regard as their stock in trade. They were even relatively new, having been replaced after the previous occasion. These had been ignored as had the packing case containing the computer from Limehouse. The small amount of jewellery I possessed was also untouched, despite being left out on the dressing table in a convenient box to take away. I even felt rather insulted. OK, it wasn't that good, but it was passable.

All that appeared to have happened was that he or they had broken in and messed the place around. But why? The strange thing was that it seemed a somehow purposeful kind of mess which had been made. It didn't have the feel of the envious lust for destruction that led bored hopeless young men to scratch the paintwork of expensive cars parked in the street or smash plate-glass windows in shopping malls. Maybe that was why I hadn't reacted so badly the previous night. What my disordered apartment was telling me was not 'You comfortable bourgeois bitch, we hate you.' If they'd cut up my underwear or trashed my china I might have felt that. It was something less hateful, but at the same time more sinister. The more I reflected on it, the message I got was, absurd though it seemed, 'We have been looking for something you've got hidden.' It was truly absurd. I had nothing whatever to hide. But that too was worrying. They, whoever they were, obviously didn't believe it.

I slid the last book back on to the shelf. Like the keystone of an arch, it seemed to hold the structure together. Order had been restored. Until the next time. I sat on the arm of the sofa and looked at my handiwork. And my life. I had measured out my life, not like Prufrock in coffee spoons, but in larger volumes. Each book represented time. Time spent reading, or in the case of the ones I had been involved in publishing, more time spent editing, arguing, speaking at sales conferences, time in meetings, lunches. One of the policemen had said as he picked his way through the scattered tomes, 'What a lot of books. Have you read them all then, miss?'

'Oh, yes, officer,' I said. 'Indeed I have.'

It wasn't quite true. I hadn't read *Finnegans Wake* even though, or rather because, it was a present from an English don at Oxford with whom I had briefly dallied. I hadn't read *The Lord of the Rings*. I had started it but quickly flung it aside in disgust at its pretentious infantile triviality. I hadn't opened even one of the volumes of *A la Recherche du Temps Perdu*. The title as much as the elephantine bulk put me off so much.

As I scanned the shelves, recalling this and that incident connected with each title, I saw with a pang of guilt another title I had never read. *The Digital Universe* by Geoffrey Reynolds.

He had given it to me not long after we first met. With a laugh. 'I don't suppose you'll ever read it. It's about computers and such. Not your usual thing, but it's one of the things I'm about.' I had said hotly that of course I would read it. Didn't he think women had minds for anything other than fiction? He had made a lewd remark in return and I had hit him over the head with a cushion. What followed was not intellectual.

I had shoved it on to the bookshelf afterwards and never taken it down again. I stood and plucked it out. I ought to read it. It was part of the man I had married, as he had said. But which part? The part that told the truth or the part that told lies?

The jacket showed a complex, presumably computer-generated pattern which the cover note said was produced from the Mandelbrot Set, whatever the hell that was. It was typical of science books. Even the covers made you feel inadequate. Out of habit, I looked at the back flap. Geoffrey stared out at me. He'd obviously selected a younger picture. He wasn't so plump around the jowls. He wore a polo-necked shirt which gave the game away. There was a biographical note. Brief, but surprising.

Geoffrey Reynolds was a Grevillian Scholar in Mathematics at Walwyn College, Cambridge. He subsequently read Economics in which he gained First Class Honours. On leaving the University, he joined Hazenbach's, the merchant bankers, as a senior statistician in their economic forecasting department, where he developed his interest in future economic and social trends. For a number of years he was the economics correspondent of the *Quotidian*. He is now the United States correspondent of the *Hobbesian*, the international financial and economic weekly.

I had never known that Geoffrey had started out as a mathematician. It explained a great deal. Mathematics was the secret language of a coterie. Geoffrey's lack of social contacts would not matter in such a milieu. Excellence in an area which most of us find difficult not to say incomprehensible, allied to his insouciant appetite for all kinds of other knowledge, was likely to make him sought-after.

It also explained another thing about him. His comparative lack of interest in money. I don't mean that he didn't need a sufficiency of it to pay for his epicurean lifestyle and grudged spending it when he got the bills. But he was never while I knew him involved in the process of making it through investments or speculation. Unlike Keynes, his hero among economists, he was unconcerned with the day-to-day juggling of funds. Keynes doubled the income of King's by his skills. Geoffrey hadn't even been bothered to take a basic economic decision such as buying his own house. Economics was a game to him. That was clearly the mathematician side to the fore. The love of games and puzzles, the pursuit of numbers for their own sake: it fitted. I could see that now.

I thumbed through the book. I had developed over the years a certain skill in assessing the type and even the quality of a book that didn't particularly interest me by skimming it. Surprisingly, I found myself reading more and skimming less than I had anticipated. It was written in a literate but relaxed and witty style, like a good after-dinner conversation – Geoffrey's speciality, of course.

It was in two parts. Firstly, there was a critical history of the computer revolution and the development of artificial intelligence machines: robots, networks for businesses such as banks and stock-market trading; home computers, games-playing machines. The whole gamut of what Geoffrey had called in an unmistakable

Geoffreyism 'Cybernetic Serendipity'. I recognized more of his liking for awful jokes and puns in other chapter headings – 'Light Programs', 'Chip Board Romance' – which some indulgent editor had let through.

The second part was quite different. It started off with a biographical sketch of an American software inventor named Roscoe D. Pennywell. He had made a pile through selling programs for weapons control systems to the Pentagon, presumably through one of those secretively cosy deals which the US military-industrial complex cooks up for itself. Having made a fortune with more noughts than the Italian National Debt by this means, he had gone on to develop and sponsor the development of much more sophisticated computer systems. Systems carried by optical fibre technology which were capable of revolutionizing, according to him, the entire assumptions on which Western society was based.

For starters, work as we knew it would be abolished. No one would need to go to the office or the factory. There would be no offices or factories in the way we knew them. The required productive capacity of a nation could be carried out in a few entirely automated factories. Distribution would be by a network of computer-controlled track systems. Any human intervention to the system could be done from the homes of the few executives still required on, guess what, a computer system. Because work had been abolished, so had many of the bad features of our present societies: there would be no traffic pollution or congestion because there would be no more traffic. Fewer journeys would be necessary because the essentials of life could be ordered over the optical fibre network which linked every home with the producer-distributors. Even travel for leisure purposes could be virtually eliminated. What was the point in spending a fortune in taking your family to say, Paris, with all the hassle that involved, when Paris could be brought to your living room by means of computer-generated images so lifelike you would really believe you were walking through the Tuileries or the Jeu de Paume?

The more I read on, the more fascinated I became. At first I suspected some kind of elaborate leg-pull, so incredible were the claims made. But there was an air of solidity about the thing: the references to research and surveys which precluded any science fictional jesting. Pennywell was deadly serious about the kind of society which was possible, if not indeed probable.

Like all good journalists Geoffrey had ended with a question. Do we want our horizons to be bounded by the on/off certainty of the micro-processor?

Yet the book wasn't just journalism. It was far too polished and well thought through. It showed that he could make the difficult transition between turning out five hundred words to an early deadline and writing a whole book. Not all of his colleagues could do that, or would want to. Offer a book contract to a journalist, and the sensible ones reacted as if you had suggested they drink hemlock. They couldn't handle the time-frame. A deadline that could be a year away seemed like aeons to them, and yet would never be long enough to complete the apparently infinite pages of typescript which a book would require.

But Geoffrey was different. He would have known that books add gravitas to a reputation that a daily journo, no matter how well known, will never have. The transitory world of the news-paper or news magazine consigns even the most careful prose, the most mordant wit, to the trash basket.

He also knew that some books make not only reputations, but money. A very few make lots of it.

Geoffrey had written one book, and done it well. What was more natural than that he would want to do it again? My mind focused once more on what I had learned from David Henderson in the pub the previous evening. Geoffrey had indeed, before his untimely death, written another book. He had written the book for publication by a man whom, as far as I was aware, he rated miles off the bottom of the scale of publishing greatness. Hadn't he said as much about Michael the last time I ever saw him alive? So what the hell had he been playing at?

My thoughts went back to the night of the storm when I was so upset at the thought of the man I loved being linked in some way to a man I despised. I had felt betrayed that Geoffrey had never told me himself about the deal with Michael. The fact that I now knew it was for a book increased my resentment of what he had done. Books were my thing. He had never even mentioned this one to me. Not a hint, not a whisper. And it wasn't any old book. Oh, no. Not some tedious students' crib to the basic principles of economics. Not even something as intellectually provocative but unspectacular as *The Digital Universe*. No, this was a mega-biggie. One of Michael's favourite telephone number gambles. A book so secret that even the most indiscreet man in publishing had managed to keep his mouth more or less shut about it. A book that had not come up when the year's publication schedule had been endlessly discussed. A book he had not thought to mention to his editorial director.

But then he wouldn't have done that, would he? Since the conversation with James Edwardes, I knew I was the token woman, the airheaded bimbo along for the ride because it suited his and Max Vincent's konspiritasia. He wouldn't consult me. Besides, I might have been the fly in the ointment. I might, knowing me, have been less than enthusiastic about the idea. Michael wouldn't have wanted someone pouring cold water on his lovely scheme, particularly not the wife of the author. Or was there something else I might have found out? Something about the deal with Geoffrey that wasn't entirely kosher? It wouldn't have been the first time his dealings with authors had been like that. But in this particular deal, I would have had a personal interest. And that would make him want to get rid of me as soon as he decently could, so I wouldn't ever find out.

I shivered and opened the liquor cabinet, its contents, thank goodness, still intact. I poured out a whisky with a trembling hand.

My mind went back to the apartment in Limehouse. That too seemed to have been the target of a pointless burglary. But that was different. There was no mess and confusion. Yet again, maybe it wasn't. Both jobs had been careful in their own way. At Limehouse they had found what they were looking for easily enough. In Hampstead, they had had to look harder. If Michael were behind the break-ins, it must be because he thought I had found out something about his deal with Geoffrey. Why else break into my apartment? And if he could break into my apartment, maybe he could also have me watched and followed – in a Norfolk forest as well as in the streets of London.

I poured another drink and wandered over to the window. Parked further down the road this time and on my side was what looked like the same nondescript saloon. The driver's window was down and a nonchalant hand tapped lazily on the roof.

Maybe I was going crazy with these imaginings. Michael was a businessman, after all, a bit unconventional but not a hoodlum. He couldn't do what I had suspected, could he? I remembered how he had been when we talked of Anna. His anger then seemed unreasoning, his threats hinted at the use of his shady connections. He had made me genuinely afraid. Oh, yes. I did really believe he was capable of anything.

It was then I thought for the first time of something I had come across which, in the light of what I now knew, seemed to shed a strange light on the matter. The scribbled note and the photostat article I had found in Geoffrey's apartment. I had put it on my desk when I had got back from there what seemed like ages ago. I hadn't seen it when I had tidied up.

With a sense of mounting panic, I riffled through the papers which I had put in their original places on the green leather surface.

As I feared, it was no longer there.

16

It was time to go. I drank the rest of the coffee, washed the mug and left it to drain. I looked out of the sitting room window. The nondescript car was there, parked in yet another position. I could see someone in the driver's seat.

I had decided to leave the car. I didn't want them – Michael's chums – to know where I was. They might realize after a while that I had gone out, but by then it would be too late.

In theory, there was only a front entrance to the block, but as it had been built in more spacious times it had a basement, once housing the coal furnace which had heated the whole place in the twenties, the days when it was possible to afford not only a resident porter but also a couple of beefy chaps to shovel the coal. The rusty iron remains were there, looking big enough to power the *Mauretania*. Nowadays it was used for the storage of ladders and maintenance equipment by the management company. The residents were allowed to use it to store bulky items: sailboards, dinghies, outboard motors, camping trailers, the sort of leisure industry junk that the urban, mainly male middle class liked to surround itself with. I didn't have anything like that myself there, of course, but I knew that the key was kept on a hook by the door. I also knew that the basement had a pair of double doors giving on to a concrete yard at the back, from where an alley went through to Rosslyn Hill.

I felt in the darkness for the light switch and went down the concrete steps past the canvas-shrouded shapes of Hampstead man's nautical fantasies. As I fumbled with the bolts of the opening leaf of the doors, I felt something soft brush my cheek. Ugh, I hated spiders.

I pushed open the door with difficulty. It had dropped on its hinges and scraped across the cement. I looked out into the yard. The coast was clear. I heaved the door closed and sprinted across into the shelter of the alley. I hoped Mrs Greenbaum wasn't staring out of her kitchen window at that precise moment.

As I emerged into the traffic-roaring normality of Hampstead, I felt suddenly very silly. Why was I behaving like a character in some cheap suspense novel? Sneaking out of buildings by the back way simply wasn't my style. Somewhere along the line I seemed to have stopped being the smart, calm exemplar of the modern working woman and turned into some kind of amateur gumshoe. Was it for real? I sneezed. I stood in a shop doorway and brushed the basement dust and cobwebs from my hair and skirt. Oh yes, it was real all right.

I took the tube to King's Cross, a grimy Victorian concoction of stock brick, cast iron and glass with a tacky modern concourse stuck on. The train, too, would have won a competition for shabbiness. I cleared a space among the abandoned cans of lager and plastic cups that littered the table in front of me, and opened the tourist map of Cambridge I had bought at the station bookstall.

'Walwyn College is not by Cambridge standards of very ancient foundation. A mere seventeenth-century stripling, it occupies a modest range of low buildings away from the picturesqueness of the Backs. It has no magnificent chapel, its library is not crammed with priceless incunabula, it has not the rollcall of famous names with which its brothers resound. And yet it is in its own way eminent among those who can appreciate real eminence.

'You see, dear lady, we are a College of doers. Movers and shakers, but not the glamour boys one reads of in the newspapers. Walwyn men get on with life. They take the rewards which come their way, but many are garlanded only with their own satisfaction. That is the real end of intellectual endeavour, is it not?'

I nodded sagely at my informant. I pointed at his empty glass.

'May I get you another?' He huffed and puffed a little, but not too much, at being bought drinks by a woman – not probably that different from being bought them by an undergraduate – and even attempted to rise arthritically to his feet to demonstrate his male independence. I got him another gin anyway. After he had demolished it in a couple of swallows, he returned to his theme.

'We have aimed to provide what Coleridge – a Cambridge man, of course – called "the clerisy": the civil equivalent of the medieval clergy, the educated men who ran not only the Church, but the administration of government and the educational system. You'll find Walwyn men in the Civil Service, in other universities, even in what were polytechnics, in the Law, in banking and in the higher journalism quietly and solidly achieving whatever it is that needs to be done.'

'Do you think Geoffrey was a true Walwyn man?'

'Oh, indeed, dear lady. Your late husband was a credit to the College, although I have to say that he did not often return for our annual Founder's Feast. I suspect he was frequently out of the country on his journalistic pursuits. I do not recollect we corresponded, although he did for a number of years telephone me occasionally when he was, as he put it, "stuck for a quote". I am pleased to say that I was able to assist him at those times. I read his work with pleasure. Much matter in few words, another mark of the Walwyn man.'

Again I nodded. I wasn't quite sure how to move the conversation on, feeling I was likely to be stuck for ever with the bland self-congratulation of this academic relic. It was like talking to someone out of Evelyn Waugh.

As Dottie Edwardes had suggested, it had been easy to arrange the meeting with her brother. He had answered the phone almost immediately the porter's lodge had put the call through, as if he spent his time waiting by it, and politely accepted my invitation to lunch at a restaurant of his choosing.

After my frustrated attempt to contact Dr Mallen, it had seemed the obvious thing to call him and arrange to visit. At least I would be able to talk to a senior member of the University and perhaps gain some information about how to achieve my aim of getting hold of Mallen. More, I hoped I would hear something of Geoffrey's early life, to fill in those gaps that yawned in my knowledge of him. After the bruising encounters in Coventry, I thought that at Cambridge at least I would discover a man who was recognizably the one I had loved.

Arthur Waddington–Smith – 'Do call me AWS, dear lady' – was a small frail man in, I supposed, his late sixties. He had chosen the boeuf-en-croute from the mainly French menu and was eating it with a relish that belied the sparsity of his frame. I had eventually coaxed him, with the help of a decent bottle of Châteauneuf du Pape, away from collegiate history into more personal reminiscence.

'I'd be grateful for anything you can remember about Geoffrey,' I said. 'How did he get on in College?'

'Dear lady, it is many years ago. I no longer have even the shreds of youthfulness which I prided myself I had then. I am an old man, with an old man's forgetfulness.'

I murmured some comforting words of demurral, at the same time being unable to imagine that he had ever been what I would call young.

'However, yes, I do well remember the young Reynolds. He was certainly one of the more memorable of my pupils. To begin with, he was remarkably self-assured for a provincial grammar school boy. None of that awkwardness or lack of polish. He was a good mimic. I suppose that helped. But under that laconic exterior there was a shrewd brain. He'd come over to me after taking mathematics in the first part of the Tripos. He had already been reading widely and I knew immediately that a First was within his grasp.'

'Why did he switch? Did he ever tell you?'

He took a delicate mouthful of the wine. 'This is really first rate. Do you know, the College sold off its cellar? Quite monstrous. "Couldn't justify such an unproductive capital asset." To be expected of these accountancy types – they have the gall to use the language of economics to cloak their lack of imagination. The bursar, now. He's an accountant. Calls himself the Chief Financial Officer these days. The College buys its wine – that's what it's alleged to be – in cardboard boxes from a cash and carry. A cash and carry.' He drank up his glass as if to reassure himself of the quality.

I poured him some more. 'Geoffrey was keen on his wine,' I said, trying to nudge him back in the right direction.

'Yes, indeed. He was a leading light in the Wine Society. I was myself its Honorary President for a number of years. He showed excellent tasting ability. I remember in particular some quite delightful things he picked up on one of his vacations – lesser known clarets, Côtes de Blaye . . .'

This could have gone on for ever. I interrupted gently. 'You were about to tell me about why he took up your subject.'

'Ah, yes. He had to justify it. I remember he said that although he enjoyed mathematics, he wanted to study something which he could have ideas about after he was twenty-five. He didn't want to be a don – he was clear about that. He said mathematics was a universal language. Now he was fluent in it, he wanted to learn something with it. He was right about that. Modern economics is highly mathematical. He had no trouble with any of the statistical stuff. He got a grasp on that with amazing speed. That's why I mentioned him when I had one of my chats with Edwardes at Hazenbach's. They took him on and the rest you know. I was pleased with his success. It's one of the things I'm here for: sending young men with talent out into the wide world. There was a time when I thought that I . . . But never mind. Cambridge is a wide enough world for me these days. Of course, economists and politicians have always been drawn together. Look at Maynard Keynes, hobnobbing with statesmen. He was another mathematician, you know. I remember young Reynolds liked to feel he was following in the master's footsteps. I never knew Keynes myself. He was dead several years before I came up. They never took enough notice of his ideas, despite his being in the thick of things. I've said it often enough and in what I hoped were the right places, but they didn't listen hard enough or long enough. Now look at the mess we're in.'

He stared mournfully at his empty plate and empty glass. He wiped his thin lips with his napkin and surreptitiously dabbed at a spot of food which had sullied his shirt front below the floppy bow tie.

The restaurant was almost empty, and the waiter was hovering impatiently. I paid the check and we emerged blinking like surprised moles into the brightness of the afternoon sun. We strolled back to the College through the crowds of shoppers and tourists. He had offered me his arm in old-fashioned courtesy, but it was he who seemed to need the support, awash as he was with gin and Côtes du Rhône. He didn't speak until we were almost under the shadow of the gateway. Then his arm tightened on mine as if with some inner tension and he stopped abruptly in the middle of the passageway. Through the arch I could see the immaculate lawn of the quadrangle and a range of grey stone buildings surmounted by a central clock tower.

'Did he ever mention to you the business with the girl?'

I shook my head, surprised and puzzled at this question. 'What girl?' I demanded a little abruptly.

He hesitated then, staring down at the worn paving stones, said, 'I'm not sure I ought to tell you if he didn't tell you himself. It is many years ago. But perhaps it will help you to know the influences upon him. I will tell you, but I will ask that the name of one of the participants must not be passed on. He is now a prominent member of the University and I think should be spared the embarrassment.' He looked me in the eyes, as if to obtain my agreement.

I shrugged. 'OK.'

He glanced down at his watch. 'It is not a story to be retailed in the midst of a thoroughfare. Perhaps in view of the time, we should take tea together in my rooms. I believe Mrs Roddon has obtained some excellent fruit cake.'

AWS's study was as I might have imagined it: dark and cavelike, the walls hidden by bookcases. A small casement window with heavily leaded diamond panes looked out over the Fellows' Garden.

It had its surprise, however. Over the mantelpiece hung an oil portrait of a man in seventeenth-century dress. My eye was caught by the easy dash of the brushwork. I went over to have a closer look. I heard A W S chuckle behind me.

'No, it isn't Van Dyck. You'll have to go to the Fitzwilliam to see a real one. School of or in the style of, I can't remember how they described it last. It's nice though, isn't it? One of my mother's ancestors. Sir Hubert Cottenham. A bold cavalier. I take after my father's side. They made hosiery. In Nottingham.' He laughed. 'China or Indian?'

I settled in one of the big highbacked velvet-covered chairs. On the occasional table at my side was a delicate porcelain cup of straw-coloured liquid and a matching plate of cake richly studded with fruit and nuts. I was beginning to feel that life as a don was fairly tolerable.

Clearly it suited A W S. He looked as he sipped his tea and bit into his slice of cake as if he were enjoying himself. I suppose it wasn't every day he got to spend the afternoon with a merry widow.

'I should say immediately that I did not make a habit of following the – how shall I say? – amorous pursuits of my undergraduates,' he began. 'The only reason I have an exceptional recollection of what happened in the case of Reynolds – I should say your late husband, er, Geoffrey, if you'll allow me that familiarity – is that I had, quite coincidentally, a family connection.'

'Family? I didn't think you were, er . . .'

'No, you're quite right. I have never tied the knot that binds so fast. I am what used to be comfortably known as "a confirmed bachelor" before the term became loaded with all kinds of prurient innuendoes. No, the family I refer to is that of my younger sister, Clara. Dorothea, whom you've met, is my elder by a year or so, although she hates to be reminded of it. Little Clara. She married, though not into a family of minor Norfolk squires.' He gave me an arch look over his bifocals to see if I appreciated this dig at the Edwardeses.

I gave a chuckle in acknowledgement.

He glanced over at the portrait. 'The East Anglian connection runs deep in the family. One is probably related on one's mother's side to any number of such gentry – not that I have particularly interested myself in that kind of thing. Been Labour from my teens, you know. You meet a far better class of person in the Party. In the great days I knew them all: Dick, Harold, Tony, Denis. And Barbara, of course. People who read books, even wrote them. Did you ever read Dick's book on Plato? First class. Quite different now, isn't it? You get the impression that for the last few years we've been governed by people who, if they ever did receive any education, despised it or forgot it once it ceased.' He seemed downcast and took a reviving draught of tea.

'You were going to tell me about your sister Clara,' I prompted.

'Ah yes, of course. You must excuse the ramblings of a silly old buffer. Clara married a well-to-do chap whose family had a department store in Norwich – Mother always said she took after my father's side – and in the fullness of time had issue, namely a daughter. Frances was a bright girl, did well at school and became an exhibitioner at Girton. Obviously I took an interest in my niece, invited her to tea, bring a friend, that kind of thing. So on that occasion she turned up at the Copper Kettle with another girl, what we used to call a real stunner. Lovely, honey blonde hair, tallish, good figure. Obviously bright, too. Girton scholar. She was an old school friend of Frances's, also from Norfolk, but her father was a doctor. She was a scientist – physics, I believe. I remember thinking at the time it was an odd sort of thing for such a pretty girl to be doing.' He looked at me narrowly, the ghost of a roguish twinkle in his bloodshot eyes. 'I wouldn't think that now. Times have changed, haven't they?'

I nodded, but felt the need to push the story along, greedily anxious to find out what had happened between the stunner and my late husband. 'This girl, she was the one you mentioned?'

'Yes. In fact, I was the sort of catalyst in the whole business. As we were strolling along the Backs together later – it was a most beautiful autumn afternoon – and I was doing my little tute on the history of the various colleges – it's a sideline of mine, as you've probably realized – who should we see but Reynolds – he was in his second year, just changed over from maths – and a couple of chums in a punt. Well, without further ado, the two girls had been not unwillingly hijacked by this disreputable gang, leaving me to waste the sweetness of my eloquence on the now desert air.

'The next day I saw Reynolds in College and he thanked me most profusely for introducing him to the most "fab" girl he had ever met. After that I heard quite a bit about the progress of the relationship, both from him and from Frances. They were quite a couple. Tall, slim and bright, both of them. Obviously meant for each other. Making plans for marriage, even. What used to be called "going steady", I believe. I suppose now they'd call it a meaningful relationship. But they were responsible too. Both destined for Firsts, and kept working hard. Competitive, even.'

I sighed, seeing them in my mind's eye. Not for the first time, I regretted I had never known Geoffrey in those days. Slim and brilliant. But would he have ever looked at me? I would have been a fat, ugly schoolgirl with a half-reciprocated crush on the English teacher. I saw them bathed in a kind of golden light, the last generation who thought they could change the world, the days before the escalation of Vietnam, before the Six Day War, before the Provisional IRA, before the souring of hope.

And there had been something elegiac in AWS's delivery. Some hint of the doomed lovers, of things not to be. Geoffrey had never mentioned anything of it. 'What happened?' I asked quietly.

'The usual thing. She met someone else. Someone she thought was far more brilliant, more attractive and, I regret to say, with more solid social connections. If she had a tiny flaw, it was that. Geoffrey with all his carefully marshalled resources of charm and intelligence was, as you know, an entirely self-made person. He couldn't offer the kind of family background which she found elsewhere. He was simply outclassed in that respect, poor chap. Oh, he fought valiantly. He borrowed money, worked at night in one of the hotels to supplement his grant, tried to entertain her back to him. Dinners, balls, that kind of thing. But it was hopeless.'

'She sounds pretty worthless, throwing him over for such trivial reasons. Shallow and egotistical. He was well rid of her I would say.' Why over the chasm of the intervening years was I leaping to his defence? Why did his pain transmit itself to me so sharply? Why was I even surprised that it did?

A W S struggled into a more upright position in his deep armchair, clearly agitated. The old-boy manner had been gradually falling away as he spoke, but now there was a crispness and an urgency which recalled him as the man who had advised a Prime Minister. 'No, no. It wasn't like that. I'm sorry if I've given you that impression. It was part of it, of course. Geoffrey was a grammar school boy with parents – I never met them and I'm sure they were very fine people – whose lives were ordinary, I daresay. But it wasn't just that. That he might have overcome. Many people do. No, that wasn't the main reason. She did fall in love. Frances assured me of that, and as she was her best friend I've no reason to believe she didn't know. And the man she fell in love with was, you have to realize, quite outstanding. Quite outstanding. Already a Fellow of his College. Already being spoken of as one of the most brilliant scientific minds since Newton. That's how they met: through science. She could understand what he was talking about, which not many of us could – or can even now. Geoffrey was clever, no doubt about it, even by conventional standards brilliant in a fitful sort of way. I remember an essay he wrote on Maynard Keynes's theory of employment, and dealing with the various criticisms of it which in its scope and maturity was quite remarkable for an undergraduate. But it was conventional: I didn't ever get the feeling that here was another Ricardo or Marshall, far less another Keynes. He produced critiques and got up the theories, but I don't think he was really creative. I think perhaps he lacked in the end some kind of vital originality. You must forgive me if I seem too candid or a little harsh. I am told it is a failing of mine. But Geoffrey's rival was not wanting in such a quality. He was that rare thing for which we have an overused word. A genius. Julian Mallen was, is, a genius.'

I was so startled the cup jerked convulsively in my hand as I raised it to my lips, spilling tea down my velvet jacket. AWS positively leapt to his feet, fussing over me, proffering a large clean white linen handkerchief from a chest of drawers with which I mopped myself, apologizing profusely for my clumsiness. Fortunately, the delicate heirloom china was intact. I set it carefully back on the mahogany table.

He stood over me, shaking his head solicitously. 'My dear lady, you've gone quite pale. Are you all right? Shall I call for some, er, more feminine assistance?'

'No, I'm fine. A headache. Please do carry on. I'm absolutely enthralled.' He returned to his chair and seated himself again. I took the opportunity to straighten my skirt and hide my trembling hands by my sides. I cleared my throat and said as casually as I could, 'So I guess she married the genius?'

'Yes, she did. Straight after she got her First. Geoffrey was equally successful. It must have been some consolation for him. On the surface he took it well, very much the gentleman with them both, sent a gift, went to the wedding. But he was terribly depressed by the whole business, as you can imagine. As can anyone who has loved and lost.' He stretched out his legs and stared down fixedly at the small feet in their highly polished elastic-sided shoes, deep, it seemed, in some more personal recollection. 'He told me he would never trust another woman again.' As he said this he remembered my presence and looked up in alarm. 'Oh, good Lord, that was a long time ago and I'm sure that he . . . I mean you . . .'

I rescued him from his floundering. 'It's all right. I understand. What you've told me explains so much about him: why he never married and his reticence about it. I suppose he must have felt utterly rejected – in favour of a paragon of all the virtues. I don't imagine that made him feel any better.'

'The awful irony was that it was Geoffrey who had introduced them. He'd known Mallen as a mathematician, had invited him to give a talk to the College Maths Society. They'd become friendly despite the difference in their ages. Sort of master-disciple thing. I can't say I ever encouraged that myself. Can lead to difficulties, you know.'

A W S was silent, apparently deep in thought. Then his face cleared. 'But a paragon. No, I didn't say he was quite that, dear lady. Mallen was . . . is . . . But you must appreciate this is information which I had from Frances who remained close even after her friend's marriage, and I do not wish to abuse her confidence. Nor do I wish to be indiscreet about a senior member of the University. That would never do. I'm sure you will not let this pass any further?' He raised a thick grey bushy eyebrow until I nodded in confirmation. 'Let me say only that the marriage was not successful. There were disagreements, conflict. Like many brilliant men, he had a strain of eccentricity. He tolerated fools not at all, and remember that to his intellect most of the rest of us must have appeared foolish. His wife was herself a woman of intellect and a don, but she was also a woman. I daresay she justifiably felt neglected as Mallen withdrew into his work. He worked alone. He was unwilling to share his work. He published, of course, but he lectured rarely and then in such terms that few could understand him. He made no concessions to his audience. He began increasingly to remind me of Heaviside, another cantankerous genius who locked himself away in a suburban villa in some absurd seaside town – near Bournemouth, I believe, and singlehandedly made discoveries in physics that are fundamental to modern technologies. He may even have anticipated Einstein's Theory of Relativity. Such men are indisputable pioneers of knowledge, but in a university, even Cambridge, genius is not enough. We tolerate a great deal, but not contempt from among our number. Mallen was not rewarded in the manner which he no doubt believed he merited. He did not proceed to the chair which Newton had held, which one might have thought was his due. Instead he became detached and isolated.'

'And his wife? What did she do? Did she leave him?'

'That, I fear, was the tragic irony of the whole business. After years of childlessness, she became pregnant. Frances told me she was overjoyed at the prospect of motherhood. She loved her work, but was not so consumed by it as her husband. It seemed to be the saving of the relationship. But sometime after the little girl, Lucy, was born, they became even more estranged. I understand they were on the point of divorce when the ending of the marriage by that means became, alas, unnecessary. Helen died.'

'But how? She was a young woman. Was it an accident? A car crash?'

'No. Far more hideous than that. She was murdered. A burglary that went wrong, they called it. You will forgive me if I spare you the details. I find the thought of it harrowing even now.' He removed his spectacles and wiped them carefully on a large linen handkerchief.

I nodded and waited, spellbound, for him to resume.

'Notwithstanding the cooling of their relationship, Mallen was quite shattered by grief. Helen was such a lovely young woman. Quite lovely. And the child was only about three years old. She was in the flat at the time and probably saw what happened.'

His voice quavered and he stopped speaking. I said quietly, hoping to channel the flow of his reminiscence to more up-to-date matters: 'What happened to them afterwards?'

'It seemed to have the effect of making Mallen even more withdrawn. The child was looked after by a succession of house-keepers until she went away to school. Mallen became more detached from the University. He had rooms in his college, but lived mainly in an out-of-the-way cottage in Norfolk, which some family interests bought for him. It's very near my brother-in-law's place, strangely enough. A small world, as they say.'

'Really?' I said. I didn't want to go into the other strange connections which were springing up all around.

'There he lived austerely like Thoreau or T.E. Lawrence, in his log cabin, occasionally astonishing the scientific community with some brilliant new paper. It was only relatively recently that he returned to Cambridge and his college.'

'Why did he do that?'

'He was offered something that any scholar would have difficulty in refusing: complete research freedom with virtually unlimited funds. Cambridge, you may know, is a centre for the commercial exploitation of scientific discoveries. The sort of thing they've always done in the United States. Well, Mallen was made a big cheese in one of these new setups. The Cambridge Centre for Physical Research, it's called, but no one who doesn't work there quite knows what it does, and no one who does talks about it. Has one of those frightful hi-tech offices out by the northern bypass. But, as I said, terribly hush-hush.'

'So he's even more hidden from the public eye?'

'Yes. It seems to suit him. I couldn't work in such a place, you know. I've had my best ideas in this very room, with a glass of port in front of me. Things have changed so much. So very much.' He lapsed again into silence.

I was about to prompt him once more when he said, 'I say, I do believe I have some photographs which I took at that time. I think your husband figures on several of them. Would it distress you to see them?'

I smiled in acknowledgement of his delicacy. 'It may do, but I should very much like to see them. Do please show them to me.'

He got up stiffly and went over to a mahogany revolving bookcase in the corner of the room and took from it a leather-bound photograph album. It was the old fashioned kind with thick black pages, the photos held in place by black gummed paper corners.

These small black and white snapshots from twenty-odd years before had that powerful ability to open up a window on the past. I seemed to be looking in on a private world, one from which I was excluded. Never before had I felt so vertiginously the chasm that had begun to yawn between the Geoffrey I had thought I had known and the Geoffrey that was.

There was Geoffrey, unmistakable, the boyish grin, the flop of undisciplined hair over his forehead. He was slim in those days, his tall figure looking almost gawky. He was wearing jeans and a white short-sleeved open-necked shirt. His arms looked skinny, the elbow joint prominently knobbed. He had his arm around a girl with an extraordinarily fragile, almost ethereal beauty, long floating hair in the fashion of the time, wide clever eyes and a serenely smiling mouth. In the background was a smudge of trees and a glimpse of river. In the foreground was a rug and the remains of a picnic: bottles, a hamper, a basket of fruit. Behind them, leaning over with his arms around them both, was another youthful figure, also clearly very tall. I stared at the slightly blurred face. It looked somehow familiar. Where had I seen it before?

I turned to A W S. 'You took this one, I suppose?'

He peered at it shortsightedly through his bifocals. 'Ah, yes, I remember. The meadows by the Cam near Grantchester. A delightful picnic. Geoffrey chose the wine. Alsace, I recall. Full of fruit but with delightful dryness. The perfect wine for a summer's day.' About those hedges blows An English unofficial rose . . .' She was, wasn't she? A delicate English rose, Helen, that is?'

'Yes. She was wonderful.' There was pain in my heart as I said it. 'They look so happy together. All of them.' To change the subject, I said, 'And who's the big, tall character behind? A chum of Geoffrey's? He seems kind of familiar but maybe he has that kind of face.'

'Ah, that was brother, Henry. He'd come down from London to visit. He was a medical student in his final year at Bart's. He and Geoffrey became friends. He was a bit suspicious at first, very protective of his sister. They were very close. But he soon realized Geoffrey was a genuine chap. I know he was disappointed when they broke up. I think he never had the same feeling about Julian Mallen.'

I was staring at the photograph as he spoke. It seemed that its dark and light areas were swirling and reforming, the fuzzy features of the tall, enveloping brother were resolving. I did know him.

'Helen and Henry. What was their family name? I don't think you said.'

'Didn't I? It was a fine old East Anglian name. Massingham. Henry and Helen Massingham. I say, are you all right? I'm sorry. This is my fault. It must be distressing for you seeing . . . well . . .'

I laid a hand on his arm, hoping he would not notice how much it trembled. 'I'm fine. Don't worry. It's been kind of you to spare so much of your time.'

He picked up the album from where I had carelessly let it fall, closed it and put it on the table.

He smiled. 'The pleasure, dear lady, has been mine. It is not often I have the opportunity to indulge my shameless pleasure in nostalgia. They were lovely days. Today, things are so different. But you have had enough of the reminiscences of an old man. There is a world elsewhere. Look how beautiful is the afternoon. Shall I call you a taxi?'

'No, thank you. It's too nice a day. I'll walk to the station.'

We shook hands under the shade of the great doorway, then I watched the small figure plod stiffly back to his rooms. Tears had started to my eyes and I brushed them away impatiently.

I heard my heels clacking on the stone pavement in the quiet street until in a few minutes I turned a corner and they were silenced in the greater sounds of the crowds hurrying to their homes.

It was quite by chance that I noticed out of the corner of my eye a man close behind me. It seemed strange to see him there, because I had last seen him walking in the opposite direction when I emerged from the gateway of Walwyn College.

I guess it's a sort of sixth sense I have picked up from spending so long in an urban threat zone like Manhattan. I notice people – men – who pass by, and I get nervous if I see them again when I don't expect to. And the business with the guy in the car in Hampstead had made me more jumpy than usual.

But what was even more unsettling about this particular individual was that I was fairly sure I had seen him before. In a quite different context. The only common factor of which was me.

It was the guy I had run away from on the woodland track near Forest House. For some reason I couldn't begin to guess at, he was following me.

17

It was definitely the same man. He wasn't wearing the waxed jacket that day. He was accommodating the urban Cambridge environment in a dark suit, and he carried a cream-coloured raincoat. It could not be a coincidence. Why should I see him walking in a Norfolk forest, then behind me in a Cambridge street if he wasn't following me around? But why?

I stopped to look in a shop window. By a covert craning of my neck, I could see that he had also halted further back down the street, casually examining some fruit on a pavement vendor's stall. I felt an overwhelming urge to go up to him, to scream, 'What the hell are you following me around for, you sonofabitch? Leave me the fuck alone!' But I knew I couldn't do that. Not only was I scared of calling his bluff directly – who knew how a character who got himself off tracking a lone woman around would react when cornered? – but it wouldn't do any good. If he wasn't a psycho, he could stay cool and deny everything. If I got a policeman, how could I convince him that it was true? There wasn't any evidence of harassment. The only way to get out of it was to shake off the bastard. But once I had done that, what the hell could I do? He – or they, whoever they were – knew where I lived, knew about the cottage. And once I had given them the slip and they had caught up with me again, they might decide they had had enough of trailing me around and decide to adopt firmer methods.

But I couldn't rely on this guy simply staying on my heels like a tame pooch. He might decide to start snapping at any moment. He sure as hell didn't want my autograph.

I realized that my staring at the display of clothing in the boutique was becoming unconvincingly prolonged. I moved back into the stream of passers-by without a backward glance. I didn't want to give any overt sign that I had clocked him. That might make him extra vigilant when I made my move. And what move was that, pray? I suppose if I had been a man I could have lured him down a dark alley and beaten him to a pulp. But that would have left the question of what to do as an encore. And why go into that 'How I wish I were a man' crap? Most men I had known were hardly capable of beating an avocado to a pulp, and would have fainted at the prospect of any real danger. No, if I was going to get out of this, I had to rely on my own resources.

I was getting near the train station. It came to me that if I really were in a bad movie, then it was a case of picking the one where it all came out right for me.

I went to the ticket office window and flashed the return to King's Cross. When was the next train? I enquired loudly of the clerk.

I got the answer I already knew and went through to the platform. It was moderately crowded with commuter types heading for the dormitory towns down the line and the occasional overdressed couples with the we're-going-for-an-evening-in-Town look about them.

I loitered by the barrier, studying the timetable pasted on the wall, watching my friend pushing a couple of notes on to the revolving tray and receiving a ticket in return. I actually felt him brush past me as he moved casually down the platform to the unoccupied area beyond the canopy. He would have a clear view there of people getting on the train. He seemed to know what he was about. But I too had a plan.

I looked at my wristwatch. Five minutes before the train was due. Time to go.

I had located the coyly entitled Ladies' Waiting Room as soon as I got on to the platform. Casually, unhurriedly, I made my way in there through the heavy wooden outer door. I was relying on two things: the natural inbuilt reticence of even a hoodlum type to go into a women's lavatory in front of a crowd of onlookers, and the fact that he would be expecting me to be ready to get on the train when it arrived. But women are always late, aren't they, darling?

Once inside I got less casual. Like most of these places, there was a kind of anteroom with benches and chairs – the waiting room proper – and beyond that another door to the loo. As I hoped and expected, it was empty.

I chose a stall in front of the doorway, slipped off my jacket and draped it over the front of the pan so it hung down like a skirt. Then I pulled the door shut from outside, stuck a tenpence coin in the projecting screw and moved the door bolt to the 'engaged' position. We used to do this at college during a party: it was amusing to see our friends with bursting bladders bent double in front of apparently occupied lavatories. They didn't think to look under the doors. Now it wasn't a practical joke. And as I was dealing with a wiseguy, I hoped the jacket would for a few vital seconds hide the fact that there weren't any feet under there. It was a nice jacket and I hated to lose it.

I left the door to the loos half open. He would see the occupied stall right away. On the other side of the obscured glass windows, I could hear the squeal of brakes as the train drew in, dead on time.

Agonizing seconds passed. Perhaps he would bluff me, hanging around outside for me to come out. When the train had gone he would have a clear field to do whatever he wanted on an unoccupied platform. But I didn't think he would be that confident. He couldn't know I wasn't going to climb out of a window and couldn't risk that I would.

So I breathed deeply. I could hear the sounds of the other passengers as they climbed on to the train and their voices, probably chatting about normal things like the show they were going to see and where they would eat dinner.

The outer door flew open, and he charged in. Immediately he saw the occupied stall through the doorway. 'London train's about to depart, madam,' he called out. He was certainly cool. When there was no response, he went through the anteroom in a couple of strides. I heard him rattling the door bolt. 'Are you all right in there, madam?'

I slipped out from my hiding place behind a bench beside the outer door, ran across the room, pulled the door to the loos shut and dropped the barred back of a wooden chair over the knob. As I hurtled out on to the platform, I could hear curses and hammering as he tried to get out.

The sliding doors of the carriage opposite were just closing as I swerved between them into the compartment. It was a skill I had honed to perfection after riding the London Underground. The doors thudded together and the train began to move.

I dropped down into a seat on the far side, hoping that by the time he got out it would be unclear as to whether I had caught the train or run off somewhere else.

I was quite out of breath and, the tension of the moment released, trembling all over. I dragged the heavy coil of hair out of my eyes and lay back on the prickly pile of the seat cushions, panting as if I had been in a marathon. The eyes of my fellow travellers, which must have been curiously turned on me as I had whirled out of the Ladies' and thrown myself into the carriage, were now mostly swivelled back to magazines and paperbacks, although one or two without other interests in their lives were muttering to their partners and nodding slyly in my direction. I got the eyes swivelling again quickly, however, as I got up out of my seat.

I had to go to the loo.

When I got up, however, I realized I had another problem. I must have wrenched the heel of my left shoe on something as I tore around at the station. As I put my full weight on it it broke off.

The countryside rolled past in a green blur. I had to decide what to do. Having given my pursuer the slip, I had no illusions that it would be any more than temporary. He would have been on the phone to his London associates and no doubt there would be a reception committee waiting at King's Cross – someone I wouldn't recognize. I had to get away from them before they turned nasty. I had to go somewhere to think through everything that had happened. I had to get off this train before the terminus and disappear. The question was where, and how?

I managed to make myself look a little more respectable using the tiny dirty mirror in the lavatory. But the fact was that not only did I have only one complete shoe, I had with me only the clothes I could barely stand up in: a thin cotton blouse and a skirt. I bemoaned the sacrifice of my velvet jacket. I didn't even have a spare pair of pants. I opened my purse and viewed its contents, hoping to get consolation from its familiarity and perhaps inspiration for my next move.

Because I was basically a tidy and well organized person, I didn't carry around the detritus in there which most women are accused of. There were the usual practical things: a purse containing notes and change to the amount of fifty-two pounds and twenty-four pence; a wallet with credit cards; a pen and pencil case; my Filofax; a spiral-bound notebook.

And an airmail envelope, containing several sheets of writing paper. Nestling suggestively next to it was my blue passport, which fortunately I hadn't returned to my desk after taking it to Norfolk. The conjunction of the two was irresistible. Lying there with Anna's letter, it was telling me something. It was saying, 'Go South, young woman.'

I had a sudden aching pang to get away from the confusion and complications which were closing in on me here. And also to see Anna. She would help me sort it out. I felt desperately in need of help. I had no one else to turn to.

Looking back on it, I realize that was the crucial moment of the whole business. If I hadn't decided to go to France, God knows what would have happened to me, even considering what did.

My hasty change of plan left the small problem of how I was going to get to a small village near Montpellier from a train heading for King's Cross. I couldn't go home. I daren't stop anywhere as it would give my pursuers time to catch up. I had to keep moving. I had to get out of the country before they even considered this as a possibility.

It was like one of those survival tests they set the more macho outfits in the army. Fortunately, although I was not six foot three and trained to kill with my little finger, I had something that wasn't standard issue to HM Forces. An American Express card.

I was awake. The train had stopped and the change in motion had interrupted my light doze. I leaned forward to look out of the carriage window.

It was a scene which was becoming familiar. A rectangular station building with a terracotta Roman tiled roof rendered in faded ochre, a dusty yard beyond that where a couple of farm trucks and a grimy white car were parked, a group of workmen in blue overalls standing by. The sound of someone unloading boxes or crates at the end of the train, and a man in railway uniform scrutinizing the documents of an elderly couple about to board. Over all this was the flawless blue of the sky, and heard even through the double-glazed window was the strident chirruping of the cicadas.

I stretched in the seat. My head was muzzy from lack of sleep and too much coffee. I looked at my watch. Only fifteen minutes to go. It was probably the next stop. Thank goodness for that. I had been travelling for what seemed like years, but was actually only about thirty-six hours.

In the end it had proved surprisingly easy. I had got off the Cambridge train in the North London suburbs, switched to the Underground and gone on to Victoria. I had just had enough time before catching the boat train – my new habit of economy had selected this form of transport, and the longer journey would give me time to think – to buy at the concourse shopping centre a sweater, a holdall, toiletries and a change of underwear. I had also got my broken shoe fixed at the heel bar.

The Channel had been calm. I had stood at the stern rail and watched the lights of Dover slowly fade into the night. It was as if a great burden was being lifted from my shoulders. Free of England, I was free for a while of Geoffrey and the tangle of his life and death.

Beneath a high white moon, the track of the ship was a faintly glowing line across the silver-flecked darkness of the sea. The old seafarers had called it the whale road. I looked on it and for the first time in ages, despite the chill of the ocean breeze and the scant protection of my cheap, hastily bought jersey, I felt within me a warmth kindling. The rising wind seized my loosened hair and set it streaming behind me. I recognized the source of the warmth, and breathed its name with my cold but smiling lips. Hope.

I had arrived. I stumbled in my awkward heels down the carriage steps on to the weed-pierced tarmac strip between the tracks. I stood back as the small yellow train accelerated smoothly away and was lost to sight as the line curved steeply around a wooded knoll, leaving only the vibration of the power cable slung overhead on grey steel gantries to mark its passing.

No one else had got off and no one had got on at the halt. As I gazed around, it was not hard to see why. There were no station buildings, only a metal sign dented with the impact of airgun pellets with the name 'Les Myrtilles' in faded lettering. There was no sign of habitation anywhere about. The fierce sun beat down from the clear sky, tempered only by a light breeze which brought with it the faint scents of thyme and rosemary.

Whilst I didn't expect there to be a taxi rank, I had hoped that there would at least be a village, a hamlet even, where someone might be persuaded to point me in the direction of the château, or even drive me there. I supposed I should have hired a car or taken a cab, but the need for economy was decisive when I discovered at the railway station in Montpellier that the halt of Les Myrtilles was only a kilometre from the village of St Gervais-les-Eaux in which was situated the eponymous château. If all else failed, I reasoned, I could walk it.

All else had failed. I crossed the line by a walkway of old wooden sleepers to a gate which gave out on to a narrow metalled road. Fortunately, there was only one possible direction, the road terminating beyond the gate in a turning head of rutted gravel infested with rose-bay willow-herb. I shouldered my bag and set off down down the hill.

After five minutes my face and body were awash with perspiration. I stopped under the shade of a huge chestnut and sat down on the warm grass. The cicadas made the small dark chamber of comparative coolness vibrate like the inside of a bell. Beyond the canopy of the tree, the sunlight was as white as a magnesium flare.

I improvised a sunhat from a copy of *Le Monde* and again strode out on to the road. Half an hour later, I staggered into the tiny village square of St Gervais-les-Eaux. I hadn't beaten any records getting there. I felt washed out by the intense heat and lack of proper sleep. The road from the station had descended gently into a wooded valley and then climbed at a much steeper angle up the opposite side. I wasn't used to exertion in these conditions – the extra pounds I carried really weighed heavily. My throat was dry and my calf muscles ached. What with my newspaper hat and crumpled clothing, I must have looked a fright. Except, of course, there was no one to see me. St Gervais was *fermé*.

Around the Place de la Mairie were the essential elements of French society: the Mairie itself, the PTT, the café, the *boulangerie* and the *boucherie-charcuterie*. But all were firmly closed and shuttered. In the dusky square itself, in the shade of the inevitable pollarded plane trees, a brown dog slept.

There was no one around to ask, but again the choice of direction was limited. The road I had come in on went straight out again. Wearily, I gritted my teeth and plodded on. Finally, at the last house in the village, there was human life: an elderly man dozing in the shade of his veranda. He woke up as he heard the click of my heels on the tarmac and nodded a wary greeting.

'*Je cherche le château. C'est la bas?*' I said in my schoolgirl French, pointing down the road.

'*Ah, oui. La dame Anglaise de grande taille.*' He grinned. '*Oui. tout droit. Une kilometre et demie.*'

Another half-hour of puffing and panting, of sweat soaking my blouse and running down my neck, of my hair falling into my streaming eyes, of salt on my lips, of sore feet and blistered heels, of screaming leg muscles, brought me to a pair of gate pillars. The rendering of both had cracked and fallen away in chunks, and one was leaning considerably out of true. On them hung open a pair of iron gates, once painted dark green but now mainly rust. Weeds grew profusely in the shingle of the rutted driveway which curved away into a green tunnel of overhanging tree branches. It was straight out of *Le Grand Meaulnes*.

It had to be the château. Please let there be a shower, I muttered to myself in rhythmic litany as I trudged up the drive. And a big, big glass of cold white wine. And a bed with crisp cool linen sheets. And . . .

I looked up and through a fretwork of green leaves I saw the château. Then I stopped abruptly, instinctively, as there was the sound of loud voices.

I stood hidden in the shade of the green tunnel and gaped out at the scene before me with amazed disbelief.

It wasn't, I hasten to explain, a château of the kind you see on the travel posters, a pointy-towered, slate-roofed confection set down in the lush meadows of a northern French river valley: a lavish country house dressed up as a castle in the way that Marie Antoinette and her courtiers dressed as milkmaids and swains. This was of the South and with the look of a real fortress, reminiscent of the *bastides*, the fortified hill towns which scatter the region as perpetual reminders of the Hundred Years War. An inverted L-shaped barrack of a place with tiny windows piercing the red rubblework façade like arrow slits in a medieval tower.

Carriage steps led up to the big oak double doors of the entrance. In the angle of the L, there was a yard, more dust than gravel, partly in the shade of the building. It was obviously used as a sitting-out area. There were rusty white metal café tables and chairs. At one of these, in a plunge-back black and white one-piece swimsuit, her long tanned legs stretched out in front of her and her long blonde hair hanging loose down on her bare shoulders, was Anna.

It was her penetrating, fluty upper-class tones which I had heard. But what stopped me from rushing forward and embracing her in heartfelt greeting was the figure who occupied the chair opposite to her, and who made it look too impossibly delicate and lacelike to contain his bulky frame. It was his deep, male rumble I had heard in counterpoint to Anna's.

But it wasn't that I hesitated to allow an unexpected, unknown third party to witness our tearful reunion. I hovered out of sight of the two people on the terrace because I knew the man very well indeed. Far too well. Seeing him there made me sick with horrified disbelief. Never in a million years would I have expected to find Anna tête-à-tête with him here, apparently laughing hugely at something he had said. I shivered, despite the blanketing heat. What, for God's sake, was going on?

I stood there, paralysed with shock, as still as if I were one of the grey-limbed trees that shaded the drive.

I watched bitterly, tears of exhaustion and anger rising to my eyes as the scene before me changed. Anna stood up to embrace the gross body of her companion, who had struggled heavily to his feet like a hippo lurching out of the mud. Ugh, how could she? The tender assignation was obviously over. He held her for a moment in his bear hug, then arm in arm they strolled away out of view.

A moment later I heard the roar of a powerful engine and a silver Daimler squealed past me, its fat tyres churning up the dust. As I shrank back even further into the undergrowth, I caught a glimpse of his jowly face and his sandbagged eyes.

Then there was silence again. I watched as Anna came back to the table, sat down and refilled her wine glass from an earthenware pitcher. I had to do something. I couldn't stay in the bushes all night.

I threw the paper hat into the undergrowth, smoothed down my hair and strolled as nonchalantly as I could over to the table.

'Hi there, Judas,' I said.

'Good morning! How are you feeling?'

The sunlight streamed into the room as Anna, in a white lace-trimmed silk peignoir, her bare suntanned arms spread wide, drew back the heavy maroon velvet curtains. She twisted the central handle of the full-length windows and pushed them open. A draught of warm, flower-scented air billowed across the bed.

I pushed my hair out of my eyes, propped myself up on one elbow and yawned. I peered at my watch on the dark oak bedside table. 'God, is that really the time?'

'Afraid so. You've slept for about fifteen hours. I was getting worried. Thought you'd died. Look, I've brought us some breakfast. Coffee and rolls. They're yesterday's but I've warmed them up in the oven.'

'They smell heavenly.' There was also a wonderful peach preserve – 'grown on the estate' – and unsalted farm butter which made the kind I had gotten used to lately seem like axle grease. I sat up in the enormous bed, leaning against the heavily carved oak headboard, munching the delicious crusty *pain complet*. Anna sat opposite in a huge wing-backed armchair, regarding me quizzically over the top of her big breakfast cup of *café au lait*.

'I suppose you're still cross with me,' she said.

'Cross? Me? Why should I be?'

'Oh, come on now. You were pretty horrid to me last evening. And I suppose you were right to be. After all, I didn't tell you about Michael. And then to find me here supping with the enemy.'

'There's no reason why you should have told me. I'm not involved with the book any more, am I?'

'Not in that way. But I feel as if I ought to have told you. It was a bit hard on you finding out like that.'

'I'm sure you would have told me eventually. And you weren't to know I would come popping out of the undergrowth and see you there together, were you?'

She laughed. 'I don't know about that. I've always suspected that under that super-efficient executive image there's a pretty impulsive emotional sort of person. But as you were so shattered and shaken yesterday I didn't get any idea as to quite why you've descended on me like this. You just scuttled up here and went to sleep. What on earth is it about?'

I blushed. 'Sorry. You're right. I was horrid. I was really taken aback by finding . . . him here. I'll try to explain. I shouldn't have called you Judas. That was awful.'

'Yes, it was a bit strong. But I'm so pleased to see you I'll forgive you – but only because I'm dying to know why you're here.'

'It was because of the burglary at the flat.'

'What burglary?'

I told her. About the break-in. About what I had heard from David and my fear of what Michael was capable of. About what had happened at the railway station in Cambridge.

She listened wide-eyed, sitting in the chair with her feet drawn up like a child, clasping her arms around her bare knees.

When I had finished, she looked at me long and hard. I waited for the outflow of warm sympathy. It didn't come. Instead she started to laugh. She threw back her head and hooted, kicking her legs in the air like a colt and slapping the arms of the chair. 'You're a better story teller than I am,' she said in the end, wiping her eyes on a corner of her robe. 'You really thought that Michael has employed some heavies to – what do they say? – duff you up? Honestly, darling, you're –'

'Crazy? OK. Why not say it? It's what you think. You really think I've gone nuts. Accusing total strangers of being fraudulent real estate agents. Seeing plots and conspiracies everywhere. Sure thing. I'm off my head since Geoffrey died. Too much stress etc., etc. Thank you, Dr Dalton. I'll go home right now as I'm obviously not welcome.'

She was out of the chair instantly, rushing over to the bed to sit on the edge and encircle me in her arms. 'Darling, I really wasn't going to say anything so unkind. I think you had a bad experience. What looks sensible in some lights becomes, well, less likely when you look at it again. That's all. And you're not going anywhere.'

I shook off her arms and pushed myself further along the bed. 'You think I imagined the whole thing? Being followed and everything?'

She shrugged. 'I don't know. All I know – at least all I think I'm totally certain of – is that Michael can't be behind it. He's not really like that. Oh, he may talk big, but he's one of nature's bluffers. His whole career is bluff, isn't it? If I'd thought he was capable of anything like that I would never have written to him in the way I did and invited him here to discuss things alone with him. He was a perfect gentleman. You saw how we were together. He was sweet. Like he used to be.'

'What do you mean "used to be"?'

'Long ago, when the world was young, darling. We had an affair, you know.'

'No, I didn't. How was I supposed to? Anyway, Michael has so many. He's an omnivore where women are concerned.'

'You sound as if you talk from experience.'

I was on the point of making a nasty retort, but instead drank some coffee. It had gone cold. We eyed each other for a minute or so. I found Anna's certainty really galling. With her track record about men, it was hard to take. But then who was I to feel superior in that respect?

Then Anna put her hand on mine. 'Let's not get horrid to each other. I don't know what happened between you and Michael. You don't have to tell me if you don't want. Michael's nothing to me now, hasn't been for years. I only told you because he's like all men: he thinks he's got a lien on me because we slept together a few times. They can still be jealous even though they have had umpteen lovers in between. I think that was his reaction when he found out I'd gone off with Pierre. A younger man and all that, too. It was the money as well, of course, and the embarrassment over the advance publicity. But more than the book, I think it was personal.'

'I see.' I paused, letting the implications sink in. 'He may be like that to you, but he hates the sight of me, I'm sure. And there's more you don't know about. Enough to make him do everything I said he had. I don't think being charming to you weighs much against what he did to me. And you should hear what he's been putting around London about me. Apart from everything else I may never get a job anywhere else in publishing.'

'That does sound like Michael. A little boy, a bit spiteful and silly. I don't know why he sacked you. He probably doesn't either. He's very impulsive. He doesn't want you to have the opportunity of demonstrating your impressive talents with anyone else. That would make him look very foolish. He'll probably offer you another job himself.'

'You don't understand how it is. There's no chance in hell I'd work for him again. In fact I think I'm rather sick of the whole scene at present. If I weren't broke I'd be happy enough without it.'

She laughed. 'I find that hard to believe. You're so dedicated to work. Unlike me. I haven't done a stroke since . . . since goodness knows when.'

'Aren't you going to finish *This Spider Love*, or any of the rest? What did Michael say?'

'I thought you weren't interested any more, eh? Look at you, you're dying for the latest news, aren't you?'

'You're my friend. That's different. Stop teasing me and tell me what really happened. You haven't given me the full story yet. I was so tired yesterday, I couldn't be bothered to ask you.'

'There's not much to tell. I wrote to Michael. It seemed silly and childish, hiding out, not facing up to things. I couldn't ask Vanessa to cover for me any longer. I'm sure she's fed up with the whole thing. You probably know Michael's got a villa on the coast quite near here. He goes there a fair bit in the summer and autumn. I said if he were around, he could drop in. So he did. I was very nervous, but as I said he was terrific. He said that as it happened he was very relaxed about schedules and deadlines because he had, in his words, something "absolutely enormous" coming out quite soon which he wanted to leave room for. "Take as long as it needs, my dear. Your loyal readers will have to wait a bit longer, that's all." I was so relieved he wasn't going to go after me for the money because I'd had some bad news on the château. Birmingham man has pulled out. Wrote a dud cheque for the deposit and skedaddled.' She switched into demotic Black Country. 'Sign of the times, innit, me duck?'

I looked around at the big room with its creamy walls and

heavy dark ceiling beams. Through the open window, I saw under the blue sky the green lines of a vineyard sketched in on the russet earth of a hillside and to one side like a smoky haze the paler green of an olive grove. 'Bad luck. Must be a real penance having to stay here when you could be in Cricklewood. If I forget thee, O my Cricklewood! London is so bloody at present. It rains the whole time. I get burgled. I'm sick of it.'

'That's the second time you've said you're sick of everything. I'm beginning to get worried. What's been going on? you keep dropping these heavy, doom-laden hints. If only I knew, etc. Tell me, have you been to Norfolk? You didn't say anything in your letter.'

I stared up at the ceiling. Between the beams above the bed, a spider was weaving away at her web. I looked at the elaborate gossamer threads, at the pattern of concentric circles intricately linked. I turned my face towards Anna's. 'I don't know where to start, except to say that Esmeralda Pym was right.'

'Begin in the middle, said the poet Horace. I always do. Begin anywhere. Start where I left.'

So I did.

18

'This is so perfect. I don't know how you could ever think of leaving.' I leaned back and the wickerwork chair creaked comfortably. Above me through the leaves of the huge sweet chestnut which cast a much needed dappled shade the sky was its inevitable clear blue.

We were sitting on a stone-paved terrace on what Anna called the *la côté du soleil*. This was of a later date than the entrance side. The windows of the rooms were larger and the views were far more dramatic. Here the ground fell away steeply into a wooded ravine, where could be seen the sandy and rock-strewn bed of a now dry watercourse. On the hillside opposite was the gravity-defying vineyard I had glimpsed earlier from my bedroom.

We were in the process of finishing lunch. My watch had stopped hours ago and I had no real idea of the time, although judging from the sun it must have been quite late afternoon. Anna didn't wear a watch and regarded my interest in the hour as some kind of strange and unhealthy obsession.

On the wooden table in front of me were the remains of lunch: a wooden bowl now empty of salad but its inside still glistening with oil and flecked with green fragments of fresh basil, a platter of some local cheeses, mainly demolished, and an earthenware jug, almost empty, which had contained a substantial quantity of the dark red wine which I had first tasted on that wet and windy night at Forest House. Norfolk seemed a million miles away, a barren and chilly place of ill omen. By contrast the Château de St Gervais seemed a glorious idyll.

'You wouldn't say that if you had the looking after of it. It's far too big for me. There are so many bedrooms I haven't counted them all. And the grounds. There are hectares and hectares. Do you know how big a hectare is? I bet you don't. It's a hell of a lot bigger than a good old English acre. You saw the state of the drive when you arrived yesterday. The whole place is like that. The only part that isn't a mess is the vineyard, and that's leased off to a couple of peasant brothers – like something out of Marcel Pagnol. They sell the wine to the Caves Cooperatives and I get a share of the profit and as much wine as I can drink. It's driving me crazy, the worry of it. No wonder I can't work.' She emptied her wine glass and stretched out her long arm to refill it from the pitcher. '"Little brown jug do I love thee,"' she sang merrily as she quaffed.

'It's actually a socking great big jug,' I pointed out. 'And you've emptied it.'

'Don't worry, there's plenty more in the *cave*. Bloody barrels of it. Enough even for you.'

'It's OK. I don't want any more at the moment. I'm not surprised you can't work if you knock it back like this every day.' I raised a hand of entreaty as she immediately made a face at this remark. 'I know that sounds prissy – and I'm the last one to talk about reducing one's alcohol intake – but it's occurred to me that if you were to finish *Spider Love* and the others, you could afford to live here. It's the perfect place for a writer isn't it?'

'You sound like my mother. "If only you'd really work at something, dear," she says. But writing's not like bloody sheep rearing. I could sit and work at it all day and still end up with nothing.'

'Anna, you've got so much talent I hate to see it going to waste. Michael seems to have given you an opening.. Why don't you go for it?'

'Because, because. I don't know. I don't feel I can any more. I know I made a bit of a joke about the Pierre thing, but I really miss the bastard. He was good for the ego if nothing else. Now I'm just an ageing has-been.'

'"Better than a never-had-been," Geoffrey used to say.' I stopped suddenly. 'I know exactly what you mean. I miss him quite wretchedly too. Despite everything I told you this morning, despite the lies and the pretences, there's still this great hole in my life.'

'I know that. And look at what they do to us – look at what we let them do to us. Look at me, reluctant châtelaine, broke, my reputation as a professional author in ruins – all because of bloody Pierre. Look at you, plunged into some mess that Geoffrey left behind, the sort of mess that's so messy you can't see what sort of mess it is.'

I laughed. 'What a wonderful way of putting it. I know exactly what you mean. But I was hoping that you, or rather Esmeralda Pym, would be on her way to unravelling it.'

'I told you I had to think about it. That I didn't want to spoil my lunch. Well, I'm not going to let it spoil my afternoon either. Let's go for a swim.'

'A swim? You mean you've got a swimming pool? For God's sake, how much perfection can we mortals stand?'

'Um, well, it's not what David Hockney would call a pool, but it's good enough for me. Come on!'

'Ooh! You didn't tell me it was freezing!'

'Don't be such a wimp! I can tell you didn't go to the sort of school I did. We didn't 'ave such a thing as 'eated watter in Yorkshire, lass!'

I bravely swam a couple of lengths in the square, concrete-lined tank and then scrambled out into the still hot late afternoon sun. I lay on my back on the tartan travelling rug which Anna had set out on the rough paving and let my naked body soak up the healing rays. Gradually I stopped shivering, and the gooseflesh receded a little. I picked up one of the thick, brightly coloured towels from the pile near my head, stood up and towelled myself roughly all over. I shook out my wet hair, and pushed it back over my ears so that it hung in a cool tangled mass down my back.

Anna propelled herself out of the water like a fish leaping for a fly and flopped beside me.

'What is this place exactly? It doesn't really look like a pool.'

'I told you that. It isn't. It's actually part of our water supply. I say, you didn't pee in there, did you?'

'Certainly not. Isn't that a public school habit? But do you mean it's our drinking water?'

'No, I'm relieved to say. That's separate. There's a spring in the hills. It gets piped down here. This tank was built to supply the bathrooms and loos in the house, otherwise there wouldn't have been enough pressure or what have you. It's because it's spring fed that it's so cold. You get used to it. You feel wonderful afterwards, don't you?'

As we sat side by side staring out across the sparkling water of the pool, the stillness of the moment was broken by a loud male shouting in French which came from the direction of the château.

Anna dragged on pants, T-shirt and jeans, hopped her feet into a pair of espadrilles and ran off in the direction of the voice, yelling out, *'J'arrive! J'arrive!'* as she went.

I pulled on my clothes rather more slowly and followed, feeling distinctly uncomfortable and stumbling slightly as the borrowed underwear was too tight and the borrowed skirt too long.

When I got to the front terrace, Anna was in animated conversation with two stocky, swarthy dark-suited men. Drawn up in the driveway was a dark blue saloon car. It didn't need a mastermind to work out who they were, but what on earth did they want? I didn't have to wait long to find out.

Anna turned to me as I staggered up inelegantly and said, 'Mary, these are policemen.' Her voice was sharp with upper-class glaciation. 'They have come to ask me some questions about Michael Underdown-Metcalfe. Apparently he did not return to his villa last night. He has not been seen since. It seems I may be the last person with whom he is known to have had contact.'

They had finally gone. *'Sales flics!'* muttered Anna as their car bumped along the drive and disappeared into the green tunnel.

'They were only doing their jobs,' I said mildly, sipping a glass of wine.

We were sitting at the front of the château, in the deep shadow of its walls. It was almost dusk, but the air was warm and the cicadas kept up their racket.

Anna merely grunted. She had become petulant, restlessly getting up and sitting down again, finally pacing the courtyard moodily.

It was obvious that Michael was to be our topic of conversation. She said: 'So what's the bastard up to? Do you think he's done a runner?'

I hesitated. In her usual slapdash way Anna might well have come up with the truth. I thought back to my midnight conversation with James Edwardes. I had heard what I had heard in confidence. For the moment at least I would keep it that way, even from Anna. 'What on earth do you mean? What's he running from? He's a rich and famous tycoon, isn't he?'

'I suppose so. But a man like that doesn't get where he is without doing something he'd rather not want people to know about, does he?'

I shrugged. 'He might have met with an accident.'

'No, there was something about the way those policemen were asking the questions. As if they thought I knew something.'

'Perhaps they think you've done him in. I've felt like it in the past.'

'Perhaps they do. Perhaps someone else has felt like that and actually done something about it.'

'Hey, this is getting serious. Do you really think that?'

'Stranger things happen at sea, don't they? Who knows what goes on in the big world? All I know is that the French police are not usually so solicitous about missing tourists who may have gone off on a bender. People like Michael don't live that sort of life anyway. Everywhere he went he would have his fax machine and his telex. His movements were organized down to the nth degree. Isn't it odd, then, that he didn't tell anyone he was coming here, not directly? The cop said he had an evening engagement in Beziers, for which, although he'd left extremely early, he didn't turn up. That set the alarm bells ringing, hospitals, road accidents, etc. It was only when his secretary started going through the papers on his desk that she found my letter with the date pencilled in in his handwriting. I didn't even know he was coming until he turned up. As he couldn't phone me, I told him to drop in and he did. I don't even know what the time was when he appeared. And there was one other thing that was a bit odd. He drove himself here, didn't he? He hardly ever did that. He didn't like driving because it meant it distracted him from acting on things straight away. Sitting in the back he could pick up the phone, send a fax or whatever. If he were driving even he would have to condescend to look at the road occasionally.'

'You didn't point that out to the police.'

'It's only just occurred to me. And why should I do their dirty work for them? It may not be significant anyway. But who knows what he was up to? He always had so many schemes on the go, even when I was involved with him years ago.'

I said nothing, but drank more wine. I felt guilty about not telling Anna what I knew, but she would no doubt find out soon enough if the shit really had hit the fan. Screw Michael. He'd got what was coming to him.

She stopped wandering about the dusty courtyard and sat down opposite me at the wrought iron table. She leaned towards me intently. 'Perhaps you were right about Michael after all. I laughed at you this morning, but maybe he's changed. This being hunted by the police. It's heavy stuff, isn't it? If there's a lot at stake, then maybe he has got really nasty. Maybe he's got as nasty as it's possible to get. We know Geoffrey and Michael were involved on a project. You said you thought it was a book, and somehow connected to this scientist fellow Mallen. Perhaps there were problems, a falling out.'

'Are you saying Michael might have had something to do with Geoffrey's death?' I stared at her in alarm.

'You always wanted to believe it was an accident, didn't you? When you told me about how he died I thought there was something suspicious about it, but you didn't want to listen. Even when that boy – Tom, was it? – told you about Geoffrey arguing with someone and driving off, you said you didn't really believe him.'

'Would you? He's half-crazy. He'd be the world's lousiest witness.'

'All right, so he's inarticulate, devious, what have you, but he might have seen something.'

'But Geoffrey and Michael . . . It's absurd! Michael surely needed him alive. What good's a dead author?'

'I don't know. Perhaps Esmeralda Pym is having a brain storm. It's hard for you, isn't it, having to think of Geoffrey being mixed up in something which might have got him killed?'

'You're right. I'm sick of mystery. I want to be able to grieve for him without this stuff getting in the way. Can't you understand that? For God's sake, whatever he did, I loved him.'

She put out a hand and laid it gently on my arm. 'Of course I see that. But perhaps in the end it would be better if you did know. Let's forget it for the moment and have some more wine.' She upended the pitcher. 'Whoops, it's empty again. I'll get some more from the *cave*. I have to have a pee anyway.' She took the jug and ran up the steps and through the big front doors.

It was almost dark, the warm velvety dark of the South. I stood up stiffly, then wandered across the courtyard to watch the moon rising over the rooftop. It was almost silent, even the insects having quietened down. I felt the tears rise to my eyes as I remembered the chillier nights of Norfolk, and the dark trees swaying in the wind across the clearing. I remembered . . .

But my reverie was broken abruptly by a shout from within the house, followed by a crash. Then came more yells. It was Anna, and she was screaming for help.

The hair at the back of my neck bristled as I hurtled up the uneven stone steps and into the entrance vestibule of the château. 'Anna!' My voice echoed in the dark. 'Where are you? What's going on?' I gazed around blindly. I didn't know where the hell the light switch was or even if there was one.

'Mary!' There was light, flooding down from the chandelier

high above the stairwell. Anna stood in a doorway at the back of the hall. She looked pale, her face smudged with grime.

'Anna, what on earth's the matter? You scared me, yelling like that.'

'Sorry. I had a bit of a fright down in the cellar.' She twisted her mouth into a wry grin. 'I dropped the jug when I disturbed the rat behind the arras. It's just coming.'

There was the sound of heavy feet on the cellar steps behind her. A deep male voice said, panting slightly, 'That's not much of a way to introduce me, my dear.' I recognized it instantly. Then its owner loomed in the dark oblong of the doorway, a bulky man clad in a crumpled cream-coloured tropical suit.

'Why, hello again, Michael,' I said. 'We can't keep on meeting like this.'

'It's your fucking fault,' he said, pointing the chicken drumstick at me before returning it to the neighbourhood of his jaws, where he tore off a great lump of flesh. It was like watching the ogre in *Jack and the Beanstalk*.

I didn't rise to this, but gave a sidelong glance at Anna, who sat next to me at the big oak refectory table. Her face remained calm and sphinx-like. She had put Michael at the head at the other end, not in deference but because it seemed appropriate to what she had in mind.

'You eat,' she had said. 'Then you answer some questions.'

He agreed reluctantly, but already he seemed somewhat diminished. Without the glitz and trappings of power, the fancy office, the big desk, the bevy of sycophantic secretaries and PAs, the chauffeur-driven limousine, and dressed in the soiled linen suit, he was just a fat, unhealthily pallid man in late middle age looking somewhat downcast, the type you find wearily legging it around the stores with a case of samples and no appointment.

He had asked to be given dinner. 'I haven't eaten for a day,' he said mournfully.

'That hardly qualifies you for food aid,' I said nastily, but Anna had been smart enough to spot an opportunity. He was up to something, that was clear, and that gave us an advantage over him, at least temporarily.

We watched as he wolfed and slurped through a mountain of cold cuts and salad. It was fortunate that the sight of him had mostly taken our appetites away, as he had chomped up most of the contents of Anna's refrigerator.

'More bread?' said Anna coldly, shoving the basket along the table.

He shook his head, downed a glass of wine in one gulp, then belched. 'You were always a generous hostess, my dear. Unlike that cold-hearted bitch. And that's not the only thing that's cold. She's got an iceberg for a c –.'

'That's enough, Michael. This is my house. Remember you're an uninvited guest here. Just because you've got a bit pissed on my wine doesn't allow you to be abusive.'

The food had restored something of his presence and his pugnacity, but he nevertheless sullenly signified acquiescence. It was advantage Anna and she kept her eye on the ball.

'Now you've finished gorging yourself, Michael, you can tell us why the self-proclaimed greatest British publisher has been hiding in my wine cellar like a fugitive. What do you think you're playing at?'

He leaned back in his chair, looking ominously more relaxed and in control. He grinned hugely. 'I don't really think it's any of your business. You invited me to drop in any time when I called to see you yesterday, so I did. As it is getting rather late, I think it's probably time you got a bed ready for me. And if either – or both – of you two lovely ladies would care to . . .' He waved a fat white hand suggestively, the candlelight glinting on the big ruby signet ring he was wearing.

Anna and I exchanged glances again. Then Anna picked up the carbon steel knife she had used to carve up the cold chicken and examined the blade in a thoughtful way. It had a wicked point and I knew that Anna, like all proper cooks, kept it razor sharp. 'That's enough, Michael. If you don't stop behaving like the Caliph of Baghdad and talk sensibly, then I shall get very cross with you.

You see, I rather suspect that those policemen who came to see us today were altogether more interested in finding you than mere concern for your good health would justify. They were very discreet, but I think they wanted you to – what do they say? – assist them with their enquiries, or the French equivalent, which is bound to be less cosy. As a law-abiding resident of this country I'm inclined to help them to that end. Perhaps we should put you back in the cellar and get them to fetch you. As for a bed, I'm sure they've got a nice cell free.'

Michael sat up sharply, his mouth a hard line, his eyes blazing. It was a familiar expression to me. I had seen grown men – well, men anyway – cower in abject submission before it. I had done a bit of cowering myself, I had to admit. But in these new surroundings, away from his own home ground, it didn't work. Anna didn't appear to be the slightest bit intimidated when he growled, 'I wouldn't try anything like that, my dear. Remember whom you're talking to.'

She gave one of her schoolgirl whoops of laughter, as if she had scored a jolly fine goal in an upper school hockey match. Still holding the knife, she got out of her place and strolled casually over to him. 'No, Michael. You bloody well remember whom you're talking to. Who do you think you are? This isn't a bloody hotel. I'm not your servant. It's not like it used to be with us. I know you're the king of bluffers, but you can't bluff your way out of this. There are two of us and one of you. There's no one else here, and as you've probably noticed there aren't too many neighbours.' Standing back out of arm's reach, she pointed the knife at him. 'Are we clear now?'

'Put that thing down, Anna. You're not going to threaten me.' He stood up, and reached out his hand.

In the murky light, I didn't quite see what followed. I saw Anna move forward quickly and Michael collapse back into his chair with a yell, then lean forward again moaning.

I rushed over to them. 'Anna, you've stabbed him, for God's sake!'

'Don't be stupid. I only kicked him gently in the balls. I was top of my self-defence class, you know.'

She went over to Michael and ruffled his thick, dark, curly hair. 'Perhaps we should move to more comfortable chairs.'

We sat in the salon, but in the French fashion the chairs were still uncomfortable. Michael had to himself the thinly upholstered, thickly gilded sofa. Anna and I sat perched opposite on matching chairs. The tall windows on to the terrace were open, the warm night breeze fluttering the long curtains, wafting in the muted sounds of the insects and the occasional hooting of an owl or the bark of a fox.

Michael, no longer nursing his private parts, was sipping coffee from a cup which looked no larger than a thimble in his great paw. The grubby double-breasted jacket was undone and flopped around him as if he had suddenly shrunk within it. In the bright light of the crystal chandelier overhead I could see that the bags under his eyes were unusually pendulous and edged with thick, black semicircles of fatigue. The tortoise skin of his face and neck was rimed with whitish stubble, which mocked the jet black of his once immaculately coiffed head. I saw that the hand which replaced the cup on the small lacquer table shook slightly.

There was a quality about Anna I had never seen before. It was as if she were high on drugs. Energy seemed to crackle from her, from her bright eyes and from the loose ends of her blonde hair, which gleamed like electrical wire. There had been violence from her – and I realized with a shock that there might be more to come. She seemed dangerous, like an avenging angel. I think Michael sensed it too. He glanced at her warily. He no longer radiated defiance, but fear.

'What's it about, then?' Anna demanded. 'I told Mary earlier you were a sweetie underneath your bluster, but now I'm not so sure. You seem to be behaving like a gangster – anonymous telephone calls to my agent, having poor Mary followed and burgled. I think maybe all that power has gone to your head.' Anna leaned forward and poked his fat knee with her long, scarlet-nailed finger.

Michael stared at her for some moments in what appeared to be genuine astonishment, then he said, 'I don't know what you're bloody well talking about. OK, I did get one of my girls to phone your old cow of an agent. I wanted to find out where you'd gone. It wasn't just the money. I thought if we could talk, we could work something out – and we did, didn't we? You thought the same. That's why you wrote to me. Not that it's bloody relevant now. But what the fuck's this about having Mary followed and burgled? That's nothing to do with me. Probably some early menopausal fantasy. She's a great one for fiction.'

I was close to tears. 'You rotten, lying shit. I didn't imagine it. It must have been you. Who else can it have been? You've been making my life a misery since you fired me. Everyone avoids me like the plague.'

He actually laughed, holding his belly to keep his fat guts in place. 'It's a tough world out there, isn't it? You should know. I'm not sorry about what I did after all you did to me.'

It was my turn to sit up in amazement. 'For God's sake, what are you talking about? I've done to you! You kicked me when I was down, Michael, don't you remember? I haven't done a thing to you.'

'You spied on me, you opposed me, you tried to interfere with my decisions. You gave information to my enemies. Isn't that enough?'

'What! I did no such things.'

'You lying bitch. No one else could have tipped off the regulators, the fraud squad, and the other fucking bastards who've crawled out of the floorboards. Only you had the means and the will to do that.'

'But that's crazy! OK, so Max Vincent did ask me to report back on what was happening at McAllister's, but that wasn't spying! It was part of a normal commercial arrangement. He'd invested millions of dollars in your lousy company and he didn't want to see it go down the tube. You're a crazy paranoid if you think it was any more than that. And most of the time he wasn't even goddamned interested!'

'Fuck Vincent! I'm not interested in what you told that scheisshund. He'd never squeal. He was in too deep. It must have been you trying to get back at me for . . .'

'Listen to me, both of you.' Anna's voice, cool and clear, had in it the peremptory impatience of the ruling class. 'I don't want to hear about your squabbles on the shop floor. I want to know why Michael has decided to inflict himself on my house in this way. For all I know I'm harbouring a crook. I don't want to hear any more accusations. No more smoke screens. Just an answer. If the police are after you, Michael, why?'

'Yes. I am on the run, as they say. The London bureaucrats contacted Interpol. Fortunately, I have some friends in high places. After I left here yesterday, I had a tip off on the car phone that the French police would be waiting for me at Beziers. I hadn't actually told anyone about coming here. It was a piece of luck for me. I drove back and found a suitable spot in the forest to hide the car, then hung around until it was dark, came back and hid in the cellar. I knew the police would come here eventually, but once they had checked it out I imagined that they wouldn't come back – at least not immediately. They would assume at first that I had already left the area and scale down the search. After a day or so, if you hadn't found me, I would have abandoned the car near a station and gone on to Marseilles by train.'

'And then?'

He shook his head. 'You don't need to know that. Suffice to say that I have contacts there who can help me.'

I could hardly believe what I was hearing. 'You mean you're going to walk out on McAllister's and all your other interests? What'll happen to them once this hits the media?'

'It'll be a fucking catastrophe. The shares will be suspended and the sodding administrators will move in. But that would happen anyway once word got out that I'd been arrested. At least this way I'll be free. They won't catch me.'

'But what on earth have you done?' There was genuine concern in Anna's voice. 'They always said you sailed close to the wind, but I thought you were clever enough to avoid being capsized.'

'It's a stupid business, really. A man as successful as I am is bound to excite jealousy in the ranks of the bourgeoisie. And that's what your famous piddling Stock Exchange is, you know. Little men. Rule-mongers. No vision, no sense of history. Petty-minded officials, that's what they are. Bankers? Wankers. They would have got their money back. They just couldn't wait. "Your repayment is now six months overdue." They didn't have the guts to speak to me in person. Hid behind some clerk or some bloody computer. "The security offered has fallen below the originally negotiated threshold value." Bollocks. Well they've been sniffing around for years, and now they've got their noses right up my arse. They really like it there. OK, so there were some deals a few years back that didn't quite gel immediately, but I knew I was right about satellite long before anyone else. If they'd given me a bit more cash, I would have cleaned up. What did someone say about TV? It's a licence to print your own money. They couldn't see it, stupid bastards. And now I'm on the brink of one of the greatest successes in world publishing this century. Instead of riding it, of seeing McAllister's take off into a global business, they choose to go after me – for what? Something I wouldn't have had to do if those stuffed shirts hadn't consistently devalued my efforts and rubbished me in their damned clubs. And because you found out and put the boot in. Like all poison it's taken a bit of time to work through the system, but when it does you're dead.'

I heard the last word with a sick feeling. 'So what he told me was right. The so-called merger really was a sham.'

He rose in his seat and shook his fist in my face. 'You see, you did know. You went to the authorities. You can't deny it. I hope you're satisfied.'

I stood up to face him. The anger that had been building in me while he had been speaking finally exploded. I slammed the flat of my hand against his flabby chest. He collapsed so heavily back on to the sofa I thought it would tip over. 'Listen to me, you bastard. I've sat through enough. For some unknown reason – some vestigial belief that you weren't a complete asshole, I suppose – I didn't want to believe the very worst about you. OK, I know you're a swindler, now I believe you're much worse. I think you're a murderer. You murdered Geoffrey.'

His darkly shadowed eyes stared into mine, his face suddenly white.

It was strange how much the accusation seemed to affect him. There was genuine shock in the way the blood drained from his face.

He remained silent, his face ashen, his eyes closed, as if struck by some gnawing pain from within. He leant forward, picked up the coffee cup and drank off the contents, setting the cup back carefully on the saucer. I saw him take a deep breath, and when he spoke his voice, that deep, too carefully English voice, had in it a note of almost plaintive dignity. 'I have been accused of many things, I have done many things, but I swear to you I could never kill anyone, least of all him.'

'You can't bluff. You had every reason to get him out of the way. You knew he'd found out what you were up to, so you had him killed. Then you thought I knew about it and you turned your attention to me. But I didn't know, not a damned thing. Geoffrey never told me. But he'd already handed over the file he'd prepared to the authorities. It was too late, but you killed him anyway.' I sank down into the chair, the tears hot on my face. I felt Anna's comforting arm around me.

For what seemed a long while, he stared at me, this time mournfully rather than angrily.

'You say that Geoffrey sent the file to the authorities? I swear I never knew or even suspected such a thing. I don't understand why he should do that. Everything he wanted was within his grasp – and I had made it possible. Why did he betray me? Don't you understand, what can I say to you?' I heard him mutter something in a language I didn't recognize. 'I did not have anything to do with his death. I thought he died of natural causes. I was as astonished as anyone. For the love of God, Mary, you have to believe me. I had no motive to kill him. I even thought he was my friend.'

I fished in my purse for a handkerchief. If he was lying then he was very convincing. I no longer knew what to think. It made me feel the pain over again. 'Why should I believe you? You might have had other motives. Something to do with the project you and Geoffrey were working on. You've done your best to make sure I didn't find out about it.'

He threw up his hands in the universal gesture of frustration. 'Once again, what do I have to say to convince you, I had no hand in Geoffrey's death. As for you, Geoffrey and I agreed you would be told in due course.'

'Well, that was kind of you, but I managed to work it out for myself.' I paused. 'To work out that you got Geoffrey to write a book in collaboration with Julian Mallen.'

He looked up sharply. 'How did you know? Did he tell you?'

'No, he didn't. I put two and two together. You're not exactly the world's expert at keeping a secret, are you?'

'Go on, then. Tell me what you think you found out, Ms Holmes.'

'I think you and Geoffrey somehow persuaded Julian Mallen to do a book about his research. I imagine that as Mallen's populist communication skills are not, by all accounts, highly developed, you needed Geoffrey to supply the readability factor. He would ghost it, in other words.'

'An unfortunate phrase in the circumstances, I think. But broadly speaking you're right. Full marks, my dear. Geoffrey was the ghost. And a very good ghost he turned out to be. Mallen, as you say, couldn't write for toffee. Endless bloody equations. No one without a PhD in maths could even start to make head or tail of what he was saying. Geoffrey did, to his credit. He realized the significance of it. You're wrong about me again, though. This wasn't one of my schemes. I didn't go to him. He came to me.'

'You mean it was his idea?'

'Of course. I'm many things, but not a scientist. Geoffrey had the maths. He had the contact. He came to me with the package.'

'Why you? As you say, McAllister's hardly has a reputation for hard science.'

'Precisely. He had the wit to see this wasn't a hard science book. It was a book which would sell not because people wanted to read it, but because they thought they had to read it, or at least buy it. It would have to be on everyone's shelves. He came to me because he knew I liked big books and could sell them well. He also wanted to make a lot of money.'

'Money? Geoffrey? He wasn't interested in money. He had enough. We had enough.'

Michael gave one of his leers. Despite the abjectness of his position – being ignominiously grilled by a couple of women who might at any minute turn him over to the cops – he was at that moment quite clearly enjoying the familiar exercise of the power that comes from superior knowledge. Particularly knowledge of things likely to hurt and distress someone else. I remembered that time, aeons ago, in his office when he had gleefully told me that he knew Geoffrey, and how he had relished the wound this had given me.

'That shows how little you knew him, my dear. Almost the first words he spoke to me were to the effect that I as publisher stood to make a great deal of solid cash from the deal, not to mention the enormous publicity and kudos it would generate, and he wanted to be absolutely sure he was going to get his cut. He mentioned an earlier thing he'd done, where he said he'd been, in his words, rather disappointed. He said he had particular reasons why he didn't want that to happen again.'

'Did you swindle him anyway?'

'My dear, how can you view me so harshly? I certainly did not swindle him. I paid him a great deal in advance and there would have been a great deal more to come. Then if what you say is true he fingered me to the authorities. If anyone welshed on the deal it was him. He must have known that my, er, enforced absence would put the kibosh on the book at least temporarily. And knowing my colleagues in publishing as I do, those yellow-livered bastards probably would have pissed it around or never had the balls to publish it. Might have endangered their peerages.'

'There was no sign of any money when Geoffrey died. If it was that much he couldn't have got rid of it. He would have told me.'

He held up his hands in a mock gesture of surrender. 'My dear

Mary, you're still quite as charming as you always were in our happy working relationship. I can assure you that a substantial wad did go into your late husband's trouser pocket. It is not for me to speculate on what he did with it thereafter. I can only assume that your domestic arrangements were such that Geoffrey did not feel compelled to share with you the unusual fruits of his labour. He was a man of the world and knew the virtues of the numbered account in the land of the cuckoo clock, where it can be kept from the rapacious hands of the female vulture.'

'You bastard!' I felt like crying again. I would have shoved Anna's knife into him there and then if I'd had it handy.

'OK, children.' Anna's tones sliced between us. 'Calm down. Michael, try not to overdo your shittiness. Mary, count to five and twenty and stop looking for the knife. Go on, Michael, things are just getting interesting. As a professional, I'm fascinated to hear what some dusty old academic has come up with that got you going like that. I have to fill my stuff with lurid invention on every page. How can he compete with that?'

'At the risk of quoting a cliché to one so skilled with the word as yourself, my dear Anna, the truth is far stranger than fiction. Certainly if what Mallen has come up with is true, then the consequences are, shall we say, earth-shaking.'

'Go on, Michael, do tell. Stop teasing us. We can still call the cops.'

He bent his large head in acknowledgement. 'You know, I'm beginning to feel like Scheherezade. Perhaps if I spin the story out long enough, you'll forget those silly threats.'

'Don't bank on it. Keep talking.'

'Actually, now I've started I'm rather enjoying it. Confession. It takes me back to my days in the seminary. Ah, yes, that surprised you, didn't it? You can't see me as a priest? Well, perhaps not these days, but I always fancied a resemblance with those really active clerics: Richelieu, Mazarin, Wolsey, or even a Borgia pope. But those thoughts came later. In my part of Poland, the priesthood was the only way for what they call in my adopted Scotland a lad o' parts to get an education, but I had bitterly regretted it in no time. Then came the war. My village doesn't figure in the history books, but it suffered as much as those that do. When the SS came, they killed the Polish men, destroyed their houses and drove out their families. They were left without food or shelter and most of them died. The Jews whom they hadn't killed straight away they rounded up and sent to the camps. For years afterwards, I would wake up screaming. You English. You can never know what it was like. You're an island. You're immune from the diseases of history.

'But I was lucky. I escaped. I was swept up in the ruin of war, joined the partisans, finally making it into Allied-occupied Europe. I conned my way on to a timber ship bound for Leith. By then I had no identity, no age, no state, nothing but a burning desire not just to survive but to succeed. And I did, I have, until . . .' He closed his eyes wearily and sighed.

We waited, spellbound, not wishing to interrupt for fear of cutting off the flow of reminiscence.

'I digress. But it does show I have some sympathy for those who succeed on their own merits. That's why I liked your Geoffrey. He was tough underneath the soft and flabby exterior. Not many Englishmen are nowadays. I gathered that he didn't come from a privileged background, unlike most of the bastards I meet in the business. He had finally woken up to the fact that after a life of so-called success, that despite being a name that one in ten of what passes in England for the intelligentsia might vaguely recognize if pressed – and in that he was doing better than most of the Cabinet – that despite the book, the articles, the well-regarded commentary, he hadn't really succeeded. He had no money. He owned no property. He lived well enough day to day, but there was nothing he could look back on and say, This will give me independence, this will give me power. And money is power. Don't let anyone fool you that it isn't. With money, you can buy anything you want. Anything, if you want it enough and you have enough to meet the price. So, as I said, he came to me with a proposition. A proposition he thought would make him money. And he knew that I, as a man who understood money, would see it too. And I saw it. Oh, yes indeed. I felt I was on the brink of something enormous. Of course, I had to check it out and I did. Discreetly, it may surprise you to hear. And indirectly. I consulted many experts in different fields through intermediaries. What I found out convinced me about the project in principle. But there was one element that was a complete gamble, one aspect in which I had to trust Geoffrey completely. One thing on which the whole business turned. That's where he showed his toughness. He said, "Do it my way, or not at all".'

I couldn't help myself. I said, 'What did he mean by that? What was the gamble?'

He smiled. 'It wasn't one that I think you would have taken, my dear. Far too risky for your little bureaucratic mind. It was that I would never have any dealings with the originator, with Mallen himself. Everything would come through Geoffrey. I could see the original work, the equations, the reasoning, before Geoffrey transformed it into the stuff the common reader could understand. But I could not meet the genius behind it. Nor would he entertain any subsequent personal publicity. An extraordinary condition. One that few of my timorous colleagues would have accepted, as they share Ms Reynolds' view of the world. That is, perhaps another reason why he came to me. I was known to favour the big picture, despite the risks. And perhaps also, although he never said this, he knew I might sympathize with one other aspect of the relationship with Mallen. Can you imagine what that was, my dear Mary?'

I stared at him. Then I saw what he meant. 'You're saying Geoffrey had some kind of hold over Mallen, that he could control him in some way?'

'What a bright creature you can be, quite top of the class. Yes, I suspected that he had, to paraphrase the immortal words of the late President Lyndon Johnson, somehow got Mallen's pecker in his pocket.'

I shivered despite the warmth of the night. It was as if a shadow flitted across my mind.

I saw Anna looking at me with concern. She raised her eyebrows in interrogation. I shook my head. I said to Michael, 'So what was it that was big enough to make you take the gamble?'

'Aha. You'll have to wait a bit for that. I imagine you're both in the position that I was when I first met Geoffrey as far as knowledge of theoretical physics is concerned?' We both nodded.

'Well, you'll know nothing, then. But I learned a good deal not only from the book, but from my associated researches. Basically, the received view is that the universe started with a big bang, a massive explosion of matter billions of years ago. And by the universe is meant everything, time, the laws of physics, the whole lot. Because everything started then, it means we can't find out what happened before the big bang. And even though it seems commonsensical – it did to me, anyway – to want to find out what caused the big bang in the first place, it's meaningless in terms of science. Because if existence hasn't begun, then there can be no scientific enquiry because there are no criteria, no tools to undertake such an enquiry. It's what the boffins call a singularity. There are other places in the universe where queer things happen – black holes, where the laws of physics don't apply.

'Mallen was very interested in the big bang and black holes because of their being singularities. In fact he thinks they are identical. Black holes are in fact big bangs from other universes, where space-time sort of turns inside out. But outside these things, where the laws of physics do apply, they seem to be remarkably consistent. Other than in these black-hole efforts, there are things like gravity and nuclear forces from one end of the universe to another. And the language of the laws of physics is, of course, mathematics. Numbers to you and me. This is where our friend Mallen gets really interested. He's supposed to be, in the opinion of those who know, one of the greatest theoretical physicists of all time. But not just that. He's interested in numbers, wherever they occur, from the level of galaxies to the level of everyday objects. Did you know, for example, that the spiralling growth of a fir-cone replicates a mathematical series, the Fibonacci sequence? And to him it's of enormous significance that, at its most basic, two and two make four throughout the universe. You can't envisage a galaxy – or a universe – where two and two make five or three.'

'But,' I put in, somewhat amazed to find myself fascinated by what he – a man I loathed – was saying, 'isn't that simply a question of definition? You say maths means that two and two will always everywhere make four. Then doesn't it become a self-fulfilling prophecy?'

'Apparently not, according to Mallen. It's the recurrence of mathematical forms like the fir-cone, like the structure of crystals, and of atoms and galaxies for that matter, which is significant. Mathematics isn't just a universal language, it's a universal source of order, of pattern.'

'But doesn't the whole thing come apart at the subatomic level? Isn't there a problem about what they call quantum mechanics the way things like atomic particles and ordinary things like billiard balls behave?'

Michael gave a triumphant bellow. 'Not any more. Not according to Mallen. The whole thing links together in some way. I don't pretend to understand that part.'

Anna said, 'I must say I'm getting a bit lost. I thought you said this book was going to outsell the Bible. Sounds so far like a number one bore.'

'That's where you're quite wrong. Mallen says it is because the universe is ordered mathematically that singularities such as creation, the big bang or what have you, could occur. Just as a mathematical series of equations can by a very small variation in the data cause what mathematicians call chaos: it sort of leaps from one pattern to what looks like the absence of pattern and then back again. The big bang and black holes are self-generating blips in the fundamental mathematical order. And once you accept that, you have to accept the order persists even throughout the singularity. It has existed before it and after it. Mathematics is mathematics even when chaotic. In other words, there is in the universe an organizing principle which is subject to chance – to probability, as the mathematicians call it – but which is not itself random. He claims that the numbers point in only one direction.'

I stared at him. 'What do you mean, "organising principle"? Are you saying what I think you're saying?'

Michael didn't reply for a moment or two. He sat there on the gaudy sofa, his hands clasped on his enormous belly, relishing the look of confusion on both our faces as we exchanged glances. He seemed calm, oriental, Buddha-like. Then he said, 'Yes, I am. Julian Mallen claims to have come up with irrefutable proof of the existence of an organizing principle. In other words, God.'

19

'. . . and I'm afraid to say that the weather at Heathrow is cloudy with occasional showers, with a temperature of twelve degrees centigrade. We'll be landing in five minutes, so please fasten your seatbelts and observe the no-smoking signs. I hope you've had a pleasant flight and we hope to see you again before long.'

The laconic ever-so-British, this-is-your-captain-speaking voice signed off in a crackle of static from the loudspeaker. I looked out of the plastic window at the wet suburban rooftops of south-west London. There was the familiar bump as we hit the tarmac, the chest-tightening roar as the engines reversed thrust, then the rumble as we taxied over the concrete apron to where the grey mobile disembarkation tunnels snaked out like hoses from gigantic vacuum cleaners.

As I didn't have any luggage, I was out into the terminal in a few minutes. In another quarter-hour, I was rattling along in a half-empty tube train back into the cold dark grimy heart of the capital.

I had decided to fly home and damn the expense. Long journeys back have none of the romance of those taken in the excited anticipation of arrival. At Green Park I broke austerity again and took a cab to Hampstead, so it was only a matter of six hours or so since my morning departure from Montpellier that I was sitting at the kitchen table sifting through the disappointingly small accumulation of mail, and that mainly junk, that had landed on the mat since I had sneaked out five days before.

The best thing was a short note from Vanessa Wordsworth – in a reused envelope patched with Scotch tape and scrawled in the blank space on the back of an old Christmas card – saying how much she had enjoyed the lunch, and 'do think over what I said'. I appreciated her confidence, but there simply wasn't space in my mind for that at the moment.

The flat was cold and had an unlived-in feeling. I turned on the immersion heater and waited impatiently until there was enough hot water for a tub. I filled it right up and sat soaking in the warmth and the aroma of Madame Rochas with a tumbler of whisky, guiltily enjoying the sensation of a bath taken in what I used to regard in the dim and distant past as working hours. Work? Did I really do that? Was I really at the beck and call of a seemingly omnipotent tycoon? Was I happily married to a man I loved and even slightly admired? How soon the whirligig of time brings his revenges. I thought of Anna, sad and lonely underneath the vivaciousness. Was she gazing into the mirror at this moment like the Lady of Shalott, watching life go by outside her castle walls?

I hadn't been able to persuade her to come back with me.

'No, I have to stay. I have to work again. That's a real priority. Who knows what's in store for us authors now Michael's flown the coop? The whole thing may collapse like a house of cards. I have to get something ready in case it does. Besides, Esmeralda's helped you all she can. It's up to you now.'

Sometimes it was tough being with Anna. She had more than a streak of the upper-middle-class obsession with standing on your own feet. If I were feeling nasty I would have said she applied it far more ruthlessly to other people than to herself, but wasn't it ever thus? Yet I knew she was right. I had dithered for long enough and I had to sort things out once for all. But not yet. I had to soak some of the gloom out of me. And the days grow short when they reach September . . .

When I finally got out of the bath, it was quite dark. I made some supper out of stuff from the freezer and sat with it in the kitchen as the rain lashed the black window.

I had picked up a newspaper at the airport, more out of force of habit than interest. The problems of the big world took less priority these days than the problems of my small one. But, of course, these worlds had just collided. The main headline story made this clear:

PUBLISHING TYCOON DISAPPEARS AFTER FRAUD ALLEGATIONS

Michael's whereabouts, it said, were unknown after he had left his luxury villa near Montpellier for an appointment in nearby Beziers. There was fortunately nothing about Anna or the Château de St Gervais. Perhaps they would get on to that later. Inside there was a whole page of Michael's complex dealings with his private companies, the loans to which had been, as far as I could understand, the reason why the Serious Fraud Office had been unleashed by the consortium of banks who had been stupid enough to lend him the money in the first place. Nothing like the squeal of a stuck bank manager, was there? I smiled to myself as I remembered the shambling, scruffy figure who was the target of this journalistic largess. He hadn't looked like a master criminal when I had last seen him.

Yes, we had let him go.

Neither of us felt like turning him in to the cops. Anna, with her unerring instinct for the bad guy, had a soft spot for him still. And I? Well, when it came to it there wasn't enough at stake for me. Yes, once I had vowed to get even, but time and chance, not to mention Geoffrey, had done that more comprehensively than I could have done. Perhaps, anyway, I lacked the hardness to take the fullest revenge, to exact the most complete penalty for how he had made me suffer. Was that the woman's failing? I wouldn't ever have another opportunity to find out.

Maybe, anyway, I had done enough. For what I had told him that night would have damaged beyond repair the self-esteem of many lesser men.

Anna and I had looked at one another. Michael sat forward on the sofa, having exchanged inscrutability for a triumphant schoolboy's smirk, drinking in our astonishment, replete with pleasure over his *coup de théâtre*.

It proved short-lived.

I said, 'God? You can't be serious. Mallen's proved the existence of God?' I shook my head. 'This sounds completely wacko to me.'

'You never had any sense of the big picture, did you? Always farting about with your little women authors – present company excepted of course, my dear Anna. When you got a real book, you'd complain about how it had no artistic integrity or some such bollocks. Whilst I –'

'You! What about *The Great Country Houses of England*? Great aristocratic beds I have screwed in, more like! Mallen's book sounds to me as if it was headed the same way as those others – to the remainder warehouse.'

'You're wrong, you're completely fucking wrong. This is a serious book. It doesn't try to prove that the Templars came from Mars or the moon is an alien spaceship. Mallen is in line for a Nobel prize. He's the greatest scientist since Einstein. If he says he's discovered God, then people will listen. People will buy the book. As I told you, it will be the biggest fucking publishing event this century. Any century. Can't you see that? And anyway you've haven't read it; no one has except me. OK. It doesn't prove the existence of God in the sense that those dirty old Polish priests talked about God. But that's the whole point. It disproves that God. The God of the Christians the God of the Hebrews: He's out of date, redundant. But it isn't just me who's saying it. *The Mind of God* has credibility. It has appendices of equations. If Julian Mallen talks about God, the whole world has to listen.'

A light was beginning to glimmer in my mind as he spoke. Some things which had puzzled me had an explanation, but not an explanation that Michael would like. That made it the more appealing.

'*The Mind of God*,' I said, pouring us all some more wine. 'Is that the title? Not bad. I can see it. A star-sprinkled void, perhaps, on the jacket. The stars in shiny silver foil and then the shout line, 'The ultimate mystery revealed'. Seal it up in plastic to defeat the browsers and you could have something.'

Michael drank off his glass. 'There you are. You might make a publisher yet. Perhaps I shouldn't have fired you and fucked up your career.'

I gave him a refill. 'Thanks, but I think I'm a survivor. I'm in a better position than you are right now. By the way, Michael, you ever hear of a guy called Clifford Irving?'

He looked at me narrowly. 'It rings a vague bell.'

'It should. What about Elmyr Hory? Tom Keating? *The Hitler Diaries? The Protocols of the Elders of Zion?*'

'What is this? *Mastermind*? They're fakers and fakes, aren't they?'

'Full marks. You've got the connection. Let me remind you about Mr Irving. He faked a ghosted autobiography of Howard Hughes and swindled a publisher out of a fortune until Howard Hughes himself came out of seclusion to spoil the scam.'

'So what?' He took a sip of wine. I could see that beneath the defiance he was worried. Maybe the bankers had seen it too.

'So.' I took a deep breath. 'Over the past few months I have made various more or less unpleasant discoveries about the man I was married to. And what I've learned makes me believe – very reluctantly – that he may belong in that elite company. A brilliant, a successful man. Skilled at artifice and concealment from his earliest years. A man who loved games and puzzles. A journalist used to putting words in other people's mouths. Used to knowing how other people wanted to see the world. It wasn't Mallen's book, it was Geoffrey's. He went much further than Mallen would have. You were set up. Don't you see? Do you think that sort of thing would have fooled anyone but you? It was tailor-made for your vanity, greed and credulity. If you say that some of the materials were genuine, then Geoffrey must have inveigled Mallen into handing them over for you to feed to your tame experts. Perhaps in the end, though, he couldn't go through with it. It would be rumbled sooner or later like all the others. So he used what he had on you to preempt that and make sure the book was never published.'

Michael's dark, hollow-eyed gaze had been trained on me whilst I had been speaking. 'He was wrong. And you're fucking wrong.

It would have sold: the Pope would have banned it' he said defiantly.

We had given him a good breakfast: eggs from the scrawny chickens living semi-wild in one of the ruined coach houses and fresh bread and brioches, warm, fetched by me early that morning from the *boulangerie* in the village, comparatively lively and blissfully cooler at that hour.

Anna had found him some old clothes abandoned by Pierre, the kind of rough garb he had used when he was painting, baggy and shapeless enough to suit even Michael's figure. She shoved the white linen suit into the coal range in the kitchen.

Dressed thus he was almost unrecognizable. He had washed his hair with peroxide, which had successfully removed most of the black dye. His springy locks were now iron grey. Unshaven, his jowls sprouted the beginnings of a vigorous beard growth in the style of Yasser Arafat. He was quite shamefaced and awkward as we said our farewells. He looked at his feet as his voice rumbled on about his gratitude to us. It was sad and more than a bit pathetic to see the man reduced to this, even though I had loathed him as he had been.

There was a flash of the old Michael, however, when Anna, bless her, had delicately enquired about whether he needed any of the readies to help him in his bid for freedom. He had laughed his belly laugh and insolently pulled up the paint-spattered smock. Around his bulging middle was a brown leather money belt. 'Don't worry your little head about me,' he boomed. 'I'm not like your fucking Royal Family. I've always carried real cash money with me. Dollars, of course. Not your toytown kind.'

I liked the 'your Royal Family'. Michael's frantic desire to be recognized as a member of the British ruling classes had always warred with his buccaneering spirit and his exuberant vulgarity. Now, when finally in reality he had become the outlaw he had always pretended to be, the pursuit of gentility had evaporated, leaving behind the atavistic shadow of his ancestors.

It might be that the police would get him in the end. Where

could he go? Would he really disappear into the underworld of Marseilles to emerge as the *capu* of some local branch of the Union Corse? It might suit him very well.

We stood in the front courtyard, watching him trudge along the drive. He even paused to wave before he vanished into the green tunnel of the overhanging trees. I never saw him again.

At least I was no longer afraid of being watched and followed. The journey to Provence had, whatever other matters it had brought to light, laid that particular demon. Whatever power, whatever motive, Michael had had to disturb and hurt me had vanished with his eclipse.

And had I indeed imagined the whole thing? Could I have imagined it? The watcher in the street outside the flat, the man in the forest, the same man – had it really been the same man? – in the Cambridge street might have been the manifestations of my confused mental state. I suppose that's how a male psychologist would have characterized it. He would have believed Michael's sincere-sounding protestations that he had not set the dogs on me. I didn't know any more. I only knew I felt free of the feeling of being observed and pursued.

The glamour of Michael's disappearance soon began to fade. As I flicked through the paper one morning a few days after my return from Provence there was only one small front-page item on the progress of police enquiries. They were following up various leads: Michael had been reportedly sighted in numerous locations around the globe from Disneyworld in Florida to a sheep station in Australia. On the financial page, there was an update on the state of what it insisted on calling the 'runaway tycoon's empire'. McAllister's was still going, just, courtesy of the administrators. That meant the accountants were now well and truly in control. Thank God I was out of it.

On the same page there was a small item concerning the resignation in New York of one Max Vincent from the post of Chief Executive Officer of Hiram and Hartstein, the quote giant

American publisher unquote. Delicately, it pointed out that Mr Vincent had been responsible for forging a link with what it referred to as the disgraced British tycoon Michael Underdown-Metcalfe.

I finished my coffee. I hadn't been idle since I got back, and now that work would pay off. This was the day when I would start to find out some more of the answers to the questions which nagged me. I was going back to Cambridge, and I wouldn't leave until I had succeeded in breaking through the barriers erected around Dr Julian Mallen. I was going prepared.

I stopped the car in one of the spaces marked 'Visitors'. I checked my appearance in the mirror behind the sun visor. I looked good: the image of the model female executive lurching upwards to the glass ceiling. Tailored jacket, replacement for the one abandoned – was it only a week ago? – knee-length skirt, white blouse and stylish cravat. The big horn-rimmed spectacles were a nice touch, I thought.

Picking up my attaché case, I sauntered over to the front entrance.

The Cambridge Centre for Physical Research, judging from its building, was well-endowed. It was brand spanking-new high-tech block, complete with a fancy glass and metal roof suspended from gantries with funny little shiny metal curlicues at each corner like table legs, presumably some post-modernist's sniggering reference to the crocketed pinnacles of old Cambridge.

I clattered up the ramped entrance way. The glass doors under the lime-green-painted metal pediment – another piece of architectural wit, I surmised – slid open with a clunk and then closed behind me. The corresponding pair on the other side of the coir-matted lobby glided apart in response to my presence and I went through. It felt like going through an airlock in one of those space movies.

The impression was reinforced by the reception area – all stainless steel and plastic. A girl so perfect in a Sindy doll way she might have been an android sat at a curved steel desk. She came to at my approach with an almost audible click as if she had been switched on. She wore an outfit halfway between a suit and a uniform, like an air hostess without the hat. 'Good morning, madam. My name is Stephanie. How may I help you?'

'I have some urgent data for Dr Mallen.' I opened the attaché case and produced a bulky manila envelope. 'It's in connection with a publication. There is a deadline, so I brought it over myself. Would you please make sure he gets it straight away? I'll wait to see if there's a reply.'

I handed over the package. It looked very convincing, plastered with red stickers: MOST URGENT. BY HAND. EMBARGOED MATERIAL. 'Here's my card as well.' I was taking a chance. She might spot that I had altered the name on my old McAllister's business cards with Indian ink and correcting fluid to read Marya Bagnold, or she might decide to ring the office for confirmation. Being an android, she relied on my convincing appearance and didn't.

She picked up the ultra-slim scientific instrument which bore as much resemblance to the old black phone as a hypodermic does to a banana and whispered throatily, 'Tracy, can you get a parcel for Dr M., please?'

Another Sindy doll appeared presently, took the package and minced away through another pair of glass doors.

I waited, pleased at the way I was concealing my tension by pretending to read with every appearance of concentration an article about lasers in one of the copies of *Scientific American* scattered on the glass and steel table.

After a few difficult minutes, there was a modulated warbling at the reception desk and Stephanie delicately applied the instrument to her ear. 'Yes, Dr Mallen. Certainly, Dr Mallen.'

'He would like to see you. Please go through the doors. Room 120. Last office on the left-hand side.'

I laid the journal aside unhurriedly and picked up my case. 'Thank you.'

It seemed a long way down the grey-carpeted corridor. I stood hesitantly outside the steel door of Room 120. There was no door handle. On the right-hand side was a magnetic card reader like the ones you see outside all-night banking halls, and a square, red, illuminated touch panel which read, 'PLEASE DO NOT ENTER'. I prodded it gingerly. The light went out, then came on again. In glowing green, it said, 'DOOR OPENING'. The door panel slid back with a hiss and I stepped through.

I was finally face to face with Julian Mallen. He stared at me, his dark eyes, deep in shadowed sockets, unmoving under the tufts of his eyebrows, the nostrils of his Roman nose flared in distaste. Where the yellowish skin of his face was not hidden by his severely trimmed full beard it stretched tight over his cheekbones and forehead. In contrast to the beard, his hair was thick and flowed in a wild mane over the buttoned collar of the severely tailored grey Nehru jacket. Both beard and hair were entirely white. His hands, as they clutched the padded arms of the swivel chair, opened and closed almost convulsively. He did not get up.

'What do you want? Who are you?' His voice did not fit his wasted appearance, being strong and harsh.

'My name is Mary Reynolds.'

He nodded. 'Ah. Geoffrey's wife. Of course. Hence your crudely minatory note amongst that waste paper. "I shall reveal everything unless you see me."'

'It was the only thing I could think of. But it worked, didn't it?'

'Mere vulgar curiosity. I could have you thrown out. We have a very effective security service.'

'I'm sure you do. But you won't. Because I do know everything, everything Geoffrey knew.'

He rose then from the chair, levering himself up with both hands. They stuck out from the sleeves of the jacket on wrists as meagre as broom handles.

Now he was standing I could see that he was immensely tall – six and a half feet at least. He towered over me, his shoulders broad but bony, his frame at once huge and shrunken.

'I don't know what you're talking about. I repeat my question: what do you want?'

'I thought there were things we should discuss.'

'Things?'

'Yes. Several things. Your relationship with Geoffrey, for example.'

'I hardly think that has much relevance now.'

'It does to me.'

'As you seem to be aware, Geoffrey and I had a business relationship. On his death, that ceased.'

'You mean you freely entered into an agreement that he should use some of your ideas and your research to produce a sensationalist piece of popular science. I don't believe you. And you know why I don't.'

'I don't care what you believe. And as I find that my curiosity about you is more than fully satisfied, I must ask you to go.'

'I've no intention of leaving yet. You see I was in love with my husband. I wasn't ready for him to die. I wasn't ready for what I found out afterwards. That gives me the right to the answers to the questions I want to ask. I've suffered for them, after all.'

'Suffering!' He sank heavily back into his chair. 'What do you know of suffering? You don't sit here every day watching yourself shrivel and diminish. Do you want me to describe the ugliness, the pettiness, the sheer vileness of the cancer that gnaws at me a little more every day?'

'You don't need to. They talk about it on the TV. It isn't pleasant, but then I don't think you deserve anything very pleasant.'

'What do you mean?' His eyes were wide with hostility and I sensed something else deeply hidden behind the cold exterior, but there nevertheless, burning within. Fear.

'I mean that, given the law doesn't prescribe the penalty, a slow and painful death is quite appropriate.'

He half rose in the chair, and feeble though he was I found myself backing away in alarm.

He crumpled, the aggression replaced by a spasm of pain which convulsed his haggard features. He closed his eyes as the agony surged over him like a breaking wave. I kept my distance, watching him with cool interest, as if I were a vivisectionist testing some particularly important product on a lower form of life. I was amazed at myself. I had felt more pity for Lucy's wounded dog.

He gradually recovered himself, the sweat beading the jaundiced parchment of his forehead. Finally, his head bent, he stared down at his knee joints plainly visible through the material of his trousers.

Then he looked up, and it seemed as if he were able to read the confused jumble of my thoughts far quicker than I was able to assemble them myself, like the person who finishes your sentences for you. I stared back as if to repel the power of this silent interrogation.

'So what is it you have come to accuse me of in this absurdly melodramatic fashion? I think I should be told.'

There was an iron certainty about him that almost broke my will to go on. I heard my voice faltering. 'Lucy. What did you do with her when you took her away from school? Where is she? What have you done with her?'

He actually smiled. 'What on earth are you talking about? What has my daughter to do with you?'

His reaction raised an anger in me which swept away my hesitation. I stood up and planted my hands on the desk top, pushing my face close to his. 'You absolute bastard. How can you sit there grinning smugly when you killed her? I know you did. You killed Lucy. You murdered your daughter. That was what Geoffrey knew, wasn't it? Wasn't it?'

He laughed aloud. I had come so close to him I could smell the foulness of his breath. He leaned back calmly in the chair and folded his skeletal hands together over his chest. 'I'm afraid you read far too many novels, Mrs Reynolds. Either that or your husband's death has left you prey to extraordinary delusions. I haven't murdered Lucy. How could I have, when she isn't dead?'

'I don't believe you. You're lying to me.'

He put up his hands. 'Please calm yourself, my dear. Very well. A scientist should never offer mere assertion, but proof. If you won't believe me, then perhaps you'd like to meet her. If you would, we can go together, straight away.'

'This is it, on the left.'

338

There were white-painted gateposts and a driveway. A discreet sign read 'Warley House'. I drove along the smooth tarmac between newly painted white post and rail fences. In the lush pastures on either side grazed plump Jersey cattle.

'It doesn't look like a . . .' I started to say.

'Hospital? No. But then why should it? There's no rule that says it must look like a Victorian Gothic prison, is there?'

'I'm pleasantly surprised, that's all.'

He pointed out the car park. I helped him to clamber out of the car. His face contracted in pain as he bent his tall, emaciated frame and slid sideways out of the seat. His large bony hand gripped mine tremulously. I gave him my arm as we walked towards the entrance. A nurse with bright red hair and freckles caught sight of us through the glass doors and hurried out to greet him.

'Why, Dr Mallen! This is a surprise. We weren't expecting you. Not your usual day, is it?'

'Evidently. I have an acquaintance – Mrs Reynolds – whom I should like to have meet my daughter. Can it be arranged?'

'Of course! Any time of the day or night you like. You know that.'

'Ah, yes. I would not be so unreasonable as to take that literally. I assume it will be our usual place.'

'The Magnolia Room. Such a shame it's not a sunnier day. I'll help you along there.'

We entered through a conservatory which extended over the whole front of the house. It was humid and there were plants in profusion, in troughs, growing up the whitewashed walls and hanging in huge mossy baskets from the roof. There was a strong and heavenly scent of orange blossom.

The nurse, who had taken the full leaning weight of the sick man on her powerful shoulders, led us down a blue-carpeted corridor to a mahogany door. With her free hand, she twisted the brass door knob and helped him inside.

'Thank you, Nora.' Out of breath, he sat down heavily on the cream-covered sofa. She gave a little bob of acknowledgement and gently closed the door behind her.

There was a bay window which looked out over a wide area of closely mown lawn. To the side as I could see a large flat-roofed building which had more of an institutional appearance. I noticed that there were bars on some of the windows. In front, on a concrete paved terrace, were outdoor chairs and tables, a few with brightly coloured umbrellas. Some were occupied by men and women in white trousers and smocks, many of them staring emptily in front of them, but at one of the tables two men played chess, one occasionally rising from his place to throw his arms in the air and kick out his legs before resuming his position of concentration.

Mallen said nothing as I stood there looking out. I turned back into the room. Apart from the sofa on which he was sitting, there were a couple of fat easy chairs in matching cream fabric and a low table in oiled teak. I noticed with interest that stout metal brackets on each leg bolted it through the cream carpet to the floor. The only other ornament was a painting of a vase of improbably coloured flowers on the wall over the boarded-up marble fireplace, which was not hung in the conventional way but screwed flat against the plaster with mirror plates. From the lack of reflection, I could see that it had been framed not with glass, but perspex.

There was a soft knock at the door. It was another nurse, dark this time, with large red hands. 'Through here, Lucy, darling,' she crooned.

I turned to look at Mallen's daughter. She was dressed in the institutional garb: white smock dress, bare legs and white socks in white slip-on canvas shoes. She was tall, but her budding figure and her full face with its ample coronet of dark blonde curls were in contrast to the cadaverous figure of her father who raised himself with difficulty from the sofa and bent his his drumskin face to kiss her formally on the cheek.

'Hello, Lucy, dear, I've brought a new friend to see you, a lady from London.' He nodded peremptorily at the nurse who was hovering in the doorway. 'Thank you, we're all right now. We'll ring if we need anything.'

340

The child stood quite still in the centre of the room where the nurse had placed her. I came forward and offered her my hand, but there was no reaction on her calm face. It was almost a shock to see how beautiful she was. She could have sat for Raphael. I remembered a photograph – of a young and laughing girl only a few years older than her daughter was now. Yes, she was like the stunning Helen Massingham, but there was something else there too – something more solid than the frail transparency of that oval face and the slender figure.

Mallen guided her into one of the armchairs and arranged her as if she were a doll. The effort involved seemed to have exhausted him, for he sank into the cushions of the sofa and for a second or two his eyes closed, the skin stretched so tight across his forehead that it seemed as if it would tear.

Lucy sat upright, her hands in her lap, her knees together in the perfect pose of a well brought up young lady. But her waxy complexion – the look of one who spent her time indoors, and the only detriment to her beauty – betrayed no animation. Instead of finely turned polite small talk and the occasional awkward school-girlish gush that might have been expected, there was utter immo-bility and disconcerting, complete silence.

'She can be like that for hours, sometimes.' Mallen had roused himself and his dark feverish eyes, the whites jaundiced with the crab that gnawed within him, met mine. 'Sometimes she walks about the room, sometimes I almost fancy I detect some sign that she recognizes me.'

'Does she hear us? Could she speak if she wanted?'

'There is no physical defect as far as the doctors have been able to ascertain. The illness is entirely confined to the brain. Its effects are similar to autism, and may be hysterical in origin. But what it is and what caused it is a complete mystery. I hope you're satisfied that she is being well cared for and in the safest possible hands. I hope you realize that the idea that I should wish to harm her is quite offensively preposterous.'

I felt my pulse rate begin to rise as my revulsion towards this man grew. It was only because he felt sure of my ignorance that he was able to say these things. I took a deep breath and said as casually as I could, 'How did she become like this? Wasn't she a normal child?'

'Entirely so. The first signs developed only about two years ago. She had a minor illness – glandular fever – which became chronic. She lapsed into a coma, and when she finally regained consciousness, she was as you see her now.'

'How utterly tragic. But surely there must be some reason why it happened. What did the doctors say?'

'There are a number of theories. Hysteria is a characteristic phenomenon of the female mind. It is associated quite often with hormonal imbalance. And in Lucy's case, I regret to say there was a history of mental instability. Her mother was highly intelligent, but highly strung. She died in the most appalling way: she was murdered by an intruder. Poor Lucy, at the age of three, may have been an inadvertent witness to what happened and the seeds of her present disability may have been sown at that time.'

'There must have been long-term effects from witnessing her mother's murder. Did you ever discuss it with her or seek any professional help?'

'No. We never spoke of her mother. She could have been the merest shadow to her. She was a tiny child at the time. I never wanted her to recall it even if she could. It could only distress her. As for what you describe as help, I have never regarded psychology as other than the merest pseudo-science.'

I had been pacing the room as he talked, but now I stood quite still. I was behind the chair in which the silent figure sat. I looked down on the dark blonde curls and I smelt the warm emanation of her body – a combination of some cheaply scented soap and the musk of sweat – which thrilled me with the recognition that behind the marble pallor and the cold white exterior of this frozen child was a living human being. And it might be that I held the key which would unlock her prison and set her free.

'I don't know much about mental illness, even less about specifically hysterical states, but isn't it the case that a severe traumatic shock could trigger such a condition?'

He looked at me narrowly. Could I detect some nervousness in his manner? 'Why yes, indeed. That was what I have just said. As a small child, Lucy may have –'

'Yes, yes. I heard that. But I'm talking about something more recent. Something that must have immediately preceded the state she's in.'

'I don't know what you're talking about. Lucy was a perfectly normal, happy child. There was no trauma.'

'Dr Mallen, you may be the greatest scientific mind since Isaac Newton, but you're also a liar.'

'That's enough! I shall listen to no more of your offensiveness. Will you please leave us in peace?'

'Oh, no. Not so fast. This time you can't bluster your way out. No trauma! Young girls have committed suicide out of ignorance of menstruation. What about going into premature labour when you probably didn't even realize you were pregnant? Yes, I know about Lucy's baby. Where is the poor little scrap? Did you kill it? Is that why she's like this? Is that trauma enough?'

As I shouted these words, I rushed at him, grabbed his shoulders and squeezed till it seemed the dry bones would crack.

He struggled in my grasp, his face a cardboard mask of fury. 'You're mad. Baby, what baby? How can you pretend to know of such things? How dare you accuse me with these filthy inventions?' He shook himself free. I pushed him back down on to the sofa. His expression had shifted into one of malevolence, the burning eyes in the ravaged face under the flowing white hair making him for a second or two seem like the evil wizard in a children's story book.

'It's no invention. I've proof. Here, here it is!' I screamed, caught up in the emotion of the moment. I dragged out of my purse the Polaroid photograph and brandished it in his face. 'Proof. Deny it if you can.'

Behind me there arose a howl of pure animal agony. I turned in horror to see Lucy on her feet, her hand raised towards the photograph, her mouth wide, and scream after scream pouring through it as if bursting up from some deep well once dry but now sprung into fountaining life.

Sick at the sight, I tried to hold her, but she threw off my arms and launched herself at the cowering figure of Mallen.

He scrambled up, dashed to the door and frantically jabbed again and again at the red alarm button by the jamb. The door was flung open to reveal the nurse with red hands and another white-coated figure.

'Lucy, my love, what ails you?' she cried as she took a firm grip on the girl's flailing arms and gently but inexorably pushed her down into the armchair. 'That's better. Quieten your noise, my darling. Even the director himself is out of his office to see what's afoot.'

All I could see of the director was a broad, white-coated back as he bent over the now prostrate form of the scientist. He stood up and turned into the room. 'He's all right. Fainted, apparently. I'm not surprised, given the row. What's been going on here?' His eyes focused on me for the first time as he saw me staring at him in speechless astonishment. 'Good God! You!'

I had no smart reply ready this time. It was Henry Massingham.

I was still shaking. The teacup rattled as I set it carefully in the saucer. Outside the window the big cedar tree shook in the freshening breeze and a few drops of rain splashed against the tall Georgian windows.

Massingham had taken refuge behind his desk. I seemed to have spent the whole of my working life talking to men from the other side of their desks. He had taken off his white coat, and, in a dark business suit, looked more like the conventional manager rather than someone who might possess real skill in some real activity.

'How is she?'

'I've given her a shot of tranquillizer. She'll sleep for several hours. As to how she'll be then, it's hard to tell. She was very disturbed. You saw that. I wonder what you thought you were doing.'

'I wanted him to know . . . I knew. And I suppose I hoped that seeing the photograph –'

'She would just snap out of it? Like in the films? "Where am I, who are these people?" It doesn't happen like that. It's a process. There aren't any miracle transformations. What you did was highly dangerous. She may have lost her equilibrium altogether when she wakes up.' Seeing my expression, his voice became less severe. 'On the other hand, she's very young. There may be no harmful effects.'

'But no good ones?'

'I doubt it. She's very ill, you know.'

'I didn't until I came here. And you're the reason I didn't.'

He rested his elbows on the pristine surface of the leather blotter and touched his slightly pointed chin with the tips of his steepled fingers.

He smiled calmly. 'I suppose you must have found out a good deal to have come here. I underestimated you. I've never regarded a woman alone as having that kind of tenacity.'

'Aren't you supposed to be a psychologist? Haven't you guys ditched the idea of the weaker sex yet?'

'Psychiatrist, actually. There is a difference. As for women, well they certainly lead the field for schizophrenia, although I have to say that most psychopaths are men.'

'I wouldn't be surprised, but I'm not here for a discussion about mental health. I should have thought you owe me some kind of apology.'

'For pushing you out of the car that time? Yes, I am sorry about that. It was the way you popped up like some kind of avenging fury. I expected you to have been safe in London. I reacted instinctively. I suppose it was rather stupid, calculated only to make things worse. I really didn't think you'd find me again, though. How did you?'

'Feminine intuition. But for God's sake I wasn't thinking of that. What about the play-acting? The Hugh Robinson bit? Or have you conveniently wiped that from your memory banks?'

'Of course not. I knew it was a bad idea. Geoffrey persuaded me against my better judgement. He could be quite persuasive, as you must know. Besides, he said he would square it with you later. It wasn't a real deception. You weren't to be a victim of any kind, but everything changed when Geoffrey, er, so suddenly . . .'

'Died, you mean? Jolly inconvenient of him, what? Right in the middle of whatever scam you two were playing.'

He took his hands away from his chin and rapped the desk top sharply. 'Hey, look here! It was nothing dishonest! I wouldn't get mixed up in anything criminal. I've got my professional reputation to consider.'

'Certainly you have. I mean to say, conspiring with Geoffrey to blackmail Mallen and defraud McAllister's, impersonating an estate agent, pretending to sell a house – that's not dishonest, is it?'

I had hit a sensitive spot, and what more sensitive spot is there than a man's integrity?

'I never said I was an estate agent. You assumed it. I deliberately didn't say I was selling it. Everything I told you was true.'

'Oh, yes? Like the fact that Mallen had gone to the States? That's what really gets to me, the fact that your lies were so obvious. You thought I was so bloody gullible, didn't you? You and Geoffrey. And for a long time, I bloody well was gullible! But I'm not any more. I know some of it, but I want to know everything.'

'All right, all right. So I admit I did sort of bend the facts a bit, but you took me by surprise when you found me at the cottage. Geoffrey hadn't mentioned you were staying on, and when the damn dog got away – God, I wish I'd had it put down in the first place; I'd only kept it in the hope that it might at some stage help Lucy – I had to look for it and . . . But I absolutely deny that I had any involvement with what Geoffrey did with Mallen. I don't know anything about it. If it ever came out that I'd . . . Oh, it's no good trying to explain things in bits and pieces. I will tell you about everything. It'll be a relief, really. But I shall have to start at the beginning. And it started a long time ago.'

'At Cambridge, you mean?' I told him about my conversation with AWS.

'Is he still going? I suppose he's not that old, just seemed that way to us. So you know about Geoffrey and Helen. And Julian Mallen. That's how it started. When Geoffrey met Helen. She told me about that first time. The autumn colours, the crisp sunny afternoon. She'd talk of it to me often, years later when she'd married Julian Mallen. Married him and regretted it.'

'That's how you came to know Geoffrey?'

'Yes. She brought him to our parents' house at Thorncaster, by the sea. Do you know it? There's a great white sand beach so flat and wide it seems to stretch for ever.'

I shook my head. 'I've never been. Geoffrey and I were going to go together.' The memory of that day when Geoffrey first spoke to me of Norfolk was fresh again. He had lied to me then, too.

'I liked him immediately. He was clever and witty. A jolly good chap, I thought. I used to visit them in Cambridge. They seemed so well suited, so much in love. I was completely astonished when she wrote to me and told me she was breaking with him. Geoffrey was devastated. I must say I rather sided with him, particularly after I met Mallen. He seemed cold and distant compared to Geoffrey. Of course he was immensely brilliant and even then it was clear he was destined for great things, but I told Helen she was making a mistake. It spoiled our relationship for years. Even when it was clear to her that I had been right, she couldn't forgive me for it.'

'So she was unhappy?'

'Yes, I think so. She thought when she married him that she could help him with his work. But he refused to let her. It wasn't that she was incapable. Far from it. He was incapable of sharing. And because his work was such a major part of his life, it left them very little in which they could communicate. He had no interest in his surroundings or even his physical comfort, so they lived in a rather hideous flat in Cambridge.'

'Why didn't she walk out?'

'You know what marriage is like. It isn't always clear what's going on from the outside. Helen was not someone who gave up easily. I think, despite everything, she must have loved him. And I know she longed for a child. When she finally became pregnant, she was radiant. Things seemed better for a while, and then there was that dreadful, dreadful day when she was –'

'A W S told me. But how did it happen?'

347

'A neighbour called one afternoon. They had arranged to take their children to a park to play. She couldn't get anyone to answer the door. She could hear Lucy inside crying, became alarmed and called the police. When they broke in they found Lucy – she was three and a half at the time – was crying that Mummy was asleep and wouldn't wake up. Helen had been strangled. She had been dead for a few hours, and the child had been with her all that time.'

My skin crawled as if underneath his words lay something even more appalling. His large head was partly turned away, staring towards the long windows set with panes of old glass which made the pleasant garden scene outside crinkle and swim as if I had a migraine. There was a set expression about his full lips. I knew what he was feeling. Grief. And anger. There flashed before me the photographs which AWS had shown me: Helen and Geoffrey brilliant in the shining light of youth.

His head was bowed now. His fists clenched and his solid right hand jerked up and crashed back on the shiny surface, making the pen on his blotter leap into the air.

'I'm sorry. It's hard to think of it even now. The police never charged anyone. They left the file open – a burglary that must have gone wrong. They interviewed Lucy, but she couldn't tell them anything. Everything that happened that day was a blank. Amnesia. It's a natural defence mechanism in people who've witnessed something dreadful. I was quite broken up by her death – despite what had passed between us – and for a long time nothing had much meaning. And there was Geoffrey to think of too. He was devastated.'

'I suppose he was still in love with her a little.'

'It was more than that. It wasn't only Helen's death. It was Lucy. It made him realize how much the child meant to him – that she could have been killed by the same psychopath who killed her mother.' He paused and stared closely at me. 'Of course, you don't know, do you? He never told you. I know he was going to. You were so much a part of it, after all.'

'Told me what, for God's sake?'

348

'About Lucy. She was the most important thing in Geoffrey's life. You see, she's his daughter.'

I drank off the whisky in one swallow. Even from a styrofoam cup it tasted good. It did something to ease the trembling which had started up over my whole body. I wasn't shaking so much as shivering intermittently. I held out the beaker. 'More medicine, please, doc.'

He poured me another slug from a big silver flask that had materialized out of his bottom drawer. I murmured thanks, and this one I sipped in a more ladylike fashion. He had gone back to his steepled fingers under the chin position, his expression watchful, as if I were going to smash him over the head with his glass paperweight. I guessed that was an occupational hazard.

'How can she be his daughter?' I finally blurted out.

It sounded as stupid to him as it had to me, because he smiled in that superior way men have when confronted with dopey women. 'The usual way.'

'You damn well know what I mean. I thought they had broken up years before Lucy was born.'

'They had, but then they met again in London. She was doing some research at Imperial a couple of days a week. Geoffrey was working on the paper then. What was it called?'

'The *Quotidian*.'

'That's it. Well, Geoffrey was a great one for nosing around centres of learning, hoping to pick up the latest ideas. He bumped into Helen.'

'Must have been some bump. Mind you, he was quite a bumper.'

'Yes. I suppose one thing led to another. The old flame rekindled, etc. The affair went on while she was working in town. At the end of the project, she went back to Cambridge and she found she was pregnant. She had been trying to get pregnant for years – and then she was. It was too much of a coincidence. She knew it was Geoffrey's baby.'

'Did Geoffrey know?'

'Yes, she told him. He wanted her to leave Mallen, but in the end she refused. She had made her decision, she said, when she married him, and had to stick by it. She told me that Julian needed her, despite his appearance of indifference. And she was still fond of him. It made Geoffrey very unhappy. He came to Cambridge several times, trying to get to see her, but she always refused.'

'Did she tell Mallen about the affair when she became pregnant?'

'No. He would have had no reason to believe the child wasn't his. They had had normal relations, and although I suppose there must have been some problem, there was never any suggestion that he had any disability. In any event, he wasn't that interested in the child. He was only concerned that it wouldn't interfere with his work. I think, though, that Helen had another reason for not telling him. She was afraid of what he might do.'

'What do you mean by that?'

'I think she felt what I had always believed of him: that he was a man of violent moods and passions. Somehow his intellectual superiority didn't always rule with his emotions, but exacerbated them. He was capable of great anger when he felt himself slighted or betrayed. And like many men of that calibre, he was prone to jealousies and suspicions – of colleagues, rivals, even those close to him. It didn't surprise me. Even Newton himself was not above pursuing the most bitter private feuds. Look at his quarrel with Hooke.'

'OK, forget the history of science. What are you trying to say?'

'I always had the feeling that if he had found out about Helen's affair he would have been capable of reacting violently. But now I don't just think that. I know.'

'Know? What do you mean, you know?'

'I know it was not a burglar who murdered Helen. It was Julian Mallen.'

20

I stared at Henry Massingham, his bland, cultivated voice seeming to contradict the words he had uttered.

'Mallen was the murderer? How can that be? And how can you be so certain?'

'It isn't so surprising, is it? No more unlikely than that she was killed by an intruder. There was obviously some suspicion at the time. He was interviewed by the police. He had no particular alibi. He was working in College, but at the presumed time of her death there was no one with him to vouch for that. But there was no evidence – no rows, no motive. Even if the fact that Helen had had an affair was common knowledge – which it certainly wasn't – there was no way to prove that Mallen knew, or to show that this knowledge had provoked him to kill her. I remember going through the whole thing with Geoffrey at the time. What would have been the point of bringing the affair and the matter of Lucy's parentage into the open, when all it would achieve would be to ruin her future even more thoroughly? We had our suspicions, that was all. The whole business cast a shadow over Mallen anyway. He failed to get the preferment he thought he was entitled to. He spent more time in Norfolk than in Cambridge. That was how the matter stood for years. Geoffrey went off to the States. I was appointed to this hospital. We had Lucy very occasionally for holidays and for weekends, but Mallen did not encourage the contact. I got the impression of a bright but lonely child. Away from school she was far more fond of her dog and the forest than of people.'

'So how is it you now say you know Mallen killed her mother?'

'That was Geoffrey. He had never accepted that the truth of Helen's death would not come out. Over the years, he pursued it. He wanted to talk to Lucy, but he knew Mallen would never agree to any contact. He had to rely on seeing her surreptitiously as a friend of mine when she came to stay. I think Mallen suspected as much: that's why he would prevent her visits if at all possible.

'It was only after she was admitted here that he could see her with any frequency, and by then, her illness made communication impossible. But he was convinced she held the key to her mother's death. He was sure she could tell him.'

'Lucy? But you said she was only a child at the time, not much more than a baby. How could she have known anything?'

'Children are very observant. The only disadvantage they have is in interpreting correctly what they see. That and the fact that their memories work differently. They seem to forget things instantly, but they're still there in their minds long afterwards. If you can be patient, they sometimes come out with things – if you've got the right way of asking – from the very bottom of their memories, from the depths of their pasts, things long ago witnessed and forgotten.'

'How could she have told him anything? You said yourself her illness has rendered her mute.'

'It was Geoffrey's doing. Much against my better judgement, he persuaded me to hypnotize her.'

It was if I had had an electric shock. I sat bolt upright, my whole body tingling. 'You did what? I mean that kind of thing is strictly TV show magic. I thought you were supposed to be a real doctor.'

The irritation and the arrogance of the man came surging back. Funny how I had been finding him almost sympathetic.

He steepled his fingers together under his chin in the familiar gesture and sighed deliberately audibly. 'That's the kind of comment I always have to deal with. The level of ignorance is extraordinary. Hypnotherapy is not magic. It's a recognized therapeutic technique for patients with mind blocks that can't be reached any other way.'

'But you were reluctant to use it on her?'

'Yes, but that was because I knew it would not be for therapeutic purposes. It was to gain information.'

'And did it?'

'Yes. Geoffrey got what he wanted. He taped the interview. He told me to forget about what had happened and to destroy any notes I might have taken. He took the tape away. I haven't seen it since.'

'I see. So that was what he used.'

'What do you mean?'

'Oh, come on. Don't pretend you don't know. You must have realized what Geoffrey was up to. He was blackmailing Mallen, wasn't he?'

'Yes. I wish I'd never got involved. If it weren't for Helen, I wouldn't have. If it weren't for Geoffrey, I wouldn't have. But when Lucy was admitted here, it seemed to bring to the surface Geoffrey's hatred of Mallen. It grew into an obsession. On top of what he saw as his failure to save Helen, there was Lucy. Another victim. He blamed himself. He should have taken more interest in the child, asserted his parentage somehow.

'He asked me what he could do. Whether he could legally get the child away from Mallen. I had to say I thought the chances were fairly slim. He would have to prove his claim. Mallen would never agree voluntarily. The whole business would be dragged through the courts. It was likely that Lucy would end up in care in a far less sympathetic environment than Warley House. Mallen could afford to pay the fees – he had been left a packet in his family trusts, quite apart from his own income – but could Geoffrey? He always gave the impression of being flush, but I knew he had no real wealth. We went over and over it. In the end, he said he would think of a way. There was a note of unusual determination in his voice as he said that. You know what he was like: most of the time he acted as if he couldn't care less about anything, but I heard a much tougher note then. It was that

353

quality which I suppose you got in his journalism: the refusal to give up until the story's been followed through or the damaging quote extracted.'

Yes, you're right. You knew him well, better than I did, really. At least you knew more about him. He could be implacable. Do you remember the wine thing he wrote about? It was a subject dear to his heart, of course.'

'Vaguely. Adulteration of some sort, wasn't it?'

'That's right, of a particularly nasty kind. Some horrible chemical that did for the kidneys. Geoffrey went for it, and all the vested interests. The guilty company was a subsidiary of some big French conglomerate and tried to deny the whole thing. Geoffrey dug it out. He spent a lot of his own time on it: the magazine wasn't convinced at first. In the end he got an award. Of course he laughed about that: made some terrible joke about being the Batman of Bordeaux, the Grape Crusader.' Through my tears, I gazed at Henry Massingham. I felt then as if a great weight were somehow shifting – not lifting exactly but shifting like driftwood lapped by an incoming tide, as if it wouldn't stay in the same place for ever.

He gave a rueful smile. 'I miss him.'

I nodded and wiped my eyes. Perhaps I had misjudged him. I said, 'So Geoffrey had got what he wanted. He threatened Mallen with exposure. He threatened to destroy his career and his ability to work, which were the only things he really cared about. He forced him to supply details of his research so he could use it to support and give credence to a book which Geoffrey had written and which purported to prove the existence of God. Geoffrey was going to pocket the advance payment and arrange things so that it was never published. He would have used the money to support Lucy. That was also part of the deal. But what would he have done in the end? Would he have left Mallen alone?'

'I don't think so. You see, I hadn't told him the real reason why Lucy was here. I simply said she had become ill. That's the story Mallen believes. You saw that today. He's blotted everything to do with Lucy's baby out of his mind. As he probably has with

Helen. But, eventually, I'm sure Geoffrey would have got it out of me, and if I had told him what happened I don't think he would have stopped at blackmailing Mallen. He would have killed him.'

'For God's sake, what do you mean? What is it?'

'I'll tell you – but you may wish I hadn't.'

We had finished speaking five minutes before but I was too stunned by what I had heard to break the silence.

'You never told Geoffrey any of that?' I said at last.

'No. As I said, I thought he might do something desperate. I felt like it myself. How do you think it's been for me all this time? Knowing that man killed my sister? Knowing how he treated my niece? But I'm a doctor, for better or worse. I can't bear the idea of taking life. I'm also a psychiatrist. I don't stand in judgement over the people who are sent here: murderers, child-abusers, rapists. I have to try to get to the bottom of why they are as they are. I'm here to help them not execute them. So why should I let myself think any differently about Mallen? He's probably as mad as they are. In any case, I had to do what I thought best for Lucy. I couldn't help her from a prison cell. So Mallen comes along every Monday afternoon to play the devoted father to his sick daughter. Until today. From what I saw of him, I doubt he'll last the week. The shock may hasten the progress of the disease. Cancer victims live on borrowed time before their charade is finally over.'

'I met the boy Tom. In rather strange circumstances. He told me he had never done what Mallen accused him of. But if it weren't him, who could it have been?'

'Mallen himself had the most opportunity, but it takes a particular type to abuse someone he believed was his own daughter. I don't see him like that: his low sexual drive was one of the things that destroyed his marriage.'

The horror of what he had told me still reverberated. I hesitated, but then plunged on. There were still the last questions I had to ask.

'And what was my role in all this business? How did I fit in, assuming I did?'

Henry looked at me. 'Isn't it obvious? Geoffrey told me that although he wanted his daughter back, he wasn't strong enough to manage it on his own. He was going to settle into the cottage – that was another part of the deal with Mallen.'

'But why on earth did he do it in that roundabout way? Why did he pretend to buy it? Why didn't he just tell me?'

'Geoffrey was a funny mixture of dash and caution, wasn't he? In this instance, the cautious side predominated. He wasn't sure how you would react. It would be a big burden to land you with, wouldn't it? A mentally ill, half-grown illegitimate daughter – particularly introduced into a relationship which was based on independence. Work, travel, the ability to up and off whenever you felt like it. The family thing hadn't come up, had it?'

I thought back to the last time I had seen him alive, the last words he had spoken. 'It had, sort of. But I have to admit he was fairly cryptic. Talked about my spending less time at the office, more at home. I thought he was completely out of line if he expected me to make jam and darn socks. I was going to tackle him about it, but I never in the end had the chance. Funny how I keep finding these loose ends.'

'He said he wanted to get into it slowly. Look for the cottage together, move in, settle down, make it a home. He thought the whole process was necessary. There would have been too many questions otherwise. There had to be some background. He couldn't just walk in one day and announce he'd bought a country cottage. It's not like a new camera or something, is it?'

'I see. So he didn't trust me. But he knew he could. I told him.'

'I'm sure you had, but you didn't know what you were in for and I don't think he had actually decided how much he was going to tell you. About Mallen. About the process by which he had been persuaded to give up his daughter. It's not very admirable is it – blackmail?'

'No. If it weren't Geoffrey, and if it weren't for the reasons you've told me, I certainly wouldn't approve of it. But why did he go to all that trouble for the cottage? He wasn't a country type. He didn't want to live there. If it comes to it, I don't want to live there. When we were together, it was idyllic, a time out of time. "Come live with me and be my love", the pastoral fantasy. But now . . .'

'It was for Lucy, don't you see? That was Geoffrey's idea. He wanted to take her there for visits, and then for weekends. He wanted her to be in familiar surroundings where he thought she had been happy, at least some of the time. He wanted her to be with two people who were happy together. He couldn't do it alone, he knew that from the beginning. He thought it would bring you all together: he knew how much you loved the cottage. That's why he went down there the day he died. We were going to try it out, take her there for an afternoon. Sarah and I would take her over there. Geoffrey got quite excited, gave her tea. He told me to bring some things that children liked. Cake and lemonade for my little girl.'

'And he decorated the room,' I said, my eyes filling with tears once more. 'He did it really badly. It was an awful mess. I don't think Geoffrey had ever used a paintbrush in his life before. I suppose that had been her room, the little one at the back?'

'Yes. He wanted me to help him get some furniture. The old stuff had got damaged – and the bed was covered in blood – that night, that night I've just told you about.'

I shuddered. 'Christ almighty. And he never knew. It wouldn't have worked, would it? Taking Lucy back to the cottage. Wouldn't she have associated it with the trauma? Geoffrey didn't know that. You let him go on planning his fantasy.'

'I don't know what effect it would have – it might have been dangerous or not, just like what happened today. I don't know what the cottage represents to her. I had to help Geoffrey. He would have done something desperate. He might have got away with his scheme. If he'd killed Mallen, then he would have been caught and imprisoned. And what good would that have done Lucy? At least in Geoffrey's plan she had a future. If she had reacted badly, then I could have explained it away. But more important than the cottage, it was the relationship that Geoffrey was offering. That might have helped. After all, nothing else I had tried myself had worked. It wasn't perhaps a conventional professional decision, but it was the one I made.'

There was silence. I stood up to go. Suddenly, the mist that had surrounded my relationship with my lately beloved husband had dispersed. I couldn't help voicing my anger and my bitterness. 'So that was it? That was what my whole marriage was about? It could have been anyone – any old mother surrogate. Anyone he happened to bump into in the street. That's how we got together, you know. He knocked me over at my offices and told me some tale about having met me in New York years before. Another lie. He wanted someone stupid enough not to have any clue as to what was going on. Do you know how that makes me feel after all this time? The one thing that I've been holding on to is that despite the schemes and the shenanigans, there was something real between Geoffrey and me. Now I know I was just a dumb broad brought in for home comforts.' I started to cry again, but this time the tears were for myself.

He got up from the desk and put his arm round my shoulders. 'Listen to me. I don't think you've got that right. When Geoffrey told me, I asked him, jokingly, whether he had anyone in mind. He said something that hasn't made any sense until now. He said: "No, not now. I might have, but it was years ago and I missed my chance." Perhaps he didn't miss his chance after all.'

With his arm still around my shoulders, he ushered me towards the door.

'The saddest thing,' he said, 'is that now she will have no one. Oh, I suppose the Mallen family trust will continue to provide for her, here or somewhere else. But she will be alone. You've seen Mallen. He won't last. And what has he ever offered her except unhappiness? As I've just implied, there was one faint hope for Lucy. It involved a medicine that doesn't appear in the Pharmacopeia. You know which?'

The answer rose to my lips unbidden. 'Love,' I said.

He nodded. 'Without that she'll decline. I won't be able to reach her any more. The white coat would get in the way even if she felt that I had not abandoned her like everyone else. She'll drift inevitably downwards into her own private hell.'

The vague shape which had loomed in my mind sharply crystallized. The shock of it made my pulse race. Before I let myself reconsider, I blurted it out. 'You don't have to worry. She was, is, Geoffrey's daughter. Now she's mine as well.'

He showed me out into the cloudy afternoon. We paused awkardly together on the entrance steps as the wind ruffled our hair and clothing. He held out his hand formally but I ignored it, instead flinging my arms around his broad shoulders. I clung to him for a moment then, recovering myself, stood back with my hands holding his arms. 'Thank you,' I said.

He turned as if to go. Then he said, 'Are you going back to London?'

'No. I'm going to stay the night at Forest House. I shan't be able to for very much longer, I daresay.'

He nodded. 'Goodbye. And take care.'

He was a conventional man and the conventional farewell had then no reasonances.

So that afternoon I returned to Forest House knowing that eventually it would be reclaimed by the Mallen family Trust, its rightful owners. The cottage was part of the fantasy that Geoffrey had created, a stage set on which he could enact his role of father. Had he really thought he could get away with it? Did he think Mallen would remain acquiescent for ever? Perhaps he would have done. Perhaps Geoffrey would have come back one afternoon and said, 'I'd like you to meet my daughter,' and we all would have lived happily ever after. Perhaps.

Until that afternoon, I had never known that was what he had wanted. And the dream had perished with him. Or had it? Had what I had said to Henry Massingham been anything other than an instinctive outburst of sympathy for a damaged soul, or had I truly reached out beyond myself to grasp in the ice-cold water a warm and living hand?

These questions still tormented me that night as I prepared for sleep. I sat on the edge of the lumpy bed and brushed out my hair in a hand mirror. There were strands of grey appearing in its blackness, and at the corner of the eyes of the face beneath there were spreading crows' feet. The face itself was thinner, its pallor, no longer touched with the warm pulse of blood at the cheekbones, was the yellowish white of old ivory. Was the ageing process really hastened by extremities of emotion? Was the prisoner of Chillon's 'My hair is white but not with years' any more than a poetic fancy? As I was beginning to feel about twice my age, I would soon know.

I turned back the duvet and climbed into bed. For God's sake, what had I let myself in for? I did, however, manage to force my lips into a smile before I set my tired old head on to the pillow.

I reached for the dangling cord of the light switch. But before I grasped it the light went out of its own accord.

'Damn!' I muttered to myself. A power cut. Strange that there had been no hint of a storm or even wind. Which could have made the rickety power lines fail. It didn't matter, though. It would surely be on again in the morning. I lay down and pulled the quilt up to my chin.

Then outside the window I heard the sound of a car engine and the noise of tyres scrabbling for grip on the loose stones of the track.

I sprang out of bed immediately and twitched back a corner of the thin curtain. I saw the gleam of headlights reflected crazily through the pines at the edge of the forest, turning them into twisted silhouettes, and then into the moonlit clearing a car emerged. It was a nondescript vehicle in blue or black. But what made my anxiety level zoom right into the red zone was not only that I wasn't expecting any midnight callers, but that as it had come out of the sheltering trees and turned on to the drive its lights had been extinguished.

It stopped in front of the house. I started to breathe normally again, controlling my instinctive panic. It had to be lovers seeking an out-of-the-way rendezvous in this country of inquisitive neighbours and, I reflected wryly, twitching curtains.

360

As I watched a man got out of the car, bulky and tall, in dark casual clothing. He was carrying a flashlight. He shone it quickly around, then turned it off. He walked briskly over the crunching shingle towards the front door, disappearing beneath the porch roof.

He was alone. I had seen that the car was empty from the brief glow of its interior light. Perhaps his light o' love had her own car. But what was he doing at the door?

There was a sudden splintering crash. I was at once in no doubt as to the intentions of my night caller. He had just kicked the door down.

A tidal wave of adrenalin swept my body, leaving my pulse beating at about twice its normal rate. I'd read often enough in thrillers of hearts hammering, but rarely had I experienced the rib-jolting reality. My head swam. I mustn't faint, I said to myself over and over. Think, think. And all the time another cliché haunted me. This isn't happening to me. It isn't real. It can't be.

The man did not seem to be in any hurry. I could hear his heavy tread in the room below, the sound of doors being opened and closed. Perhaps he was a burglar looking for the kind of loot that burglars like. But there was none of that here.

I heard him mounting the stairs and the squeak of the timbers. He paused on the landing. I saw the flash of the torch through the gap under my door. I breathed shallowly, hoping that the silence in the house would convince him it was empty. But as I heard him open the door of the adjoining room, enter it, and the boom of his footsteps on the bare boards as he walked around it, I knew he was searching it. And that, whatever I did, he would soon find me.

The memory of the Ladies' waiting room at Cambridge railway station floated into my mind. I grabbed the ladderback chair by the fireplace and stealthily tilted it under the doorknob. Then I pushed up the lower pane of the sash window as far as it would go. There was only one way out. The night air was cold on my naked shoulders as I leant over the windowsill. About six feet below was the ridge of the porch. If I could get on to it, I could drop safely to the ground. What then, I didn't speculate.

I heaved myself up and over the sill and dropped my legs out into the darkness. I could feel the rough pointing of the brickwork of the outside wall with my bare toes as I hung there, elbows hooked over the bottom frame of the window, fingers in claws gripping the rounded edge of the sill.

In the room I heard the doorknob rattle, then a thump on the door panel as he pushed the door and a grating noise as the canted chair legs slid a little way then stuck fast against the raised edge of a floorboard. There was a muttered curse.

I lowered myself further out of the window, in agony as my upper arm muscles took my full weight, my feet waving desperately, seeking the ridge tiles of the porch roof. Now more than ever I regretted my lack of inches and athleticism. I thought of Anna, who could probably shin down a drainpipe like a squirrel on a branch. It was no good. I couldn't reach. And I was terrified to let go. If I slipped and fell, I would at the very least break bones. I hesitated, and then there was no longer a choice.

In the bedroom there was an almighty crash, then the pounding of feet. Two powerful gloved hands grabbed my arms and heaved me with effortless strength over the windowsill and back into the room. I heard the rip of cloth as the shoulder strap of my nightdress tore away. Then the hands released their grip and I fell with bruising force full length on to the rough floorboards.

I crawled into a kneeling position. My shoulders ached as if they were dislocated. I saw in the light of his powerful torch that my attacker, ignoring me, had turned out my suitcase and thrown my things on to the floor. I heard a tearing sound as he shredded the case's fabric lining. Then he dragged out the drawers of the chest and upended them, pawing at the contents with his gloved hands. Next it was the turn of the bed. He tossed aside the mattress as if it were a sheet of newspaper to examine the bedstead. Then there were more tearing sounds as he ripped open the ticking of the mattress itself. He must have a knife. Apparently unsatisfied, he shone the torch on the items spread out top of the chest: various bottles of scent, moisturizer and lotions, talcum powder, a jar of cold cream, deodorant, a cardboard carton of tissues. With a casual movement of his arm he swept the whole lot to the floor. There was a crash of glass as something shattered.

Then he came back to the window and shone the torch on me.

I put up my arm to shield my eyes from the blinding beam. He reached down and twisted it back down to my side. 'Keep your hands where I can see them.' It was a heavily accented voice but I'm no good at recognizing such things. He moved the torch away from my face and played it over my body. The broken shoulder strap dangled at waist level at the end of its triangle of drooping cloth, exposing my left breast. It wasn't, however, an occasion to worry about modesty. I could feel gooseflesh springing up over me in the cold breeze from the open window. He turned the torch back on my face, but this time not directly in my eyes.

I suppose I should have been cowering with terror and begging for my life or my virtue at this point. It was after all one of every woman's worst nightmares come to life. But instead I felt an enormous anger at the unhurried, almost casual way in which he had broken down the door, careless of any noise, the confident manner in which he had searched the house, as if he had his own system, the way in which he had rooted through my things efficiently and ruthlessly, the dispassionate way he was now sizing me up.

Most rapes I'd ever heard of, the guy was jumpy, only too anxious to get himself off, full of threats and bluster. This guy was calm, calculating, as if he had all the time in the world. He made me wild.

'You bastard! You get the hell out of here.' It wasn't great as a piece of defiance, but it made me feel better.

He hit me across the mouth, not with full force but hard enough. It made my eyes water. My lower lip split, and I got the salty taste of my blood.

He watched how I reacted for a second or two, allowing me to experience the stinging pain, then he hit me again, in the same place but harder.

Then he said: 'I haven't got all night. Any more of that talk, I'll break your fucking arms and legs. You tell me what I want to know and I'll leave you alone.'

I could only think, What the hell is he talking about? What do I know that this hoodlum needs? I said, 'OK, ask me.'

'You've got a thing my guvnor wants. Your feller gave it you. You know what it is. Tell me where it's hidden, then we'll go and get it.'

Now I was really afraid. I hadn't a clue what he was talking about. Something Geoffrey had given me? He hadn't given me anything. No package I was to guard with my life. No letter I was to open 'in the event of my death'. The only problem was this guy was not going to believe me. He did not have the look of one to whom rational discourse was second nature. I was under no illusions as to what was going to happen. They might not be the greatest limbs ever, but I was rather attached to my arms and legs the way they were.

'It's not here. It's in London. At the flat.'

He said nothing, but hit out at me with his gloved fist. I flinched away and it missed my face but caught me on my shoulder with terrible force. I screamed in pain, rolling over, clutching myself.

'I warned you not to piss me about, cunt. We've done that flat. If you'd hidden a mouse turd in there, we'd have found it. Tell me where it is.'

He came forward as he spoke and his booted foot lashed out. The kick landed on my ribcage, just below the breastbone, and flung me back against the wall. I felt or heard something inside me give soggily. I almost blacked out with the pain and ground my teeth to stop myself from screaming. It would do no good and I wouldn't give him that satisfaction. The most dreadful thing about him was his calm manner by which it was clear that this was an everyday job which wasn't even all that interesting.

In my agony, I had rolled back over to the chest of drawers. I was on my hands and knees, my hair loose and hanging in tangles around my face. Despite myself, the tears were rolling down my cheeks. All I could say over and over again was, 'Bastard, bastard bastard.' He stood by the window, playing the long rubber-covered torch on me.

Then he took a step towards me. 'All right, you stupid cow. I'll give you ten seconds to tell me, then I'll smash your right arm so you'll never fucking use it again.'

Ten seconds. It was like some children's game of bluff. But this guy wasn't bluffing. He wasn't even excited. Why couldn't it have been a nice peaceful rape?

Instinctively I crawled away from him into the angle between the chest and the wall. As I did so, I jabbed the palm of my hand down on something sharp which dug in deep. It was a piece of broken glass from one of the cosmetic bottles he had hurled on to the floor. I winced, lifted up the hand and put it down again. This time, my fingers closed over a cool metal cylinder. It was the aerosol deodorant.

'Time's up. On your feet!' He reached down, yanked my arm and started to twist it slowly over the wrong way so I could feel the tendons cracking. I came up level with his chin. I could smell the aftershave. What a nice clean boy. I lifted up my left hand, pressed the stud of the can and sprayed its contents into his eyes.

He yelled in pain and surprise, letting me go to rub at the stinging fluid with both hands. I picked up the long heavy torch from where he had dropped it and swung it with all my strength again and again at where his fingers clawed. I must have hit his nose, because something seemed to give. He gave a cry of pain, his head dropping forward. I raised the torch above my head and brought it down as hard as I could. He reeled under the blow. His groping hands found only the curtains which ripped as he fell forward. I shoved hard at his curving back and he tumbled into the pale rectangle of the open window. Then I reached up and slammed the lower frame of the sash down on the back of his neck.

The strength of will and defiance I had summoned up from God knew where left me at that moment. Drained and appalled, I could think only of flight. I dragged aside the smashed remains of the flimsy bedroom door and went down the stairs two at a time. At the bottom I stumbled and fell heavily on to my knees, but I could no longer feel pain. The front door hung ajar on one hinge.

I ran across the starlit clearing, my feet flying over the sharp flints and shingle of the driveway. I ran heedless of thought, my only feeling that I had to get as far away as possible. Every second I expected to hear the panting breath and the pounding feet of the dreadful man I had wounded, savage for vengeance.

Ahead the dark forest beckoned as a place of safety, a place for a wounded animal to hide from the ravening wolves. I staggered as I hit the ruts of the track, and then I was running along it within the shelter of its bordering trees, their branches arching out and up on either side, and above their darkness the silvery channel of the star-sprinkled sky.

I had never run so fast for so long. My breath scorched through my lungs like molten metal, a white-hot skewer impaled my battered ribs. My whole body seemed on fire with agony, but still I ran on. Suddenly I was pitched headlong on to the stony surface as I tripped over a projecting root or broken branch. I lay there for a moment, smelling the scent of the soil and the sharp tang of the pine needles, moistened with the dew. In that moment I longed to close my eyes, to rest there in the darkness under the friendly heavens, and to wake in a quiet morning of soft mist rising through golden sunlight. I heard the rasp of my eyelashes against the flesh of my cradling arm as my eyelids closed.

Behind me an engine roared into life, then revved into a mechanical scream. He was in pursuit.

I was on my feet again but with a kind of lethargy. I had done so much to be free, but I was to be caught and killed at last. I slowed and looked behind me at the headlights raking the sky as he circled the car in the clearing, like terrible eyes seeking prey. And then came the howl of the engine, the squeal of the tyres and the white glow through the trees as he turned to come after me.

I ran again, but without conscious energy, without hope, with only the will to survive, the last ineradicable portion of the spirit which against the odds wishes for life and not death.

In a few seconds he would be on me. In one last desperate attempt, I turned off the track where it curved away out of sight of my pursuer and ran over the grassy verge, into the forest proper, wading ankle deep in the prickly pine needles. But I was at the end of my strength and I was slowed to less than walking pace by the close-planted young firs with their sharp spurs of broken branches. I looked back to the track at the few yards of freedom I had gained. Soon he would come with his torch and his implacable determination to find me, and on the barren forest floor, in that night without end amongst the slender tree trunks, there was nowhere to hide.

At that moment, to my amazement, I heard the sound of another car, approaching more slowly from the opposite end of the track. There were headlights shining through the trees in front of me. The newcomer braked sharply and stopped: he must have seen the other headlights. Clinging out of breath to a low branch in the futile shelter of a pine trunk, I stared at the apparition: an accomplice, no doubt, coming to assist in the capture.

It was then that I became aware of the silence. There were no more sounds of the pursuing vehicle, and whoever was in the second car had turned off the engine. A man climbed out. He walked to the front of his car and into the beam of his own headlights where he stood, a dark figure wreathed in the softly rising spirals of mist.

A voice called out, 'Who's there?'

Scarcely believing, I realized it was a voice I knew. He called again, 'Mary, is that you? What is going on? Mary, are you there?'

It was no time for caution. I stumbled forward into the pool of light and fell into his arms. 'Thank God, thank God it's you,' I said over and over again. 'Ross, Ross. Please help me.'

21

'Hello, my duck. There's someone to see you.'

It was the nice nurse, the plump, motherly one with grey hair and the lovely smile. The grumpy one, the one who clearly disapproved of me, the one who had asked me whether I had had a bit of domestic, was off duty.

She helped me to sit up in the bed, and I gritted my teeth the while.

A large bunch of exotic blooms advanced into the room, clasped by a pair of brawny, bare, tanned arms. Then the flowers were lowered to reveal a broad face under a severe grey crew cut, with a big grin.

'Well, hello there. How're you doing today?'

'Ross, what lovely flowers. You shouldn't have.'

'I don't see why not.' He gave them to the nurse who, clucking approvingly at the pleasant scene, bore them away to find a vase.

We stared at each other for a few moments. Then he seemed nervous, ill at ease. I said, 'Aren't you going to sit down?'

He found a chair and drew it up to the bedside. 'This is a nice room. For a hospital, anyway.'

'Yes. The Royal Norfolk Infirmary is great. I feel a bit guilty, though, not being on the ward. But I kept up my private insurance . . .'

'Sure, why not?' he said without interest.

'Something bothering you? You looked pleased to see me when you came in.'

'Of course I am. Dammit, I am.' He reddened slightly as he said this.

'Then what is it?'

'It's nothing. It's just that guy, the guy . . .'

'I know what you mean. The guy I killed. What about him?'

'The police were asking questions. They came to the pub again yesterday.'

'And?'

'And I had to go through it all again. How I served the guy a drink earlier that evening. He leaves the pub after about a half-hour. Then when I go out for a stroll and a breath of air after locking up about eleven I see him again, sitting in his car, on the other side of the green. Then I'm going to bed when I hear a car drive off and I look out and it's him. Then I go to bed, but I can't sleep and I remember that I've seen the guy before, a day or so ago, kind of hanging around the track through the wood by your place. So I get kind of worried and I get in the car and go round to see if you're OK and . . .'

'And I'm not OK. And neither is the guy because although he drove after me down the track, he was so badly injured he died at the wheel of a brain haemorrhage from a fractured skull before he could catch up with me.'

'Right. I still look at you and think, Christ did she do that? The guy looked like he'd been hit by a cruise missile.'

'Ross, what's the problem? The police have been through it with me a half-dozen times too. They have to. To them it was a suspicious death. They have to investigate it. It's their job. Plus around here it makes a change from checking up on stubble burning.'

He stared intently at the immaculate white of the hospital sheet, then he looked up, his clear, grey eyes on me, questioning. I stared back at him frankly. 'I repeat, what's the problem?'

He banged his hands together sharply and got to his feet, pushing the chair back. Then he went over to the window and spoke to his reflection in the glass. 'Goddamn. I don't want to say this, I don't want to even think it. But the police now seem to know who this guy is. He didn't have any identity stuff when they found him, but this time – I guess because they're a bit pleased with themselves – they let slip that they think he might be an Northern Irish guy the London cops have had tabs on. Not a political but a guy who does, well, commissioned jobs. A hit man, in other words.'

'I see. Or rather I don't see. What's that to do with me?'

He turned back from the window. 'For Christ's sake, of course it's to do with you. Someone sends a hit man, there must be a reason.'

'And you think I know what this reason is, or might be? You think I haven't been entirely honest with you?'

'I don't know. Maybe. Perhaps you haven't had the opportunity to think about it.'

'Listen, Ross. Come over here and sit down. That's better. Let me tell you something. I swear to you I don't know why this guy came after me. I don't know him from Adam. I don't know why anyone would want to have me rubbed out by a professional killer. I'm in publishing, for God's sake, not the Mob. Also, I did not set out to kill him. I acted entirely in self-defence and in my humble opinion I was bloody lucky to get away alive myself. As it is, I've been kept in here for three days already with two broken ribs, a punctured lung, a dislocated shoulder, a broken collar bone and God knows how many bruises and lacerations all over me. I can hardly move and I couldn't bear to look at myself even if I could. Even the police were kind enough to say at the beginning that although they were sending the file to the DPP they didn't imagine I would be charged as it was obvious I had been under severe danger of death. So I don't care whether or not this guy is first cousin to the Jackal. To me, he was a psycho who broke into a woman's bedroom in the middle of the night and for a change got more than he bargained for.' I sank back on the pillows, exhausted with the effort of this speech.

Ross reached out a large brown hand and patted mine, heavily padded and bandaged from where they had dug out the splinters of broken glass. 'I'm sorry, Mary,' he said softly. 'Sure I believe you.'

I nodded and closed my eyes. I'm sorry too, Ross, I thought as I drifted into sleep.

I came out of a light doze after breakfast the following morning to find the grim-faced nurse standing over me, arms folded across her flat bosom. I strongly suspected she had poked me awake.

'Get a lot of visitors, don't you? Lady here to see you, if you're up to it. And there's a letter, handed in at the desk it was.'

For a delightful moment I thought it might be Anna, or that the letter at least might be from her. But the envelope the nurse put on my bedside table was in a cheap manila envelope with my name and the address of the hospital in crude block capitals. Probably a bill. A creditor hoping to collect before it was too late. And the figure who followed the nurse into the room confirmed that Anna was a thousand miles away, oblivious of the latest Perils of Pauline.

It was Sarah Massingham.

She was even more translucently pale than when I had last seen her.

There were no preliminaries. 'I had to see you. Firstly to apologize for the way I behaved to you. I hope you can understand that I was only trying to protect Henry. And secondly . . .' She was sitting with perfect poise on the hospital issue wooden chair. She paused and glanced down at her long hands. I let the silence run on, unwilling to help her out. Finally, she looked up again, and I saw by the brightness at the corners of her eyes that she was weeping. She took a deep, snuffling breath. 'Secondly, I wanted to tell you about Geoffrey and me. I want you to know that it was over before he met you in London. It was over for him anyway.'

I felt tears in my own eyes, but I wouldn't let myself cry. 'Is that really true? I thought for a long time when I saw you together in Breckenham . . . well, that you were the reason he wanted to buy the cottage. And even when I knew it wasn't, I thought that you and he might –'

'That time, at the hotel. It was the last time I saw him. And before then, I hadn't seen him since he met you. Our affair ended when that happened. I was desperately unhappy. I just hoped, despite what he'd said, that his coming to Norfolk meant that I would see him again, but he told me it was no go. And he got furious when I flounced out of the main entrance in full view. How on earth did he cope with that?'

'He denied the whole thing.'

'Very Geoffrey, wasn't it? I even wrote to him at home, I was so desperate for a reaction. He didn't answer.'

'I remember the letter. He got it the last day I saw him alive.'

'I miss him as well, you know. God, I do. But I can't expect you to understand that. I saw how you looked when you came to the house in search of Henry. You recognized me. I suppose you had guessed about Geoffrey and me.'

'Yes, I had. But it was the perfume as well.'

'Perfume?'

'You left a scent bottle in Geoffrey's flat. Norfolk Lavender. It has a very distinctive odour. You were wearing it.'

'I like it, funnily enough. Limehouse. Yes, we used to go there. I told Henry they were shopping trips, or I had to see my dentist. I don't think he cared very much. He's far more interested in his work. I think he cares more for his patients than he does for me. But it's not very good, is it? An affair with your husband's best friend?'

I put out my hand to touch her arm, wincing at the effort it cost me. 'I'm not judging you. These things happen. I can see how you feel. Were you very unhappy?'

'There were a whole lot of reasons. Yes, I suppose I was bored, frustrated, neglected – the usual things. God, how I hate it here sometimes. Living in that damned house. Oh, I know it looks all *Homes and Gardens*, and it is when the sun's shining and we've got friends down from London for the weekend. Sunday lunch, drinks in the conservatory, that kind of thing. But you try living there the rest of the time. There's no one to talk to: only boring landowners and their even more boring wives. Henry's working all the hours that God sends. He hardly says hello to me some days. And in the winter, when the evening closes in before the afternoon's hardly started, that's when I really hate it.'

'Henry told me you were a nurse. That you nursed Lucy when she was first admitted.'

'Yes, I did. I did what I could for the poor dear child. I used to be at Great Ormond Street. That's how I met him – he was at some Bart's reunion that I'd gone along to. I know what you're saying. I would like to work. I miss it. I felt that so strongly when I was with Lucy. But that was special, in special circumstance as you're aware. Henry won't let me get a nursing job. Status is all-important in the country. Can't have me emptying bedpans for the kids in the daytime, then hobnob socially with the parents in the evening. I love children, working with children. Henry wanted me to be some sort of administrator at the hospital. That would be OK, apparently, but I couldn't stand it.'

'So you and Geoffrey . . .?'

'Yes, at first, I just wanted a fling. To get back at Henry – not that I would have told him. Despite everything I still feel something for him. It had been ages since I'd been treated like a real woman. But also I hoped that . . .' She paused, and I could see she was making an effort to continue. 'Henry and I . . . we haven't got children. He doesn't want them. Says he knows too much about the harm that parents do. But I've always wanted a child.'

'And you hoped you might get pregnant from the affair.'

'Yes, yes. I bloody did hope that. But it never happened and now I've got nothing.' She was crying openly, twisting her handkerchief over and over in her hands.

There was nothing I could say.

Eventually she stopped crying. When she turned to me again, she was more composed. 'His death was so sudden, wasn't it? I had no idea he had a heart condition. You can't always tell, though.'

I shifted uncomfortably in the bed. I hoped she would go soon.

She moved solicitously to help me. Once a nurse, I supposed. The slim shoulders concealed considerable strength. She settled me and plumped up the pillows behind me. I caught a waft of lavender from the front of her white silk blouse.

She sat back in the chair and regarded her handiwork. Then she said, 'If I were you, I would think what happened was a bit too much of a coincidence.'

'What do you mean?'

'Geoffrey, then you. By all accounts, you were nearly killed.'

'By whose accounts?'

'Hasn't anyone told you? You're in the papers. You're a heroine. "Plucky Mary fights off rapist" and so on. They'll be queueing up for your story when you get out.'

'Famous for fifteen minutes, I suppose. But what did you mean about Geoffrey?'

She lowered her voice and leaned closer to me. 'I'm not the world's greatest intellect, but I know he was fooling around with some powerful people. I overheard them, Geoffrey and Henry, talking about it. Henry thinks that because I'm not highly educated I'm stupid. It suits men to think their wives are thick, doesn't it? Well, I thought what Geoffrey was getting up to was absolutely crazy. I told him as much.'

'He wanted his daughter back.'

'And he wanted revenge.'

I closed my eyes. I was suddenly back in that dreadful night, pursued by that dreadful man, my heart pounding as if it would burst. As if it would burst. 'Oh, God,' I said.

She reached out to touch me. 'You've gone quite pale. It's the shock still. They ought to have you on a drip. I'll get a doctor.'

I shook my head. 'No, I'm OK. I think perhaps you should go. I forget how tired I get at the moment.'

When I was sure she had gone, I turned my face into the pillow and let the tears flow.

I struggled to sit up, my aged body racked with agony at my slightest movement. I might as well look in the envelope. I had nothing else to do.

I managed to swing an arm over and grab it. I stuck it under my chin, gritted my teeth and levered myself upright by clenching the muscles of my bottom, about the only ones which didn't hurt, and shoving with my elbows. I made it, panting, and pulled open the envelope. In it was a cutting from a newspaper – *The Times*, by the look of it – and a plain sheet of white paper.

I picked up the cutting. The surviving part of the masthead showed that it was that morning's edition.

Dr Julian Mallen, the physicist and mathematician, died yesterday from cancer in Addenbrooke's hospital, Cambridge. A hospital spokesman said he had been suffering from the disease for some time but had been admitted the day before as a result of the sudden worsening of his condition.

Dr Mallen, at fifty, was regarded by his peers in the scientific community as one of the most brilliant scientists produced by this country for generations. He made many important advances in quantum mechanics, particularly in the mathematics of probability, and contributed a stream of seminal articles to scientific journals even as he struggled with terminal illness. Although it appeared that he had failed in his search for the unifying principle in nature – a quest which had defeated no less than the great Einstein – colleagues believe he may have been on the edge of a great discovery. His death at such a comparatively early age is therefore a tragedy for the world of science.

Dr Mallen spent his entire working life in Cambridge, latterly at the Cambridge Centre for Physical Research, of which he was a Senior Director. A full appreciation will follow tomorrow.

I was about to crumple up the envelope, the cutting and the paper which had enclosed it when I noticed that it was not blank as I had at first thought.

On it were four words, rough capitals scrawled in a cheap biro, the ink from which had smeared and blobbed: 'LET'S CALL IT QUITS.'

There was something about this bald, enigmatic message that set my heart racing. I knew it had come from the world of violence which had so savagely obtruded into my ordinary, protected, middle-class existence.

Despite what I had so vehemently told Ross Earle, I knew my assailant at the cottage was no random burglar or rapist. He was after something specific – he had said as much. The attack had been of calculated viciousness, to frighten and compel whatever it was out of me. What it was I had no idea. I had only the sick feeling that it was in some way connected with Geoffrey. Geoffrey and his labyrinthine scheme.

And here was more of the same. A missive in the language of hoodlums and cowboys. Self-consciously macho, an apparent grudging tribute to my capacity for survival. You sure did good, honey. He was one of my best men.

But why quits? Why that particular word? It implied an equalization, a settlement of an issue between me and my anonymous correspondent. But of what issue?

And then all at once I knew. The cutting said it. Mallen had been the issue. Now he was dead, the threat which Geoffrey and I as his supposed accomplice had posed to him was cancelled.

Geoffrey's elaborate scheme to enrich himself and destroy the reputation of the man he had hated had had a flaw. It had assumed that Mallen stood alone. But behind him, I had no doubt, were ranked forces which had things at stake which would brook no interference from amateurs in the field of extortion.

For having seen the place, I didn't for one moment believe that the Cambridge Centre for Physical Research was set up for the disinterested pursuit of academic excellence. A W S had implied as much. What were they doing there? Probing the structure of the universe, to find the secret of the energy that powered the stars? Looking for the ultimate weapon, the ultimate defence system?

How proud the leaders of the military-industrial complex must have been to recruit a man like Mallen, a man slighted in his profession and willing to cooperate with anyone who would fund his work. How unwilling they would have been to have their best asset taken from them.

Was it really to be quits then? I had escaped with my life, but Geoffrey had not. The inference to be drawn from the message was that they – whoever they were – would leave me in peace. But only provided, presumably, that I did not rock the boat by attempting to pursue the matter.

The shadow world of those powerful conspiracies which actually controlled our lives had stretched out of its obscurity and touched me for but an instant with its spider's claw, then receded. How could I ever hope or dare to find it again?

As in the flickering light of a phantasmagoria, I saw Geoffrey driving in terror down the forest track, stumbling out half-dazed after he had hit the tree, fleeing into the forest where his heart had given out before they could seize him.

I knew then that discover it I had to. I would not give in. I would not rest until I found something of substance on which to lay the responsibility for my loss and grief and anger. Behind the words, there was a person, a man. And I would unmask him.

But how? As I lay there in the hospital bed, my mind wandering from the pain-killing drugs they fed me, the images floated before me. I tried to bring back every detail of my visit to the Cambridge Centre for Physical Research, as if amongst the steel and glass itself there lay some vital clue.

I saw myself cross the foyer, speak to the receptionist, sit down and pretend to read the magazine, gazing around with curiosity. There was something I had seen there which I knew lurked in my memory. What was it? What?

As I was tiring with the effort, my mind begging for sleep, I had it. The roll-call of sponsors discreetly displayed on the wall opposite the entrance. And amongst the bland corporate identities was one I recognized.

As I drifted into unconsciousness, I knew that the path to the shadows had been illuminated.

A few days later, the consultant pronounced there was nothing further that the hospital could do for me. It was time to go home. I should take it easy for a few more weeks – no strenuous exercises, he said with the ghost of a wink – until my injured lung had fully healed and my battered ribs and collar bone had knitted together. As I was a fit and healthy young woman – thanks for that – I would eventually make a full recovery.

I certainly hadn't felt either young or fit as I had tottered out of the hospital on the arm of the nice nurse and into the waiting cab which was to take me to the train station.

I had winced at every jolt of the train into Liverpool Street, staggered to the cab rank feeling white and drained, and graciously, like an elderly dowager, accepted the help of the young cabby up the slippery marble steps of Nightingale Court.

Before going inside, I stood on the top step, looking out into the London afternoon, feeling the wind ruffle my loosened hair, smelling the damp air and hearing the branches of the sidewalk trees creak. Soon would come the autumn. I remembered those lines of . . . was it Housman? 'And beeches strip in storms for winter and stain the wind with leaves.' I too felt stripped for winter, naked and shivering, awaiting the ruthless storm, unready for the task I had set myself.

I hobbled up the endless staircase. As I came to my front door, I saw it was open.

Oh no, not again, I groaned, putting out a hand to the jamb to hold on to. Then standing in the doorway was a figure, tall and blonde in a flowing garment of many hued and shimmering silk.

'Anna. Anna!' I said, before I collapsed weeping into her open arms.

22

'So are you going to accept Vanessa's offer?' Anna mumbled, her mouth full of *tortellini alfredo*.

The Cento Cypressi was at its lunchtime fever pitch. Waiters ran hither and thither bearing plates of steaming pasta – ugh! – and, worse, still had the energy to belt out maudlin tenor arias by the dozen.

I wrinkled my nose. 'I don't know. That'd mean I'd end up coping with you and your problems again. It was bad enough being your publisher. God knows how it would be as your literary agent.'

'Beast. I'm a reformed character.'

'Scattergoods may have agreed to extend the deadline on your contract but that doesn't mean you're out of the wood yet. They're new to the publishing game and aren't familiar with authors like you. They will expect you to write the books. What have you managed so far? One page, or is it two? And how long have you got left?'

'I haven't a clue. It shows I need someone like you to keep an eye on me. Anyway, I've been doing some more research. Don't laugh, I really have been. Number three is going to be brilliant. I've got a wonderful title. *Riding Westward*. Evocative, *non?*'

I shrugged. 'You need more than a title. And that reminds me, I'm riding eastward myself at the end of the week. I have to get the car back. I've been putting it off. It's been over six weeks. I'm pretty much recovered and can drive again, I don't have any excuse.'

She stared at me in amazement. 'You're not serious. What do you want to go back there for? Can't you get somebody to drive it here for you? Seems crazy to do it yourself.'

'No, I can't. It's very awkward. The car's at the pub in the village. Ross took it there afterwards. He's been looking after it. If I suggested I couldn't get it myself, he wouldn't let anyone else bring it. He'd insist on doing it himself, and I don't want him to do that. I don't want him to come here. Does that make sense?'

'Are you sure that's what you want? He sounds nice. All brown and hunky.'

'There is another reason for going. The cottage. I want to say goodbye. That's silly, isn't it?'

'Of course it isn't. It's quite an important part of your life. You need to say goodbye to places as well as people. Leaving's grieving as they say. It was with me, with the château. Even though I was desperate to get rid of it, when the time came to hand over the keys and walk down the drive for the last time, I had to brush away the tears. Mind you, by the time I got to those crumbling gate pillars, I was whooping for joy. The money. The money. Those people. They didn't mind what they paid. Hong Kong must be paved with gold. I've never been there. Is it?'

'No.'

'I say, I'll come with you to Norfolk if you like.'

I gazed at her sadly. 'I'm sorry, Anna. This time, I'd like to go alone.'

I was sorry, too, that I hadn't told her everything. But if Anna had known what else I intended, she would surely have done everything she could to stop me.

I paid off the taxi, and then stood shivering in the biting wind which swirled over the village green. It was half past ten and the pub hadn't opened yet. I had wanted to get there early to avoid the scrutiny of the habitués of the public bar.

I went round the back to where the living quarters were and banged on the door. There was silence for a while, and then I heard the heavy sound of his footsteps.

He was wearing a sweat shirt as usual. The hand of one tightly muscled brown arm gripped a wrench. 'Well, hi there. Come on in.' He put down the wrench and wiped his hands on a towel. 'I was down changing over one of the barrels. I hope you haven't been standing out there a time.'

I shook my head. He motioned me inside. I didn't sit down but stood by the window looking out into the yard. I could make out the scarlet nose of the BMW in the gloom within the old cart shed.

He followed my glance. 'There she is. Safe and sound. Cleaned and polished. A beautiful auto. I wish I could afford one.'

'So do I.'

He smiled uncertainly. 'I'll get us some coffee.'

He bustled around in the kitchen area. It was cold in the room and the furnishings looked even more drab than they had in the summer.

He gave me a mug of coffee and said, 'I'm sorry about what I said in the hospital. It's been bothering me. It sounded as if I thought you hadn't levelled with me about what happened.'

'Would it matter if it turned out I hadn't?'

His brown face and grey eyes betrayed no emotion. 'Does that mean you didn't?'

'I asked first.'

'You know damn well it would. I'd like to think you could tell me . . . well, whatever there is to tell. That you could trust me.'

'Ross, listen to me. You don't want to get involved with me.' I stopped, irritated at my lack of assertiveness. It sounded like something they said in the movies. 'No, let me rephrase that. I don't want to get involved with you. There's no point in it. There's no future in it. I don't know anything about you. You don't know anything about me. You helped me. I'm grateful. That's all there is. I'm sorry.'

He turned away to stare out of the window, then turned back. For a moment I thought he would start to argue, but instead he shrugged and mumbled, 'I guess I never should have even imagined that you could, well . . .'

'Let's get the car, Ross,' I said.

He carefully manoeuvred the car out of the cart shed, and parked it in front of the pub. He polished off a few specks with a wetted finger – the coachwork had been burnished to a finish it had not had for months – and handed me the keys with a ceremonial flourish. As I took them, I leant over and kissed his cheek. 'Thanks, Ross, for everything.' He started hesitantly to put his arms round me but I gently disengaged. The time for that had passed.

I waved a hand out of the car window as I drove away, but I didn't look back.

A little way out of the village I stopped the car in a layby, got out my handkerchief and cried for a while. He was a nice guy. I was grateful to him. I felt sorry for him. But that was all. I cried all the same.

I dried my eyes and repaired the damage to mascara and make-up in the visor mirror.

It seemed strange to be sitting in the driving seat of Geoffrey's car again. It would always be Geoffrey's car. The slightly sagging leather of the driving seat even carried the imprint of his ample form, the worn-down rubber of the gas pedal a reminder of his driving habits.

In the door pocket were his maps, on the centre console behind the gear stick was the box in which he untidily stored his music tapes. I rummaged around in it, keen for the first time since his death to play something typically Geoffrey to suit my mood of remembrance.

But instead I came across something I thought a bit odd. Mozart. Geoffrey didn't like Mozart. 'Too predictable,' he would say loftily and, I always thought, rather pretentiously. So what was he doing with Mozart's Concerto for Two Violins Op 13, K4913, 'The Swiss'?

I stared at it with a strange feeling of anticipation. I wouldn't call myself a musicologist, but I did know that the Kochel numbers of Wolfgang Amadeus' oeuvre did not have four figures and that he never wrote a violin concerto called 'The Swiss'.

With fingers that trembled slightly I prised open the little plastic box. Inside was a perfectly ordinary tape cassette. Impatiently I pushed it into the slot of the tape player and jabbed the playback button. What I heard from the speakers was not Mozart. It was not even music. It was the voice of Henry Massingham.

I walked up the narrow sandy lane between the tall hedgerows – now nearly devoid of leaf and hung only with bunches of dark red haws – which for generations had sheltered the fields from the unseasonable winnowing of the north-easterlies.

Although I had come this way before, I seemed on this occasion to be looking around me with eyes newly opened, so sharply did every detail of my surroundings impress itself upon me. Perhaps it was the freshness of the day, brightening into one of those cold, dry interludes in the damp progression into winter; perhaps it was the effect of absence which caused this preternatural concentration of vision.

I still felt physically quite weak and dawdled along. I paused for breath, leaning against a gate and gazing out over a huge field which sloped down to the hidden tarmac road running in the dry bottom of what passed in this country of gentle undulations for a valley. Through the gaps in the pines on the other side I could see the occasional flash of a windscreen and the accompanying noise of an engine. In the spring, the field had been greener than any grass with seedling wheat. Now the light brown earth had been turned by the plough, and lay bare and expectant. From afar, I heard the metallic cough of a cock pheasant.

The sound awakened other noises in my mind.

'Lucy, it's Uncle Henry. I've got Uncle Geoffrey with me. Can you hear me? Nod your head if you can hear me. That's good. I want us to have a little talk. There's so much we can talk about. So we've gone to a special place where we can talk without anybody hearing us. It's a very special place, Lucy. It's a place where you're only three years old. We can talk about Mummy there. What do you see in that special place, Lucy? Can you see your Mummy? I know you want to talk about her because you loved her very much and she loved you. I know she did because she used to talk about you to me. I loved her too, Lucy. Can't we talk again as we used to?'

There was silence, the sound of someone coughing, the creak of a chair. Then her voice, small, toneless and disembodied. I tried as I listened to fit the voice to the lovely silent girl I had seen. I shivered, as if a statue had given utterance or words had come from within a tomb.

'It's very dark. It's like looking down a dark passage. I don't like it there.'

'You're quite safe. You're just watching something happen. Yes, it's like the television. What's going on there, Lucy?'

'I can see Mummy. She has long hair and it's all golden. She looks very tall. She has a lovely red dress with big yellow flowers. I'm standing on tiptoe in my new shoes.'

'That's wonderful, Lucy. Do you see anything else there when you think about Mummy? What else can you see there when you're only three years old?'

'I don't know.'

'Please, Lucy. You're quite safe.'

'A horrid thing. Don't want to.'

'Is it because Mummy went away?'

There was a sob. 'Mummy went away.'

'She didn't mean to, Lucy. Can you remember that day, the day Mummy went away?'

There was another pause, some muttering and a whispered shh! Then Lucy's voice again.

'She's standing at the stove, and she's putting a cake in the oven. Mummy and I have been making the cake. I feel very warm and happy. We're going to the park this afternoon. Then Daddy comes in. Mummy's surprised to see him. She says, "Why aren't you at work?" Then Daddy shouts at Mummy. He's saying horrid things because Mummy starts crying. She runs away and Daddy runs after her. They're in the bedroom, and I'm standing at the door. I can see Daddy standing in front of Mummy. He's got his hands around her neck and he's still shouting at her. Mummy looks very frightened. I can see her hands hitting Daddy's back. She's making funny noises. I'm very scared so I run away to my bedroom and hide under the blankets and I make myself very small so that everything will be all right.'

'It is all right, Lucy. What's happening now?'

'I can smell the lovely cake in the oven so I come out to see if Mummy says it's ready. But it's just Daddy in the kitchen. He looks at me and says that a bad man has taken Mummy away. She isn't ever coming back. He was a very bad man, but he's gone away now. If anyone asks me I have to tell them about how the bad man took Mummy away. If I don't then the bad man will come back and take Daddy away too. If anyone asks where Daddy is, I have to say that he's at work. Otherwise the bad man will come back and take him away for ever. Then Daddy goes away, and the cake starts to smell funny and I go to tell Mummy in the bedroom, although I'm frightened of the bad man. But Mummy looks funny on the bed and she's asleep and I can't wake her up. Then I have to go away and hide again in the bed and play with my dolly like a good girl so that everything will be all right. Then there are lots of men, and Daddy is there and he's crying. And there's a kind lady and she's asking me about the bad man, and I tell her how he hurt Mummy. I didn't want the bad man to come back and hurt Daddy. I wasn't a bad girl, was I? Is that why Mummy went away, because I was bad? Is it?' Her voice dissolved in sobs.

Then there was the voice of Henry Massingham, speaking calmly and gently, but even over the hiss of the tape I could hear the catch as he struggled with his emotion. 'No, Lucy, you're not a bad girl and your Mummy loved you very, very much. You need to cry now, but then you'll have a little sleep. When you wake up, you won't any longer be three years old. You'll be safe here in your new home with Nora.'

There was the snap of the stop button as the tape ended.

★

I had sat there, my mind numbed by what I had heard, trying to imagine Geoffrey's thoughts as he listened to his daughter's voice, so full of long-suppressed emotion. At what point had he veered away from a mere violent act of revenge to the creation of Mallen's own special punishment cell? Once again, I marvelled at how little I had known of this man.

Automatically, I reached out and ejected the tape cassette. I flipped open the small plastic box to put it away safely. As I did so, I looked more closely at the paper insert with the glossy cover picture of the Swiss mountains. It was a very clever fake. How typical of Geoffrey. The last leg-pull of all. He must have been thinking of Poe's story, 'The Purloined Letter'. Where better to hide a letter than in a letter rack? Where better to hide a tape cassette than in a box of them?

The clumsy searcher who had beaten me half to death looking for this wasn't up to Geoffrey's subtlety of invention.

But Geoffrey had left the best joke till last. Printed at the bottom was a note of the kind frequently seen these days. 'This recording has been made possible by the generous sponsorship of the Union Bank of Switzerland. Special thanks to Herr Muller for his combination of musical and financial knowledge.'

Fighting back the tears, I managed in the end a smile. I knew now where Geoffrey had lodged his ill-gotten McAllister's gains. Michael had been right, up to a point. It took one to know one. But he hadn't meant to conceal it from me. He would have expected me to work it out.

He would have been very surprised if I hadn't finally got around to asking Mr Muller at his office in Zurich for the contents of account number 4913.

I walked on. The field ended abruptly at a wire fence, and beyond a rough grassy fire-break the forest began. I hesitated, suddenly daunted by what faced me. I had to summon up the will to go on, to confront the devils which hung grinning from the twisted branches and peeped from behind the fissured trunks of the Corsican pines. Under them lay darkness, and dread was in their heavy drifts of dead brown needles.

I went on. The sunlight fell on the track only in patches. About me was the medicinal scent of resin. In the enclosure of the forest, the atmosphere was chill. I felt almost suffocated and every pace was an effort of will. At times I felt I was almost dragging myself along against the attraction of some restraining force, some gravity holding me in an orbit from which I had to escape.

When I finally emerged from the cover of the forest on to the open plateau before the house, I no longer felt that once-familiar stab of pleasure, of recognition.

It was silent. Even the breeze had died away. I gazed for a few more minutes. Then, reluctantly, I made my way slowly over the mossy turf to the front door.

In the kitchen the lovely old brick floor, the colour of autumn beech leaves, was still solid beneath my feet. The big butler sink and wooden draining board still stood beneath the brick-silled casement window through which the early afternoon sun streamed. The huge Welsh dresser still occupied the whole of the wall opposite me. The massive range still glowered from the fireplace. But there the familiarity ended. Gone was the warmth born of the excitement of a new beginning. Gone was the feeling of sharing. Gone was the life I had thought to live in this place.

I wandered into the sitting room. Its bright clean paintwork seemed a mockery of what I had intended here. It looked and felt unoccupied. There were no untidy piles of books, magazines and newspapers, no scattered files covered with scribbled notes on yellow. stickers, no half-drunk coffee mugs as pointers of a life in hasty progress. That life had ended, and a new one not begun.

The garden had reverted to wilderness. I had got word to Norman that his services wouldn't be needed. The grass browned by the first frosts was waist high again. Dotted through it were the greying husks of nettles, gathering strength for their spring resurgence. Next spring maybe some other couple would wander round, this time in the company of a genuine estate agent, and make their plans. Would they fall in love with this place as I once had?

I strode through the wet grass to the post and rail fence and stood on the bottom rail looking out at the dark line of the forest. I remembered that day when Ruff the dog had appeared in my life and brought Lucy Mallen with him.

Lucy. Whose short life had been a mockery of childhood. I trembled as I forced myself to remember what Henry Massingham had told me on that dreadful day at the Hospital, what I would have to overcome in her mind if she were ever again to trust and love.

'I've never told anyone about what happened the night that Lucy was admitted here. Sarah was there, of course, but we've never talked about it. Now, I feel I ought to tell you. You have a right to know after all. And it will be a relief to unload the whole mess.

'Mallen phoned my home late one evening nearly two years ago. He was speaking from the call box in Barton St Margaret. He had driven there from the cottage. He couldn't bear the telephone and had refused to have one put it in. He sounded quite desperate. He appealed for my help as a medical man and a relative. I knew then that something was very wrong, because he and I were hardly on the best of terms, as you can imagine. At first I was inclined to tell him to go to hell, then when I realized that it was Lucy who was ill I agreed to come at once. I took Sarah – she used to be a pediatric nurse.

'When I got there, I was glad I had done that. In my profession you get used to dreadful things. It isn't fashionable to say so but madness isn't somehow just being a bit abnormal. It's a glimpse of something subhuman, almost elemental. It's very frightening to anyone who hasn't witnessed it before. And Mallen was terrified. I felt almost sorry for him, his only daughter turned into a raving wild thing. You saw it yourself only an hour ago, but on this occasion it wasn't just madness. There was death.

'As you know, she had had a baby. As far as I could make out from Mallen, he hadn't found out that she was even pregnant until a few days before. He said the boy Tom was responsible, flew into a terrible rage and threw him out. Poor Lucy had hardly known what was going on. Mallen had raved at her for hours – she told

Sarah that Daddy had shouted at her. He said she was as big a slut as her mother and that he didn't care whether she lived or died. No one would care about her ever again after what she had done. She locked herself in her room and there went into premature labour. She must have screamed to high heaven in agony – I know she was bleeding heavily from the state of her bed. Mallen said he hadn't noticed anything as he'd been working on something which took all his attention. Can you imagine it? The callous indifference of the man disgusted me beyond anything I had ever experienced.

'As far as I could make out the child – a little boy – had lived only a few hours. It was very premature. Mallen said she came down with him in her arms, wrapped in an old tablecloth. At first Mallen thought the bundle was a doll. Then he realized. The baby was probably dead by then.

'When Mallen tried to take the baby from her, she fled to the attic and refused to come down. Every time he went near, she screamed at him. Finally that night even Mallen realized he had to get help. And he went to me. To keep it in the family.

'That was how things stood when we got there. She got wind of why we had come and screamed down, "You're not going to take my baby away. He's mine." I tried to reason with her, but it was useless. When I told her the child was dead, she kept on repeating, "He's just been born, he can't be dead. I won't let him be dead."

'In the end I had to take him away by force. She was clearly in such a state that something had to be done. It was the most appalling thing I think I have ever had to do. While Sarah and I engaged in this awful wrestling match, Mallen just stood there. Pathetic, frozen. Well, we managed it. The poor little scrap was still wrapped in the cloth. I can see him now: his red face all shrivelled, as light as thistledown.'

He stopped speaking, overcome by the recollection. I was crying now, the tears leaking hotly from my eyes.

I heard him start speaking again, oblivious of me, apparently once more in the darkness of that night. 'I didn't know what to do. I knew I had a duty – the law, that sort of thing. But what could I do? I didn't want to put my niece through the publicity which would follow. What gain would that have been? And Mallen begged me to help him. He was abject. He thought such an open scandal would destroy his work. That was what he was really worried about. That the University – and this hush-hush research outfit he works for – would come under pressure to cancel his fellowship if it had come out that he had through ignorance or wilfulness concealed his daughter's pregnancy and through it caused or at least not prevented the death of the baby. He had a horror of being in the public eye. Maybe he was also nervous of what else would come out once the reporters started digging into the circumstances of Helen's death.'

'So you agreed to hush the whole thing up?'

'Yes, God help me. Not for Mallen's sake. I despised the man, I wanted him to be ruined. But I wanted Lucy to retain some chance of regaining a normal childhood. We buried the baby in the forest somewhere. I don't remember where exactly. It was too dark. And I sedated Lucy and admitted her here. When the drug wore off she wouldn't speak, hasn't spoken since. Sarah nursed her personally until she was over the physical effects of the birth. I made sure no gynaecological examination was carried out for the hospital records. None of the staff know about it. Her file says she's suffering from an hysterical trauma of unknown origin. Mallen has paid the fees which are, have to be, very substantial. She's been here for over eighteen months now.

I shivered at the memory and looked at my watch. Nearly time. As I walked back to the house across the overgrown lawn, I heard the sound of heavy feet crunching over the gravel of the front drive. Punctual to the minute, my visitor had arrived.

I couldn't bear to invite him into the house, so after an awkward moment we ended up strolling together in silence along the track into the forest.

He was in virtually the same clothes that he had had on the first time I had met him, the day, centuries ago, that he had shot the dog, Lucy's dog. Waxed jacket, high rubber boots and a peaked checkered cap. Under his arm he carried the same single-barrelled shotgun. He could have stepped straight from the pages of the *Field*, the very model of an English country gentleman.

After five minutes or so, we sat down by the side of the path on the trunk of a felled tree and for a moment the silence continued. Then he said, leaning the shotgun carefully against the timber, 'It's a jolly nice day for a walk, but I don't think that was what you had in mind. Your note was a bit more pressing: "It is imperative that you meet me." Rather emotional, eh?'

'You know what we womenfolk are like. A bit hysterical, what? Particularly when it concerns what I have to discuss with you. I think you know quite well what it is.'

'I have to confess I don't.'

'You can hardly have forgotten. Or perhaps you have. It may be an everyday occurrence for you. Murder.'

He was on his feet, the picture of indignant rage. 'Are you mad, woman? Do you know what you're saying? If you were a man, I'd –'

'Have me horsewhipped? Please, James, let's not put on the aggrieved country squire act. Let's pretend we're grown-ups. I know and you know that I know.'

He sat down heavily, his huge hands resting on his knees. When he spoke again it was in the voice I imagined he used in the board room of the bank. 'All right. What do you think you know? Tell me whatever preposterous yarn you like. Whom am I supposed to have murdered?'

'Geoffrey,' I said.

This time he didn't get to his feet. 'You excel yourself, to accuse me of the murder of a man who died from natural causes. And even if he had not, what conceivable reason could I have had for doing such a thing?'

'The usual. Money. Power. Leaving your mark on posterity.'

'There's no doubt: you're completely mad. Your husband's unfortunate death has obviously left you utterly unable to distinguish fantasy from reality.'

'No, I'm not mad. I thought I might have been when I imagined I saw people following me. Then I realized that they really were. It was a little late for that, as by then one of them had come crashing through my bedroom door.'

'Yes, I heard about that. It can't have improved your mental state. Though because you're attacked by a burglar doesn't prove you've been – what did you say? – followed by people.'

I ignored this. Stick to what you know, I said to myself. Hold on to that. Don't be persuaded by specious logic. This man is trying to undermine you. Don't let it happen.

I felt in the pocket of my coat and waved the small shiny object at him. 'Remember this? You gave it to me soon after we met. After you'd shot the dog. You gave me the collar tag. A good performance, wasn't it? Squire Western to the life. What was it you said? "A boffin. University man. Didn't know him." Of course you bloody well knew him. An eminent Cambridge scientist living on your doorstep. Your brother-in-law a Cambridge don. You knew about him. If you hadn't, you would have found out. You're the Lord of the Manor and a merchant banker, not a hick. It was me you didn't know at first. You didn't know who I was, because I wasn't supposed to be there, was I? You blundered in chasing the dog – and found me. Perhaps you'd heard rumours about people being seen here. You covered up your surprise well, though you did let slip something which didn't register with me until later. You said that you hadn't known the house had been for sale. You hadn't known, because it hadn't been. Then when you discovered my name, you must have heard the alarm bells ringing. Reynolds – of course you recognized the name. A well-known journalist, former economist at your bank. You knew. And I bet that the minute you got back you were on the phone to Mallen wanting to know what the hell he was doing letting his house be used by a journalist, of all people. You'd had no indication from Mallen that he had had that in mind. After all, he'd left it empty for a year or so. Perhaps you sensed something was wrong. How does it sound to you so far? Am I still crazy?'

I could see he didn't like it. His well-fed florid jowls tightened, and what had remained of the avuncular amiability had evaporated. Squire Western had turned into Captain Bligh.

'Quite unbelievable, but fascinating in its way. But why do you imagine I should have any concern over what Julian Mallen did with his house? What was he to me?'

Underneath the aggressive mask I could sense his growing uneasiness. 'I didn't know that for a long time. You put up such a smoke screen of stuff about McAllister's and Geoffrey. And I don't even think that Geoffrey himself realized the connection, otherwise he might have been much more careful about moving into this house. It was his one big mistake and the one that cost him most. It wasn't until I went to the Cambridge Centre for Physical Research that I saw it myself. And the significance didn't dawn until later, when I started to work things out in the hospital. But even such a secretive outfit has to have room for corporate vanity – and also no doubt to give an impression of openness. As you know, displayed in the foyer there's a list of sponsors and donors. Everything has them nowadays, including trash cans in the street. And in discreet letters in the long list is the name Hazenbach's. It would be a bit odd if the boss of the bank didn't know something about the place he'd put money into, wouldn't it?'

'A charitable contribution only. The bank makes many such. It doesn't presume a personal relationship with one of the employees.'

'One of the employees! I like that. So Mallen was just the doorkeeper, was he? The next winner of the Nobel Prize for Physics. You can't still pretend you don't know him.'

'Nothing you have said indicates proof of anything which can reflect to the discredit of either the bank or myself. All right, I knew of Mallen. Just because a fellow lives on your patch doesn't mean you are acquainted with him. And the centre is the kind of thing the bank has been proud to support. Successive governments have been obsessed with short-term benefits – immediate industrial applications, technological spin-offs in the modish term. Hazenbach's has always taken the longer view.'

'Oh, very public spirited. Nothing to do with even larger

393

returns, of course. But you weren't merely a contributor, you were the origin, weren't you? It was your idea. A chance remark by your brother-in-law over dinner, the gossip of the University: Mallen passed over for Newton's old chair, first-class mind becoming disillusioned with the University. I suppose it set your mind working. Your chance to make your contribution to history, not just as a banker, but as a sponsor of discovery. Not in a vulgar obvious sense, but in the solid discreet style of your ancestors. After all, it was Edwardes' money that went into the foundation of Walwyn College, wasn't it? Subtly done, but there nevertheless. I noticed it when I visited the college: the Edwardes Tower, the seventeenth-century's quiet reward for sponsorship. AWS didn't draw attention to it. Probably thought his fellowship would smack of nepotism, which wouldn't do for a socialist. Let me think the connection was entirely his creation. Rather sweet, that, don't you think?'

'One doesn't like to boast of such things. It's not our way. But none of this supports your original ridiculous accusation that your husband's death was other than an unfortunate accident.'

'I'm coming to that, don't worry. So you made the pitch to Mallen. You had him installed here so that you and he could work on plans for the Centre discreetly. Perhaps you bought the house for him? But what you failed to do was what any modern corporation in the States would have done. You failed to check out your man thoroughly. And believe me, I know that can be a big mistake.' I allowed myself a brief and bitter smile.

'You relied on his being a Cambridge chap. You didn't listen enough to your gossiping brother-in-law. You didn't wonder enough about why he had been passed over by the University for honours of public significance. Otherwise you might have gathered that despite being a genius in his specialty, he was a child. He was like one of those chess players: of enormous intellect but emotionally immature. As he had aged this had been accentuated, making him antisocial, paranoid. Capable of great unreasoning anger. In the wrong circumstances, a danger to others. And a man with a guilty secret. A man who would do anything to prevent that secret being revealed in public.' I stopped to watch his reaction. He remained sunk in immobility, his hands clasping his knees, his broad back curved as he leaned forward, the green waxed jacket's faint sheen in the sunlight like the hide of a reptile.

'When you taxed him with his involvement with Geoffrey, at first no doubt he denied that there was anything other than an innocent motive – lending the cottage to an old University acquaintance, perhaps – but under pressure eventually he confessed the truth: that Reynolds, in possession of a damaging allegation, was forcing him to put his name to a work of popular science for which Reynolds as the ghost writer and impresario would receive a vast fee. In order to make this farrago convincing, Mallen had given him access to his research notes. I'm sure you were horrified at the enormous risk that was being run. If the book were published to scientific disdain – no matter what the commercial success – Mallen and his work could be so discredited that the other funders would pull out before any results could be gained. Public corporations are vulnerable, unfortunately, to public opinion, unlike your own cosy family set-up.

'And that wasn't all. If Geoffrey had in the end gone on to reveal what he knew about Mallen's past, Mallen would not only have been utterly discredited but very likely imprisoned as well, thus effectively closing down the research project. So you decided to stop Geoffrey from going ahead with his scheme. You had him killed. Isn't that right? A thousand years of breeding and you end up a common murderer?'

There was silence for a few moments. Then he raised his head. His pale eyes were expressionless and cold. 'You have no proof of any of it, do you? It's all supposition, ingenious but based upon nothing more than circumstances and your own vivid imagination. Who will vouch for any of it? Reynolds? Mallen? That publishing fellow? He may be dead by now as well. And if he isn't he's hardly going to return to help you. Documents? There are none relevant. Go ahead. Go to the police with your cock-and-bull story. They won't be interested, except in your being an accessory to your husband's fraudulent activities.'

'Police? Who said anything about them? I don't need proof for what I have in mind. I was married to a journalist, remember? I have the contacts. They'll take great pleasure in sifting through the doings of the Cambridge Centre for Physical Research. That'll probably scare off most of the more sensitive donors for a start. Mallen's private life will occupy a few more scribes. As you said, he's dead so he won't be around to correct even the grossest exaggerations. After that, they'll start on you personally. I wonder what you've got hidden in your closet, in addition to what I know already?'

For the first time, I saw a flicker of real fear pass over his blunt features. As I watched, his nervousness seemed to grow. He got up from the log and walked off a little way down the path. Then he wheeled round and came back to stand over me. I looked up, forcing myself to remain completely calm, doing my best to stop the inner trembling that was threatening to erupt into an almighty fit of the shivers.

Then he said, 'I don't think we need to get involved in further unpleasantness. What's done is done. Nothing will change the past. I never meant it to be like this. Through my own foolish desire for, as you said, a place in posterity. You were right. I should have seen through Mallen. He was more than half-mad, I think. I saw only the genius, the genius that could have discovered the ultimate nature of matter and energy. Just think of the applications of that: the ability to generate limitless power, to tap the brightness of the stars. And Mallen could have done it – if he hadn't been misled. Yes, I did persuade him to come here. I bought the house from the Forestry Commission through a nominee company the bank controls. Mallen told Reynolds it was a family trust, I believe. He was trying to sort the matter out himself. He didn't realize I would recognize who Reynolds was, hoped I wouldn't notice, I suppose, the idiot. They're all fools, these so-called intellectual giants. Vain, and arrogant. The truth is that your husband hardly had to persuade him into that wretched book. He'd had crackpot ideas himself for years about a mathematical proof of the existence of God. Theological ontology, he called it. Reynolds remembered that from his Cambridge days. He was a clever fellow, wasn't he? You have to give him credit for that. Mallen was like Newton, with his crazy obsession with alchemy. I couldn't allow him to have that over the Sunday papers. Would have made us all a laughing stock. Ruined everything the Centre stood for.'

'So it was you who pulled the plug on McAllister's, not Geoffrey? You let me think it was him. Why?'

'I thought it would distract you away from his real involvement with the ghastly man. Make you think he was collecting information to expose the fellow. Our little tête-à-tête also showed you didn't at that time have a clue what he was really up to. Actually, he had made a dossier on Underdown-Metcalfe and his activities. It was on one of the disks removed from his flat. I suppose that was Reynolds' own insurance policy, in case things went wrong. Careful man, in some ways. I didn't like stooping to such nefarious activities but I had to make sure we had his master copy of the typescript. I was going to have McAllister's burgled as well, to get their copy – fortunately Metcalfe had kept it as quiet as he was capable of up to then – but when I read Reynolds' dossier, I made sure that the information went to the appropriate places. The Fraud Squad is much better at breaking into offices and safes than most burglars. One of the black plastic bags full of documents they took away in the full glare of the television cameras went astray. And as a result, Underdown-Metcalfe isn't in a position to publish even his own name, what?'

He turned away again to stare into the trees on the other side of the track. When he turned back, his face was sombre, his eyes full of careful sincerity. 'I was shocked, you know, when it happened. There was no intention to kill him. I want you to know that. It was entirely an accident, because of his weak heart. It could have happened at any time, I understand. I had always a great regard for the man. You must know that. A great regard. It was only that he was in danger of prejudicing a very substantial and important investment. I went to try to talk to him the afternoon he came here by himself. To try to persuade him not to pursue the course he had begun, not to use the material he had. But he was very stubborn. He listened, then he showed me the door. When I sent my chap round that night, it was merely to, well, frighten him a little. I never meant what did happen. Geoffrey panicked, I think.'

I felt faint, and my hands gripped the rough bark of the tree trunk I was sitting on. Despite everything I thought I knew, this casuistical confession of his role in Geoffrey's death, so blandly retailed, shocked me to the marrow. Then fury welled in me. 'You expect me to understand that he was prejudicing your investment? You had him killed for that. You're insane. Your whole view of the world is insane. Who are these people whose investments have to be protected by murderers?'

'My dear Mrs Reynolds, Mary, the world is a larger place than you conceive of. I had hoped that if I was frank with you, you might appreciate exactly what was at stake. Don't you realize how many billions, trillions of dollars turned on Mallen's researches? Your husband's death was an unfortunate accident. He could have died as a result of any over-exertion.'

'Such as being hunted down like an animal. And what about me? Does your rational version of history forget that your goon was going to kill me?'

'Believe me, I had no part in what happened to you. Some of our associates took a different view of the risks you posed. You were of course kept under observation. The search of your flat indicated you had somehow obtained a document linking Mallen with Reynolds which had escaped our original searches. Then, foolishly, you took steps to evade the surveillance. When you reappeared in London, and then subsequently made contact with Dr Mallen, they were of the opinion that you were involved in your husband's scheme, or had discovered it. Your actions contradicted my earlier advice that, having talked with you, you were unlikely to be a threat. There was another factor. It was only after your contact with Mallen at the Centre that he begged my colleagues and me to do something about you. You see, up to that point he had concealed from us the real nature of the threat that Reyolds had posed. He had pretended that the book was the only matter between them. He had kept secret that Reynolds had some kind of proof of his involvement in his wife's death. He thought you had it or would find it. There was no alternative then but to get from you directly whatever this proof was. I have to say I still disagree with their methods. I know that this is quite inadequate, but for what it's worth you have my apologies for what you've gone through. In the event, Mallen's death has made fools of us all. He gave us to believe that his illness would spare him for a longer period. I daresay your intervention was not helpful in that regard. The best laid schemes . . . I hope you can now see that there really is no point in raking the business over. After all, your husband's part in it was hardly blameless.'

For a moment, I almost bought it. His tall, massive figure radiated the magisterial propriety of his age and class. The calm, authoritative male voice, with its unspoken consciousness of its own superiority, over the ages had been accustomed to exact obedience and adulation. Who was I, a mere wife, a mere widow, to say that my husband had not died for some glorious but futile cause? An unknowing soldier in the battle for human enlightenment. Then I said, 'You really are insane if you expect me to nod my head and say I understand. I'm not going to.'

'You're being extremely stupid. If you won't listen to reason, I have to warn you that any attempt to take the matter further could lead to very serious consequences.'

'You mean the goons will come back? Forget that. If anything happened to me there would be a major investigation. There are too many people who would make sure of that.' I spoke with a confidence I didn't entirely feel.

'But. what would be the point? Revenge for Geoffrey? You're not the kind for that, are you? It would be a pointless act.'

'I will do it, believe me,' I said. 'Geoffrey may have been doing things which weren't entirely honest, but he didn't deserve to die. I think that's reason enough for me.'

I walked away.

I had gone only a few yards when I heard running feet behind me. As I turned, he caught up with me, grabbed my shoulder and threw me to the ground. The fall jarred the collar bone which had been broken and I cried out, screwing my eyes up with the pain. When I opened them again, he was standing over me and his shotgun was pointing at my head.

'You were a damn fool to continue with this, Mrs Reynolds. Now I'm going to have to shoot you, just as I shot Lucy's dog. With as much compunction.'

'For God's sake, this is Norfolk, England, not the Wild West.'

'Stay down, damn you! You forget, a shotgun blast doesn't raise an eyebrow in these parts. You'll have simply disappeared. Hundreds do every year, you know. There are miles of forest. They'll never even find your body. I know places no one else knows. Known them since I was a boy. I'm sorry, but there it is.' His big thumb hooked back the hammer with a click. The black hole of the muzzle looked as broad as the entrance to the Lincoln Tunnel.

I stared back into it. I never thought I would be able to feel the blood draining from my face, but I could. It was ridiculous. He really was going to kill me.

I suppose in extremis the mind works in a funny way. I'll never know quite how I made the connection, what made me pick up on what he had just said, as if I had tripped over the insignificant protruding root of a vast and spreading tree.

I said, 'If you kill me, you'll never know about your son.'

I saw his eyes widen with shock. The shotgun which had been held stiffly to his shoulder wavered then sank. 'What the blazes do you mean? You know I have no son. You're trying to gain a few more miserable seconds.'

'You have a son. Lucy Mallen bore him, after you'd raped her.'

'No! No, curse you! That's a damned filthy lie. You're lying.' The gun was now held loosely in the crook of his arm, pointing at the ground. I could see tears at the edges of his eyes.

'James,' I said softly, struggling into a sitting position. 'It's not a lie. Put down the gun. You're not going to shoot me, are you?'

It was as if something inside him had shrunk. His face grew pale, and his expression haggard. He sank down on the grass opposite me. I gingerly put the shotgun to one side, well out of reach.

'How did you know? How in God's name did you know? You must be a witch.'

'You said "Lucy's dog". When you shot it, you said it belonged to Mallen. You were so careful to make out that you didn't know Lucy Mallen. You didn't even use her name. "There may have been a child", you said that day. Of course you knew Mallen had a daughter. You were surprised when you recognized the dog. I saw that in your face, but you hid it with all the theatre over the tag. You didn't need the tag to tell you, because you knew Lucy.' I took a deep breath 'You met her in the forest. She roamed here like you, with her dog. You met her and you raped her.'

'My son, tell me about my son.'

'In a moment. There was another thing. Lucy left a letter addressed "Dear Boy". I thought at first she meant it for Tom Fincham, but he had merely found it somewhere. She wouldn't have left it for him. He couldn't read. She hoped you would find it. I've listened when you talk about your childhood. You seem grown-up, you do grown-up things, but deep down, like a lot of men, I suppose, you want to be a boy roaming the greenwood, don't you? Is that what you told her – before you attacked her?'

He started to sob. When he spoke again, his voice was almost a whisper. 'I want you to understand something. It wasn't like that. It wasn't rape. It wasn't like that at all. I swear to you that I never intended . . . I mean we were friends. We would meet in the forest. That's where I first saw her. She was so lovely. She seemed to dance above the grasses like a fairy creature. And yes, I told her how I had known these woods as a boy. I said I was still a boy at heart. She didn't know who I was or about my business connection with her father. I never met him when she was home from school, and he was under strict instructions never to speak of our relationship. He was a ghastly fellow, didn't speak to her from one day to the next. And she had to look after him. It was no life for her.'

'I suppose what you did improved it?'

'I didn't mean anything of that sort. I swear to God. I'll tell you how it happened.'

'It doesn't matter. I can guess.'

'You don't understand. Please listen. I met her in the summer two years ago. Oh, I'd seen her from a distance before then, playing with the dog near the cottage. But this time, she'd become more adventurous and gone much further from home. I came upon her suddenly and I think we were both surprised. She was sitting on a fallen branch in the central opening of the wood of Douglas fir that my great-grandfather planted. It was a long way from the track. It was a most beautiful sunny day. She had the dog with her. We talked. I told her about how I loved the woods, showed her the orchids that were growing in a boggy hollow at the edge of the trees. When she had to go home, I asked her if she would come back the next day. We could be friends and this could be our special place. She did come the next day, and the next. I looked forward to seeing her. She was a most beautiful child. One day when she came it was later than usual and I had almost given her up. She seemed sad. She had had an argument with her father about going back to school. We sat together, and I put my arm around her, to comfort her . . .'

'I don't think I can stand any more of this. Did you know how old she was, for God's sake?'

'I don't know, yes, but it had no relevance to me. All I knew was that we were friends, that she enjoyed talking to me, that I was better company for her than her own father. "Daddy never listens to me like you," she said. "Even though you're grown-up, you still want to hear what I've got to say." I didn't will it, you know. She looked so sad and I gave her a kiss. I hugged her close and I kissed her. Her hair smelt so wonderfully clean, like the breeze from the pine woods. And then I put my hand on her little breast. She wore no brassiere, only a T-shirt. I felt her nipple with my fingertips. She didn't protest, I swear. She smiled at me. I felt so full of love and tenderness, and she was so soft and her skin glowed like a pearl. Good God, I loved her, don't you understand? I was so gentle, she hardly cried out. She may have been a child in years, but her body knew what was happening. She moved with me. I wouldn't have hurt her for the world.'

I fought back my growing nausea. 'Then afterwards you told her not to tell.'

'God forgive me, I said it had to be our secret, that it meant we loved one another.'

'How many times? How many times did you . . . meet her again.'

'I don't know. I don't remember.'

'Yes, you do. What did you say? That you wouldn't like her any more if she didn't come back, that you'd tell her father she was a bad girl? Did you threaten her? How many times was it?'

'I don't know, I don't know. Three times. She had to go back to school, and that was the last time. I came to my senses then. I stayed away from that part of the wood.'

'I'm sure you did. You'd got what you wanted. You abandoned her. You left her to suffer the consequences. A child of eleven. Did she tell you about the baby?'

'Dear God, I never even knew that she was pregnant. Mallen said she was ill, that she had to go into hospital. I didn't know anything about a baby. Please tell me where my son is.'

'So you knew she was in hospital, but you made no attempt to find out what was the matter with her?'

'You have to realize that if anyone . . . if Mallen had found out . . . God, it was so damned stupid of me! I risked everything. A man in my position –'

'You've done this before, haven't you? Haven't you? Dottie told me about rumours of another child in the village, how that was hushed up. Did you buy off the parents? Is the Chief Constable a good friend of yours? You let people think it was poor Tom who did it. And everyone thinks you're the generous squire.'

'Please. You have to understand. I told you, I never meant any harm. Tell me about my son. Please. Tell me where he is.'

I stretched out my arm and pointed at the dark line of trees. 'There. Somewhere in there is your son's grave. He was born prematurely to a girl who scarcely knew what was happening. He didn't have a chance. He may have been stillborn or lived a few minutes. Only Lucy can tell you that. She's recovering, you know. I expect soon she'll be well enough to want to talk about what happened.'

He gave a cry of an intensity which almost made me pity him, then his head fell into his hands and I saw his massive shoulders shake. 'Please, I can't, I wasn't really going to kill you. You've got to help me. You know the girl. Talk to her. Think of Dottie. If she were to find out, a thing like this would kill her.'

'No, it won't,' I said. 'That's what men always say, isn't it? It's their self-justifying way of trying to wriggle out of owning up, trying to pretend that whatever they've done their womenfolk will suffer worse out of undying love. And it's a kind of moral blackmail on anyone who feels inclined to turn them in. Well, I've never heard of anyone who would feel obliged to leap into the flames: suttee's been abolished, hadn't you heard? I'm sure Dottie will regard you as I do. With contempt.'

'Please help me. I'll confess to the business with Mallen and your husband. Face the music for that, if you want your pound of flesh. But the girl, she's nothing to you, is she? You've no reason to tell anyone.'

'The girl, is that how you think of her? So much for love. Shall I tell you who she is?'

I had finished speaking several minutes previously.

He seemed sunk in thought. Then he said, 'My God, I see now. You will do it.' He looked up, his eyes moist.

I stared back at him and said nothing, all the tension having left me. What would be would be.

He picked up the shotgun, and spoke quietly, almost to himself. 'Perhaps there'll be no need for that.' He hefted the weapon. 'It's a good gun, this one. One of my father's. Single-barrelled. Sixteen bore. Local gunsmith. We don't go in for those fancy makes. They're not working guns – only for ponces or the Japanese. My father. He and I never really got on. One doesn't, I suppose. I've no one to pass it to. Not now.'

He paused, as if uncertain as to what to do.

404

I stood up and dusted the pine needles from my skirt. 'Goodbye, James.'

I turned and for a moment felt a chill between my shoulder blades as if the gun were pointed there. Then I walked on quickly, and didn't look back.

It must have been only a couple of minutes later that I heard the shot. It could have been a poacher taking a pot at one of the pheasants that were as common as sparrows round about.

But I didn't think that likely.

I stood on the shingle looking up at the house for what I knew would be the last time. As I did so, I thought I noticed at the edge of my vision a movement in the scrub at the fringes of the forest. I turned quickly, but whatever it was was still. I stared out for a few moments, struck with the indefinable sense of being observed.

Then I knew what I had to do. I thrust into my pocket for the heavy old-fashioned door key, and held it aloft. I hurled it as far as I could towards the forest. It fell short and I heard it clink on the stones.

'It's all yours now, Tom,' I shouted, and my voice echoed in the clearing.

There was no reply. Only a gust of wind cold from the Arctic which set clattering a few early roosting pigeons.

I drove fast down the long straight road. Forest House was already ten miles behind. Every tree that flicked rhythmically by marked the lengthening of that distance and I felt my thoughts pulling free of what had held them to that place.

For months, I had grieved for bereavement, for loss. Not only for Geoffrey's death, but for the loss of those illusions which had sustained me through my life. Illusions of perceptivity, of intelligence, of my firm place in the world. Unlooked-for, the monsters had risen from the dark abyss of the past and consumed those illusions and all but destroyed me as well.

But I had survived. In the words of the Sondheim song, I was still here. But I was changed. I had learned to suffer and to feel pain. I had come near to death, and I had hit back against it. I was not proud that I had killed a man, but I felt no guilt, no thirst for expiation. It had been a moment of pure animal instinct in which the Johnny-come-lately constructs of human morality had no place.

As for James Edwardes, I had not set out to cause his death. I had wanted to satisfy the hunger in myself for the truth about how Geoffrey had died. And, yes, I had wanted to see the discomfiture, the disgrace of the man I held responsible. But not his death. Not until I heard him talk slightingly of her whom he had supposedly loved and had abandoned in so cowardly a fashion. Only then had I lied to him about her recovery.

But despite that, I could not have pulled the trigger. I had learned that about myself, and felt glad in the knowledge. James had chosen his own death, secure in his myth-making to the last. Death before dishonour, to the extinction of the species.

And what now of the future? What of the commitment I had given to be a mother to Geoffrey's daughter? Was I bound by my declaration given in the grip of an overwhelming atavistic emotion? Had I really reawakened a capacity within myself which I had for years regarded as irrelevant to how I wanted to be? Or was I only responding to what the man I had loved had wanted of me?

It was true that I longed for the day when Lucy's alabaster face – that face like a Della Robbia image of the Virgin – would lose its stone pallor and blush with the warmth of returning consciousness, when her eyes would brighten and she would once again talk and laugh and cry, when at last she could leave her institutional prison.

But even as I longed for it, I felt daunted by the responsibility. Other women might have assumed it easily. But I was myself. Could I after everything I had been through, everything I had been put through, allow myself to be anything other than honestly myself?

Henry Massingham had said that only love would save her. And he had meant a mother's love. Would my love be strong enough to undo the anguish, the betrayals which had driven her mind into its hidden cavern? Did it have to be my love alone?

★

As I reflected on this, fearful and confused by my conflicting emotions, I remembered a woman's face.

Henry, coldly selfish in his marriage, consumed by his profession, had been unable to see what should have been obvious. But I too had lacked empathy and perception.

Why had I not shown more compassion to Sarah, whose loveless misery I had interpreted as shallowness, lost in my own feelings of jealousy and mistrust? It had been she who had nursed Lucy through those terrible first days. I had failed to acknowledge that properly, to recognize the depths of her feelings, how much she might fear losing her to me. I had heard how she had longed for a child. She would love Lucy, had already loved her. I was sure of that.

And I could have a role. I might be uncertain of my capacity for motherhood, but I did not lack warmth or the capacity to give and receive love. I would tell her of her father, of his wit and brilliance, of his passion and, eventually perhaps, how he had schemed and fought for her sake, how through his ingenuity he had raised a fortune to safeguard her future. I would on high days and holidays bring gifts and gossip from the big city. I would, as far as I could, through what I had of culture and intellect, enrich her narrow provincial world. In these ways I could play my part in reclaiming her life from the enveloping darkness.

But was that enough for Geoffrey's daughter? Was it not my duty to respond again to that reasonless physical imperative at the core of my being, and to take the torch proffered by his dying hand?

I had left the trees far behind, but I was still deep in the dark wood. I looked at the dashboard clock. If I wished, I could be in Cambridge and with Lucy before dusk.

And if I were looking for a sign, one was to hand: a white on green trunk road sign. It was decision time.

The roads diverged in one mile: straight on for Cambridge, filter left on to the slip road for the motorway to London. My hands lay steady on the steering wheel. On the clock, the second hand swept inexorably on. There was the first countdown marker for the junction: three strokes. Then two, then one. I held my course.

Almost as the white broken lines to the slip road gave out, I swung the wheel left to a cacophony of hooting from the cars close behind. Bloody woman driver. I didn't care. They weren't close enough to see the tears streaming down my face.

I drove on automatic pilot. The next thing I was conscious of was the glare of the sodium lights like those of a great airport runway which indicated the beginning of the vast penumbra of suburbia which surrounded London. London. The flower of cities all. And at last my home.

There would be letters to write. A difficult one to Sarah Massingham. And one much easier to Vanessa Wordsworth, accepting her offer of a partnership in her literary agency – even if that did mean coping with Anna's foibles.

But before I started on my new career, I owed myself a little holiday. In Switzerland, I thought. Not skiing. Ugh, all that horrid snow. Somewhere dignified and calm. Zurich would be most rewarding at this time of the year, particularly for holders of numbered bank accounts.

I might as well end there.

What should I say of the rest of Geoffrey's legacy to me? I loved him and he deceived me and caused me pain. But he also gave me love greater than I had ever before received. For that I shall forgive him everything.

I find it strange – though others who read this may not – that, after this telling, these events which I believed would continually resonate in every moment of my existence seem already to be sinking silently into a great sea, down beyond the reefs and wrecks which litter its shallows, then into depths from which I believe they will hardly ever re-emerge into the bright sunlight and the dancing waves.